I0600731

Praise for
Eve of the Pharaoh

"Enthrall[ing,] action-packed ... vivid scenery, complicated characters, and unexpected turns that erupt around an ancient mystery ..."
— Jennifer Anne Davis, author of The True Reign Series

"Rich and vivid imagery ... sucks you in ..."
— Barbara Kloss, author of the Pandoran Series

Era *of* Shadows Series

BOOK ONE

Eve *of the* Pharaoh

R.M. SCHULTZ

Copyrighted Material

Eve of the Pharaoh: Era of Shadows

Copyright © 2018 by R.M. Schultz. All Rights Reserved.

No part of this publication may be reproduced, stored in a retrieval system or transmitted, in any form or by any means—electronic, mechanical, photocopying, recording or otherwise—without prior written permission from the publisher, except for the inclusion of brief quotations in a review.

For information about this title or to order other books and/or electronic media, contact the publisher:
R.M. Schultz
email: rschultz.imaging@gmail.com
website: https://www.facebook.com/historicadventurestories/

ISBN: 978-0-9988918-1-1 (print)
       978-0-9988918-2-8 (eBook)

Printed in the United States of America
Cover and Interior design: 1106 Design

To all the great mentors I was lucky enough to have in my life and who inspired me: my parents, brothers, teachers, and coaches—Lou Kallery, Bob Fischer, Mark Plumlee, Russ Tucker, John Graham, BPak, Erik Wisner and so many more. To Matt, my best friend, for all of his help and insight. To those who said I never could. And above all, to Creslin and Jocelyn, who lie at the heart of my emotions and teach me everyday what it is to be human.

This story is based on numerous written records
referencing historical events and people of ancient Egypt.
The discovered monuments, temples, and architecture are factual.

Ancient thread character list

Akhenaten: Second son of Pharaoh Amenhotep III and Queen Tiye

Aten: The sun and god

Ay: Nefertiti and Mutnedjmet's father, brother of Tiye the queen of Egypt

Beketaten: Akhenaten's sister, Nefertiti and Mutnedjmet's cousin, daughter of Amenhotep III and Queen Tiye

Croc: Heb's pet cat

Dark Ones or The Shadows: Mysterious monsters from children's tales

Devouring Monster: Creature that is a mixture of a crocodile, lion, and hippopotamus—from the underworld and devours the hearts and souls of men

Heb: Main character of ancient thread

Kiya: One of Akhenaten's significant foreign wives

Mahu: Akhenaten's captain of his personal guard

Mudads: Egyptian soldier

Mutnedjmet: Nefertiti's younger sister, daughter of Ay, cousin to Akhenaten

Nefertiti: Mutnedjmet's older sister, Akhenaten's cousin, daughter of Ay

Pentju: The royal doctor

The son of Hapu: The royal magician, supposed reincarnate of Imhotep

Suty: Akhenaten's bodyguard

Thutmose: Akhenaten's older brother, son of Amenhotep III and Tiye, the crown prince of Egypt

Tiye: Amenhotep III's wife, mother of Akhenaten, Thutmose, and Beketaten, Ay's sister, aunt of Nefertiti and Mutnedjmet

Prologue

K NUCKLES RAPPED AGAINST WOOD. I jumped in my seat, and my book smacked into the desk. Beyond flickering candlelight stood the door of the meager hotel room, but the sound hadn't come from the hall. The ruckus arose from the other side of the door to the adjoining room.

Grabbing my cane in a shaky hand, I crept across the floor. The knocking ceased. I didn't know anyone else staying here. Someone who'd had too much to drink? Pressing my good ear against the thin partition, I held my breath. Cool air seeped under the door, like an evil spirit trying to slither in. Floorboards creaked inside the adjacent room, drowning out a man's muffled ranting. The tapping of metal on glass followed. Was this neighbor trying to get out to his balcony, or was someone else out there attempting to break in? I wiped the sweat from my trembling palms onto my pants.

A fist pounded on the door again, rattling my skull. I stumbled backward as my heart thundered against old ribs. The crushing grip of terror squeezed my chest, allowing only faint breaths to spew in rapid succession. Should I wedge a chair against the door and jump out a second-story window? I took a deeper breath. No, I'd pretend my room was vacant and hope the disturbance would disappear.

Silence. Could he be in serious trouble, like choking or a heart attack? I might not have been much of a hero, but I wasn't the type to ignore suffering because of fear and the late hour. Gurgling followed, and maybe a muted cry for help. Guilt gnawed at my gut. Maybe I should just peek in. I inched over to the deadbolt and quietly unlocked it.

The door burst open, revealing an unkempt man in a suit and fedora. He leapt at me. Grabbing the front of my waistcoat, he yanked, pulling me within an inch of his face. Bloodshot eyes bored into mine. My fingers slipped off the cane and it clattered to the floor. A rank stench of smoldering whiskey billowed through my nostrils. I couldn't move or breathe.

"L-listen!" the man whispered. His stinging breath poured over my face as he swayed, his words slurred. "D-don't let 'em know I talked to you. Get this out of the country! Please, for the sake of mankind, take it and contact Dr. Shelsher's office in Cambridge. I'm the last of his colleagues here. Find another who knows!"

The man's hand dove into his jacket and produced a small picture frame, thrusting it against my chest. Instinctively seizing the object, I acted more in defense than desire. He spun around on one heel and retreated back into his room. A drawn curtain veiled the door to his balcony, but the glass shuddered, and muffled voices clawed their way in from the outside.

Glaring back at me, he pointed. "Hide it, lock your door, put that flame out, and go to bed! You never s-saw me. Best depart first thing in the mornin'." He eased his door shut. A metal bolt slid against wood, issuing a scratch and a dull thud.

I slammed my own partition door shut and bolted it. Forcing deep breaths, I braced myself against the thin wood. What had just happened, and what had that crazy man given me? My knees gave way and I slumped to the floor. My hands held a sepia-style portrait of a group of men in suits. They wielded tools and stood outside an excavated tomb in the desert—an immediate reminder of the recent discovery of a new pharaoh of ancient Egypt, King Tut. Howard Carter had uncovered the boy king's tomb last fall, November 1922.

But this picture wasn't of Tut's tomb. I brushed a hand across the surface in wonder, disturbing a thin layer of dust. Something sharp poked into my other palm. Wincing, I jerked my wrinkled hand from the frame. A gap revealed itself between lengths of wood. Something was tucked inside. My pulse quickened in anticipation, and I stuck my fingernail through the slit.

A gunshot exploded next door, penetrating the walls of the hotel and resonating out into the desert night. Dogs barked and hotel guests screamed.

I dropped the frame and extinguished the candle, hiding in the dark. Quiet. Sneaking over to the bathroom, I huddled against a far corner.

Pain compressed my throat, reminding me I still had to breathe while listening for intruders. Seconds dragged by like hours. I remained frozen, even as my muscles cramped in displeasure. Ten minutes later someone pounded on a nearby door in the hall. I lurched. "Open up—police!" a man shouted in Arabic. A door creaked opened. More shouting. Banging and muttering carried through the adjoining wall for hours.

Before sunrise, I departed for Cairo. But as I shuffled through the lobby, a clerk whispered to a bellhop and mentioned a suicide. My blood turned cold. Stopping to eavesdrop, I feigned innocence by rifling through my luggage as if I had forgotten something. The clerk described a gruesome fountain of blood spewed across a room. The victim had supposedly taken his life with his own gun. A feeling of defenselessness came over me, and I hugged my cane. A suicide? Or perhaps a murder committed by the strangers out on the balcony last night. I needed to escape with this secret or I might be the next to die.

—*From an unsigned letter, dated the 3rd of April, 1923.*

Chapter 1

Present Day

PALE MOONLIGHT PEEKED OVER my shoulder, and my core tingled with anticipation. Wind whipped across my face, stinging my dry eyes. Noting the GPS coordinates, I probed the sand with gloved fingers and a shovel. As dirt spilled up my forearms and into the glove, I grimaced with disgust. Touching grime sent chills through my limbs, but this pursuit was too important.

The cool soil encasing my hands made it difficult to imagine that a few short hours ago, the same dirt had baked under the relentless Egyptian sun. Also, as others often imagine, I didn't stand upon a vast desert. Mountains dominated the skyline, encircling me like shadowed guardians of the valley. The Valley of the Gates of the Kings.

Damn, nothing but pebbles and more earth. Was this the wrong location? If not, did we still have enough time, or would someone catch us? I tipped my fedora back and wiped thick sweat from my brow and stubble-covered cheeks.

The jagged, black script upon the ninety-year-old parchment raced through my mind. Dr. Shelsher's final words had appeared scribbled in haste or fear. *"What transpired on this, my last expedition, has intensified beyond words. If you find and read what I've hidden, I didn't survive to share my discovery of the lost secrets of the ancients, the legendary Hall of Records. The Hall, the mystery I've been fascinated with and have chased all of my life."*

A shudder of unmatched excitement vibrated up my spine. How had my dad even found these letters? Recalling more, I searched through the darkness. *"I was the first person, nay, the first living being, to enter the Hall of Records since it was constructed, sealed off, and hidden over 3,000 years ago."*

The beam of a flashlight arced over, blinding me. "Gavin," a soft female voice spoke from the shadows beyond, "if you want to become one of the greatest living Egyptologists and join the ranks of Howard Carter, we have to keep digging. This is the last night I can help you."

My body locked up with apprehension, but I forced a slow nod. If I discovered the lost tomb of Amenhotep, then I could attempt to follow the path to the Hall of Records and its treasures, legendarily unmatched in the ancient world. I'd publish related scientific articles and books for the rest of my life; I'd be saved from my current path and dilemma. Back home, my family all expected me to do the right thing: follow their dreams and become a doctor. But a lack of enthusiasm had led to carelessness—and a terrible medical mistake. I'd transformed from a kid with a brilliant future to a continuous disappointment. This trip could change everything. It had to, no matter the risk. Even if I died out here, it'd be easier than returning home ...

"Maddie, you still think we interpreted the professor's letter correctly?" I asked, kicking a mound of excavated dirt in frustration.

The wind picked up, and she shouted, "What? You're mumbling again!"

I yelled back as loud as I could, trying to enunciate, "The papyrus everyone has access to says one hundred twenty cubits below the horn of the mountain, but I'd say we're at least five times that ... if the horn is the summit!"

Soaring into the night sky, the mountain peak blotted out half of the moon. My stomach cramped with pain. Popping a couple antacid tablets into my mouth, chalky grit caked my tongue as I chewed and tried to swallow. This bout had better pass. We couldn't turn back for a hospital now, not after coming this far.

"But we're north of the House of Amenhotep-of-the-Garden," Maddie said. She had an obsession with ancient Egypt as all-consuming as mine, but she also pursued a PhD in Egyptology.

Throwing back a swig of warm water, the chalk thickened to a paste before washing away. "The entire Valley of the Kings is north of that. Plus the lost tomb of the first Amenhotep may've already been discovered in Dra Abu el-Naga, and they didn't bury pharaohs here until after—"

"*Allegedly* discovered," she said. "Not everything you read online is accurate. What if his wasn't the last royal tomb of the New Kingdom to be built outside the Valley of Kings, but the first within? Or what if he was relocated—"

The clang of steel on rock filled the night, originating from our guide's—Mr. Scalone's—sunken shovel-head. My heart leapt with excitement. Had he found something?

Swinging her flashlight around, Maddie focused the beam on our guide. The whites of Mr. Scalone's eyes glinted under the artificial light, like a crocodile sighting prey. He wiped large hands on tight jeans and straightened a white shirt, buttoned only to his rippling upper abs. A smirk expanded across a ruggedly handsome countenance. "You kids may've taken classes, but you need a man with experience to find anything out here," he said with a thick Italian accent, tossing back wavy locks of black hair.

My stomach cramped again in painful anticipation as the guide stood basking in glory instead of prying at the buried object with his shovel.

Shaking my head in irritation, I gritted my teeth. Unfortunately, this muscular Italian whom I already didn't like and two local hands made up the remainder of our current team. A couple of others had stayed back in Cairo. I had hoped Maddie and I would work alone, but how could *we* pull this off? We didn't know anything about the complexities of foreign antiquities regulations, not to mention illegally exhuming artifacts.

I imagined I'd excavate the tomb and help Maddie inside. We'd lift our flashlights, gazing upon glistening images of wonder, figures not seen in thousands of years. She'd slip her little hand into mine and squeeze as we'd descend into the unknown, our hearts pulsating with exhilaration. Maybe a linen-wrapped mummy would stagger toward us, moaning, its arms reaching out for our throats. I'd protect Maddie by fighting the walking corpse off with a pickaxe. But just as a rotting hand would nearly crush my beating heart, I'd use my knowledge of the past to dispel the ancient curses of the dead and save us. We'd find answers to all of life's biggest questions, reinvent history, and I'd carry Maddie out in my arms—

Mr. Scalone cursed and flung a cluster of rocks at my feet, bringing me back to the present. My fluttering stomach crashed back down in disappointment at the sight. He hadn't found the burial chamber after all. So many meaningless stones lay under the desert.

A howl carried through the gorge, echoing off the cliff faces. The two local guides whispered to each other in Arabic, their flashlights darting about. An inbound breeze pricked the stubbly hairs on the back of my neck and blew the fedora off my head. A dark cloud blotted out the moon. Splattering raindrops broke upon my back, soaking my shirt with their chill. Our piles of parched dirt released a musty odor.

My hand cramped with tension and something snapped, digging into my palm. "Ouch!" I yelled in surprise, tearing off my glove and shining a light downward. Blood streamed over my thumb and dripped into the night. A large splinter from the shovel had embedded into my skin. My quivering fingers plucked out the shard, and I sucked thick liquid oozing from the wound.

"What was that howling?" Maddie asked, her light scouring the nearby ridges.

"Probably a jackal," Mr. Scalone said. "They won't come after the living, so don't run away." He glanced about. "The Egyptian militia and police are our biggest concern. If they catch us, we'll spend our lives in a cell resembling a medieval dungeon. That is if they don't shoot us dead first. Reminds me of the time I was tracked by bushmen in Botswana ..."

The guide's words faded under the screaming wind and pounding rain. Squeezing down on the bronze bracelet I always wore on my left wrist and forearm eased my escalating fear.

Forgotten crypts still lay buried in these canyons, the work of millennia-old flash floods carrying tons of silt. We stood at the bottom of a natural pyramid, the one Maddie hoped Dr. Shelsher alluded to. Writing on the backside of the professor's letter had appeared as nonsensical notes referencing the Egyptian trinity of man, woman, and child, but combining the third letter of every word had revealed a message: "*Inside the lost tomb of Amenhotep the path begins. An enduring clue still suppressed by time. Primeval units of measure are stated on papyrus, but shrouded is the buried location. Expose the ancestral base, the oldest pyramid of them all, athwart the tomb of the boy-king. Feel the eye of Horus give way ... a secret entrance!*"

Expeditions utilizing sonar had even revealed anomalies across from King Tut's tomb, although no one had yet unearthed anything. The reason why remained a mystery to me and all of Maddie's peers. But I'd convinced myself of glory before, only to be thoroughly disillusioned.

Shaking my head in disappointment, I shined my light up through cascading rain to the triangular peak of the mountain. Rock composed the summit. My jaw fell open in realization.

"Forget the sonar scans and modern technology," I yelled to Maddie through the gale. "The ancients wouldn't bury their pharaoh beside a pyramid, even if the divine symbol was a mountain of solid rock. A god-king would be sleeping *inside!*"

Scrambling up the wet slope, I perspired and heaved for breath. Eventually arriving at a location matched by 120 cubits and a specific orientation encrypted by Dr. Shelsher, I kicked to drive my shovel into the incline.

"Wait!" Maddie yelled, climbing up beside me. "How do you suppose we find a secret entrance along the face of a mountain this size?" Extending a small arm from behind her flashlight, she motioned at the massive ridge.

"Trust the professor?" I said, panting. "Maybe the base he referred to is where the dirt ends and the actual rock of the mountain peak begins. Wind and rain could've altered the visible transition line significantly over the millennia, even to some degree since Dr. Shelsher's time."

Mr. Scalone arrived, followed by his hired help. Grunting like a powerlifter performing squats, probably to emphasize his strength, he dropped our gear against a rock. "We're running out of time," he said. He and the two locals set to work, digging faster than ever. Laboring as a single unit, they alternated shovel and pick, flinging a stream of soggy topsoil down the slope.

My stomach churned with worry. I couldn't let this male model of a guide steal this opportunity. Working vigorously over the next hour, my hands grew raw inside the leather gloves. I would unearth the secret entrance of the tomb and let the world see. Riches and ancient history would leak up through the sand, calling my name. I'd swim through artifacts, and Maddie would cheer—

The wooden handle shuddered in my hands. No rocks loosened with further digging and prodding. Whatever lay hidden beyond the remaining layer of soil was much larger than a standard desert stone. My eyes, wide with elation, burned in the wind and rain. "The base was once here!"

The beam of Maddie's flashlight bounced off of the plummeting water droplets between us like falling stars. "You doubted?" she asked. A faint reflection of white revealed a teasing grin. Dashing over, she assisted with the packed dirt that was transforming into mud.

Sucking in a deep breath, I plunged my hands into the softened hillside. A large stone waited beneath. I heaved with all my might. The block didn't budge. Running my fingers through loosened dirt and mud, I searched for a symbol. After another hour of following the edges of pristinely carved slabs, my thumb fell into a shallow defect. Tracing the course of the indentation, the wedjat eye, the eye of Horus, formed in my mind. This was the hieroglyph! I shoved again, my heart pounding hysterically. The faint grating of a loose block vibrated through my arms, but the slab didn't give a millimeter. "Help!" I screamed, my voice cracking.

"Stand back," Mr. Scalone said, sprinting over. "Your scrawny twigs won't help anymore here. Dig another tunnel over there." He nodded back a few feet. "Give the men room."

I didn't budge, searching for another option.

Mr. Scalone shoved me with one muscular arm. Tripping on a pile of debris, I tumbled over as he and his men propelled themselves against the stone inside the mountain. My hands clenched in anger. Douche bag. Jumping up, I hoped with the excitement Maddie hadn't noticed how easily he had tossed me aside. But I'd have my glory soon enough.

They all heaved, leaning into the earth. A massive limestone brick shuddered as it crawled inward, rumbling for several feet, and then plunged into darkness. Thunderous crashing erupted from the inner shadowy unknown, as if the block tumbled down a long stairway. Given the hollow character and fading depth of the echoes, the interior must have stretched far into the roots of the mountain.

Everyone stood in shocked awe. As if in a dream, I stepped past the others and climbed across the threshold, beyond the lighted world. Ancient air swept into my lungs with a burning sting as the eons of time crawled inside my soul, jolting my bones. My breath quickened, and its labored rasp broke the age-old silence of the inner sanctum.

"Get outta there quick!" Mr. Scalone yelled.

My body turned chill with terror.

Chapter 2

Present Day

I STOOD ATOP A TWISTING staircase of stone, just inside the secret chamber. Steps led down into a vast darkness that swallowed the beam of my flashlight.

"Send one of these guys in first," Mr. Scalone said. He aimed his flashlight at the hired hands, who wore the typical *thawb* of the Middle East. One's beard reached to his chest; the other's lay sparse and patchy upon his chin and cheeks.

No. I was going first. But dread paralyzed my limbs like a dead person who saw no light waiting for him at the end of the tunnel. I had imagined shoving the guide back into the dirt and taking Maddie by her hand into our own adventure, but I couldn't. This was no longer a fantasy.

A presence hovered around me. Like a hot breath on the back of my neck, the sensation created a blanket of goose bumps on my arms. Shuddering, I swung my flashlight around. No mounds of treasure or statues of gold stared back at me, but something else lived in here. The feeling drew near.

A massive block appeared from the shadows, swinging at my face. Leaping sideways, I tripped and fell upon a stairway a split second before the object smashed into my nose. The stone crashed into the tomb wall and sent a stream of dirt down around me before slowly swinging back and forth across the width of the inner chamber—like a pendulum through the darkness. Then it dangled precariously overhead. Yelling, I rolled farther away as my chest constricted in panic.

After a moment I stood on trembling legs, my heart racing like an Olympic sprinter's. Mr. Scalone yelled from outside the secret entrance. Grabbing my flashlight and fedora, I brushed my pants off and inched away from the dangling slab—its momentum and swaying had subsided. Thick rope anchored it to something in the shadows above. I released a clenched breath. But something else made of stone had tumbled downward when we'd pushed the false block at the entrance inside … Was this dangling block the false block or a booby trap? I glanced around.

Twisting stairs ran down to the lower chambers, the symbolic descent of the sun into the underworld.

The heat of fear rose and spread throughout my body. But this was it, what my life was meant for. Intoxicated, I clutched my bronze bracelet, and like a small moth drawn to the searing flame, I wandered down the ancient path. Mr. Scalone's shouts faded behind me. The walls closed in, and the temperature plummeted as I descended several stories into the mountain.

A chunk of stone lay at the base of the stairs—what must've fallen when we'd pushed in the larger false block still dangling near the entrance. Maybe this was a piece of the false block that had broken off, or an appropriately placed stone that'd been set just inside the entrance to create echoes and frighten people away … or to awaken something within the tomb?

A cartouche-shaped antechamber emerged, its once-sealed stone door smashed to bits. Creeping along, I placed one foot inside. My flashlight beam swung along the path of my trembling hand, lighting up a billow of disturbed dust particles. I coughed. Echoing broke the deathly silence, like a ghost wailing in a cemetery.

The chamber didn't overflow with colorful artifacts, furniture, chariots, or boats of gold as I had envisioned. Only a few discarded objects lay scattered about, dust laden and dull under the abrasion of time. A twinge of defeat pulled my shoulders down. Like most others, this tomb had probably already been raided in antiquity. Damn it! Punching my thigh, I bit my lip.

My flashlight arced around, searching for anything of value. No treasure. But soot-covered images adorned the inner stone. Hieroglyphs. I studied them.

Reflected light glinted from the floor at the far end. Something lay there … a desiccated body. I froze, keeping the light fixed on the leathery corpse. Then a presence hovered over me again. Could this be a trap? I glanced around, my heart pounding.

Nothing moved inside the tomb other than disturbed particles of dust. Holding my breath, I scrutinized the body. Dressed in an old-fashioned brown suit and wearing large, round glasses, this carcass still had tufts of brown hair.

Dr. Shelsher? He clutched something to his chest in a gnarled hand. I inched closer. Drained of moisture and deeply wrinkled by the arid climate, the body appeared like a mummy. The skull's empty sockets swallowed the intrusive shaft of light. My stomach crawled like fingers toward my throat, but I couldn't look away. In a death grip, he clutched a leather-bound book.

Maybe some answers could be found inside. Reaching for the journal, I paused. The hairs on the back of my neck stood up. A warm breath floated by amidst the eerie silence. Casting my light around the room, I prepared to bolt.

A face flashed right in front of me, under my swinging beam. Dark eyes and waves of loose hair approached! Dropping the light in sheer terror, I spun away. But a strong hand clamped down on my shoulder and held me fast. A mummy? The curses were true? A blinding light struck me in the face. I screamed.

Chapter 3

Present Day

"MY GOD, YOU SOUND LIKE a twelve-year-old girl," Mr. Scalone said, shoving me away.

I fell down beside the corpse, embarrassment burning my cheeks. There was no animated mummy in the tomb, only our guide …

"Are you okay?" Maddie yelled from the darkness above. "What happened?"

"He's fine," Mr. Scalone said.

I snatched the book from the mummy, accidentally breaking off a curled finger. Tissue vaporized into a cloud and settled as a brown powder. I sneezed. Drumming echoes resounded throughout the tomb. Maddie screamed.

Mr. Scalone shook his head before studying the body. Had he seen me take the journal?

I turned my back to the guide, pulled my fedora low, and stumbled away. Untying the cracked leather bonds that sealed the book, I spotted a layer of brown dirt on my thumb. Dust from the corpse? Tensing with a combination of fear and disgust, I rubbed the area vigorously on my pants until no particles remained. Then opening the cover, I peeked inside—

A wooden handle skittered across the floor, making me jump in surprise. Mr. Scalone cursed as he kicked aside scattered objects.

Maddie and I should probably sort through the artifacts before our guide, Mr. Ego, ruined them. This find could still impress her, my perfect girl whom I'd fallen in love with when we were both freshmen in college. "Come down, Maddie," I tried to yell, but my voice never grew very loud. "You need to see this."

"Treasure?" Maddie called from above. "Gold beyond my wildest dreams?" Angled rays of light arced over my head. Her approaching footfalls quickened.

The sole of a small boot and a shovel tested the antechamber floor, as if anticipating being struck by a trap or falling into a pit. My light illuminated her. Maddie, a shorter woman in her mid-twenties, slid her thin but shapely frame against the broken limestone slabs at the room's entrance. Her chest, underneath a blue tank top, arched around the blocks as she lifted a pant-covered leg over the debris.

Gazing upon her initiated a flutter in my stomach, even down here. The woman of my dreams. But the distance might as well have been miles. To her I was just a friend. But if I discovered the Hall, maybe she wouldn't be able to resist the influence, wealth, power, and fame that would follow. Maybe she could love and respect me then.

I squeezed my abs and cleared my throat to crush the sensation. "There's a body," I said, "without an obvious cause of death."

"Well, it's what we assumed must've happened," she replied. "Poor Dr. Shelsher. I wonder how he got in here—"

"I don't think it's Dr. Shelsher," I said. "This person's too young, or he was when he died. And there's something else … something more interesting."

"More interesting than three thousand, five hundred-year-old Egyptian artifacts fashioned of pure gold, hidden inside one of the last lost tombs?" Her sarcasm coated the words.

"Just …" I didn't know what to say without piquing Mr. Scalone's curiosity, so I waved her to come closer.

"Watch your step," Mr. Scalone said from the far end. "Egyptians made traps for tomb robbers, and they built things to last. There might be more than curses to protect the secrets of this tomb." He shined his light back up the stairway.

An image of the dangling slab that nearly crushed me popped into my head. I shuddered with fright.

"What is it?" Maddie asked, her brown eyes darting about behind fashionably sheer glasses.

"Looks like a narrative," I said, running a finger over the translations inside the journal.

Creeping past me, she glanced around at the scattered tools and broken furniture. "I meant, is this the lost tomb of Amenhotep?"

"I'm not sure yet," I said, scratching sparse stubble on my chin as I eased through crackling pages. "Looks like a translated ancient Egyptian story."

"Like the 'Tale of Sinuhe'?" she asked, finally studying the book in my hands. "But Egyptians typically used papyrus for stories. Could it be translated from the hieroglyphs on the walls of a tomb or pyramid, or the Hall of—"

I shrugged. "Not from these walls—I studied them. And, no, it's more recent than Sinuhe and similar stories," I said. Maddie stared at me now. "Where're our guides?"

"They said they would not be coming inside. Their faces turned as pale as ghosts, and they wouldn't move."

"Why?" I asked.

Maddie shrugged. "Worried about disturbing the dead, maybe? Curses?"

I shook my head in disbelief. "But look at this." Flashing my light onto the tomb walls, ancient but still vibrant hieroglyphs glowed in yellow, green, red, and blue. Ornate symbols coated in dust adorned the face of every surface, rising to twice the height of a man.

Maddie's petite jaw fell open, and her lips grew slack. "Gavin, could this tell us how to locate the Hall of Records?" Her voice cracked, and her flashlight shook. "Are these clues or a map to the treasure ... to the secrets and answers to the most important questions people have asked since the beginnings of civilization?"

"There isn't anything of real value in here," Mr. Scalone said, tossing an object aside.

I gritted my teeth in frustration. "It's going to take a while for me to interpret these hieroglyphs," I said. "Morning will bring guards and tourists. We'll be arrested."

Leaning over a dust-covered object, Maddie ran a hand through her straight, brown hair and tucked it behind an ear. A sparkle gleamed in her eyes as she whipped her flashlight around the scattered artifacts. "We better get started, then," she said, her pupils dilating. "I'd like to see the treasures, learn how to become a god, read the formulas from the magical Scroll of Thoth, learn the secrets of the heavens, the universe, and the earth, and understand what the animals of the world are all saying."

I scoffed with skepticism. Even I didn't believe in the legend of the Scroll of Thoth, although I needed the Hall of Records to be real. The Hall could unveil secrets about the past, and possibly the present and future. But how could it possibly grant the knowledge and power for apotheosis—for a man to become god-like on earth, like a pharaoh?

Mr. Scalone snatched the journal from my hand and thumbed through it.

"Hey!" I said, reaching out to take it back. He shoved me away. "Be careful!"

Anger rose inside. I imagined myself in a caged ring, circling Mr. Scalone. He'd hold the journal. A crowd would watch in hushed silence. Maddie would sit in the front row, twirling her hair with nervous tension. I'd rush Mr. Scalone and we'd lock arms, sprawling down with the sharp slap of bodies on canvas. He'd punch at my face, but I'd grab his wrist and pull it back. My legs would wrap around his torso, locking his elbow. He'd scream and pound the mat, tapping out. The crowd would erupt with cheers, and Maddie would run into the ring, handing me the journal as she kissed my cheek—

"Oh my god!" Maddie's shrill cry echoed through the chamber.

I spun around in shock, my stomach catching in my throat.

She stood before a pile of broken stone, which obscured a dark passageway.

Mr. Scalone dropped the journal and ran over to assist with moving debris.

Scooping up the book, I brushed it off and placed it in my messenger bag.

Maddie and Mr. Scalone crawled over the shattered rubble of another once-sealed doorway. I ran after them.

Inside the next chamber, light darted amongst objects from millennia long past—broken, but of academic value—and settled on an opened granite sarcophagus. Reflections danced off of gold, black, and ivory engravings encrusting the coffin. My heart raced, and my throat dried in anticipation, forcing a swallow.

"The lost tomb of Amenhotep?" Maddie whispered, studying a broken figurine at her feet—a *shabti* statuette. "This is the burial chamber. A treasure room should be adjoining this one!"

Mr. Scalone reached down for the discarded object.

"You probably shouldn't touch anything else," Maddie said. "Not yet."

"Why?" he asked, his heavily tattooed hands and arms hovering over the blue and red hieroglyphs upon the statuette. "Will we be cursed? Like the coincidence during the discovery of King Tut's tomb? It wasn't even the workers; it was Lord Carnarvon, the man funding the expedition, who died suddenly in times when medicine was hardly advanced."

"But he died from a mosquito bite," Maddie said. "Then his dog died and other mysterious deaths followed. We need to catalog this all correctly first."

The guide didn't reach farther but still eyed the treasure.

My trembling fingers squeezed the bronze bracelet on my forearm as I attempted to steady myself. Breathing came in tense, shallow gulps. I didn't believe the tales, but reality faded down here. The ancient spells said death would come swiftly to whoever disturbed Pharaoh's rest. "Something down here killed the professor's student. And how could anyone else have gotten in or out?"

"How do you know it was his student?" Maddie asked, standing on her tiptoes to peek into the sarcophagus.

"The name on the inside cover of the journal is John Walsh," I said. "He was a PhD candidate under Dr. Shelsher."

Mr. Scalone's large fingers brushed against the crushed face of the *shabti* figurine. He chuckled, grabbed the statuette, and thrust it up into the light. The air turned cold, and the walls shuddered around us, releasing a musty stench.

Chapter 4

Present Day

A BOOM SHOOK THE MOUNTAIN around us. I jumped before realizing thunder had cracked outside the tomb.

Mr. Scalone dropped the crushed artifact. "A piece of forgotten crap compared to what I was expecting," he said, walking away.

Maddie examined the once-colorful female figurine, crafted of bronze. "This one's supposed to be Pharaoh's concubine in the next life." Laughing, she placed the damaged artifact into a plastic sack before nestling it into her messenger bag. "Gavin, maybe you should take one. You know, since you can't get anywhere with Kaylin."

I almost dropped my flashlight in shock. What? Did Maddie really think I wanted Kaylin, our mutual friend from college whose rich dad was backing this expedition? She must be teasing, attempting to relieve any tension from turning me down in the past.

A reflective sparkle momentarily blinded me. The wavering beam of my flashlight settled upon the outer sarcophagus of the glorious dead. I gulped stale air, awestricken. Eerie images of a twisted mummy, the fallen god-king sleeping within the eternal granite, flooded my mind.

"Just one souvenir," Maddie said. "My mentors will love it." Her light also focused on the sarcophagus, whose worth to history would be more precious than anything else in the burial chamber.

Forcing a deep breath, I stepped forward. Our flashlights wavered over the coffin, the beams hunting for crevasses beneath the gaping lid. Leathery brown skin from a gnarled leg lay exposed. I gasped in astonishment, and sweat trickled down my brow. Maddie clamped a hand over her open mouth and froze. Leaning over, I cast my light farther inside the stone box, half expecting to be yanked in.

The stinging reek of embalming agents permeated the inner confines, even after all these years. But no inner layers of coffins or precious artifacts remained. The crumbling mummy of the ancient pharaoh stared toward the heavens, surrounded by dust—

"There's nothing in the next room either," a voice echoed from the darkness. I jumped back in surprise. Mr. Scalone reentered from another side passage, one that would have led to the pharaoh's treasure room.

"Nothing?" Maddie asked.

"Just discarded junk," Mr. Scalone said.

"Maybe I should collect what's left," Maddie replied.

"We don't have time," I said. "It'd take days to catalog it in your ivory tower format. I'm going to read the hieroglyphs and could use your help."

"Meet you there in a minute," Maddie said. "Just gonna peek inside the treasure room."

My head hung in growing disappointment, like a wilted plant. I needed to find a clue about the Hall, like Dr. Shelsher's letter said we would. Stepping back into the antechamber, I pushed the brim of my fedora up and located the beginning of the hieroglyphs. The images started due east, carved with perfectionist precision, just as the tombs and pyramids. I faced the origin of life itself, the rising sun. Blowing a layer of dust into a swarming cloud, I touched the ancient symbol of a man. A tingle ran throughout my body, connecting me to the ages. The presence of men and women working the tomb by oil lamps, the artists with their brushes, and the rasp of their breathing floated around me.

The intricate detail of the figures evoked sounds or thoughts. Attempting to form English sentences, I started slowly and awkwardly, but soon the artwork came alive. Descriptions and translations sprang into my mind. Grabbing a notepad from my bag, I jotted down important ideas, potential clues, or anything that seemed out of the ordinary for typical tomb jargon.

I was becoming lost in the timeless words, the tingling of discovery fueling limitless energy, when a boom echoed through the walls of the tomb, spilling gritty dirt onto my head. Grating from stone on stone rattled the stagnant air. This wasn't thunder. My muscles tensed with apprehension. What had Maddie and the guide been doing? Jumping to my feet, I dropped my pen and paper and crept toward the commotion. Maddie sprinted past me to the stairway, bounding up two steps at a time.

Barreling out of an adjoining chamber, Mr. Scalone crumpled papers against a camera. What was happening? I raced up the ancient steps, following them back to the entrance.

"No!" Maddie screamed, heaving for breath as she reached the summit. Her fingers arched like claws beside her face. "The opening!" Leaning over beside Mr. Scalone, she tried to push and pull against a sliding stone slab filling the exit, which had ropes attached to the upper surface that slid into a perfect semicircular defect carved into the block in the wall above. The false block entrance that had dangled over the doorway …

My heart skipped a couple beats. Someone was trying to trap us inside the tomb!

I assisted, but pulling on the edges with all of our might couldn't match the strength of whoever was out there. Rumbling into the void, the block's margins fell even with the inside bricks and ceased moving.

We shoved outward, but the slab wouldn't give. The smooth surface and now-flush edges yielded nothing to pull on. Yelling, I clenched a fist to punch the stone but took a breath and rapped it with my knuckles. Maddie screamed and repeatedly smacked its surface with the flat of her palm. Bellowing as loud as he could, Mr. Scalone cursed and shook his fists and tattoo-encrusted forearms. He jumped and caught the ropes protruding from the wall above the false block. Hanging on them and tugging, he shoved his feet against the wall. The block didn't budge.

Pounding and tamping rang from outside, vibrating the walls of the tomb. Earth rained on us from above. We fought against the stone long after the noises outside ceased. Darkness engulfed us, broken only by the pale beams of flashlights. We were trapped.

Hyperventilating with disbelief and dread, I searched the area.

"Someone really didn't want us to find this place," Maddie said, slumping down onto the stairway. She held her face in her hands, and terror revealed itself in her trembling limbs.

My heart melted with sympathy. "I …" I wasn't sure what to say. We could all die in here. My body sank onto the stairs in defeat. "I'm sorry. But we might still get out of here."

Storming along the wall, Mr. Scalone cursed and shoved on everything.

"I knew the consequences," Maddie said, not exposing her eyes. "I could've stayed home or in Cairo with Kaylin." Two tears rolled out from under her palms and glided down creamy cheeks, gathering below shaking lips. "I wanted to believe in something bigger, like you do. The mystery got to me. What a mistake."

Remorse for bringing her along created a hollow sinking feeling deep in my stomach. Could my wild ideas have gotten us both killed? I'd messed up plenty of times on my own, but now I'd taken Maddie with me. If something happened to her, I'd never forgive myself. I wanted to reach out to comfort her, but my quivering hand didn't respond. "Maybe there's another way out," I said, yanking my phone from my bag. No service.

Maddie's hands fell to her side, her eyes cloudy behind fogged lenses. "Out of a tomb in the desert, buried by the sands of time?" Grabbing her own phone, she clicked through a few screens.

She was right. Secret exits weren't common in ancient Egyptian tombs. Burial complexes were flawless and designed to protect Pharaoh and his treasures for the next life while denying thieves access. Tapping my foot on the steps, I tried to speak through parched vocal cords and fought back tears of my own. "Maybe time has loosened a stone or two. We could dig our way to the surface."

The resonating silence tugged my torso down even further into despair. If we somehow escaped this, I'd head home and follow a normal career path, like I was supposed to. I wouldn't interfere with Maddie's life anymore. The hope of a grand accomplishment kept life exciting and made me forget the things I didn't want to remember. But I just ended up crashing and burning harder and harder.

"It's just as much my fault," Maddie said. "I've laughed you off before, Gavin, and I'd have dismissed this, too, if I didn't want to believe you so badly. Damn it!" She slapped her knees. "Well, I think we know what happened to the student in here."

Glancing down into the darkness, images of both grisly mummies and their stark, sunken eyes sockets appeared in my mind. The corpse of the student lay gaunt and preserved in the moistureless environment. Dehydration must've killed him. How long had it taken him to die? How long would it take us?

Chapter 5

Present Day

MR. SCALONE CURSED, grabbed his pack, and stomped down the stairs, back to the lower chambers of the tomb.

"What happened to his hired locals?" I asked, examining the once again sealed secret entrance and walls.

Maddie shrugged. "Mr. Scalone found them. He guaranteed they were the type of people who could be trusted, for the right price. They make their living digging for artifacts. Maybe they ran off … or betrayed us."

"Those two couldn't have replaced the slab themselves, could they?"

"How did anyone else know we were here?" she asked. "Anyone besides Kaylin, her little brother, Aiden, and their bodyguard? They will find us … unless someone is guarding the mountain."

My eyes sprang open with new hope, but the feeling faded like dew under the desert sun. The remainder of our group in Cairo knew our destination was the pyramid mountain in the Valley of the Kings, but they didn't know we had climbed up and dug inside. Kaylin, her brother, and the bodyguard, Jenkins, were probably lounging in the hotel waiting for our call. Maddie had convinced me this crew would be the minimum to try to pull this whole thing off. I knew a lot about ancient Egypt and possessed textbook knowledge of modern medicine, but my talents ended there. I hadn't been on any adventures before … or traveled much of anywhere. Reluctantly, I had agreed to let the others join us.

Through Kaylin's father's funding and influence, we had been granted an informal meeting with the Egyptian Minister of Antiquities. As I'd sat outside a small Cairo café, sweat had accumulated in the crook of my elbows and back of my knees. Compact cars raced along the nearby street, flinging dust and honking so often the racket grew into background noise. Aiden, a beanpole teenager, stared absently as music blared out of earbuds partially concealed by red dreadlocks. The hired bodyguard stood silently against a nearby wall.

A black limo had parked at the curb. Two hulking men in gray stepped out, flanking a man in a white suit. Striding directly for our table, the man in white sat down. He sipped from a steaming cup, which wafted an herbal aroma, while scrutinizing us and our story. Speaking with only a slight accent, he said we could apply for excavation rights, but it'd take years, and we'd probably be denied amidst these times of civil unrest and terrorism. He warned us that exhuming artifacts illegally carried stiff sentences, then patted his wavy gray hair, donned dark sunglasses, and excused himself.

We hadn't revealed Dr. Shelsher's letter or our true purpose of locating the Hall of Records. But despite Kaylin's wealth and Maddie studying Egyptology, the Minister of Antiquities couldn't or wouldn't grant us access to sites not open to the public. Our childish excitement crumbled.

Maddie had slapped the table, rattling our cups. Not wanting Kaylin, Mr. Scalone, or the bodyguard to know too much, she briefly explained my letter and the opportunity of unearthing a tomb. Grinning, she suggested a vote.

Temptation had dangled before us like a golden fleece, creating a tingling in my stomach. Maddie, Mr. Scalone, Kaylin, and I decided to take the risk in hopes of discovering the Hall now, rather than waiting for a potential opportunity in several years. The police and military remained preoccupied with internal conflict, anyway. Tourist attractions had become a secondary or tertiary commitment. Also, once we revealed the secrets of the Hall, the Egyptian government should be grateful. We'd shine a positive light, distracting international attention from recent transgressions such as shooting unarmed protestors, locking up dissenters without trial, and terrorist attacks. Kaylin also mentioned that if we were really thrown in prison, her dad could buy us out.

Maddie and I had flown to Luxor to visit the Valley of the Kings. The others would stay behind in the comfort of the hotel until we unearthed the tomb—except for Kaylin's hired expert, Mr. Scalone. He insisted he come along, as he knew the country and had much more experience with explorations than either of us. After hiring a couple of locals in Luxor—

Gritty antacids broke between my teeth, returning me to the present. A painful cramping in my stomach climaxed, doubling me over before it subsided. "Did you share the letter with anyone else?" I asked. "Someone who might come looking for us?"

"No," Maddie said, her chin slumping onto her chest. "I had a lab technician corroborate the date of the paper and ink to the 1920s, to convince me it was genuine. But I didn't let him read all of it. In academia, the head of the department gets all the credit for their student's accomplishments. I wanted our stamps on this before inviting professors into the mix. My entire career could've been fashioned and funded from this discovery." More tears rolled out, cleaning streaks of dust from her skin before trickling off of her chin.

As I pondered our deaths, a shiver of terror ran through my body.

"You discover any clues about the Hall?" she asked, running a finger across a pile of dirt she'd formed at her feet. "I read about Pharaoh in his coffin text but didn't find much in the treasure or annex rooms."

"There're no obvious clues in the hieroglyphs," I said. "Typical spells from the Book of the Dead, the Book of Gates, and tales about Pharaoh and his allegiance and offerings to the gods."

"And what's inside the dead guy's journal?" Straightening, she cocked her head and moved her eyes as if reading. "Didn't you say it looked like he translated a story?"

"Yes," I said, tipping my fedora back. "There could be clues about the Hall buried in there, but it'll take a while to read."

"Unless that book tells us how to get out of here, we're in serious trouble. And nothing the student knew worked for him. If we don't escape, everything the professor discovered, including the Hall, will be lost again." Her voice grew tense, as if history were more significant to her than her own life. "And this time it'll be lost forever." Brushing aside her tears, she rolled her dark locks into a bun on top of her head. "Maybe Mr. Scalone has some ideas."

Shuffling down the stairs, she dragged a shovel along behind her. The grating of steel on stone followed her into the darkness.

My spirits sank as I watched her go. How could I make her feel better? "At least if we die, it's in a place we always wanted to be part of," I said.

She glared from the edge of the shadows created by my flashlight. Not even the corner of her pink lips turned up. "We only have enough water to survive a couple days."

My stomach cramped again, this time with anxiety. Rifling through my messenger bag, I pictured my pack with most of my supplies against the rock on the mountainside.

"Get off your asses and find a way out," Mr. Scalone said, stepping back into view. "I've been in worse situations. Like the time I was thrown into solitary in Colombia. They didn't think I'd make it out of that one, either. Must've been pretty surprised when they opened my cell."

Maddie stomped her foot in defiance—creating a hollow echo—and stepped down alongside Mr. Scalone. "Come on, Gavin, don't give up yet!"

I gritted my teeth in frustration. Damn tour guide. He made her feel better, being a cocky bastard. But what could I do? Maybe he was our only hope.

Rushing down to the lower chambers, I prodded every inch of the crypt with my shovel. Mr. Scalone took pictures and tapped along with his own tool. Hours dragged by. No shouts of excitement echoed through the dark halls, and I couldn't find a crack wider than a hair's width. We hadn't slept for over twenty-four hours. Fatigue and a parched throat slowed my progress.

Sipping warm water, I washed gritty dust off my teeth and hacked. I felt along smooth walls, entering the cobweb-encrusted treasure room. The air lay heavier in the narrower confines and smelled of damp earth. An external presence hovered, growing more intense. Clanking from shovels echoed from the antechamber or annex room, their rhythm slowing.

Beyond what must've been the middle of the following night, I collapsed in exhaustion. In dreams past, I had played the champion, but recently, nightmarish scenes unfolded. As I slipped into sleep, the nightmares awoke once more.

I searched for something, hunting. Then I saw her face, the old woman's.

Chapter 6

Present Day

I DREAMT THAT BLOOD POOLED *across my gloved hands as I lifted a dismembered foot from the operating table. Blue drapes slipped away. Aching from standing in one spot for at least an hour, I offered a hemostat to Dr. Banks. I couldn't observe much through the small opening in the blue towels and had been contemplating what I'd do if the surgeon fell over from a heart attack. The patient's anterior tibial artery might shoot blood across the room like a pulsing water fountain. The nurse would scream. I'd catch the collapsing doctor in one hand, so I could keep the other sterile and clamp off the bleeder. The splashing against the far wall would cease. Then the nurse would care for the surgeon while I saved the patient … or maybe I should let the doctor fall and save—*

Dr. Banks yelled, ruffling the blue mask over his nose and chin. The head nurse laughed at me, her swollen midsection jiggling under purple scrubs. The surgeon motioned for me to place the amputated tissue aside as he closed the subcutaneous layer over the tibia. The heat of embarrassment rose in my cheeks.

The dark foot in my hands felt like a hundred-pound weight. But this old woman had suffered from poorly controlled diabetes and needed the amputation. I opened a black bag. The slippery blood released my grip on the foot and it dropped onto the floor with a splat. No signature lay on top of the foot or on the arch. Freezing in panic, I barely registered Dr. Bank's shouting or the pointing from students who observed through the partition window. Springing over to the operating table, I threw up the blue drapes. The surgeon screamed. His face flushed as red as the blood on my gloves. But it was too late. I'd already seen the signature on the anesthetized patient's other foot. That foot had been the one we were supposed to remove! And I was in charge of making sure she was marked and draped appropriately. Collapsing, I hit the hard floor with a crack. Everything went black.

Familiar images arose in the dream, and my heart rate slowed, my ribs expanding for deeper breaths. I wandered through a barren desert and stumbled upon a gleaming white city beside a river. Searching for friends, I found buildings filled with horrors, although I couldn't put a face to any of them. No reanimated mummies chased me, but the monsters appeared no less ghastly. A cold fog swirled around my feet as I fled in terror.

Waves then slapped against wood as I sailed upon a boat with several companions, unable to recall their faces. I longed to meet them. Then I could almost make out a semblance of her features. A biting nostalgia sprang forth, caking my eyelids with tears. The smell of citrus—

A boot sank into my ribs, jolting me awake just before I saw the woman who haunted my dreams. Scrambling away in surprise, I flailed like a seizuring animal.

Maddie stood over me with a flashlight beaming into my eyes. "You scared the crap out of me!" she said. "I thought you were dead."

"How long was I out?" I asked, trying to hide a yawn.

She glanced at her watch, a pale blue light reflecting off of her tired features. "Maybe an hour or two. It's seven in the morning."

"Already?" I asked, rubbing my scratchy eyes and running a hand through my short brown hair. "Did you sleep?"

"How could I sleep in this situation?" she asked, folding her arms across her chest. "I just took a break."

My head slumped in shame, and my stomach cramped with biting pain. Digging through my bag for pills stronger than antacids, I said, "I don't think well without sleep." I clicked on my metal flashlight. The beam reflected off cobweb-covered walls, quickening my pulse. Recent memories rushed back in a flood, and fear turned my body cold. Stringing webs clung to my pants, shirt, hair, and even the inside of an ear. I squeezed my eyes shut, trying not to picture spiders crawling on me, and brushed myself off in a frenzy.

Maddie smirked. "Just pretend we're back in college cramming for a final. You didn't even look at the material until the day before and had to stay up all night." She paused. "What excuse did you give your teachers for being gone? You'd probably need a pretty good reason in med school. Can I assume they won't be looking for you anytime soon?"

Locating the gray herringbone pattern of my fedora, I hid my disgrace. Maddie finally huffed and stomped away, back to the outer chambers. I searched the tomb for a couple more hours before stumbling back to the steps and collapsing in failure and exhaustion. Escaping this crypt was hopeless.

Maddie sat beside me, absently gnawing on a granola bar and sipping water. I gobbled a handful of cashews. The salt shriveled my tongue and forced me to take a gulp of precious water.

Resting with his back against a wall, Mr. Scalone shoveled down a handful of dark jerky. His stuffed backpack lay beside him. How much food and water did he have? So far he hadn't offered us anything or asked if we had enough. Would he if the time came?

"I have a few packs of batteries in my bag," Maddie said, "but maybe we should turn off the flashlights when we're just sitting here, to conserve." She clicked hers off. Mr. Scalone and I followed suit—suffocating darkness swallowing us. Teeth crunched on food. The rasps of breathing grew in volume as my eyes darted about in escalating panic.

A light flashed back on. "I can't take it!" Maddie said, her voice faint as if she'd just sprinted a few laps. "While I have the option, the lights stay on ... even if it means we live our last hours in the dark." Standing, she shivered as if she'd just seen the dead. Something in the distance caught her attention, and she inched away. I clicked my flashlight on, watching her go. Extending her face as far from the student's corpse as she could, she searched his pockets. She dug a cracked wallet and timepiece from his suit, examined the items, and placed them into her bag.

"Okay," she said in a high-pitched tone, trying to sound optimistic. But the dirt and sweat stains covering her clothes and her tangled hair clashed with the ruse. "Kaylin's probably already sent a search party, and I'd like to learn the greatest secrets of the human race before we … Gavin, maybe it's time to crack open that journal again. What if it grants us the power of a god-king?"

Intelligence, optimism, and just a hint of sarcasm radiated from her.

She was still beautiful. My head felt light under the influence of attraction.

Who could control who they desired? Well, I wish she could so she would pick me instead of the hunkier types she usually went for.

"How 'bout I read?" she said, sitting beside me. "I'm probably a faster translator. You know, years of education."

"You could give a flawless interpretation," I said, "but it looks like he wrote the English version. And I worry …" Pausing, I considered my words. I didn't want to offend her and her training. I looked down, my hands sliding under my thighs as my shyness controlled me. But I didn't want to hand over my one prize from my only expedition. "I've spent my life on this subject too, even if not academically. And we wouldn't be here if I hadn't picked certain clues out of the letter."

Maddie's eyes narrowed, but the bridge of her nose wrinkled and one corner of her lips lifted. "Okay, you can read it to me."

I let out a long sigh, releasing an aching tension. The horror of our situation mildly subsided. Discovering something new about ancient Egypt would ease our minds. What else could we do at this point? Hopefully the others would find us and dig us out.

"Idiots." Mr. Scalone grunted between moist chomps of meat. "We don't need a goodnight story; we need to get outta here." Grabbing his pack, he disappeared into the darkness.

I blinked my gritty eyes and ran a hand across my face. At least the air was cool in this tomb, compared to the 90 to 115 degrees Fahrenheit in the desert outside. I dug out the leather-bound book, its cover peeling like scales of a reptile. Turning the first crinkling page, I read, "You who can read this have truly entered the Hall of Records. Behold the secrets of the grandest and longest-reigning civilization that will ever exist in this world. This is The Legend, as old a tale as has ever been recorded by man. The greatest story ever told."

Chapter 7

Journal Translation

LET MY VOICE ECHO from this eternal hall of stone and carry throughout the ages. May these words be heard by those with the ability to discover them. When you interpret the past you may perceive the future.

If you're reading this, then I'm already dead, passed from this world to the beyond—my attempt to achieve immortality, the birthright of the privileged few, failed.

Many times I have struggled to tell this tale, to comprehend the truth of what really happened. I shared only pieces with friends and family, to spare them the horror and despair. This is my final rendition.

The world is already old. Tens of thousands of years passed before the first god arrived and united us, when we were nothing but wandering nomads. The writings at Karnak, Memphis, Abydos, the Palermo Stone, and the Turin Royal Canon indicate the god-kings ruled our empire for over 1,500 years before my time. So many pharaohs lived and passed into the beyond, blessing or destroying our kingdom.

I was an ordinary man, born to a common man and woman. Not a god-king, but I lived with the splendor and the heinous, never forgetting the day I overheard Akhenaten's dreams. These ramblings succeeded his own death, but God, the Aten, had previously resurrected him before my very eyes. We were young when his brother, the crown prince, would soon die and leave behind a trail of mystery. Akhenaten claimed to have witnessed it all when he visited the underworld.

"The gods are dead," Akhenaten said into the shadows, waving his gangly limbs. Firelight danced behind him, outlining his form like a demon. "They destroyed each other in a great war following their human deaths.

"Remembrances of deific struggles have scarred our lands. Apart from the river and the black banks, there is only the red desert … a wasteland. A thousand years ago, it was not so. Lush oases decorated the sands, and herds of animals roamed. It has all crumbled to ash and dust."

Crouching into my hiding spot, I eavesdropped on the evil thoughts buried beneath Akhenaten's façade. The cold sweat of fear trickled down my back, causing me to shudder. Flames crackled, twisting his shadow into a monster. Thick smoke burned my nostrils, carrying the reek of something haunting. A slit of light eked beyond his body and landed upon my face. I held my breath, my heart pounding in my ears.

"This world is the only one left in all the universe, after the passing of the so-called gods." His oddly deep voice resonated, as if speaking to someone. But he appeared to be alone. "All of the gods except the Aten, the sun itself, have fallen. The living sun-disc is the giver and taker of all life in our world. The sun is dominion! The sun and Akhenaten, we will be one and the same after Father passes. I will become the Aten and control all of existence!"

What madness boiled beneath my master's eyes and his twisted shadow? I should've run, but I couldn't force myself away.

Holding a white blade above his head, he twisted the knife and watched shadows tread across a golden hilt. He sliced into his forearm. My eyes and jaw popped opened like those of a fish being yanked from the Nile. Dark blood streamed from the gash, running down his wrist. Cupping his hand, he cradled the liquid before it crawled over his fingers and dripped onto the floor. Leaning his head back, he closed his eyes in pleasure. His shadow flickered in a direction opposite his body. I gasped in shock. Slamming an open palm over my mouth, I held my breath in fright. What sinister force could explain what I had just witnessed, some kind of magic? Or had terror manipulated my mind?

Snatching a pitcher, Akhenaten poured liquid onto his wound. Fizzing bubbles erupted. Screaming in pain, he shoved a wadded rag into his mouth. Muffled shrieks ran on for nearly a minute but didn't carry down the dark hall.

He eased the cloth from his lips; strands of saliva clung on like spider webs. "That is why only the strong thrive and reproduce in this world.

There are no gods who reward kindness or dignity, you ignorant fool! The ravenous and avaricious obtain power over the meek, only to be rewarded.

"Do you still not understand? Our world is the world of the gods, with the Aten and Pharaoh. The underworld is for mortals; I've seen it! God chose the laws of this land. And he is capricious. He may favor you now but could turn on you in an instant. We currently exist in what people believe is the glorious afterlife, our *Duat*. Breathe in the moment. False promises of a more comfortable life after death should never dictate how you live today."

He turned his head, and firelight flashed in the corner of his eye. My heart raced with fear. Swooning, I nearly collapsed. Had he noticed me spying? Or had he been speaking to me the entire time?

Chapter 8

Journal Translation

B UT MY SITUATION DID NOT begin this way. Father said a phoenix cried the moment the sun sank behind the western hills, suffocating my mother's final scream as the doctor pulled me into this world and she departed for the next.

Entering with the sunset—the repeated cycling death of the Aten—I wailed as Osiris took hold of the earth. A child of darkness who executed his mother, or so they told me.

Father worked himself weary to earn servitude to Akhenaten's father, one of Egypt's greatest god-kings, Amenhotep III. Throughout Pharaoh's extensive reign, he developed and nurtured the country. People swam in wealth and prosperity, enjoying comforts previously unknown. But given the peace Amenhotep III cast across Egypt and all the lands of the outer world, the military's strength began to wane.

As a servant of the only immortal in the world—an honor that God bestowed upon Father—Father would be granted access to communion. This would help our family blossom in the eyes of the Aten. God helped the faithful pass divine judgment and be reborn in the underworld, once they had completed the first two steps of the life, death, and rebirth cycle. We only needed to work hard and pray often throughout our short time in this world. Then we'd live together in eternal happiness.

Luck smiled on this common boy. I grew up alongside Amenhotep III's second son, Akhenaten, originally named Amenhotep IV. He was several inundations older than I—the inundation represented our annual flood and measure of time. And after Akhenaten's previous servant went mad,

Pharaoh appointed me as his son's personal subject. I'd serve and learn from a direct descendant of God.

But everything changed. After I received my life's position, following an ordeal I cannot yet relive and discuss, Akhenaten and I played together. Relentless sun and overlying sky surrounded us, stretching infinitely blue. The desert aridity parched my tongue and throat, but I hadn't known anything different. We sat in white, knee-length kilts upon the sand, a board game resting between us. Rays of heat rained down, but he insisted on remaining under the living sun-disc, the Aten our God, the creator and destroyer of all life.

For the first time, Akhenaten allowed me to play the board game *senet* with him, to hone his skills for future contests. He'd claimed the title of Reigning Champion of the kingdom years ago and had no intention of ever losing. The most popular game of our time put strategy, wisdom, and blind luck to the test.

From where the future god sat in front of me, his disfigurements were subtle. At the time, he was not meant to rule, but perhaps the Aten changed its mind after the birth order of Pharaoh's sons. Perhaps the Aten fashioned him peculiarly because he'd be different. His father didn't carry those spindly limbs, the elongated face with thick lips, or the prominent cheekbones. Despite his thin frame, his stomach and chest sagged, but his most striking feature was his elongated skull. Destined to wear the red and the white crowns of Lower and Upper Egypt, his head was already cast in their shape.

Akhenaten's eyes flashed up, cast in shadow below thick, black eye paint. "Your turn," he said, his floral and leather-scented body oils mingling in the heat.

I sat captivated by his grotesque appearance.

"Stop staring," he said, his voice growing deeper as his lips thinned and pulled back. "My other servants are old and boring, but you watch me like them." As he shifted his hunched form, a dark cloud settled over the sun. Spidery fingers reached for his walking stick, which always rested nearby. But his eyes turned misty, drifting off into another world. "Do I intrigue you? Am I not fit for the eyes of a mere servant?" Tapping his finger against a sunken cheek created a hollow echo.

I shook my head, my gaze sliding away.

"I will grow out of this appearance. My father, the god-king, told me so." A single tear pooled in the corner of his eye.

The sinking sensation of pity filled my heart. Did he play with me to avoid judgment from the other royal children? Were we not friends? "I was only admiring your tactic on passing the water test," I lied, trying to deflect attention to the *senet* game. "You're from the family of the Aten and will achieve the afterlife and greatest glory we all hope for. If I look upon you, it's only with envy."

Snarling like a lion, he hesitantly let his words fall. "If I were to be Pharaoh I would understand. But coming so close without ever transforming into God himself ... I do not think I am favored, and I curse those responsible."

An uncomfortable sinking sensation arose in my gut. Swallowing, I stared at the sand.

"It is your move," he said.

I counted along the thirty squares with the game piece for my soul, *ba*, and the piece for my life force, *ka*. Landing upon a square of power, I earned a spell from the Book of the Dead.

Yelling, I jumped up into a victory dance, my legs and arms swaying to the rhythm of the *sistra* rattle in my head. "I passed judgment! I'm on my way to the afterlife!"

"Impossible!" Akhenaten said. Placing one hand on his stick, his other clawed through the dirt. The sun's rays faded again, and a chill wind rustled my hair and kilt. My master's knees bent backward slightly as he planted his feet. His hunched form rose, fan-shaped shoulder blades sliding under thin muscles like wings of a great bird.

My stomach grew empty with worry, like an endless hunger. I'd made a mistake.

"You cheated. A commoner will never receive power before me!" Lifting his face to the sky, he opened his palms and shrieked, "Why?" His ribcage expanded before his gaze settled on me. "You passed the water test because of my assistance. I believed you would be a good servant in the next life. But I said four spaces. You did not roll three and receive a spell from The Book."

"I must've misheard ... I thought—"

"Silence!" he said, thrusting a long finger at me. "You do not even know how to count or read. I tell you what the dice say. You are just a servant with no education, and you know nothing. But you are a cheater." His elongated eyes narrowed, the black on his upper lids stretching.

I spoke in my meekest voice, fear rising inside like a flood. "No, a mistake. I barely know how to count."

"Grab a stick," he said, pointing behind me.

Shuffling to a nearby mud-brick wall with my head down, I kicked up dust before arriving at a stack of poles. I fumbled around and picked a sturdy stick, its surface knotted and blanched from the sun. The object emphasized my scrawny frame. What did he plan to do?

"Come over here."

I inched my way back. "Are we going to play the bat and ball game?" My lips quivered.

"We will let God decide," he whispered in a hollow voice, striding up to me with a stiff-legged gait. "You are too ignorant to understand the significance of the bat and ball. The ball is the eye of the evil serpent, Apep. If you smite his enemy, the Aten will grant you power in the underworld." He stalked me. "I see Apep now."

Swallowing a touch of my apprehension, I said, "I can throw the ball so you can hit it harder." I motioned with a fake toss. "It'll be fun and grant you even more favor!" Plucking a ball from the ground, I lobbed it at him. He batted the toy directly into the earth.

"Games prepare us for the trials of the underworld, before the Aten and the judges," he said. "You, I fear, will never pass into the next life. Your *ba* will be consumed by the Devouring Monster, even if you stumble upon the chamber of judgment—"

Laughter from approaching children floated on the wind, drawing his attention.

His words bit deep, stinging my heart. I'd heard stories of the Devouring Monster. When God judged a person, his heart was weighed on a scale against a feather, representing the divine and righteous order. If the objects were of equal weight, the heart belonged to a person who had lived a decent life. If not, the organ would be cast to the vile beast, a monster with the face and jaws of a crocodile, the body of a lion, and the rear of a hippopotamus. When a man's heart, the essence of his thought, personality, and memory, was consumed by the Devouring Monster, he'd cease to exist in any world. No greater punishment could be dealt.

Akhenaten spoke in anger but knew more about these matters than me. I only learned what he taught me, as in recent years Father had turned peculiar. When I was young, Father had educated me in the ways of the world, but now whenever I asked about obscure and deeper matters, he grew fearful. He assured me that I'd learn all I needed to know about God from my master. After all, Akhenaten received daily mentoring on all manner of subjects from the most educated scribes, court advisors, councilmen, high priests—

My master's head snapped back, and he eyed me like a great cat about to pounce upon the weakest of the herd. Hoisting my stick in shaky hands, I attempted a feeble defensive stance. His thick lips pulled back into a smile, only a few feet from my face. A crushing sensation ensnared my throat and chest like the jaws of a crocodile. I gasped for breath. Quaking with fear, I coughed and attempted to scream for help. Only gurgling came out. Fog swirled across my vision as darkness closed in. What was happening? Magic? Frantically tearing at the nothingness around my neck, I attempted to free myself. The pressure released.

Heaving for air, I leaned over. Muddled thoughts stirred as my vision returned. I'd heard tales of mysterious powers flowing in secret throughout our world, but I'd never seen proof of their existence—

The strangling and compression on my chest returned, this time stronger. I fell to my knees.

Chapter 9

Journal Translation

M Y EYES FLUTTERED LIKE shutters, alternating night and day. Thoughts whirled in confusion. Akhenaten towered over the board game, kicking my *ba* and *ka* into the dirt. He cursed names I'd never heard with violent defiance, dust swirling around his feet and a hot wind whipping his kilt.

A group of young girls raced toward us, one standing out. Nefertiti, Akhenaten's cousin, was young but the most beautiful woman I had or would ever lay eyes on. My mind clouded just looking at her. I attempted to rise. Nefertiti's younger sister, Mutnedjmet, ran beside her. The smaller girl was cute with gentle features, and her feet floated through the sand. The third arrival was one of Akhenaten's five sisters, Beketaten. Although Beketaten didn't display Akhenaten's deformities, her frame swung awkwardly and her face stretched out like a horse's. I gazed back at Nefertiti, and our eyes met.

"What did you do?" Nefertiti asked her cousin, brushing long, dark hair away from her arching cheekbones. She knelt beside me, a deep floral and citrus bouquet teasing my senses. Her tender hands caressed my neck as she brushed my sidelock—the braided hair youth wear at the side of their heads—from my face. The most beautiful girl in the world, and royalty, no less, tried to assist me to a standing position. My dizziness from the strangling or her touch might have affected me, my foot slipping as I collapsed into the dirt. "Oh no!" she said, holding a delicate hand over her open mouth.

Akhenaten laughed. "Leave him be. He is nothing more than a servant and is not worth your time."

"You shouldn't treat anyone like this," Nefertiti said, shaking a finger at him. "Especially your only friend!"

Lunging at Nefertiti, Akhenaten raised his walking stick. She stood her ground, glaring up at him. Twisting his core like a serpent squeezing a rodent, he wound up for a strike.

"No!" I yelled, reacting faster than I had thought possible. Jumping to my feet, I lifted my own stick. But despite Akhenaten's build, he wielded inhuman strength. Striking like lightning, his weapon knocked my defense aside with a clap. Another sharp crack followed and resonated through my skull. I tasted metal …

✳ ✳ ✳

My head pounded, the kind of throbbing that radiates through your temples and down across your neck and shoulders. A dim light flickered, illuminating white walls strewn with vibrant paintings. I lay upon a bed of reeds in my cramped room. The smell of roses clung to the air and mingled with citrus. Something wet pressed against my face, and drops of cool water rolled down my forehead and cheeks. Nefertiti smiled. A purple ring encircled her eye, showing through her deep green eye paint.

"What happened?" I asked, my mind racing. I tried to sit up, my eyes focusing on the injuries marring her sculpted face. My lower lip cracked, and I tasted the saltiness of fresh blood.

Pressing her chest against mine, she forced me down. "Rest now," she said. Relief washed over me. "Are you all right?"

"I'm fine." She ran a hand through her hair, and dark locks cascaded down and bounced against a swollen cheek. A trail of dried blood led away from her nostril.

My muscles tightened in anger. Had Akhenaten hurt her? "No, you aren't—"

"You're my savior," she said, her smile partially veiled behind shiny hair. "You tried to protect me, risking your own life. I pray Akhenaten will forgive you." Gliding a tender hand across the dark stubble on my head, she tucked my sidelock behind my shoulder.

My heart beat like a drum. I was falling deeply in love. "What can I do to make you feel better?"

"Listen," she said. "I am thankful for what you did—it was very brave. But Akhenaten is from the line of Pharaoh. You shouldn't question him, or you'll suffer greatly in this life and the next. Pharaoh is fond of your father, but not more so than his own son."

Such was the world we lived in.

Giggling erupted inside my room. Nefertiti's little sister, Mutnedjmet, and Akhenaten's sister, Beketaten, sat across from us.

"Are you okay, Heb?" Mutnedjmet asked in a high-pitched voice, her bright eyes vibrating with energy. "I hope my stupid cousin didn't hurt you too badly and—"

"My brother could've injured you permanently if he had wanted to," Beketaten said. The tip of her nose twitched as she talked, her voice nasal. "He's very well trained in combat."

I couldn't speak, shocked to see so many females inside my room. But Mutnedjmet and Beketaten faded in the presence of their glamorous family member. Nefertiti blushed.

Was I staring? My tongue slowly responded. I didn't want her to ever leave. "How long can you stay?"

"Not long," Nefertiti said, scooting away. Her dark eyes sparkled beneath green paint.

"Who cares? He's just a servant boy," Beketaten said, glaring at her cousins. "It's like if your cat scratched you, you wouldn't starve it. Akhenaten will take him back."

"I'll stay with you, Heb," Mutnedjmet said, a smile crossing her young face.

I froze, confused. Was she really interested in my well-being? The sentiment sounded sweet, and I hadn't ever received female attention like this. But I desired to be alone with Nefertiti. The curious Mutnedjmet could become a nuisance.

"Mutnedjmet," Nefertiti said, "you'll be leaving with me. There'll be no girls in this boy's room after sunset."

Mutnedjmet's lips parted, but nothing came out. Her face flushed to a deep shade of crimson.

I wanted to say something to Nefertiti, so she wouldn't forget me in a couple of days. But my stomach burned with anxiety, and my tongue felt like a limp worm. "I wish I could serve you instead of him, my lady."

Nefertiti smirked with sealed lips. As Beketaten stormed out of the room, her sandals stomped the tiled floor.

My forehead wrinkled in confusion. She couldn't have cared about a poor servant boy's attention. Was it envy or resentment, then? Perhaps every boy favored Nefertiti.

"You were born to serve Akhenaten," Nefertiti said, watching Beketaten's steaming trail with wide eyes. "No one can change that." Standing, she took Mutnedjmet's hand, and they both departed.

Watching them disappear into the dim hallway, I fantasized about my next encounter with Nefertiti.

I had always tried to assist Nefertiti in anyway possible, often standing in her presence with my master, her cousin. But before today, I never thought she knew who I was—

Something landed on the floor beside me, making me jump. Sauntering over to my bed, an orange and white cat flopped down. The stripes over his trunk relaxed. He had entered through the room's single window, positioned so high I could barely reach it. The opening was fashioned only to provide ventilation from the day's heat, but even the papyrus-reed curtain for deterring bugs and sunlight didn't discourage him. I smiled with joy.

This creature was my best friend. I called him Croc, for crocodile of the Nile. In years past, I'd spotted something orange hiding amongst the reeds on the sunny riverbank. I had crept closer. A scrawny kitten! His dark orange streaks enticed me to sneak up behind him while he remained entranced with the water. Meowing, the awkward creature navigated through the foliage. I pinched his scruff, and he reacted quicker than anything I'd encountered. Gangly limbs thrashed, scratching my hands to shreds as he hissed like a snake. But I refused to let go. He bit, sinking needlelike teeth into my flesh.

Howling in pain, I'd released the miniature terror. He splashed into the river, swallowed by the calm waters. I gasped, my heart wrenching with guilt. Seconds crawled by without any hint of orange or white. The ripples faded. Sucking in a deep breath, I plunged headfirst into the cool water.

I scanned around erupting bubbles, diving deeper. He drifted amidst the blue with frozen limbs, appearing paralyzed. I propelled myself into the depths. He sank deeper, pawing at the water as if mystified but still unable to swim. He'd have to take a breath any second and drown. His suffering and death would be all my fault.

My hand had wrapped around his bony torso as he was about to gasp for air. Clamping down, I hoped to stop his chest from expanding so he wouldn't inhale the fluid. Unfortunately, I was also not a swimmer. Thrashing with one hand and flailing my feet, I writhed back toward the shore. My chest constricted as the air drained from my lungs. The surface remained too far away. My muscles contracted in panic, and my mouth opened on its own accord. Stinging water crashed against my closed throat, causing me to shudder violently. I clenched my lips and teeth. My chest heaved and spasmed. Then, with my hand raised, we broke out into the world together, choking and coughing as I crawled onto land. Releasing the tiny creature, we spewed water like clay drinking vessels.

"Careful, there're crocodiles," an old voice had said. A bald man with facial wrinkles so deep they appeared like crevasses clutched a reed net and backed away from the bank. He had not been there when I dove into the river. "Fishermen and those washing clothes are attacked most often. And we know not to splash around like wounded prey—and to avoid the surface and shore. That's their attack zone. You're going to get us killed. Now get out of here!"

Croc had remained immobile, wheezing for breath between fits of coughing. Tearing off my kilt, I wrapped him in it to protect myself in case he started biting again. I cradled him in my arms and ran, as naked as the day I was born. I glanced back; the fisherman was gone.

I raised my skittish new friend, and after months of feeding him, he warmed up to me. The awkward kitten grew into a regal cat and allowed me to stroke his soft fur, purring while he ate. His deep humming warmed my heart and comforted me whenever sadness or loneliness set in. Then he returned and slept on my bed every night, as if he owed me a life debt.

Petting the orange fur along his back, I followed his stripes. He purred and kneaded his toes on the reeds of my bed. A sense of calm rose within me. "Where were you when Akhenaten attacked me?"

Croc shut his eyes. I chuckled in spite of the aching in my head and recounted the events to my little companion. "What should I do if anything like that happens again? I can't tell Father. He'd be worried sick but unable to do anything. Perhaps if I hadn't killed Mother, she could have helped."

Croc stretched, his coarse footpads brushing my arm.

"I can't stand up to Akhenaten; he's God's son. But I don't want him to hurt Nefertiti."

Croc's eyes popped open as he let out a hiss. Sharp claws tore into my forearm as he leapt against the wall, scrambling up and out the window. Ouch! I glanced in the direction Croc had cursed in his own tongue, and eyes appeared. Horizontally elongated by black makeup, they glinted through the darkness of the hallway. The torch in my room flickered and grew dim. I swallowed, my stomach knotting with fear.

How long had he been there? Pretending not to notice, I closed my eyes.

"Sleep is boring," Akhenaten's airy voice whispered from the doorway. The smell of smoke followed. "Pharaoh tells me to lie down, to dream. I linger in boredom most of the night. If I have to be without the Aten, I would rather wander and watch what others do in his dark absence." A pause. "What do you do when he sails through the underworld? Do you sleep?"

I opened my eyes. Akhenaten's face hovered just inches from mine, his hot breath swarming me. Jumping back, I hit the wall and released a cry of surprise.

He chuckled. "I hope your head does not hurt too badly. Just do not stand in my way, question my actions, or cheat ever again. Do you understand, my sleepy little servant boy?"

I nodded, trembling with apprehension.

"I need to begin preparing," he said, stepping back. His eyes drifted, staring into nothingness. A moment later they refocused on me. "It is time for you to stop talking unless I ask. Do not address anyone. You are an inanimate object who serves me. Nothing more. You only trust what you hear if it is the sound of my voice. You only trust what you see if it is me you are watching. And you only trust what you feel if it is my emotion."

My gaze fell to the floor, the heat of shock and embarrassment rising in my cheeks.

"You will assist me in the morning, following this sleep."

Nodding, I didn't look up.

He slipped into the darkness of the hallway. "I may wander a little first, unless Father catches me again." His voice echoed down the corridor. "Even Pharaoh sleeps like a mortal. I have wandered into his chamber, and he has no idea I am even there."

Silence. I released a stifled breath and fell onto my bed.

"And do not get any ideas about Nefertiti. She is mine!" His mask of black eye shadow emerged. Then he vanished again, his footfalls fading into the distance.

Chapter 10

Present Day

MADDIE STARED AT THE book in my hands, and her shovel and flashlight clattered to the stone floor of the tomb—which we were trapped inside. "Oh my god! That's from the Hall of Records?" She pointed at the journal. "Akhenaten and Nefertiti? Two of the most famous of all ancient Egyptians?" She jumped up and down with her hands in the air, her bun bouncing.

I smiled at seeing Maddie's happiness in spite of our horrendous situation.

"Yes!" she yelled, her eyes sparkling behind dirty glasses. "We'll find out what really happened and obtain limitless knowledge. That's the promise of the Hall of Records, right? Or at least enough ancient knowledge, gold, and power to become god-kings."

Doubt gnawed at my conscience. "Maybe this is their story, but it's probably just ancient lore the student was piecing together."

I turned back to the diary to read aloud. Something about the words and the corresponding hieroglyphs appeared strangely familiar. The translation must've taken the professor or his student months. A chill slithered into the subterranean chamber. I adjusted my fedora by the pinched-front of the teardrop-shaped crown and buttoned up my shirt.

"You two gave up completely, huh?" Mr. Scalone asked, stepping into the antechamber and unleashing a heavy body odor. "You shouldn't be wasting time reading. I would like to survive this predicament." He motioned with his head. "Why's this mummy down here, anyway? Aren't they supposed to be inside pyramids?"

I responded first. "Pharaohs and their families were placed here hundreds of years after their deaths. Priests gathered them, wrapped them in linens to preserve their bodies, and made a great trek through Egypt. They hid the mummies from tomb raiders here in the Valley of the Kings. In the eighteenth dynasty—the time of Akhenaten and Nefertiti, actually—they built tombs here rather than constructing pyramids. The ancients began separating the mortuary temples, where the dead received offerings, from the hidden tombs so Pharaoh's final resting place wouldn't be disturbed or plundered. If we get out of here, look at the mountain's summit. Mount al-Qurn, literally the Horn, or what the ancients called The Peak. Its rocky apex resembles the pyramidion, the capstone of a pyramid, too obviously to be coincidence."

Maddie remained silent, probably agreeing with what I had said. But she could be a little condescending because of her formal training. She knew more, but sometimes our ideas didn't coincide. No one force-fed me their beliefs, so it was easier for me to think outside the box.

"How the hell would you know?" Mr. Scalone said. "This place was disturbed and plundered." Motioning for Maddie to follow him with one hand, his other large hand made a stop sign for me.

My brow tensed with suspicion. What was this guy trying to do now? They stepped out of sight, their voices becoming muffled. I crept after them.

The dull reverberation of wood tapping on hollow stone filled the air. The sarcophagus? Whispers followed. The echoes sounded like someone trapped inside a deep well. My mouth dropped in realization. There should be an actual well inside this tomb! But not in the burial room.

A murky image of the lowest chamber of a tomb popped into my mind. Something sparked inside of me. People often considered the wells built into the tombs in the Valley of the Gates of the Kings as magical. But in reality, wells were subterranean chambers meant to drain condensation and rainwater, so the tomb wouldn't be damaged. They were constructed near the entrance, where water typically worked its way in. Maybe there was another way out.

I snatched my shovel and leapt up the twisting stone steps with exhilaration. Climbing past the false block, I continued to the original sealed doorway and prodded the floor and the walls. I'd be a hero yet.

Something touched my back. Jerking, I spun around.

"Relax!" Maddie said, trying to hold my arms down as they instinctively rose into a defensive position. "There're no walking mummies in here, or they'd have taken you when you were sleeping."

Mr. Scalone ascended behind her, dragging the tip of his shovel along the wall. A frightening screech of grinding metal chilled my bones. What had he talked to Maddie about? Killing me off, so he'd have more water?

Chapter 11

Present Day

"ALREADY SEARCHED this area," Mr. Scalone said, nodding to the original sealed doorway of the tomb. "Looked here first because it's the closest to the surface."

My beam of light reflected off the rock beside the stairway. The margin against the wall tilted and angled like a gutter, falling into a long, narrow shaft the beam wouldn't penetrate.

"The well?" Maddie said.

"You think we should look down there?" I asked.

"I'm not," she replied. "You're not the type of guy I'd trust to protect me down there, or get me back out."

My heart buckled under the crushing fist of her words. So that was how she really saw me, a weakling. Even though I maintained a regular workout schedule, I could never really build up my thin limbs. My gastrointestinal disease didn't help, as it decreased nutrient absorption—

"I could do it," Mr. Scalone said, his head high as he hovered over me and the dark pit.

"That's why you're here," Maddie said, examining his muscular body. "But you still might have a hell of a time getting back out. Going farther down into what should be a chute and blind chamber doesn't sound like a good idea." Tilting her flashlight, she scanned the walls beside the shaft. Her light settled on a smooth layer of dirt at the base, just to the right of the original sealed doorway. "Is that where water worked its way through over the centuries?"

My muscles jolted. Here was my chance! Kneeling, I pushed a handful of dirt aside to reveal a small area of erosion on the edge of a limestone block. "Maybe we can dig our way out," I said, squeezing the shovel handle.

"I already prodded there," Mr. Scalone said. "The blocks aren't loose. We'd have to mine through them, and that'd probably take weeks."

"They might've grown soft, and limestone's already friable," I said, ramming the steel edge of the shovel into the cracks. I jumped on the handle in an attempt to lever the slabs, but they didn't budge. Flying into a frenzy, I jabbed the corner again and again. The steel created large indentations, but the work stung my hands with shuddering vibrations. Within minutes, I'd exhausted myself. Heaving for breath, I leaned over with my elbows on my knees and cursed. Mr. Scalone laughed.

Maddie settled a hand on my back. Shrugging it off, I stood up and kicked the stone in irritation. Did we have enough time and supplies to get through a single block? What other option did we have? I hadn't discovered any clues about the Hall of Records, and we wouldn't have enough time to read the entire journal. I'd seen thinner novels. Time was running out.

Maddie darted off but quickly returned wielding an ancient bronze pickaxe. Hoisting the tool over her head, she screamed and aimed for the wall.

"Wait!" I said, grabbing the wooden shaft, which jerked her out of her wind-up. "You can't use that! You'll destroy an artifact."

Rolling her eyes, she threatened a kick to my groin. "If we don't, we'll be history for sure!" She swung again. Ancient metal contacted stone, clinking and sinking in. The withered handle shot vibrations up her arms, contorting her look of determination into a grimace. She pulled back, but the tip had lodged into place.

Helping to pry the axe out, I wiggled it in a circle.

Mr. Scalone approached with his harder, steel shovel and thrust the tip into the indentation. It sank into the soft stone with a crack, and a small chunk broke free.

I almost shouted in glee, but the tiny fragment appeared miniscule beside the original slab. Using my shovel to hack at the edges, I alternated swings with Maddie. Not having enough room for all three of us to work on the erosion, Mr. Scalone retreated back into the lower chambers. I would quarry this rock and carry Maddie out with me.

After a couple of hours, Mr. Scalone gave up searching and taking pictures or whatever it was he was doing. Relieving Maddie, he mined into the block.

Constant darkness made it difficult to judge time, but at least a couple of days of intense work followed. I longed to see the sun. My gloves wore through, and my hands blistered and drained. My muscles and joints burned and ached. Guarding his pack, Mr. Scalone never offered us anything.

✳ ✳ ✳

The pickaxe head flew off the cracked handle and clattered down the stairs. Wedging the piece back on, I jammed my pocketknife into the top of the wood. I hoped that would expand its fitted end and keep the head in place. Blood from my raw hands oozed across the tool.

"Take these," Mr. Scalone said, holding out wrinkled gloves covered in brown stains.

I shuddered with disgust. He finally offers something, and it's nasty gloves? What kind of grime and dead skin hid in the filth inside those things? They smelled like forgotten gym socks. But they might ease the burning of my hands—

"Take the damn things," Mr. Scalone said, shaking them.

Grabbing the stiff leather gauntlets mummified to a bent-hand shape from dried sweat and blood, I closed my eyes and slid them on. We set to work again, excavating chunks of crumbled rock. Rubble broke loose and tumbled down the stairs with diminishing echoes.

An area large enough for one of us to fit in tunneled into the base of the wall. But no light streamed through. A rising sense of accomplishment faded. What if the hired hands had sealed us in and waited outside to make sure we never escaped? But we had no other options. I crawled into the gap.

Desert dirt and rock lay solidified just beyond the slab. Tapping it with my shovel emitted a muffled sound that didn't lighten my mood. Sighing with chagrin, I dug on.

✳ ✳ ✳

Our food disappeared, as well as the extra batteries. I offered Maddie the last swallow of my water while we dug our graves.

"How many feet do you think we'd have to dig through in total?" Maddie asked, wiping her dirt-encrusted brow with a gaunt hand.

I grimaced. Probably more than either of us wanted to hear. "Depends on where this entrance is in the mountainside compared to the secret block," I said.

Resting her shovel, she glared. "Tell me. I've already accepted we may not make it out."

"Five to ten feet … if we're lucky," I said. My stomach growled with hunger. Thankfully, the painful cramping bouts had subsided with the lack of food over the last couple of days.

"Maybe we can find some honey down here," Maddie said. "Food meant for Pharaoh's next life. It's been found in other tombs and doesn't go bad even after a few millennia, but water will be—"

"Could be twenty feet," Mr. Scalone said, kneeling and peering through the opening. He hadn't grown as gaunt or desperate as us.

Nodding, Maddie's face turned pale. My heart sank into my stomach, pulled down by an anchor of remorse. It was my fault Maddie was here. I had set up a medical externship in Cairo, through the university and Doctors Without Borders. The administration had been happy to get rid of me while they sorted through my blunder and endless paperwork. And I couldn't get into as much medical trouble in a developing nation. They'd probably expel me, but I didn't want to go back anyway. How could I face anyone?

Finishing the externship over a week or so ago, I'd had some extra time. To be truthful, although I was a bit embarrassed about it, I'd waited over a month to set up the clinical rotation. I'd waited until Maddie would be in Cairo working on the fieldwork portion of her PhD. I'd emailed and messaged her a few times before I'd left the States, but she'd blown me off. She was too busy working on her thesis to even meet for a meal. So eventually I let her know I possessed something capable of altering her career. After a few short replies and several days of skepticism, she agreed to lunch.

A few weeks ago, inside a dim restaurant, I shared the professor's letter over slippery grape leaves and hummus drowning in garlic. She deciphered a few clues, and her enthusiasm escalated. In just a day or two she managed to convince Kaylin to fly out with a hired guide. Kaylin's younger brother, Aiden, and a bodyguard also arrived. The teenage sibling had probably been thrown out of the house by their dad, who'd funded the trip. And the father might have thought hiring a tour guide and a bodyguard would keep his children safe—

Gritting my teeth in resentment, I returned to the present. I crawled inside our burrow, buried my shovel, and loosened the rock and dirt. With every scoop, I hoped for a glimpse of sunlight, but it never came.

As the passage lengthened, the three of us took turns squirming up the slope and scraping at the barrier.

During one of my rest periods, I sat on the lower steps. A suffocating gloom of depression weighed me down. Sighing, I adjusted the ancient-appearing bracelet on my left arm—a gift from my dad. My love affair with ancient Egypt had begun when I'd first picked up a magazine packed with photos of ancient tombs, jackal-headed men, and gold funerary masks. I hadn't even started kindergarten at the time. But my dream of becoming an Egyptologist drifted away with my dad's death. He'd encouraged me to chase the stars, but once he passed, my mom demanded I give up his crazy notions and make something of myself. Then, after developing a sometimes crippling gastrointestinal disease, it became nearly impossible for me to travel like he had. So I finished my undergraduate education and applied to medical school.

Unfortunately, I'd received my last infusion for the disease over a month ago already, and I would need another in a week or so. But I shouldn't have to worry too much about that if I didn't make it out of this tomb.

Pulling out my wallet, I fished around for a picture—a black-and-white photograph that carried deep wrinkles and worn edges. A middle-aged man in a fedora beamed for the camera. He had an arm wrapped around his young son, who wore the same type of hat but grimaced in an attempt to display strength or at least determination. The Sphinx, the guardian of the Giza pyramids, towered over the background. The picture was fake, but I treasured it. My dad had had it taken at a traveling King Tut exhibit back home, in front of a backdrop. He'd pointed to the Sphinx and the pyramids and said, "I'll take you when you're old enough, and we'll see *a lot* more than tourist attractions."

Not knowing what he meant, I still couldn't wait to go. I studied up on everything from ancient Egypt nearly everyday since. Every book I read for leisure and every magazine article had been in preparation. Now I stood inside a forgotten tomb. My dad really had brought me to Egypt; he just wasn't here. Tears trickled down my cheeks, and my eyes burned as I wandered back to the entrance and the others.

"Do you have any more water?" Maddie asked Mr. Scalone as she wriggled out of the tunnel. The guide shook his head, his dark locks flat and oily. "Food?"

"No," his accented voice croaked. "I'd have given you some already."

✳ ✳ ✳

Another day passed before Maddie and I collapsed beside each other on the ancient stone. Utterly spent, we lay beside a massive pile of deformed limestone, rock, and dirt, awaiting our fate. I wished we could've finished reading the tale from the Hall of Records together. My mind drifted, and my vision faded.

Chapter 12

Journal Translation

THE PRECEDING INCIDENTS with Akhenaten and Nefertiti raised deep questions. Having stood out amongst the royal servants like the tallest papyrus plant of the bunch, I'd been hacked down. I'd become an outcast. For the remainder of my childhood, I didn't question authority or my responsibilities, as such behavior was detrimental to civilization. I'd only resisted once, to protect the girl I loved. And although the societal scar healed, its memory remained too jagged to be disguised.

Serving Akhenaten, I performed whenever he commanded. I bathed and dressed him, fed him, played his silent shadow, and cleaned up after him. He kept me in my place but at times still grew angry. Becoming overly meek, I worked as fast as I could manage.

Obedience to the royal family burned away months and years. My company primarily consisted of Akhenaten and his extended family, including Nefertiti, Beketaten, and Mutnedjmet. I spoke to Nefertiti every time we entered the same room, if Akhenaten stood out of earshot. Our time together never lasted long, but the elegant beauty always smiled when she saw me.

As I grew into adolescence, Akhenaten came into his early twenties. We'd not played together in years, but soon we'd share adventures I never could have dreamed.

"Heb, my boy," Father said, his broad face appearing at the palace's bedroom door.

Smiling with delight, I lifted my weary head from the elevated neckrest of the reed mattress, fashioned to keep scorpions away from the face.

"I'm so sorry I don't see you much anymore," he said, stepping inside. "I'm only allowed to depart after Pharaoh has retired and we've completed our chores. You're usually still attending Akhenaten then, and we're both spent." A pair of tears slid down his flat cheeks, but he quickly wiped them away. "I wish we could retire in the same room, but now, as one of Pharaoh's lead servants, I must rest in his wing. Families aren't allowed, only royal servants and soldiers."

Sympathy tugged at my core. Poor Father felt so bad. He loved me and did the best he could. "I know, Father," I said. "You've explained it a hundred times."

He plopped down beside me. "If only we could lie in the garden all day, under the cool shade of the tamarisk tree, and watch the soaring clouds play with the sunlight. Like we used to. But I wish the best for you, and you are in a prestigious position. The first servant of Pharaoh's second son is not to be taken lightly. Many would fight for your status."

Nodding, my head sank, and I bit my lip with regret. I couldn't tell him how appalling Akhenaten was. He might think I was ungrateful or would worry all day and night about my well-being. "Didn't you want me to become a scribe, to be educated about this world and the next? I'd earn respect and be able to work my way up among the elite of society."

"That is indeed one of the most noble of professions." He patted me on the back, his eyes glassy. "I cannot control fate. God had other plans for you. I think you will do quite well, however. We work long and hard but have access to every comfort the palace has to offer. Beyond its walls lurk dangers you couldn't imagine. Men, beasts, and nature ever await their opportunity to overpower the unprepared. You are on the right path. But if for some reason you find you are not, hope can always shape radiant dreams out of the nightmares of the present ..."

I pondered the situation of my life, dark thoughts pulling at my heart. Tugging on my sidelock, he hugged me, and his bronze bracelet dug into my back. "My only regret is not having more time with you." He yawned, rubbing a wrinkled hand over his short, graying hair. "You need sleep." Squeezing my arm, he waved and left.

Lying back down, I stared at the cracks creeping across the shadowed ceiling and drifted off to sleep.

Akhenaten woke me with the repeated tapping of his sandaled foot on my head, just as the Aten peaked over the Red Sea Hills. I jumped up, afraid he'd been waiting too long. Rubbing my scratchy eyes, I bathed him and shaved his body—typical of any civilized man. After dressing the young royal, I adorned him in black eye paint. He admired himself in a bronze mirror, turning his head side to side.

"We're sailing today," he said.

I held my breath in apprehension as I placed jeweled bracelets on his arms and legs, slid in his earrings, and anointed him with oils carrying scents of musty leather and pungent flowers. I set a thick, black wig on his head, and he made incremental adjustments until satisfied.

"Sailing?" I asked. "Where?" Akhenaten rarely ventured outside of the palaces or the Temples of the Aten in the two major Egyptian cities of Memphis and Thebes. Perhaps he didn't like the outside world, or perhaps Pharaoh was afraid others would stare at his hideous son.

I followed Akhenaten out of the baths, and my stomach growled with hunger. We wolfed down a breakfast of starchy vegetables and crusty breads. The thick, earthy liquid we called beer—which we drank at all meals for energy—rolled down the back of my throat. Akhenaten's teeth sank into a pomegranate as I dowsed his sweet bread with honey. Akhenaten spat a mouthful of seeds across the table as he snagged the bread.

"Along the Nile," he finally answered. "We will be traveling past all the people and lands of the kingdom. A hunting expedition …" His lips parted and his forehead wrinkled as he pondered something.

"Hunting fowl on the river?" I asked, forcing a hunk of tough bread down my throat. Rising dread rattled my nerves, but I knew I shouldn't ask too much. "I'm not feeling well," I lied. "I probably shouldn't go."

"It is custom for royalty," he said. "I have trained with the throw-stick, and Pharaoh says I am the best he has ever seen. He warns me about venturing out, but I will delay no longer. A boat and ten of my closest guards await us. We leave as soon as we finish."

I choked in surprise, a sputter of beer spewing from my lips. Akhenaten spat and more seeds scattered before he licked at the honey on his bread. "Contain your excitement, little servant boy. There are threats in the great world incomprehensible to you and your pampered life. You will not be secluded with me inside the royal barge as typical. You will stand in the open air on a small vessel … and you will not be partaking in the hunt. You only come to serve."

I nodded with apprehension, and somewhere a hint of wonder sparked within me. I'd see the kingdom. "I'll tell Father."

"No!" He hammered a fist onto the table, causing our plates to leap into the air and rattle back down. "My own father does not know." His brow furrowed. "I, however, must understand my country and what is about to happen. We sail south with the winds, against the Nile herself. To Elephantine and the edge of the kingdom, beyond the city of …" He clenched his jaw, thin but striated muscles standing out. "Past the city of Thebes."

My eyes wandered in confusion. We resided in Memphis, the capital of the government, but the royal family spent more time in Thebes—the religious and economic capital. I'd known only a sheltered life in the confines of palaces. "What's wrong with Thebes?" I asked.

"The troubles with Thebes are far beyond a servant's comprehension," Akhenaten said as he tossed the red-stained rind of the pomegranate onto the table. "All you need to understand is that there are atrocious people attempting to undermine Pharaoh. They strive to divide Egypt into upper and lower countries, to obtain power for themselves."

The bridge of my nose knotted in bewilderment. Questions ran through my mind, but I didn't push Akhenaten any further. If I remained his faithful servant, I'd see more than I ever dreamed, but the road was too dangerous. Inching for the doorway, I planned to dash off straight to Father—

Akhenaten snatched my arm, guiding me down the hall.

What I didn't yet understand was that the more I learned, the less I actually knew about this world.

Chapter 13

Journal Translation

STUMBLING DOWN THE dusty streets of Memphis, I trailed Akhenaten. Sacks of supplies buckled my thin frame, although I attempted to stand proudly. The captain of Akhenaten's personal guard led us through the city, his tall and lean physique commanding authority and parting noisy pedestrians.

Ten royal soldiers in total marched around us as we passed between shops on the ground level of two- or three-story family homes. Armed with the traditional spears and rawhide shields, the guards wore padded caps. A few carried curved swords at their waists, while a bow and arrows were strapped to the backs of two.

The bow had fascinated me ever since I had watched a soldier release an arrow years ago. An ability to propel a small spear through the air with greater speed, distance, and accuracy than a thrown weapon must be magic. Father said God gave us the bow, and that it was one of two reasons for our victories over the lands of chaos surrounding ordered Egypt and its river of life. He described barbarian hordes and pirates to the north and Nubians to the south, as well as inhuman monsters, the Dark Ones, lurking amongst the shadows. I'd asked about the second reason he had mentioned. He said the horse and chariot had revolutionized war, especially when utilizing a mounted archer. Desire to draw the bowstring and release an arrow, to taste magic, filled my waking dreams—

Shouting from a man with a dark beard erupted as he bartered over a loaf of bread. But he stopped and stared at us. The hearty aroma of fired grain mingled with dust, clay, and freshly shaven timber. A short, plump man stopped writing on a small palette in mid-stroke. Those working pottery, stone, wood, and jewelry fell quiet, watching Akhenaten. I pulled back my slouching shoulders, and we tramped on.

A bald, thin man in a white sash and kilt emerged from a shop.

"Please, magician, don't!" A woman burst out behind him. "Son of Hapu—" she said, but she froze when she saw us. The man's head swung around. Black eye paint traced the trenches of deep wrinkles running across his face, accentuating the tangled pattern of a spider's web.

My blood turned cold. The streaks running across his face ... Never before had I seen a magician, but tales ran in whispers around many a dinner table. Both respected and feared, these men commanded an ability to control the world in ways others could only imagine. People begged for their aid only when need grew greater than their distrust. Fortunately, under the prosperous reign of Amenhotep III, such services were rarely sought.

A stark-white cat leapt onto his shoulder and perched. It appeared twice the size of Croc, rolls of fat billowing from its belly as it eyed Akhenaten. As if in slow motion, sound faded. The cat twitched, its crystal eyes fixating on mine. Stumbling, I nearly fell. A soldier grabbed and shoved me back up as we passed, my head careening around.

The magician waited, his face grimacing. Pulling something from a sack, he concealed the item inside his hand and traced symbols in the air. What was he—

A clap rang out to our right. As I spun around, a stack of pottery toppled down at us. I jumped aside and tripped, falling. Pieces shattered as they collided with the street, while others rolled in tightening circles.

The guards, with weapons raised, glanced about.

"Get this out of my path!" Akhenaten said.

The captain reached down, not for a broken drinking vessel, but for his own bow, which had fallen onto the street along with his arrows. The arrows lay spread out in a flat semicircle, evenly spaced and all pointing at Akhenaten's feet as if to suggest he turn around.

My master kicked the bolts aside, his face reddening as he scanned the crowd. A horde of people stood in the street, but the magician was gone. Dread rose inside me along with a shudder. How could someone control objects in such a way? Or was it just sleight-of-hand, a magic trick?

"Go!" Akhenaten said, snarling at the onlookers.

Striding forward, his captain gathered the fallen weapons.

Mud-brick buildings and dirt streets opened up to a magnificent view. The shimmering waters of the Nile emerged, halting my breath as I soaked in their beauty. Early sunlight sparkled across the surface of gentle waves and ripples, the Aten's rays dancing and blurring my vision. A fresh scent wafted into my nostrils, and a softness hung in the air. As a child, the river had been my favorite place, but lately servitude had me standing ever-patient at Akhenaten's side.

The blue belt of water stretched impossibly wide across the desert, but the soldiers muttered about the river being at its most shallow this time of year. The annual inundation, the life-giving flood of our land, was about to begin. This trip's timing had been premeditated.

Small sailing ships and skiffs composed of bundled reeds littered the port or glided across the water. Boxes of cargo were hauled in or out of Memphis. What strange wonders lay hidden inside those crates?

Pushing me forward, the tall captain pointed to a spectacular barge and said, "Over there." A pure-white sail rippled at its attachment to the central mast. Fashioned solely of wood, the vessel clashed against the other ships. The bow curled up and outward, carved into the shape of a sphinx.

I was struck with wonder; my breaths came quick and shallow as we climbed aboard. Hollow echoes sounded beneath my sandaled feet—I was walking upon wood! How many Egyptians had ever experienced such a sensation? I was lucky indeed.

Akhenaten barked orders. The soldiers untied us from the dock; oars broke water in unison and guided us out into the river. The sail billowed open into a white cloud as a strong gust snagged the fabric, tugging us southward. Magnificent walls surrounding the white city of Memphis began to grow smaller. My hands shook with apprehension and excitement. Father would have no idea where I was.

How long would we be gone? Where did the waters of the river come from? Where did they go? How many other cities were there?

At the stern, the captain shifted the rudder, and the bow veered left.

The guards set aside their oars, allowing the howling wind to power us.

We skimmed atop the ancient river like a falcon catching the air currents, and the surrounding banks blurred. I sat out of the way, near the stern and anchored supply crates.

Forcing his hunched posture upright, Akhenaten paraded across the hull as the wind whipped his kilt. People on the shore stared as we slipped past. Once at the bow, my master rested one foot on the edge of the barge, basking in glory under the morning rays of the Aten.

Movement flashed at the corner of my vision. Something rustled underneath a white canvas covering the supply crates. Holding my breath in suspense, I glanced around. The captain hadn't noticed. What new surprise waited? The sheet rustled again, and a feminine hand popped out. Grasping the edge of the cover, fingers slowly drew it back.

Dark hair flowed beneath, followed by beautiful eyes surrounded in deep green. My heart jumped with elation. My favorite person in the world lay hidden beneath!

Nefertiti's eyes bulged when she saw me watching. Motioning with a finger to her lips to remain silent, she winked. I grinned and nodded as she covered herself again. But my stomach churned with worry. What might Akhenaten do when he found her?

Memphis faded into sand and water. On both sides of the river, farmers prepared their parched fields and irrigation canals, hungry to receive the life-giving floodwaters. The acres cracked, peeled, and curled upward like a crocodile's scales. But after the floods came and receded, the soil would turn black. Then the green life of vegetation would rise from the earth.

The workers' skins had burned to a dark tan, similar to Akhenaten, who contrasted with the pale elite of the rest of his family. Guiding donkeys and oxen, one farmer worked on a *shaduf* machine. The *shaduf* held a weight on one end of a long arm and a rope attached to a bucket on the other. Pushing the end with the bucket into the river, the hunched farmer utilized the counterweight and with minimal effort lifted the pail of water. He poured the liquid into his irrigation ditch, where it ran toward his fields. Smiling with fascination at the simple marvel, I took in this grand new world.

Farther to the west, beyond the strips of farmland, red desert and hills sprawled to the horizon. To the east lay a smaller expanse of rocky desert, before the Red Sea Hills marked the edge of the world. Akhenaten was right: there wasn't much out here apart from what life the river brought. But the Nile also had to be feared, given the countless stories of lives being taken by the eternal waters. Its power and speed were vastly greater than its modest waves would suggest.

The northerly wind gusted in my ears and tore at my hair and kilt, bringing a taste of dirt as we picked up our pace against the current. Only the occasional cacophony of ducks protesting our passage interrupted the howling of the wind.

"We'll be gone a few weeks," the captain said. "Perhaps you could learn to row ... or even steer during the slow times."

My jaw must've hit the deck in surprise. "I want to learn both!"

"Don't get too excited," the captain said. Pulling the handle of the rudder to him caused veins to pop along his forearms and a deformed foot and lower leg to brace against the hull. A twisting scar ran from his knee to a half-missing foot. The outer portion of his sandal sat empty. "Once you know how to row, it's just work, struggling against the Nile herself. Thankfully, she isn't so temperamental this time of year, but you're scrawny and probably unable to row hard."

I glanced at my frail body, embarrassment rising before I could gather my nerve. "I'll try my best. There're nine other soldiers, so you can put me on the side with only four."

He grinned as he scrutinized our watery trajectory. "It'll have to wait. Akhenaten doesn't want you wasting anyone's time or energy on something you'd never be good at or needed for."

I couldn't force my gaze from his half foot with two twisted toes. "If I can row as well as one of the soldiers, will you teach me about your bow?"

Narrowing his eyes, the captain studied me. A thin smile crept onto his lips. "A servant will never excel with weapons. Only if thousands of the Nine Bows—our traditional enemies—hunt us and the mysterious Dark Ones sweep up from the south, only if they wipe out our armies and ravage our homeland would you be called upon to fight. So dire a situation will never again befall this kingdom. Because of the Aten, we're all created and born into the role necessary for the god-king and our country to thrive. It's been this way for eternity; it's the way of the world. Order over chaos.

Only when we forget do we fall victim to the madness swirling in the raging storms around us."

I sighed, eerie images of the Dark Ones flooding my mind, probably called forth from childhood tales. Black humanoid forms shifted amongst a rolling fog. The monsters surrounded me and pressed in. Shuddering with terror, I shook my head and blinked to dispel the vision. "Akhenaten taught me the ways of the world. I am what I am, but I thirst to loose an arrow … just once."

The captain's smirk opened up into a full smile, although he wouldn't look at me.

The wooden frame of his bow lay still but powerful beside his hideous leg. How could the sun-disc give the chosen people a weapon of wood? Wouldn't it have burned? As I pondered Father's explanation, it suddenly sank in that the captain had said we'd be gone for weeks. My stomach knotted with anxiety. Father would be very upset.

Hours passed as we skimmed through the countryside under the blazing sun and roaring wind, which drowned out the soldiers' conversations. Akhenaten remained at the bow in regal pose while commoners dropped everything to stare.

What was he was doing? Displaying his royal presence? Or perhaps he wished people would recognize him—

"Hi!" a female voice shouted, making me jump. Nefertiti stood beside the crates and waved, a beaming smile on her face. She held something in her other hand, something she shouldn't have been holding.

Akhenaten turned, his sunken cheeks burning red. Orb-like eyes narrowed into shadow as deep as his makeup.

Chapter 14

Journal Translation

NEFERTITI HELD AN orange and white cat in the crook of her arm as she stepped away from the crates at the rear of the boat.

"Croc!" I yelled.

"What have you done?" Akhenaten asked as he approached, planks shaking under his feet. He punished Nefertiti with his sneer, and I recalled the look he had cast when he'd struck me for disobedience.

Her beautiful smile vanished, giving way to quivering lips. "When your brother hunts, he brings cats to flush out the fowl," she said.

"I am not the crown prince Thutmose, and I do not care about an insignificant cat." He clenched his fists, and his knuckles blanched. "We carry a cage of felines, trained to hunt fowl. They are not strays like that one." He pointed at Croc. "What are *you* doing here?"

"I can help," Nefertiti said in a merry timbre. "Pharaoh doesn't know you left. My father doesn't either, but they'd probably want to keep an eye on this expedition. I'll be able to tell them a story of valor ... or one of failure." The escalating tension made me swallow. Nefertiti's father, Ay, was the great court advisor and a military commander, amongst the most elite of society. Even though Pharaoh might not know everything that occurred in his kingdom, Ay certainly did.

Akhenaten's jaw clenched, his fingers wringing the shaft of his walking stick. "No woman can help a man hunt. You will swim back to Memphis!"

"Hatshepsut did things she wasn't supposed to," Nefertiti said, sticking out a hand to slow Akhenaten's advance. "And she became the only woman pharaoh."

"Hatshepsut's been erased from history, her mummy and monuments defaced." Spit flew from his lips. "She will never experience the afterlife and will soon be forgotten. Do you desire a life after this one?" He raised his walking stick.

Cowering, Nefertiti sank to the hull. I attempted to leap over and protect her, but my body didn't respond. My toes curled in horror.

Raising his walking stick, Akhenaten swung and struck Nefertiti across the shoulder, releasing a crack. My heart jolted in pain. Crying out, she slumped over. Croc scampered from her arms and disappeared behind the crates.

Grabbing Nefertiti by the hair, Akhenaten yanked her to her feet as his trembling lips dripped saliva. "We've come too far to turn around." He dragged her to the edge of the boat.

Nefertiti screamed, tears brimming in her eyes. My legs finally responded.

Stepping between them and the water, I hung my head in meek opposition.

Flinging me aside, Akhenaten shoved Nefertiti's head over the edge. She wailed and pleaded, her limbs flailing. Biting agony, more painful than any physical ailment, sank into my soul. I attempted to—

"Perhaps I can take her back," the captain said, standing and stalling the horrific scene. "In the next city we can take a skiff back to Memphis."

"Sit down, Mahu," Akhenaten said, his voice low.

The captain sat back down at the rudder.

Akhenaten tapped his chin. "But I may have a use for you, cousin." Snatching her shoulder, he then dropped her onto the wood planks. The thud caused my jaw to tense and clamp shut. "But we sail for weeks, and I do not want to hear any complaining."

Nefertiti sobbed uncontrollably.

"The peasants wish to gaze upon me," Akhenaten said. "They must know who I am, and I do not want to be seen with a woman. Not yet. You will stay out of sight, or you will be tossed into the river."

Curling into a ball, Nefertiti clutched her shoulder and shivered. Akhenaten strutted back to the bow, his wing-like shoulder blades crawling under thin musculature as he utilized his walking stick for support.

Crouching at Nefertiti's side, I placed a hand on her back.

"Don't touch her!" an enormous guard at the side of the boat said.

I jerked my hand back but stayed by her side. "Are you okay?" I asked.

Tears cascaded down my love's creamy cheeks.

"Thank you for bringing Croc," I said. "He bites anyone who tries to pick him up, but must've sensed your kind soul."

She chuckled through her whimpers, warming my heart. "I didn't want you to be without your Croc," she said. "He's opened up to me over the years. I don't know what I thought would happen. In my heart I knew I'd be punished, but I overheard Akhenaten and wanted to come. He's plotting something, and I don't want to sit around waiting only to be forced into the typical woman's role. I want to be like Hatshepsut." She sobbed. "I feel so sorry for Akhenaten's girls."

"His girls?" I asked.

The burning light in her eyes faded to a glimmer. "He's of the line of the Aten and has owned women since becoming a man several inundations ago. One has already borne him a child, even though several other pregnancies didn't survive. He doesn't allow other men around them, so maybe you were unaware. I had assured him you're only a servant, not a male he needs to worry about ... so we can still see each other."

My heart sank into my stomach. Is that what she really thought of me? A friend, but hardly a man? I'd risked my own life for her, because I loved her. But I'd always be *his* servant. Something deep in my soul stirred and boiled over. My cheeks flushed as I looked to the sky and the blazing sun. But I had accepted what I was long ago. My shoulders hunched and my knees wobbled as a fog rolled over my thoughts. Anger passed as fast as it'd come.

"You don't want him to see you as a threat, or he'll have you castrated," Nefertiti said. "Or worse."

Perhaps she'd told Akhenaten she didn't see me as a man just to pacify his aggression and jealousy. Either way, I couldn't ask. The answer could destroy me.

I shuffled back to the crates, a shell of a man. An orange and white ball sat wedged into a gap between boxes. Two dilated pupils stared back. Hissing, Croc thrust lightning-quick claws into the air before sitting quietly. I scooped him up as he hissed again, this time quieter. As I scratched along the soft underside of his white chin and cheeks, he purred but kept watch on the others. Tears brimmed in my eyes, but I wouldn't let them fall or let anyone see.

We sailed along the twists and turns of the river, and darkness started to descend.

"We dock at the bank," Mahu ordered, pointing.

Inching over to Nefertiti, I asked, "What're we doing?"

Her dull eyes didn't focus. "It's too risky to sail at night. We could crash into a sandbar or rocks, especially when the waters are low."

The port side of the vessel eased against the left shore. Akhenaten always preferred east, the direction of the rising Aten.

After stepping ashore, the soldiers hauled on ropes to anchor the boat into the sand. Two pitched a large tent while others unrolled blankets.

Pointing at the hulking soldier, Mahu said, "Suty and two others sleep on land with me. The rest of you stay on board. If the river comes up quick and pulls the barge away, Akhenaten will have our heads. It's happened before this time of year." The tall, lean captain glanced down at me. "Sleep anywhere except within the tent. And remember," he scratched his smooth chin and looked east into the desert, "nights can get cold. Shelter and warm torches of the palace won't be found out here. We need to conserve our fuel and supplies. Stay close."

I glanced around with trepidation, and something hit me in the face, knocked my head back, and bounced onto the ground. Suty roared with laughter, pointing to a rolled blanket.

I gritted my teeth in frustration, swept up my sleeping gear, and climbed back onto the boat. Picking through the supplies, I chose the best-looking loaf of bread for Nefertiti and several of the worst for the others. How long before the mold started, infecting loaves with its decay? Then we'd have to eat grain. I snatched a blue jar of honey, one of wine, and a vine of dark grapes, stacking everything in my arms.

As I walked to the tent, the Aten sank into the underworld, its twilight leaving only fleeting rays and long shadows to crawl across the desert floor. God would wage his nightly battle with Apep. Only after defeating the vile serpent could he emerge again. What if just once the Aten couldn't overpower the evils? Would day become night? God's might was irrepressible, but how could a snake continue its attack unless it were also powerful? Father told me not to worry, but how could I not? The entire world would end if the sun-disc did not rise.

"Servant awaits with food and drink," I announced outside the royal tent. A rustling sound carried out of the flap doorway before an oddly deep voice replied. "Get in here, I'm famished."

Parting the flaps, I stepped under the towering canopy. A central torch warmed the air, sputtering below a small vent. Akhenaten sat upon a wooden chair at the head of a short table, his hungry eyes staring. Huddled in a corner with tear lines staining her cheeks, Nefertiti clutched the top of her white linen dress—

"Leave the food and drink and be off," Akhenaten said, pulling my attention from her.

My gaze fell to the ground. Placing the food on the table, I turned to leave but cast Nefertiti another glance. Her dark irises glazed over, conflicting with her green eye paint. My breathing quickened with fearful curiosity. What was going on?

"Get out!" Akhenaten yelled and gnashed into a hunk of bread, pointing to the exit.

I hurried away.

After serving dinner to the soldiers, I spread my blanket on the sand beside the tent. I felt closer to Nefertiti here. Lying down, I gnawed at earthy bread and gazed up at the expansive sky painted with stars. Captivating beauty radiated from the heavens, even in the absence of the Aten. Shapes took form amongst the points of light. What did the scorpion or the man represent? How long had they been in the night sky? Stars flickered back and forth, as if communicating. The twinkling stopped. Was that a sign? For me?

A female's scream pierced the night, followed by a thud. The sounds originated from Akhenaten's tent. Springing to my feet, I lunged for the entrance. The two guards stationed outside beside a torch looked at me as if I'd sprouted wings like a locust.

I advanced.

Suty, the hulking monster of a man beside Mahu, shook his head. "What do you think you're doing?" Hefting and twirling his curved sword, he winked. The motion revealed a jagged scar that wound down the side of his face and through a hideously deformed ear. This appendage looked like the pointy ear of a pig. His monstrous appearance drove fear into my heart.

Did Akhenaten's personal guards all have disfigurements? To help mask his own? "It sounded like someone was hurt," I said, my teeth chattering as I looked at the captain.

"You have no business in there unless Akhenaten asks for you," Suty replied, in a more uneducated dialect than his comrades. "No exceptions. Probably going to hear a lot a noises on this trip."

I stood immobile and horrified. Noises? Only Akhenaten and his cousin were inside!

Another muffled wail. Suty's scarred eye popped open, and his deformed ear twitched downward. "Your master's in there, and you are his servant. Act like it or take your punishment!"

I stepped toward the tent.

Suty rammed the edge of his shield into my knee with a crack, bringing a sharp jolt of pain. I collapsed in a heap. He kicked me in the stomach, launching me into the distance as if I were made of papyrus. Air rushed from my lungs, and I landed with a thud, sliding through the dirt and choking on grit. Several minutes passed before my chest could expand and suck in a breath. Groaning and pleading escaped the confines of the royal tent. Forcing myself to my feet, I turned to face the guards.

Chapter 15

Journal Translation

"PLEASE! I BEG YOU, Nefertiti's being hurt!" I yelled to Mahu, but I watched Suty—who was standing just before the entrance to Akhenaten's tent alongside the Nile.

"Boy, you come back and I'll decapitate you," the beast of a man snarled, broken yellow teeth flashing in the night.

I leapt for the tent. Suty raised his sword, and Mahu leveled his spear. What could I possibly do? Whirling around, I dashed off into the desert, unable to accept the situation. Nefertiti's wails of protest carried out from the tent. I squeezed my eyes shut and clamped my hands over my ears. Stabbing needlelike pain pricked my heart.

I ran until I collapsed, sobbing. The Aten blessed my life, but I couldn't accept this. How could the world be this way? Was it true what Akhenaten believed, that those near to God could act however they desired, and others had to live amidst their shadows? Howling in despair and hopelessness, I punched and kicked the dirt until my knuckles and toes bled. I should've given praise and offerings to the Aten, to right the wrongs, but at that moment I cursed the sun-disc—God himself—and wished he wouldn't reemerge in the morning.

"I pray Apep will swallow you whole this night!" I screamed into the heavens. "Let his chaos digest your sphere like the devoured lump of a rodent winding through a serpent's entrails!"

Staring into the night sky with teary eyes, I shook my scrawny fists. A flapping sounded in the dark, followed by the outline of a great bird passing across the thickest river of stars. Massive wings rode the wind before disappearing into the black. Straining to locate the strange beast amongst the backdrop, I spotted a pair of stars arcing across the sky. Horror squeezed my young heart. Those where not stars, but the whites of hunting eyes circling back for me! Trembling, I blinked away the tears. Had the Aten already brought forth punishment?

The bird-like creature swooped closer. An unmistakable head of a man sat upon its feathered neck! I cowered in terror just as the creature vanished into the darkness again. A *ba*—the piece of a person's soul that can travel the earth after death! But a *ba* should never roam outside its tomb at night. These invisible souls could travel the world by day but must return to their mummies before the Aten descended, or risk being lost forever.

A hollow thud resonated behind me. Jolting, I spun around. The monstrous avian loomed over me, feathers stretching out like fingers from the underworld. Recoiling in horror, I attempted to scramble away, but my hands slipped through the sand like water.

"Hear me!" a gaunt face cried into the night. Its echoing voice sounded as old as the halls of eternity and reeked of decay. "I cannot stay or my *ba* will be lost. I already risk too much!"

My heart drummed and my limbs trembled, but I couldn't move.

"Remember!" Its neck snaked out at me. I flailed backward. Crocodile teeth flashed in the moonlight and descended. "Do not turn around. Whatever you do, do not turn around!"

The head advanced, and I spun away. Mutilated parts of a human body lay strewn in the sand before me. The corpse's decapitated head faced the heavens, its eyes frozen in terror. I recognized the face—one of Akhenaten's soldiers. My body jerked, and I screamed—

The first pink and purple rays of the Aten crested the Red Sea Hills, consuming the adjacent stars. I lay in the sand shivering and baffled. The body and the *ba* were both gone ... A nightmare? I'd had my share of peculiar or terrifying dreams, but never with a *ba*.

Memories of last night flooded my mind, and I rose to my knees. I punched my thigh in frustration. My actions would cast me out of favor with the Aten. I needed to salvage what hope I had left, as I'd never survive in this vast desert alone. Neither would Nefertiti, and she couldn't stay with Akhenaten. She needed my help.

Running under the expanding light, I retched and coughed. My limbs remained numb, carrying bluish undertones. God must've stricken me ill for my blasphemies, my body no longer able to receive his life-giving warmth.

But what did the mysterious *ba* want? Not to turn away and see the mangled body, or not to return for Nefertiti? The soul could've been a trickster, or more likely just a dream. Little did I know its words should've been heeded, but that they had nothing to do with returning to the barge.

The river snaked into view, and all lay quiet. The Aten hadn't yet crested the horizon, but its red light shone all around. Hopefully in the underworld God couldn't hear all my thoughts and screams.

Orange and white fur rose and fell in steady breaths, snuggled onto my blanket outside the tent. One bed lay empty, that of the missing soldier who was the dead man from my dream …

Scooping Croc up, my purple fingers, feeling thick, didn't respond as expected. A fit of coughing and shivering spiraled through my body.

"You look like death," the captain said, rolling over.

I headed to the barge.

"Listen, boy," Mahu said with a hint of sympathy as he rubbed his eyes and sat up, "there're things in this world you may not want to accept, but the sooner you realize you can't change fate or the will of God, the better everything is."

I continued marching away, without acknowledging him.

"I was once like you, having a terrible time with things. Everything I had believed in and thought to be true changed. I'd resisted a transition with my comrades but watched friends suffer or die. Eventually I gave in to the way things are, designed by powers far greater than my own. Now look at me. I've been rewarded, promoted to captain of Akhenaten's personal guard. I married a beautiful woman, have three happy children, a house, enough rations for my entire family, and I serve the line of god-kings. What else could a man desire?"

Wrinkling my upper lip in annoyance, I boarded the boat. Even though physically smaller, Mahu carried more power than the scarred beast, Suty. I respected and wanted to be like the captain, but at the moment I couldn't accept it.

"What's your name, boy?" he asked, following me.

My voice cracked through chattering teeth. "M-my father calls me Heb," I said, rummaging through the crates for breakfast.

"Whenever you say your name, say it with pride. Put your trust in the Aten, and you'll be rewarded." Mahu pounded on the side of the boat, the hollow thudding waking the others.

Serving breakfast, I overheard fearful whispers about our missing comrade and what might've befallen him. Soldiers mentioned magic and curses, Dark Ones and Shadows. The image of the mutilated corpse from my dream released a shudder along my spine.

I sat and ate, not entering the tent. Warmth gathered in my chest, and my fingers grew more flexible.

"I am ready," an eerie voice called from the desert. Akhenaten stepped into view, holding a throw-stick—a short, curved hunting tool carved into the shape of a snake. The carcass of a large rodent dangled in his other hand, along with his walking stick. Flinging the corpse aside, he said, "Commoners use traps and nets to snare fowl and fish, but royalty hunt game with skill. I am among the most adept to ever throw. Perhaps even my servant will linger over the juices of meat for the first time." He grinned as he approached, grabbed me by the neck, and ran long fingers over my scalp and growing stubble. Kissing his own hand upon my head, he said, "I will take care of you, my good servant."

A warm feeling blossomed inside. Finally, praise and appreciation. Perhaps Mahu was right, I needed to get over what I felt was proper and follow orders. But something inside me arose in defiance, suppressing the urge to capitulate to the order of things.

Tapping me with his throw stick, Akhenaten caught me low on the back. Somehow sharp pain shot down my legs, making me cry out in surprise as he let me go.

The soldiers collapsed the tent. Nefertiti sat in the dirt with tousled hair, staring blankly. Gobbling down his breakfast, Akhenaten strode over to her. He kissed her cheek and straightened her hair, whispering in her ear and smiling. Pain and jealousy clawed my heart.

With a broken posture, she shuffled to the barge and boarded with the last soldier. I tried not to stare, but I couldn't control myself. Dark bruising encircled her neck, and her dirty cheeks carried clean tear paths beneath smeared eye paint. She sat at the stern, alone.

If only I could help her … but I couldn't. I was powerless.

"We sail without him, then?" a stocky soldier asked Mahu, scanning the eastern desert for their missing comrade while wringing callused hands.

"Disembark!" Akhenaten said.

The crew cast each other uneasy looks but took up oars and pushed off. As we sailed with the humming of the wind, my emotions screamed for justice. But the Aten blessed the journey with a strong northern gale. Days blended together and became routine. Nefertiti slept in Akhenaten's tent but never spoke to him during the day. The horrible wailing that haunted the first night in the desert did not recur. But her cries had burned themselves into my soul, never to be forgotten … even in the next life.

Chapter 16

Journal Translation

"WE HUNT!" Akhenaten said early one morning, pointing out over the Nile as we sailed. "Take us to the marsh." Reeds grew in thickets along the margin of stagnant water at the western shore. Hundreds of vibrant birds and ducks chirped and pecked through the muck under the golden rays of the Aten.

I shivered in the cool dawn air as two soldiers collapsed the sail, slowing our momentum. Mahu guided us in without a sound, rank swamp odor sweeping over us like a fog. The buzz of swarming insects followed, after the wind had died down, and the occasional prick of a bite arose somewhere on my exposed body. The fowl chattered and dove for cover amongst the brush. Akhenaten cocked his throw-stick back and paused, scanning around. Releasing a breath, he unwound his torso and flung the weapon. The stick twirled end over end with a whirling hiss and disappeared in the foliage, creating a dull thud. A duck's blue-gray body fell from the reeds and plopped onto the water's surface, floating on its side. Picking another throw-stick from a stash, Akhenaten continued his massacre.

"Dock and release the cats," Akhenaten said, motioning to the crates. The boat drifted into the vegetation, and a soldier released three gray cats from a cage. One crouched low and repetitively stomped with its hind legs before pouncing and vanishing into the green. Five ducks flushed from the brush and took flight, screaming curses in their own tongue.

Akhenaten displayed deadly accuracy as his cats continued to drive prey out from hiding. Within an hour, all colors of fowl littered the area as if a rampant disease had decimated the population. My eyes closed and I caught my head in my hands, sadness and guilt rising in my chest. We couldn't possibly eat them all before the meat spoiled. What would become of the wasted lives and souls? Would they return, hatching again next spring? Perhaps they could be reborn as different creatures or live in the afterlife.

Akhenaten held up a hand. "My faithful servant shall be granted a chance to partake."

I swallowed hard with trepidation. Akhenaten motioned for me and I obeyed, keeping my gaze low. Shoving a throw-stick—fashioned in the shape of a snake—into my hand, I tentatively grasped the tail.

"Choose a target, envision success, and throw," he said.

"Hunting is a great honor," Suty said, eyeing the weapon in my hand. I didn't feel honored. Hitting a bird with a stick would be nearly impossible, and my gut told me I shouldn't succeed in front of my master. But I didn't want to look foolish to Nefertiti. As I raised the stick, the snake's eyes burrowed into mine. The object felt heavy, and a power emanated from the wood, carrying into my hand and up my arm. Its mouth opened, revealing wooden fangs and a moving tongue! Heat scalded my palm. Yelling in surprise and pain, I hurled the stick with all my might. It landed short of a long-legged bird, and the stick splashed, creating weak ripples before bobbing on the water as if to mock me. Steam arose from the murk around the weapon. Snorts and roaring laughter burst out from the soldiers. No one seemed to have noticed the magic of the stick.

"The hunt is only for those who wield physical prowess," Akhenaten said between bouts of roaring merriment as his lower belly jiggled. "I do things for you, things you will never comprehend." His amusement halted, his eyes unblinking. "You were only created to serve. God made it so. Do not forget!" He swung an open hand, landing a firm pat on my back, and I stumbled away.

Embarrassment and rage spiraled together in my heart and hot blood rose into my face. I wanted to punish Akhenaten, but I'd never be able to do anything to him. Shuffling to the rear of the boat, I plopped down to sulk. Nefertiti sat there but hadn't even lifted her head to witness the spectacle. A touch of relief settled over me. Croc lay beside her, his ears perking up when a hunting cat hissed. Launching from the boat, Croc landed amongst the reeds.

Gray cats emerged from the papyrus with birds dangling in their mouths, only to have soldiers pry away the spoils. Popping out of the brush,

Croc lugged a large duck. Suty reached out to snatch the game. Croc hissed and swatted the approaching appendage. Jumping, the soldier jerked his hand back.

"You little …" he said, reaching for his sword.

My throat tensed with fear. Sprawling over the boat, I crashed face-first as reeds poked into my eyes, mouth, and nose. Croc scuttled away, his tail puffing to twice its normal size.

"Please don't hurt him!" I begged, reaching out. "He isn't trained!"

Suty seized the dead duck, snapping its body in his fists with a sickening crunch. "He bites or scratches again, I crush him."

Scooping up Croc, I sloshed back to the boat. Suty swatted him on his back as we passed. Croc tore out of my arms with claws bared, racing onboard and hiding amongst the crates.

Akhenaten tapped his foot. "Enough!" he said. "You have all seen how many I killed and will commemorate the event on the walls of my future tomb, a record amongst even the ancient kings. Leave the cats and the dead. Now we sail!"

Pushing the boat back toward the flowing river, the soldiers remained quiet. The morning mist had burned off, the air still. Complete silence.

A horrible roar erupted from the depths of the marsh. The boat bucked underneath me and tipped violently toward the water's surface.

Chapter 17

Journal Translation

THE BOAT SPUN AROUND and dipped to the opposite side, tilting farther over. Murk from the marsh we'd hunted in rose over the edge, sloshing in. Another pounding blow. Sliding into the railing from her sitting position, Nefertiti pitched overboard. Soldiers launched into the water along with Akhenaten and myself—shrieking in surprise.

Soldiers' screams rang in my ears before my body smacked horizontally into the wet surface, my head sucked under. Turbulent water and bubbles erupted around me, disrupting my vision. My blood thickened with fear. What terror could capsize a barge? And did it lurk beyond the swirling debris? I thrashed through the filth, tasting muck—I hadn't become much better of a swimmer since I'd rescued Croc years ago.

I resurfaced, a net of algae clinging to my face and neck, threatening to suck me back under. My breath came in panicked gasps. Massive jaws and teeth smashed into the barge, the creature's smooth skin, large eyes, and small ears not resembling a crocodile. What was—

The vessel spun again, sending Suty and Mahu teetering. The larger man managed to hurl his spear. When it plunged into the water, the weapon's velocity diminished. If the bronze pierced the creature's hide, it did not carry enough power to even distract the beast. The gaping jaws of the brown-skinned monster reached for the hull. Tremendous tusk-like teeth struck wood with a loud crack as an arrow buried into the side of its face.

Bellowing, the beast plunged under water with an elephant-like splash. Violent thrashing arose on the far side of the boat. The eyes of another creature submerged. A soldier treaded water in front of me, but his chin slipped beneath the surface. His frightened screams ended in waving hands, gurgling, bubbles, and then ripples.

Terror engulfed me with compressing force, and my arms and legs thrashed on their own.

Another soldier disappeared. How many creatures waited below? Would they suck me under at any moment? A body resurfaced, bitten in two, blood pulsing out from the wound traversing the torso. Panicking, I kicked away from the boat.

Nefertiti screamed. My arms kept stroking, but my head turned. Her limbs flailed. Pain struck my heart. Was she being attacked, or could she not swim?

Forcing a couple of deep breaths, I struggled toward her despite consuming fear. "Are you wounded?" I yelled.

Her eyes pulled open wide as her mouth emitted deafening screeches. I swam closer, reaching out. Grabbing my shoulders, she climbed and thrust me under water. My air disappeared as I blew bubbles of surprise. In her terror, she wanted to stand on me for leverage. My lurching strokes—no one had ever taught me to swim—weren't enough to pull myself to the surface. My lungs and throat ached.

I did the only thing I could—I dove deeper. When Nefertiti's head sank under, she immediately let go. I swam away, but a giant form plunged toward me through the swirling murk. My heart stopped. Massive jaws unhinged. I rolled as fast as I could. Teeth snapped shut. A leviathan-like body smashed into me, sending me spinning with disorientation.

I expected to be crushed, but the jaws did not ensnare me. Several seconds passed, and I resurfaced. Nefertiti squealed. Eerie suspense from unseen death waiting below summoned a fear unlike any other. The emotion so thoroughly haunted my mind, I still cannot help but recall it whenever I enter water.

Grasping Nefertiti's dress from behind, I paddled with all my might. She screamed and splashed, which might draw the attention of the creatures. The prospect of something lurking below and pulling me under was the only thought in my mind.

Massive jaws snapped off another soldier's arm. Blood swirled in the water around me as we approached the boat. The shore was too far away.

Arrows and spears rained overhead. Clinging to the edge of our vessel, I pulled Nefertiti against the wood. She still wasn't coherent, but Mahu hauled her up and extended his hand for me. Squeezing his palm with as much strength as I could muster, I kicked as he pulled. But it was too late.

An unbelievable crushing pressure clamped down on my lower leg. Something pierced my flesh and grated against bone. I cried out in shock and blinding pain, and Mahu let me fall back into the river. But an arrow whistled over my shoulder. The compression on my ankle released. Mahu yanked me up, and I collapsed into the shallow water filling the hull. Blood pulsed from my lower leg, intertwining with the murk.

Mahu continued loosing arrows until the last surviving soldier hauled himself in. Crawling and splashing through the boat, I clawed my way to the stern.

"Row!" I yelled in my cursedly quiet voice.

The remaining soldiers took up paddles as Mahu scanned the ripples, releasing an arrow. Oars broke water, and the boat lurched. Tilting the rudder, we angled toward the open Nile. Reversing the handle veered us to shore. "Keep rowing!" I said. The vessel pitched while I attempted to keep it straight, summoning all of my strength.

"Stop!" Mahu yelled. "Take us out to the river!"

I shook my head in disobedience. Now I understood my life-given duty as clear as the blue sky. The short conversation with Mahu was as deep a discussion as I'd ever shared with someone other than Father. "We can't leave without my master's body!" I said.

Mahu screamed, his face contorting like a possessed man's. "He's gone! The hippopotami got him! The royal son is dead! Get us out of here!"

My existence would become the consequence of my own decisions and actions. I did not desire a mediocre life.

"There!" I yelled, pointing. Wing-like shoulder blades floated along the surface. Akhenaten's body lay face down. No blood swirled around him. The boat bucked under a blow, and the men cried out. But they continued to row, in spite of the dread permeating the air. Mahu signed at the waters with his index and little fingers extended before reaching out and hauling in the gangly corpse.

"Row hard!" I said, shifting the rudder. Another impact vibrated the hull and shook my bones. Wood splintered as the boat rocked, but we weaved toward the body of the Nile. I held my breath. Overwhelming pain arose in my leg.

Mahu rolled Akhenaten onto his back. Examining the body, he placed a hand upon the royal son's neck. No visible wounds showed themselves, but Mahu shook his head. "Once I witnessed a doctor save a child from drowning … but I'm not gifted in medicine or magic." Raising a fist into the air, the captain drove it down onto Akhenaten's chest. The body jerked under the blow, and Nefertiti screamed.

Red-tinged water erupted from Akhenaten's mouth, sending him into fits of coughing. Mahu turned my master onto his side, and sputtering and convulsions followed.

I dropped the rudder in utter shock. A man—no, a god-favored man—had risen from death before my very eyes. What kind of dark magic did my master wield—

"No!" Nefertiti said, but she clamped a hand over her mouth.

Stories of magic carried in bloodlines, in the descendants of the Aten, were true. They possessed power over death itself, even resurrection! Akhenaten was surely the Aten's chosen one. But disappointment overwhelmed me, dragging my shoulders down. I had hoped to bring the body back to Pharaoh, as we should, imagining my bravery would be justly honored. But now … awe and fear solidified in my soul.

Akhenaten continued to gag and choke as a soldier draped a dry blanket over him. After opening and securing the sail, the men bailed water from the hull and assessed for structural damages. No boards were broken on top, but they'd have to inspect the underside when we were long gone from this place. Hopefully we wouldn't sink.

A strong wind whipped the sail, and we flew along like an albatross.

The wet hair of my sidelock blew into my face. I felt like a hero and more alive than I ever had.

I'd saved my master.

Steering the vessel, I learned by making incremental adjustments, some correct and some incorrect. I just never repeated the same mistake.

Rolling onto his stomach, Akhenaten propped himself on his elbows. His entire body spasmed, his eyes vacant. Placing a knee underneath himself, he tried to stand but failed multiple times. Mahu offered assistance, but Akhenaten pushed him away. Crawling to the bow, he sat with his back to me.

Nefertiti sobbed while the pain in my leg intensified. A deep purple encompassed my entire lower leg, a puncture wound at its center.

Chapter 18

Journal Translation

A HIPPOPOTAMUS TUSK HAD pierced my flesh and bone, and blood still cascaded from the wound. I felt faint. Clenching my teeth, I tried to concentrate on steering the barge. But the throbbing pain became unbearable.

Warm hands caressed my skin as Nefertiti applied pressure to the wound and wrapped it in a dry cloth. Circling my leg and purring, Croc sniffed and licked the bandage. A glimmer returned to Nefertiti's eyes as she whispered, "I'd hoped Akhenaten was dead." Her lower lip trembled, and a tear ran down her cheek.

Sympathy stung my heart. "Things will be different now … after that," I said.

Her plump lips turned up into a faint smile as she finished dressing my wound.

Mahu stood and spoke. "We return to Memphis. The omens say this voyage is cursed and should be abandoned."

"We stay the course," a resonating voice echoed from the front, followed by a fit of coughing. Akhenaten trembled but didn't turn around.

"But, Your Majesty," Mahu said, "we are in no physical or mental condition to continue to Elephantine, much less the borders of the empire."

"You have not seen what I have!" Akhenaten screamed, turning and coughing red-tinged fluid onto the deck. He wiped stringing saliva with the back of his hand, his black eye paint streaking across his cheeks. "We need to visit Thebes now more than ever. The wheels of this ancient world grind quickly. I must seize the moment … *my* time!"

Akhenaten's dilated eyes contained a madness beyond what usually lay veiled beneath.

No one argued.

"We sail day and night," Akhenaten said. "The rising level of the Nile will cover any sandbars."

Thankfully, the red tinge of silt now flowed in the river, indicating the commencement of the inundation.

Mahu conceded to Akhenaten but folded the sail to half its breadth at night. The captain and I alternated navigation duty and slept when we could, the pain in my leg a constant. Croc purred and yelled high-pitched meows, growing uncharacteristically affectionate and clingy.

"What was it you were doing before pulling Akhenaten from the marsh?" I asked Mahu one evening, the moon's faint light illuminating the water's surface. "Pointing at the hippopotamus like this?" I extended my index and little fingers.

"Not now!" Mahu said, his eyelids pulling back as he waved at me to stop. "It's a simple spell to ward off crocodiles. I was trying whatever I could, but don't waste magic! People are born with mystical powers but must learn how to wield them. Most carry so little you'd never see its effects, but a rare few possess powers no man should."

I sucked in a breath of surprise. Could I possibly hold magic within me and be special without anyone ever knowing it? Hope broke into the dark world like sunlight. I'd try this magic if we ever encountered a crocodile, to determine if I had the capability. But did my predetermined status as a lowly servant mean that I'd not control enough magic to matter? Shadows lingered over my excitement, optimism ebbing as quickly as it came.

Suty yelled at his sulking comrades, who slouched and hung their heads, "Pay attention, you fools!"

Akhenaten continued to stare south.

One short soldier leaned over to another, his voice tight with tension, "Seth's chaos and his serpent, Apep, are trailing us on this voyage."

My lips pursed in wonder. These men probably needed to mourn their three dead comrades, and contemplate the bizarre disappearance of the other, rather than voyage on.

"Thank you for everything you've done," Nefertiti said as she unwound my stained bandage. "The crew risked everything for Akhenaten, but you did more for all of us than anyone would expect of a servant … more than we'd expect of a royal man."

The honor of being appreciated rose as a tingling through my face and cheeks. I knew what heroes felt, and my life took a new course. Mahu's advice was all I needed. Nefertiti would see me as a man and would fall in love with me. She'd love me for how I felt about her, and for the lengths I was willing to go. My current status wouldn't matter, but I'd climb through the ranks of men for her if need be. For the first time, I didn't feel like a servant.

My wound burned when she removed the cloth, as if my limb had caught fire. Pain ascended into my thigh. Reeking like the carcass of a rodent covered in maggots, the wound also drained gobs of thick yellow fluid. My toes curled in disgust. But Nefertiti no longer ignored me as a man and I couldn't jeopardize that. I clenched my jaw to hold back a whine, as any hero would. This injury just needed more time to heal, like the lacerations I'd sustained as a clumsy child.

Nefertiti secured a new bandage, wrinkles of concern arising on her smooth forehead.

✳ ✳ ✳

Days blended together upon the vast waters among barren desert, scattered trees, shrubs, and farmland. My thoughts turned cloudy, and I tired easily.

I awoke, startled to find I'd blacked out at the rudder. Nefertiti knelt by my side, and my leg throbbed. Lifting my kilt revealed that my injured leg had swelled to twice the size of my other leg. Streaks ran upward under my skin, twisting into black and purple near my groin.

Nefertiti pointed as her mouth fell open. "Mahu, look!"

Striding over with wide eyes, Mahu said, "The marks of death reach for his heart. We need to get him to a doctor, magician, or priest soon, or he'll be lost."

Something loosened in my throat and my jaw trembled with dread. I could die? Now that I was a hero and had accomplished something, I was going to die? Fear and loneliness overwhelmed me, and I started to shake. I'd never pass the underworld's judgment. There was still so much I had to learn and assist Akhenaten with to gain favor. And what would happen to Nefertiti?

Standing for the first time in days, Akhenaten wheeled around. His eyes dilated with anger. "Who placed the servant boy in charge of steering this vessel?" His cracked lips twitched, eye paint still running ragged across his countenance. "He is always stepping beyond his boundaries, and it is detrimental to us all. We are falling out of favor. Remove him!"

I sat frozen in shock. Akhenaten should treat me as his savior!

Suty tossed me aside. Crashing into the hull with a smack, I lay there drifting in and out of awareness for an unknown duration of time. Nefertiti and Mahu's faces swirled in a fog of feverish nightmares.

My eyes opened, but everything was blurry when we ran aground. Awaiting us, armed guards motioned to come ashore. Mahu carried me off the barge while Akhenaten led his soldiers into a mysterious city.

We were escorted into a magnificent temple. However, unlike any house of worship I'd seen, this one was enclosed and dark. My breathing changed to shallow panting as anxiety mounted. How would the healing light of the Aten reach me? Or was this where they brought the blasphemers, people who cursed God?

Placing me upon a cool mud-brick slab, several men examined me under firelight. One with a white sash across his chest touched my wound. Blinding pain shot up my spine and into my head. I screamed and tried to thrash away but was held firm. They poked and prodded my leg, muttering amongst themselves.

The magician wearing the sash shook his head. "Amputation won't help if the marks extend to his body," he whispered. "At least he's only a servant."

Loneliness gripped my heart, and my head slumped back as I lay dying in the temple. Tears rolled down my cheeks. Father … Croc wasn't here either, or Nefertiti. I would die alone, journeying into that desolate darkness without love or friendship—

A man in a leopard-skin cloak with a clean-shaven head entered the hazy scene. Another followed, wearing the typical white kilt with a writing palette suspended over his shoulder by rope. The doctor with the palette inspected my wound, made notes with his instruments, consulted a stack of papyrus, and whispered to the other two. "The hippopotamus planted the seed, but now the disease seeps through his blood."

Circling me, the man in the white sash set down a series of statuettes. He produced a bronze wand in the shape of a cobra and shook it in my direction, speaking gibberish.

Cupping my forearms, the priest in the yellow animal-skin cloak nodded. The magician set the cobra wand on my chest and tied knots up a length of rope, placing it adjacent to my leg. "This servant has been bitten," the magician said. "Give me breath. A shriek shall call out from the malignant humors that are scattered throughout this body. If the poison passes the seven knots, I will not let the sun shine. I will not let the inundation rush forth!"

The priest produced an ivory knife, shadowed hieroglyphs inscribed upon its blade. Blackness consumed everything for a moment, but the lamplight flickered and returned.

"It has taken hold in the tibia," the doctor declared.

The priest held the knife high before plunging it down into my leg.

Chapter 19

Journal Translation

THE MAGICAL BLADE THE PRIEST stabbed me with sank into my wounded leg. I jumped with surprise and blinding pain. My vision flashed white and my ears rang. But the magician and doctor held me down onto the mud-brick slab inside the dark temple. I screamed as the knife grated against bone, the smell of burning flesh stinging my nostrils. The scraping sensation rattled through my head as thick, yellow pus erupted—

My eyes fluttered as I awoke. Nefertiti now sat beside me in a small room under dim light, staring at the floor. "What happened?" I whispered, not having the strength to sit up.

"You're alive!" She settled a hand on my head. Sweat dripped from my brow, but I felt colder than when I'd spent the night out in the desert. "They said the disease festered under your skin, in your bones. The magician, the doctor, and the priest were all there. They released the poison, but it'd already spread …" She sniffed, but a tear rolled down to the tip of her demure nose. "They said you probably won't make it through the night—"

I gasped in horror.

Squeezing my arms, she said, "But if you do wake tomorrow, you should live. Hold on, Heb. Hold on to me if nothing else." She sobbed, laying her face on my chest.

Nefertiti's raw emotions granted me strength and a profound purpose. "I will make it," I said confidently, as Mahu had taught me. "I'll do it for you."

Staring deep into my eyes, she said, "There're priests helping, but you need rest."

"Where's Akhenaten?" I asked.

"Settling business here in Thebes." Her freshly painted green eyelids closed. "But his affairs will conclude in a couple of weeks, and when he's finished, he won't wait for you. Either you'll be healthy enough to travel, or you'll be left behind."

I gasped as I attempted to rise.

"But we'll come back to Thebes soon; we always do." She forced a thin smile. "And I'll find you … or I'll find you in the next life."

Tremoring, I let my head fell back down. The thought of losing Nefertiti twisted my heart like the gnarled trunk of an olive tree. But she stroked my damp hair and kissed my cheek. My heart raced with excitement. Desperately wanting to kiss her back, I attempted to sit up. The room spun, and she pressed me down. Relaxing, I fell into a sleep teeming with dreams of love and desire.

Billowing clouds raced across the endless sky in my dream, sunlight flooding between the obscure shapes of animals and men. A tree sparkled under the heavenly light. The tamarisk tree. Father. A pink petal released its hold on a branch and drifted to the earth. Another and another followed, floating on the wind. The branches grew bare …

I blinked my eyes open. The light of the Aten drifted through an open window. I was alone inside a small room. I forced myself to a sitting position on a pile of reeds, my limbs trembling under my meager weight. A glistening substance was smeared over the wound on my elevated leg. The puncture had contracted and the red lines had vanished, along with much of the swelling. Days must have passed. I touched the shiny layer around the injury, my fingers sticking to it. Pulling away, I rubbed the substance and smelled an earthy, sweet tang that initiated memories of Akhenaten's breakfasts. Honey. But used as a salve? My stomach released a low growl of hunger.

A hunk of bread sat on a plate beside me, a jug of water nearby. I swallowed the ration whole and guzzled water. Something wasn't right. Nausea rolled through my body, and I heaved the contents back onto the floor. My vomit appeared as a pile of mush.

"Small amounts," a shaven man in fine fabric said, entering. "You've barely held down enough water over the past week to ward off death. Your stomach must expand slowly."

Wiping stinging vomit from my lips, I spat more out of the back of my throat. Chunks landed beside a figurine on the floor. The visage of a stout dwarf with a mane and beard like a lion stared back at me. Fashioned of strange material, the statuette shone a deep blue.

"What's that?" I asked, retching.

"That is Bes," he said, his naked eyebrows narrowing as if surprised I didn't know. My silence dragged on. "He is your protector, warding off evil of all kinds. Helped save your life, he did. Take him when you go; you never know when you may need him again." The man held out a dangling necklace, the spinning face of the lion-dwarf emblazoned upon dried mud. Gratefully accepting the token, I slid it over my head.

I'd already survived that first initial night and at least several more days, but another week passed before I could eat whole meals and limp about my room. The blue dwarf still watched over me. My body had turned gaunt, more so than ever. I wanted to grow strong in order to protect Nefertiti, but the struggle turned into a never-ending battle. Could I ever become the man she desired? I slumped down.

Shaking my head, I forced the dark thoughts out. This allowed curiosity to seep in. I was in Thebes, and prior eavesdropping had educated me. The city of Thebes was the largest in the world, and the only city I knew of besides Memphis. Thebes had always been the capital of Upper Egypt, where the royal family spent most of their time. Uprisings crept up within the city, but Thebans loved Pharaoh and built him a monumental temple and palace. Pharaoh often ruled as one of them, but court duties to keep the lands united had sent him to northern Memphis.

I took a deep breath. Would I witness the grandeur of hundred-gated Thebes now that—

Shouts of frightened men rang outside, startling me. I stood on shaky feet, my lower leg throbbing as blood rushed downward. After hobbling outside, I stumbled through an open courtyard and entered a magnificent temple. Pillars of stone surrounded me, supporting a solid roof. Firelight danced at the margins of the darkness, and a scream pierced the inner shadows.

My vision adjusted as I crept toward the commotion.

Akhenaten held something above the man in the leopard skin who'd been present during my treatment. Three of our soldiers also pinned him to a stone slab. Several other men, who I assumed were priests, given their clean-shaven heads, unsuccessfully attempted to negotiate or yank the guards off. Shrieks erupted beneath the yellow, spotted hood.

Suty, as if a monster, flung a priest aside. The man sailed through the air before smacking into a wall. The monster's scimitar cut down another, and his spear pierced the chest of a third.

"Bring him out into the light of the Aten," Akhenaten said. "The people wait."

The hooded priest they'd been holding down kicked and screamed as the soldiers now dragged him out. A flash of light landed upon the priest's aged eyes. Terror stormed in their depths and ignited my own. What were they going to do?

"Akhenaten!" I said in a pathetic voice. "This is one of the men who saved my life!"

My master followed behind the soldiers and shook his head. "You would not understand, my servant." Grabbing my hand, he squeezed as if to console me. "You could be replaced in seconds. This man committed crimes against Pharaoh, Egypt, and God." He shoved me aside.

In my weakened state, I fell onto my back, the procession continuing out into the courtyard. Clambering to my hands and knees, I crawled after them. The Aten's rays beat down upon the sand, which burned my knees. I grimaced in pain, but continued on.

More people than I'd ever seen in this world gathered in the distance, creating a rumble out of mere whispers. Frightened expressions ran across their faces. The soldiers stopped, holding the priest down. Would they tear off his cloak and strip him of his title or bury him in the sand?

"This will create greater conflict," Mahu whispered to Akhenaten. "Please consider a more subtle approach."

"People of Thebes!" Akhenaten roared. "Your high priest has plotted to usurp power from Pharaoh Amenhotep III, the god-king who calls Thebes home. I am Akhenaten, his son, the son of the Aten! I have come to ensure that the rule of Upper Egypt is never questioned. Such treachery must be punished!"

He revealed an object hidden beneath his kilt, a knife with a gold handle fashioned into the shape of a crocodile's head. Out of its shinning jaws erupted a blade of bone, the actual mandible of one of the great beasts. A multitude of teeth formed one serrated edge, the other curved to a sharpened point.

"The Devouring Blade of the Aten!" Akhenaten yelled, holding the long knife over his head. "A weapon of such power, no one can feel its bite and survive, just as nothing can oppose God. This blade drinks the spirit of its victim like the Devouring Monster consuming a heart. A soul will be lost forever. Do not let this be your fate, people of Thebes!"

Chanting in a strange tongue, Akhenaten drew symbols in the air with the blade. Then he plunged the knife into the high priest's stomach, just below his ribs. The man screamed, writhing about. His cries reached out to the heavens, but his head arched backwards.

Akhenaten sawed flesh with the serrated crocodile teeth and shoved a hand inside the gaping wound. Reaching up toward the man's chest, he ripped aside inner organs as his arm buried up to the elbow. His grasp settled, but when he yanked nothing budged. Plunging the knife in through the wound, he twisted vigorously and cut. He withdrew his hand and thrust it overhead. Within his blood-drenched palm sat the high priest's beating heart.

Chapter 20

Journal Translation

THE HIGH PRIEST'S EVISCERATED heart pumped several times in Akhenaten's hand, and shrieks erupted from the watching Theban crowd. Its beating slowed and then ceased, dark liquid rolling in streams over my master's forearm. The high priest's body writhed on the ground and shriveled, as if the blade drank the very liquid inside the body's tissues.

"I wield the consuming power of the Devouring Monster!" Akhenaten said. Plunging his teeth into the heart, he ripped off a large piece of flesh as blood spurted across his cheeks. The vilest of demons in my nightmares didn't compare to the sight. I gagged with disgust.

Basking in the Thebans' captivation, Akhenaten breathed in their fear. After chewing the moist tissue, he swallowed. Blood flowed out of the gaping hole in the organ before spilling over his hand, running down to the tip of his elbow, and dripping into the sand. Closing his makeup-covered eyelids created the illusion of solid black orbs for eyes.

The crowd wailed. Clenching my teeth, I suppressed the vomit rising in my throat.

"The traitorous high priest's soul is no more!" Akhenaten said, dark spittle flying beyond red teeth. "It is as if he never even existed."

Howling, people fell to their knees and recoiled in agony. The body desiccated before my eyes, the heart mummifying in my master's hand. For a moment, awestruck wonder transcended horror.

"Do not make this your fate, people of Thebes," Akhenaten said. "God placed Pharaoh above you. Do not ever doubt this!" Dropping the wrinkled heart onto the sand beside the corpse, he motioned to his guards. "Bring Nefertiti."

Suty reached behind a pillar and dragged out a struggling Nefertiti. He followed Akhenaten, who strode away from the watching Thebans. My mind still reeled in disbelief of what had just occurred, but I limped after them. The Thebans were silent. But then a single angry shout was followed by another and another.

After marching out of sight of the mob, Akhenaten and his soldiers broke into a run. I hobbled as fast as I could on my aching leg. The woeful cries behind us turned to anger and intensified.

Tense minutes crawled by as we raced along narrow streets between mud-brick houses. Falling farther and farther behind, I lost sight of the group. My heart thumped with panic and exertion. Which way was the river? The clamor of a pursuing horde echoed off the buildings behind me.

I pushed my body as hard as it would go, and pain radiated up my leg.

Veering left where the soldiers had last turned revealed only another empty road. I glanced down all the side streets. Would the people of Thebes accept me as a wounded man? Or in their fury would they link me with Akhenaten?

The hum of flowing water sounded to the west, calling to me between buildings. I hobbled on. Wind and heat blasted me as I emerged from the city's edge, the Nile dead ahead—as well as Akhenaten's docked barge. Dirt transformed into mud, pulling my feet deeper with each stride. I grunted in misery as the squishy ground suctioned my afflicted limb like a giant leech. Was I in a terrible dream? The sensation of trudging through quicksand with an enraged mob in pursuit reminded me of nightmares. I faltered.

I hadn't crossed half of the flooded bank when Akhenaten's soldiers started to board our vessel. Figures wearing faces of rage and anguish poured from between the buildings at my back like hornets from a nest. Screams carried across the open space. Out of utter fear, I waded faster.

After Nefertiti climbed aboard, she glanced back. Reaching out a shaking hand, she motioned for me to hurry. I staggered through the mud of the early floods, but my body remained weak. The Thebans closed the gap between us as our boat sailed away …

I'd never make it. The Thebans would tear me limb from limb. They'd only know me as the servant of the madman who had brutally murdered and devoured the soul of their high priest.

How could I escape this? Akhenaten's plan to sail to Elephantine crossed my mind, but what if that was only a cover for his business here? They would have to sail against the current to continue to Elephantine. With the approaching mob, that would be risky. Mahu should want to sail north with the river, as fast as he could go, back to Memphis. But picturing the captain lowering the sail to face the wind, I imagined Akhenaten might object.

I had to guess. The only chance I would have to get out of Thebes alive would be to angle across the shore and shallow water, to intercept their trajectory. Pivoting to my left, I was barely able to breathe as I anticipated the folding of the sail. Would Akhenaten choose north?

The boat slid into deeper waters, the white sail billowing open with a gust of wind. They were continuing south, to Elephantine ...

Chapter 21

Journal Translation

I'D CORRECTLY ANTICIPATED Akhenaten's unpredictable commands and objectives—something deeper than fleeing the angry Thebans. I splashed into the Nile. Our barge was only a short length behind me but much farther out in the water. The Thebans, after seeing the boat launch, turned and chased me.

I struggled in a diagonal direction against the current. Thankfully, near shore, the river's pull remained feeble, but fear still strangled my heart. The possibility of unknown terrors waiting below scared me more than the mob. But hippopotami and crocodiles wouldn't live within the waters so close to the city. People would have driven them out long ago.

Reasoning eased my trepidation, and my arms and legs stroked more easily through the water. Most of the Thebans stopped at the bank and shouted, but a few waded in. Our vessel approached, accelerating. Yelling, Mahu and Nefertiti motioned for me to swim farther into the belly of the Nile. I struggled with strokes but swam slightly better than during my last attempt.

I fought with all my might. The boat neared, but I was too far away. The bow and Akhenaten passed, then the hull, and the stern. Reaching out, I was still twenty feet away. The crew made no motion to drop the sail or turn around. Mahu ducked into the shallow hull while Nefertiti's arm movements encouraged me to swim faster. Waves lapped against me. My body and spirit sank in disbelief that they wouldn't slow down to catch me.

Reappearing, Mahu flung a rope. The line flew through the air and landed only feet from me. A couple of quick strokes and I grabbed hold. My exhausted body wouldn't allow me to haul myself in, so I tied the end of the line around my chest. Mahu reeled me in and reached out with an open hand. Falling onto the wooden hull, I gasped as my body shook and my head floated in a rush of fog. Nefertiti hugged me even though I was dripping wet and emotionally and physically broken. Her warmth made it all worth it. A flicker of hope ignited in my heart.

"Thank you," was all I could mutter, bracing myself on all fours.

"You were forged with the will of a lion," Mahu said, "even if you were given the body of a rodent." Slapping me on the shoulder, he knocked me back to the hull, where I rested.

Akhenaten sat with his back to us. I wrinkled my upper lip in resentment. What had been his intentions in Thebes? Perhaps he desired to instill fear but hadn't brought enough men. Or perhaps he yearned to fuel Theban anger to gain the support of his father. Then he could return with an army. Would starting a war between Upper and Lower Egypt benefit him, or was he just mad?

Days and nights blurred amidst the howl of wind and water, quacking ducks or chirping birds, and rocking waves. Mahu navigated during the day, and I took over for short periods in the dark when he and Akhenaten slept. My open wound had sealed over with a bed of red tissue, and the edges reached out for each other. Croc remained at my side, and after several more days, I walked the length of the boat without too much pain in my leg.

"Elephantine!" Akhenaten said, pointing ahead.

A mysterious island appeared within the morning fog, and wonder filled my mind. The Nile parted around protruding earth, as if the isle would never succumb to even her powers. The howling wind died.

We glided closer, and the acres within the river expanded. The stone base of the island reared from the waters, appearing like majestic elephants. Atop their backs, buildings towered over the land. One structure soared above the rest, a watchtower. Sailing past, we turned around after reaching the far side of the isle.

The five remaining soldiers took up oars as Mahu guided us to the rock base. As the barge settled against stone, a contingent of spear-toting guards appeared. They stood motionless within a man-made passageway in the rock.

Akhenaten didn't acknowledge the Elephantinians but said, "I am Akhenaten, son of Amenhotep III, Pharaoh of Upper and Lower Egypt. I request access to your island, to speak with your high priest, and to stand upon the watchtower."

The local guards saluted with outward palms—the sign of adoration—and the tallest among them spoke. "The men and women of Elephantine are ever faithful to the god-king. We and the Aswanians defend Amenhotep's southern lands from the barbarian hordes of Nubia, the Dark Ones, and the Shadows. We do not ask for aid in this service unless dire need arises, and under Pharaoh, we've grown strong. We will assist with all that you seek."

Akhenaten ordered his soldiers ashore. Following, I slipped in surprise when I splashed into ankle deep water in the doorway. The natives led us deep into a flooded tunnel where the Aten's light disappeared, replaced by the flicker of oil lamps. Layers of horizontal lines were carved into the walls, a measuring device for the water level. The life-giving inundation was underway. But how did the river rise if no rain had fallen?

Continuing upward through a narrow staircase, the Elephantinians' footfalls echoed throughout the tunnels. We emerged through the subterranean level of a small island town. The wind howled in my ears and whipped around buildings. An old man with a shaven head and deeply wrinkled face stared from the roof of an adjacent mud-brick house. He sat unmoving, unblinking. I glanced away, unnerved. Egyptians typically used their roofs as balconies, but something wasn't right with him. Stabbing pain from my wound climbed up my leg as I glanced back … he was gone.

The guards marched down the rock streets without a word. Anticipation of something awful happening restricted my breathing, but the pain in my leg receded. Why were we here?

A great wall and watchtower rose beyond a stone temple and blotted out the southern sky. This temple was also covered with a roof. But before the situation in Thebes, I'd never seen a temple not open to the light of the Aten. Why would someone worship God without basking in his rays?

Steep stairs circled the tower, and we climbed into the sky. Stepping up to the highest level, we overlooked the world. I gazed in awe upon indescribable beauty—beauty like Nefertiti's.

A chill wind tore at my hair and kilt, threatening to blow me off. Land spread as far as I could see, cut by the snaking blue ribbon of the Nile. My gaze followed the river south toward its origin, but the waters didn't have a beginning or end. Where did it all come from? Farmlands didn't stretch beyond the border of Elephantine. But this wasn't the end of the world; so much more fertile earth lay beyond. I realized what a juvenile crocodile must feel when thrust into the endless river, forced to fight for survival. But I also needed to undertake the search for my own meaning in a vast world.

Black spots dotted a green plain far to the south, wavering across the landscape. A herd of roaming animals? Cattle, donkeys, horses, sheep, or pigs, like we had back home? After what I'd seen on this trip, I'd keep an open mind.

Darker figures appeared at the edge of the grassland, enshrouded in fog. Stopping, the herd lifted their heads and scanned the brush behind them. The new arrivals crept closer. Breaking into a dead run, the herd streaked across the plain. But the predators' hunched forms, running on two legs, moved with greater speed, a life-and-death chase on the earth below, me a spectator in the heavens. I shuddered. Was this how the Aten saw us?

Multiple animals toppled over, overtaken by the predators obscured inside their gray fog. Then the mist crawled back to the tree line, hiding whatever lurked inside. The remainder of the herd raced on.

I yelled and pointed, turning to the others. But only Nefertiti and two Elephantinian watchmen remained.

"They went to visit the high priest," Nefertiti said over the gale and giggled. "You were distracted."

"How could I not be?" I asked, motioning at the panorama as my stomach sank. What would transpire between Akhenaten and the high priest of Elephantine? My hands trembled with anxiety, thoughts of having to flee from angry locals filling my mind. But I looked north over Nefertiti's shoulder. I couldn't see the city of Thebes, only the unchanging landscape pierced by the river.

Stepping close, Nefertiti whispered in my ear, "The view's amazing, but I think Akhenaten wanted to come up here to see if we're being followed."

Chapter 22

Journal Translation

"This was once the southern border of the world," an Elephantinian watchman said without turning, his voice old and hoarse. He studied the unending countryside beyond the Nile and his island, far below the watchtower. "I've watched from these walls for over forty inundations. The land to the fourth cataract is claimed by Pharaoh, but it is largely uninhabited."

"Did you see the animals taken down by the predators in the fog?" I asked.

The guard turned, one shaven eyebrow arching onto his wrinkled forehead. "The lands beyond are ours, but they still run wild. You'll see strange things if you look long enough. People whisper about the return of the Dark Ones and The Shadows, humanoids living amongst the chaos. Monsters from children's stories. If they exist, they haven't challenged our lands, but whispers say their strength and numbers are growing."

A dark fog rolled through my mind. Images emerged inside my head—faces bound with white linen beneath black hoods. Glowing green mist wisped by.

I stumbled to the edge of the precipice.

Nefertiti yanked me back. "What're you doing?" she asked.

Lunging to safety, I shook with dread. That was the second time the images had appeared; the first after Mahu had mentioned the Dark Ones when we'd sailed away from Memphis. Had I seen them before? In nightmares? "What are the Dark Ones?" I asked.

"I've never seen one," the watchman said. "They're only children's tales, but Nubians speak of humanoid creatures wielding great magic. Supposedly they rose against Egypt millennia ago and sent us spiraling into darkness. Not until the god-king who could command the sphinx came were they wiped out. If any of that is real, it is ancient history."

I could no longer see the herd. "Who could command a sphinx? They're statues."

"Legends, boy," he said. "But we still mold sphinx from stone, to strike fear into the hearts of our enemies. The days of the old kings and their power are gone. People once said, 'He who could command the sphinx ruled Egypt.' But no one has done so for eons."

My forehead wrinkled in confusion. I looked west and then east at the vast desert stretching to the horizons. Not far down the east bank sat a town flanked by a towering mountain of rock.

"That is Aswan," the Elephantinian said. "It was once our southern frontier and a wealthy trade city along the routes to Nubia and to the east. The roads have grown cold and stale."

"The mountain is impressive," I said.

"Holy," he replied. "Granite stone with a grandeur unmatched any-where in the world. Many of the great monuments and temples of Egypt were carved from the mountain itself." He nodded to the southeast. "The mud-brick walls marked the edge of the world at the first cataract, before Egypt's influence extended beyond—"

"What's a cataract?" I asked.

Pointing a gnarled finger at the blue ribbon, he said, "Man cannot sail around those granite outcroppings teeming with rapids. The wall and the natural cataract protect the organized world from the chaos beyond." He paused. "That and a crocodile breeding program we borrowed from the northerners and their Walls-of-Snefru."

"What?" Nefertiti said, holding a hand to her mouth.

"We infested the moats," he said. "No one has breached it in centuries. Would you try?"

Nefertiti's face turned ashen. Images of creatures lurking in crocodile-plagued waters summoned jitters and constricted my throat.

Massive clouds rolled in, and a gust bent my body under its force. Huddling over Nefertiti, I gazed up at the purple peaks floating against a blue sky.

"Sorcery is at work," the watchman said, his knuckles blanching upon his spear's shaft.

"Why do you say that?" I yelled over the incoming squall.

"The thunderheads ride a ghostly wind out of the west." He pointed with his weapon. "Days grow darker in the south yet rain seldom falls here, even during the inundation. But we'll feel this wrath."

The clouds sailed across the sky with the speed of a cheetah, putting my nerves on edge. I wasn't sure how I felt about magic after seeing the display in the streets of Memphis—those arrows encircling Akhenaten, the magician with the white cat, the lady referring to him as the son of Hapu.

Slipping her hand into mine, Nefertiti braced against the wind and stared into the tempest. Excitement and fascination sparked as I too stood against the storm. She kissed my cheek, bringing a burgeoning smile of elation to my lips. My body tingled with excitement, and I turned to gaze upon my love with more wonder and awe than when gazing across the open world. I studied her dark eyes, deep green makeup, lustrous hair, high cheekbones, demure nose, shapely chin, and full lips. She smiled but didn't turn her head, allowing me to indulge in her beauty. For a moment *I* was king of the world.

Cold water pelted my bare shoulders, snapping me back into reality. Streams from the sky assailed the watchtower just as Akhenaten, his soldiers, and a group of Elephantinians stepped upon the landing. Nefertiti jerked her hand from mine.

"Are any boats trailing us from the north?" Akhenaten asked.

"No, son of the god-king," the watchman answered.

Leaning into the wind and rain, Suty and Mahu peered in all directions. Akhenaten was subtle but leaned on his walking stick as he carved symbols into the air and whispered under the racket of the downpour. He motioned, as if turning pages of papyrus in the wind. "Time to return to Memphis," he said. "We will pass Thebes under the cover of night." The rain pounded harder. My master led us away, the descent accentuating his awkward gait.

I released a long sigh of relief. Surviving several weeks on a perilous adventure across the world, I'd experienced more than most servants. It was time to return home.

As we proceeded through the town, people celebrated the great inundation by dancing in the rain. But when we passed, they stopped. Following the stairwell and tunnel, we stepped back into the flooded basement of the island. The hash marks confirmed the water had already risen.

I waited for my turn to board, and an eerie sensation overcame me, followed by images of the past. Glancing back, I half expected a mob of angry Elephantinians to be chasing us. But no men stampeded. Only a small group watched from the cellar. The old man from the rooftop balcony was there, his stark face sending chills along my spine.

I stepped aboard, giving one last glance over my shoulder. Whispering amongst themselves, the Elephantinians pointed but showed no hostility. The old man remained silent, unblinking. His face also resembled the watchtower guard I'd talked to … But that was impossible. The guard had stayed behind and had been armed and armored.

The torrential downpour soaked through my kilt as I sat near the stern. Shoving away from the island, we angled into the belly of the Nile. Mahu steered as the raging river lifted and propelled us. Red-tinged waters swelled and rolled over the banks, pushing rocks the size of boats while uprooting shrubs and trees. The power of the current summoned feelings of vulnerability and insignificance. Did all this water come from precipitation emptying into the Nile? We sped downriver, although we now rode into the howling wind.

Land whisked by in a blur, the rain subsiding beyond Elephantine. Akhenaten again ordered us to sail through the nights. We passed Thebes under the cover of darkness, which gave me some comfort.

After about a week, the white walls of a grand city emerged on the horizon, as if rising out of the river itself. Memphis. My heart burned with nostalgia. I missed Father, my home, and the comforts of the palace.

We entered between the guardian sphinx and the great walls, and the vast emptiness of the outside world disappeared. But a crowd of people awaited us at the port.

Chapter 23

Journal Translation

WORD OF OUR RETURN TO Memphis—the capital of Lower Egypt—must've been sent upon swift wings. A troop of royal guard, the god-king himself, and his queen awaited us inside the great, white walls. Pharaoh's blue and gold striped *Nemes* headdress flowed over his ears and godly shoulders.

I stared with submissive awe. The golden beard of the god-king protruded from leather straps—the false beard—matching a massive gold necklace stretching across his chest. Much of Pharaoh's exposed flesh shone gold, his skin transforming to that of God. Glinting under the light of the Aten, he appeared too magnificent to belong to this world. But despite all his power and godliness, his face and body sagged with age and exhaustion. His belly protruded beyond his thighs, not aided by his hunched spine. Even god-kings must grow old inside mortal bodies. Tiye, the great royal wife and mother of Akhenaten, stood beside Pharaoh. Her lustrous red hair blew freely in the wind, her white dress and gold adornments sparkling.

Standing behind them was Father, his broad face taut. My stomach cramped with anxiety. He should be overjoyed to—

"Oh, no," Nefertiti whispered, digging her fingernails into my arm. "Father's here."

Ay, a handsome man of middle age, stood at Pharaoh's right and patted down a thick, black wig. I'd have to break my back trying to impress him if I ever wanted to marry his daughter. Towering beside Ay stood a more handsome, younger man whose muscles rippled—the crown prince of Egypt, Thutmose. My insides shriveled, and I felt weaker, becoming less of a man just beholding the prince. This wouldn't turn out well for us, but what could I have done? I'd had no choice.

Stopping their work, the people of Memphis hovered around the docks and watched. The racket of the port and wind faded to a whisper. We docked and stepped ashore, Akhenaten leading us with a tall posture and puffed chest. The soldiers and I fell into salutations, kneeling in the dirt and holding our palms out to the god-king in adoration.

Nodding to his family, Akhenaten said, "Father, Mother, Brother."

Pharaoh's eyes narrowed with suspicion or anger, the tortuous veins on his hands popping out as he squeezed the royal crook and flail. "Welcome back, my son," he said, his voice withered. "You never informed me you were going hunting. Did you know we will return to Thebes after I address a few last pressing affairs here? Probably within the month."

I held my breath in suspense. Was he going to strike Akhenaten down or let him pass? Pharaoh's insides must've been boiling, but the man retained diplomacy.

"Come, we have much to discuss," Pharaoh said, hobbling away.

After surrounding us, Pharaoh's royal guard—who must've totaled fifty—prodded and steered us toward the heart of the city. Walking at Nefertiti's side, I hung my head with regret and worry as to what punishment might follow. Ay stomped between the soldiers, snatched his daughter's hand, and yanked her away.

"Did you see the countryside, Brother?" Thutmose asked, his fists clenched as he attempted to walk casually after Pharaoh.

"I had business to attend to," Akhenaten said, his gaze fixed ahead.

The tense march concluded at the palace. Grabbing me by the back of the neck, Suty shoved me into the dirt. "Servant, you're not needed for this," he said. "Prepare your master's room and a hot meal."

The procession continued into the palace in a whirl of dust.

✳ ✳ ✳

Screams and shouts rang throughout the palace's halls for hours, but no words were distinguishable inside Akhenaten's quarters. I waited, nervously tapping my foot.

Nefertiti appeared in the hallway, her hair reflecting the flickering lamps. The sandals of her inquisitive sister, Mutnedjmet, and Akhenaten's sister, Beketaten, slapped along at her side. Tears cascaded down Nefertiti's cheeks while little Mutnedjmet held her hand. They passed by without noticing me.

Stepping out behind them, I watched. Mutnedjmet looked up at Nefertiti, smiling. "Don't be sad, Nefertiti," she said, "Akhenaten may be punished, but Pharaoh won't flail him."

Beketaten's long face displayed no emotion.

"That's not what I'm worried about," Nefertiti said, sinking to her knees.

"Did something happen?" Mutnedjmet asked, her soft face wrinkling with concern.

"Akhenaten deserves everything he gets," Nefertiti said, covering her head with her arms. "I never should've snuck onto that ship. I hope Father and Pharaoh don't find out."

"They know you went," Mutnedjmet said.

"I know …" Nefertiti fell silent, her hands falling to the floor. "I mean …"

"Did Akhenaten do something?" Beketaten asked as she stepped back and placed a hand on her chest, her voice more high-pitched and nasal than usual.

"I …" Nefertiti's mouth fell open, but no more words came out.

Trying to think of something to say, I approached in hopes of comforting Nefertiti. Mutnedjmet noticed, brushing tangled hair out of her face.

"Heb was there to protect you," Mutnedjmet said. "He always looks after you."

Nefertiti glanced back with teary eyes, her dark green makeup smeared. All of her bruises had faded, but the glow behind her dark irises, the radiance I'd fallen in love with, had not returned.

"But he has no power," Nefertiti said. "He couldn't help me or the priest."

My heart crumpled, as if being stomped on. She still thought I was weak! I hadn't been able do anything else that first night but grow angry and curse God for my miserable fate.

"Heb's desire to care for you should provide more comfort than any words I can offer," Mutnedjmet said, patting her sister's hand.

My jaw dropped in surprise. The girl's intelligent words clashed with her appearance, taking my speech away. A feeling of self-worth washed over me in a warm tingle. Did I hold some kind of power? Love? Would Nefertiti realize it?

"Is there anything I can do?" I finally asked, kneeling and placing a hand on Nefertiti's shoulder. Hoping for some simple or even great task, I yearned to make all of her cares and concerns vanish.

Nefertiti shook her head. "There's nothing a servant can do for me right now."

Smirking, Beketaten nodded.

"I—" I tried to say.

Emerging from the shadows at the end of the hallway, Akhenaten strode up to us, his ever-present stick clacking on the tile. I removed my hand from Nefertiti.

"Servant," he said, his dark eyelids closing to complete his black mask. "If you have gathered a meal and tended to my room, leave us. Your father is anxious to see you."

My forehead furrowed. I didn't want to leave Nefertiti; she needed protection. Glaring with narrowed eyes, my master folded his arms. Perhaps she would be safe now that we were back inside the palace. Pharaoh gave the orders here, not his second son.

"What did Pharaoh do to you?" Mutnedjmet asked her cousin.

"Never question me!" Akhenaten's face contorted like a beast's as he lunged forward, reaching for her. But Mutnedjmet jumped behind Beketaten. Growling, he spun on me, his teeth flashing in the lamplight. "The expedition has not altered anything between us." As he poked a gangly finger into my ribs, his eyes locked on my chest. His hand snaked out, ripping the amulet of Bes from me. Twine bit into my neck before breaking and causing warm blood to dribble down my back.

I raised my hands in defense and cowered in fear as he flung the necklace against the wall. It issued a crack, and fragments clattered to the floor. "Do not wear false idols! You witnessed my capabilities. You saw me take a man's *ka* and swallow his *ba*! He is gone. Few have wielded such magic, and they guarded it viciously. But I've been trained and have joined the ranks of the most powerful men in the world! I am second in line to be pharaoh, and my dominion will not stop. Do not give me more reason to become angry." He shoved me down the hall. "And never again go into the closet in my room," he said, pointing to his doorway. "Is that clear?"

"Like the afternoon sky," I replied. I hadn't cleaned his closet since before we'd left.

"Fetch me a meal as well, servant," Beketaten said, the tip of her nose twitching as she chuckled. "Before you see your father."

My chin collapsed onto my chest, and a feeling of powerless resentment tightened my insides. Was Beketaten trying to get me into trouble, or should I obey her, too? Hurrying off, I glanced back and witnessed the four discussing something quietly. Akhenaten had arisen from the dead and swallowed a man's soul. How could I ever hope to protect Nefertiti from such power? After everything I'd been through and accomplished on the river, my situation had turned even darker than before we left.

I assembled a meal from the kitchen and raced off to Father's room.

"Heb, my boy!" Father said, his broad face brightening. He stood up, failing at blinking back his tears.

"Father!" I ran into his open arms, so glad to see him.

"I'm so happy you're home," he said, hugging me tight and tugging on my sidelock. His bronze bracelet sank into my skin, and I felt safe for the first time since our adventure had begun. "You must've experienced so much. Come, tell me everything."

Sitting on the floor of his room, we chugged aromatic beer as I recounted my first tale. I showed him the jagged wound from the hippo, still red and tender. He coughed up a spray of chewed bread particles. Falling to a whisper, I described Akhenaten's crimes at Thebes.

Standing, Father cringed and looked past the walls painted with vibrant floral designs, glancing out the open door into the hall. He turned his attention to the high window, peeking under the reed curtain before whispering, "There's much you need to learn about this world before becoming a man or falling victim to its chaos. Things haven't turned out as I had hoped. Pharaoh's son is squeezing you in his fist, not letting you see the ways of Egypt. Only glimpses."

"Why?" I asked, my mind reeling in confusion.

He rubbed a wrinkled hand over his short, graying hair. "You have a good idea about your role here. I serve Pharaoh as you serve his son. It's a blessed life, but there're more important affairs, things beyond this world. Matters of the west hold a deeper meaning and purpose. You must follow your own path if necessary," he swallowed, "something I've always been afraid to do. Your mother—"

"What?" Hundreds of questions began to cry out in my mind.

Swinging the curtain aside, he glanced out the window again. The sky stretched like a blanket of darkness, spotted only with pale starlight.

"What's the big secret?" I asked.

He held a finger to his lips. My hands shook with suspense, but his eyes bulged as his gaze fixated on something outside the doorway.

Chapter 24

Journal Translation

From the blackness beyond the doorway of Father's room, two narrowed eyes reflected the flame of candlelight. My stomach knotted.

"Hello," Akhenaten said as he stepped inside, his walking stick tapping the floor. "Father and son together. So precious, especially when one's wife and one's mother is gone. A traitor, I heard."

My insides lurched in surprise and fear, but I remained silent. My mother? She had died when I was born. Had she not been faithful to Egypt or to the Aten?

"Akhenaten, Your Highness," Father said, bowing low and placing his palms outward. "We were discussing my son's adventures. The journey was a great life experience for him, and he is blessed to have you as his master."

"He is," Akhenaten said, placing a long finger on his chin. "But it is time to sleep, and I will need his services early." He spread his slender arms, and his lips twisted into a sinister grin.

"Of course," Father said, bowing lower. "I just missed him after he was gone for so long."

Akhenaten grasped my palm, yanking me to my feet as if I were a child. Placing an arm around my shoulders, he guided me out.

"Goodnight, Father," I said as I waved; longing for my family pulled at my heartstrings. The last couple of hours were not enough to make up for the weeks without him.

Father waved back, his bronze bracelet glinting in the lamplight like a beacon. "Goodnight, Heb; see you again tomorrow night …"

We shuffled down dark hallways, the tension only broken by the flap of our sandals and the tap of my master's stick. Exiting Pharaoh's corridor,

Akhenaten marched me to the wing for servants and guard of the royal family, and he departed.

I entered my room and spread the blanket I had kept from our sailing adventure over my reed bed. Croc dropped from the window. Sauntering over, the orange cat curled up beside me. The mattress felt luxurious. Closing my eyes, I focused on Croc's soft purring.

An hour passed as my curiosity amplified and consumed me. What did Father want to tell me? Did he know more about what had happened in Thebes, or about the mysterious disappearance of the mutilated soldier in my dream, or about the *ba*? Why was he being so secretive? But I had another problem. The hollow eyes of my love flashed in my mind, her spark lost. Sorrow, twisting like Akhenaten's knife into my heart, caused me to wince. How could I restore the light, Nefertiti's love of life, her hope, and happiness? I needed to be her hero again, like with the hippos, and prove to her I wielded power. But what could a servant do?

I stroked the warm fur of my comrade, whose chest was rising and falling with sleep. Rolling over, I settled a hand onto my bare chest, and an idea sparked. Perhaps the magic of Bes, the magic within the amulet I'd carried, could restore Nefertiti's spirits. The idol seemed to have done its part in saving my life. I'd gather the pieces as soon as I could and bring them to her.

Waking early the following morning, I strode into the hall under dwindling oil lamps and pink dawn light. I arrived outside Akhenaten's room, stooping to gather three large pieces of my amulet and hiding them inside my kilt.

I returned to the menial chores I'd averted during our voyage, and hours faded into days. Akhenaten's needs grew more urgent and extensive, his temper shorter. I found no opportunity to talk to Father or to wander to the royal female wing and Nefertiti's chamber.

I worked inside Akhenaten's room, his lair, as I often thought of it. Stretching beyond several high windows, the chamber's interior was decorated with beds, chairs, chests, tables, paintings, and potted art radiating yellows, reds, purples, and blues. I avoided the closet, recalling his odd request. I dusted off an ornate chair covered with images of men and the sun, and a fine powder lifted into a swirling cloud. My nose tickled, causing me to sneeze.

"She still doesn't eat," a heavy female servant said to a thin woman as they hustled through the hallway, their foreheads glistening with sweat. "Can't sleep, either."

"Poor thing," the other said, whisking by.

My stomach churned with concern. Creeping over, I stepped out behind the pair.

"Ay can find no way to comfort his daughter." Their chatter faded around a corner.

Nefertiti! I had to bring my amulet to her. But how could I get inside her quarters if only females were allowed? Akhenaten's selfish needs filled my every waking moment while she suffered. Spinning back into the room with clenched fists, I bumped into a chair. The furniture slid away with a grating rattle, revealing a hidden figurine. Cast into the shape of a hippopotamus, the object glistened in blue, its surface as smooth as river rock. Horror sank into my heart as I recalled our encounter on the Nile.

Leaning over to scrutinize the object, I kept my distance. Could this hippo be magical? I placed the chair back over the statuette and searched for secrets underneath other potential hiding places. Nothing. My gaze fell upon the closet. Peeking back out the doorway and down the hall, I saw no sign of anyone.

Parting the hanging reeds over the recess in the wall, I reached into the darkness. My fingers brushed against an edge. Grabbing the object, I yanked it out. A stack of papyrus. Writings and bizarre images sprawled across the pages, but I couldn't read any of it. I dug out other stacks of paper, amulets, and wands I'd never seen before. Similar blue statuettes of a lion and a crocodile sat tucked into the corners of—

"Boy!" a voice called from outside. I jolted with surprise. "Your master's classes are nearly over. Fetch his dinner." The stern face of a graying servant stared back at me.

"Yes, sir," I said, shaking in terror as I tucked my discoveries away. Would the lead servant think it was abnormal to be cleaning the closet? Hopefully he wouldn't think of mentioning it to Akhenaten.

I ran for Pharaoh's audience chamber, but six female servants in blinding white dresses turned down the corridor in front of me. Gossiping, the largest woman waved her flabby arms about. The others laughed. I lowered my gaze and followed close behind, stepping quietly. Two short men stood guard alongside the corridor ahead, but we didn't even capture their attention as we passed. I'd entered a hall I wasn't supposed to—the women's wing.

The thick aroma of baking bread and fired vegetables billowed out from a room ahead, along with a chorus of high-pitches voices and laughter. The women I followed bustled on, and my breathing turned rapid and shallow. I feared I'd be caught. Could I say I got lost?

"Hey," a quiet voice said. I froze, filled with dread. The women, still involved in a reenactment of someone's conversation, continued into the dining area. I turned, and a smiling face appeared, her bright eyes vibrating with energy. Mutnedjmet. She brushed a strand of dark hair away from her face. "How's your leg?" She pointed to the hideous scar swallowing my ankle. "I heard all about the hippos and what you did. It was unbelievable. Wait, why are you here? You shouldn't be in this hall."

I held up a hand to slow the girl's intensity, my mind racing. "I made a wrong turn. Been gone too long."

Her eyes narrowed. "No, you're not as dumb as the others. Are you trying to look at girls?"

"No!" I said, glancing around in embarrassment. Nothing but burning lamps lined the hall. I whispered, "I need to see Nefertiti."

"Why?" she asked, playing with a lock of hair as if it were a stringed instrument.

"I need to go." I turned to leave.

"I might be able to help you if you tell me why you want to see her."

Temptation tickled my insides, which was probably her plan. But what else could I do? I might not get another chance. Removing the pieces of the broken amulet from inside my kilt, I held them out in an open palm. "These were parts of a necklace given to me by a Theban priest. It helped save my life, and I want to give it to Nefertiti. My wish is to make her happy again."

Laughing, Mutnedjmet clutched her belly. "That is sweet, Heb, but Bes is completely broken. He can't help anyone like that. He's supposed to be an invincible guardian."

Heat rose in my cheeks with humiliation. I was a fool. Spinning around, I shuffled away.

"I know where we can get another," Mutnedjmet said. "A complete talisman."

I stopped.

"I'm not sure if it will lift her depression, but we can try." Mutnedjmet hopped over and grabbed my hand, tugging. "Come on." She skipped off down the hall.

I trailed Nefertiti's sister around sharp corners under dancing flames, and we ventured into regions of the palace I'd never seen. We passed servants, all of whom eyed me suspiciously and made my skin crawl.

"It was boring here after you and Nefertiti left," Mutnedjmet said over her shoulder. "I had to spend too much time with Beketaten, listening to her opinions about everything. Was it fun? The trip, I mean?"

Fun? Stabbing pain climbed up my bad leg, causing me to wince. "I became a hero for a moment and saw the world. I remember a lot of pain but also so much wonder. And I met people who owed me nothing but were willing to save my life."

She smiled, pointing. Fading sunlight streamed through a doorway, and my throat constricted with worry. I knew I'd better get back and assist with Akhenaten's dinner and bedtime rituals before he grew furious. He'd be waiting on me soon.

"Why's no one around?" Mutnedjmet asked, tiptoeing to the doorway and peeking inside. "The magician should be here. Let's check his lab." She inched down the hall to the adjacent room.

A light glimmered within, dark green but faint and without an obvious source. So many objects littered the chamber that there was no clear walkway. I stalked after Mutnedjmet in deathly silence, the eerie light washing our skin in green. Blankets of gooseflesh arose on my shaved arms and legs.

What a mess. But the jumble was created by oddities with lingering odors I did not recognize. Jars sat upon overflowing shelves, stuffed with assortments of unidentifiable contents. Statues and statuettes of men and animals swarmed around everything. Powders of brilliant colors spilled from containers, creating mounds on the floor. Creatures and pieces of creatures floated in yellow liquids. An unmistakable hippo bobbed inside a jar, but my head was bigger than the entire creature. Wrinkles ran over its pink body, its eyes closed in death. Sticking out of its belly was an umbilical cord. Eerie curiosity consumed me, making my stomach crawl inward. The familiar head and chest of a cat seamlessly blended into the hind end of a fish, floating in suspended animation. I gasped. Could magic really combine animals into horrid beasts? Or had someone sewn them together?

Mutnedjmet didn't seem to care, which shocked me just as—

I jumped back. The creature I feared more than death itself floated in a jar in front of me. A miniature beast that combined the head and jaws of a crocodile, the body of a lion, and the hind end of a hippo, a fetus of the Devouring Monster—the greatest fear of any man or child! My heart skipped along with my breathing, rapid with terror. Blood pounded in my ears. How could this be? Squeezing the fragments of my necklace, I leaned closer.

A reptilian eye popped open, staring directly at me.

Chapter 25

Present Day

A THUNDEROUS ECHO RESOUNDED, shaking the walls of the lost tomb we'd recently discovered. I awoke from dreams of the mysterious woman and unknown friends. One flashlight was dead, the other faint. Maddie lay still.

A shudder ran through my bones as I tried to gasp, but my dry throat and cracked lips barely created a painful whisper. I swallowed in fear. Was she dead? Reaching out, I touched her shoulder and shook her. Nothing. My fingers stretched toward her neck, to check for a pulse.

"Don't think because you showed me one tomb that I'm going to let you put your hands on me," Maddie croaked as she opened an eye. One corner of her parched lips formed a faint smile, beneath streaks of dried blood. "Gavin, I give you a lot of crap, but …" She might have winked, although it could've just been a blink.

Smiling, I imagined grabbing her in one arm. I'd hoist her over my shoulder and run up that tunnel, my palm open in a violent stiff arm. The barrier would give way in an explosion of rock and dust. We'd both emerge like immortal action heroes or super—

"I can't go on," Maddie said, "even if there's only a foot of dirt left. I wish I could've seen the Hall of Records … or finished the tale with you."

"I wish we could have shared that too."

The grating of a shovel on rock carried down the shaft. I rolled over but couldn't see Mr. Scalone. Something sat beside the entrance. A water bottle, still holding over a quarter of its height in liquid!

Anger and desire flooded my body with conflicting tremors as I crawled desperately toward the container.

The walls of the tomb trembled, followed by a boom.

"What was that?" Maddie asked, her voice hoarse. She wouldn't have seen the bottle.

"I had hoped someone was digging us out, but now I think it's thunder." Yes, it was fall, the time of year the desert could actually receive rain. We'd been caught in a downpour a few days ago, just before entering this tomb. Maybe some rain would work its way through our tunnel and we could all drink! Not much water remained in his bottle.

Snagging the container, I threw back a swallow. Cool wet washed over my shriveled tongue and throat, like a stream across a cracked field. Hacking, I nudged Maddie and handed her the rest. She gulped it down.

I dragged myself up the shaft, rage from being lied to rising like heat up my neck and face. I would confront the arrogant bastard and unleash all the emotion I had left.

Lying on his stomach, Mr. Scalone barely fit within the tubular confines. The beam of his flashlight reflected off of the enclosure walls. A trickle of something dark formed along the edge of the ascending tunnel. The stain grew larger and glistened.

I reached for his ankle.

Dirt spewed forth with a massive roar. Raging water, mud, and rock engulfed us. The deafening torrent lifted me from the floor and whisked me away like a stick. Fighting to keep my head up, I gasped for air. Everything gave way beneath me as I toppled into the pitch black of the well. The liquid rolled and twisted like an underground waterslide. My body spiraled, the gauntlet battering me at mind-numbing speeds. But the churning water also acted as a cushion.

Landing with a splat in what should be a blind chamber at the bottom of a sloping shaft, I swallowed dirty liquid. A bellowing waterfall continued to gush downward with a vicious current. The swirling of a flashlight intermittently illuminated a cramped room with dirt walls. Terror compressed my chest, making it even harder to breathe. A river must be rushing in, the funneling of rain and silt from the mountainside into a low spot. The simple reason why the tomb had been buried and remained hidden for so long—it had been covered by feet of silt after flashfloods absorbed and evaporated.

I fought to gain my footing amidst the pandemonium, and the water-fall pummeled my weakened body. My knees anchored into the mud as the water rose to my waist. "Maddie!" I yelled amidst the tempest. A muffled screaming carried over the roar. The cry came from above.

The current swept my knees out from under me, and I slipped into the wet. Bracing against a wall, I scrambled to my feet. Water climbed over my chin in a matter of seconds. A ray of light burst out overhead, like a beacon of hope after days in hell. Energy came in a spurt of optimism, shooting through my body. I treaded the surging rapids, which lifted me back into the shaft of the well chamber. Rising higher and higher, I clawed through the dwindling stream along the incline of loose mud and dirt. I hoisted myself back onto the stairway and coughed up a mouthful of water.

Kneeling beside the far wall, Maddie had anchored herself with her axe by wedging its head into a large crack in the floor. She'd clung onto our bags beyond the edge of the torrent, now a creek rolling down each step to the tomb below. Mr. Scalone was nowhere to be seen.

Pointing to the faint daylight streaming through the shaft we'd dug, I couldn't say a word or even smile. I shuffled on my hands and knees through the mud and dwindling water, and I squeezed into the tunnel. The last couple of feet had been smashed through by the flood. I broke out into the light. My chest heaved for oxygen as my limbs sank into the mud. I crumpled into a shallow pool expanding across a small plateau on the mountain.

Maddie's scream of elation rang out and echoed through the valley. Then, crawling on all fours beyond the edge of the pond, she started coughing. White water spewed down a gulley in the mountainside before crashing and spraying sloppy mud in all directions. Wobbling to the water's edge, I turned onto my back and gazed into the sky. An expansive curtain of dark clouds rumbled overhead as rain splattered my face. Maddie fell flat onto her stomach beside me. Cradling her head in her arms, she sobbed.

Relief washed through my body, relaxing every muscle. Had my exhausted mind invented this escape because it refused to come to grips with reality? Maybe my body still lay inside the tomb, slipping off into the realm of the dead ...

The cool sprinkle of precipitation on my shriveled lips created a euphoria that started in my core and swept outward. Opening my mouth to catch the falling droplets, I burst into laughter.

Resting in the mud for several hours, we slurped on dirty pond water. Maddie's sopped hair was caked with mud, the same as her face, chest, and pants. Reaching a hand up to her head, she touched a mound of sludge entwined in her dark brown locks. She grimaced while attempting to tease out a large chunk. I chuckled.

A gray fedora floated by, like a duck. Lunging, I retrieved the hat as well as Maddie's glasses, which had partially sunk into the silt. Water soaked most of our belongings, and our phones that we'd turned off wouldn't turn back on. The books in our bags appeared intact, though damp. Easing the transcription papers out of my bag, I nestled them inside a travel book for protection.

Mr. Scalone rested on a nearby rock, his head in his meaty hands—he must've fled the tomb before Maddie or I, when I'd been down in the well. I even felt sorry for him, sorry for this entire debacle. But we needed to get out of here.

I gazed down across the empty valley. Rain and flooding must've driven away the tourists and workers.

"Let's get back to the river, and then to Cairo," Mr. Scalone said, his voice like a frog's. "Then we can decide what to do."

I'd fly home and go back to school.

With Mr. Scalone in the lead, we avoided the main paths to the Valley of the Kings in case whoever had trapped us remained in the area. The rain dwindled from torrential flash flood volumes and then ceased. My mind remained in a dark tunnel until we arrived at the Nile and entered a small terminal. After purchasing water by the case, we located a departure schedule. Thankfully, turmoil within Egypt had drastically dropped the number of tourists, which allowed for more flexible spur-of-the-moment traveling.

"Let's split up," Mr. Scalone said. "If someone's watching the area, they'd be looking for three people. I'll take a flight. You two take the train." He marched away.

My forehead tightened in suspicion. But maybe he was right.

Maddie and I would wait for the night train—it was already evening—but our filth didn't help us blend in.

"Looks like you two got caught out in the rain." A robust tourist with a full beard chuckled, his belly bouncing as we strolled by.

Maddie flashed him a beaming, irritated smile.

Spotting a quiet area in the corner, we ordered and devoured plates of lumpy beans and lukewarm falafel. Rank garlic wafted through my sinuses as the sun set, emitting an orange light.

My stomach cramped. A new fear emerged—my Crohn's disease. Not being able to prepare my own limited-ingredient meals could be disastrous.

The intestinal affliction sporadically invoked excruciating pain and vomiting, and it could force me into the hospital. Luckily, so far I'd never had a surgery for the condition, but the doctors had said I might need it at any time in the future. My old man's damn immune system. But I had it much worse. Eventually, but hopefully not for a few more decades, I'd end up withered and weak, confined to a chair like my dad.

I took a smaller bite.

Chapter 26

Present Day

I AWOKE TO THE LURCH and squealing of brakes halting the night train. Jumping in my seat, I struck my head on the bench. The chill air conditioning raised goose bumps along my arms. Had we arrived in Cairo, near the ancient city of Memphis, already? Or just at a stop along the way? I adjusted the towel guarding my seat. Who knew what kind of germs bred in the fabric of such communal furniture?

Maddie slept beside me, her face resting peacefully upon the red bench seat. Dried mud dangled from her dark hair. I smiled, glad the professor's letter had enticed her. But she also made me nervous—like no one else—because she was my perfect girl. My fidgeting and inability to articulate well when speaking with her probably made me unattractive. Why was the world this way? The more you desire something, the more important it becomes, and the more important something is, the more doubt and nervousness chew away at your confidence like roaches, making you less likely to attain your desire. People who don't care are relaxed and poised. They land the prettiest girls and best jobs. Maybe that was why I'd been able to get into medical school, because I hadn't truly wanted it and had therefore been confident during my interviews.

I released a deep breath. At least when Maddie and I worked together on a project, my nerves settled, but what she desired still remained a mystery. Placing her on a pedestal like she claimed she wanted never worked.

I found myself staring. Her perfect teeth peeked out from her open mouth, reminding me of the first time I'd seen her smile. I'd been walking under falling maple leaves, through campus with a mutual guy friend. She waved at him as she approached, and he introduced us. Her natural beauty, intelligence, and something else … her vibrating energy struck me. And, I have to admit, so did her backside in those black yoga pants. It popped, not wide, but out and round. My friend referred to that full appearance as "Pop to her boom."

Attempting to say something funny but still entranced, I'd ended up only stuttering, "H-hi." Our initial awkward meeting and my nerves rubbed off and made Maddie uneasy around me. But we shared many classes and a limitless fascination with ancient Egypt. Eventually we became good friends.

My stomach churned and cramped in protest, curtailing my thoughts. I held my breath in fear. The tightness receded. Throwing a handful of antacids into my mouth, I washed down the fruity chalk with half a bottle of water. At least I'd had a real adventure, although it wasn't anything like I'd envisioned. I should return home and face my failures.

My fingers brushed against cold metal, settling on the bronze bracelet I typically hid beneath the sleeve of my shirt. The ancient Egyptian-style artifact made me feel like the worldly adventurer I wanted to be. It also made me think of my dad. Complications from the same gastrointestinal disease I carried had led to his passing years ago. But in his day, he'd been the adventuresome type who toured the globe, selling medical supplies to hospitals all over the world.

Had my dad encountered any excitement like I'd just experienced? He'd brought the bracelet back after a trip maybe fifteen years ago and told me he purchased it from an Egyptian man on the black market. The seller claimed the artifact originated from a tomb he had uncovered and would have belonged to a simple man in ancient Egypt over three thousand years ago. These salesmen were untrustworthy, but the story had overcome my dad, forcing him to make the purchase. He'd never brought the bracelet to an expert, either, because he'd wanted to believe it was genuine or feared the artifact might be confiscated.

Not until after his death, when packing to leave for college, had I found the bracelet and started wearing it. Even on my scrawny wrists it clamped tight, but I could squeeze it on with a little work. And all ancient people were small compared to today's standards. This could've been the decorative wear of a large man in those times. The thought made me feel bigger and stronger.

Running my fingers across the cool bronze reminded me not only of my dad, but of the man I wanted to be. To desire something so old, rather than the latest thing, felt right. The connection to the souls of the ages never ceased to send shivers up my spine. I hoped the previous owners were heroes but felt more connected to good, simple men. What had their lives been like? Their hopes and dreams? What about regrets, and even secrets? And how had my dad received the photograph with Dr. Shelsher's letter? Possibly from my great-great-grandfather, who had also spent a lot of time in Egypt. But why not go after the tomb himself? My dad had always pushed me to chase my dreams … And how had he mailed the letter and photograph to me after his death?

To my astonishment, I'd received a package from my dad several months ago, years after his death. It arrived on my birthday. Maybe an old friend had mailed it. I tried to get to the bottom of it over the next couple of weeks by contacting everyone he knew, but they all seemed just as surprised.

My hands had shaken with excitement as I'd read my dad's simple "Happy Birthday!" note and gazed upon the picture of an excavated tomb from the 1920s. My dad would never just give me something; a secret riddle or clue was always hidden. Every birthday and Christmas present I ever received needed to be discovered, some not until months later if I couldn't figure out his puzzles. After locating the professor's and another unknown man's letters wedged into the cracked frame, I poured over the words a thousand times.

Chasing clues enthralled me, but at first I hadn't believed any of it. The information encrypted into the professor's letter wasn't corroborated anywhere. With my knowledge, I would've had some inkling or would've found a connection during extensive library searches. My dad wouldn't lie to me, but he was the type to believe anything that promised excitement and adventure. I'd stashed the letter away.

Then, when I'd been cleaning out my apartment after the medical school mishap, my dad's gift resurfaced and offered me another path. I'd been plotting a new life ever—

"Trouble sleeping?" Maddie asked, startling me.

Nodding, I tapped the cover of the cracked leather journal in my lap and said, "This story can't be true. Too much unexplainable magic."

"Ancient Egyptians had rare men whose profession was listed as magician," she said. "They must've explained the unknown as magic. How would *your* mind react in a scary, ancient world?" She smiled. "Remember when Mr. Scalone grabbed you in the tomb and you screamed like a little girl? Did you think he was a mummy?"

Staring out into the moonlit night in shame, I clutched my bracelet. She had a point.

"You still wear that thing?" Maddie asked, eyeing the bronze on my wrist.

The train started moving again. I placed my fedora over my face and closed my eyes. If she only knew.

Chapter 27

Journal Translation

THE ELONGATED PUPIL of the miniature Devouring Monster—which floated inside a jar— collapsed inside a deep yellow iris. Lurching backward, I tripped over stacks of papyrus inside the magician's lab and fell to the ground with a smack. Parchment spilled everywhere.

"Careful!" Mutnedjmet said.

"Did you see that?" I pointed a shaky finger at the monster inside the murky bottle.

"I see a lot of scary things in here," she said.

"No, the miniature Devouring Monster looked at me!"

She examined it, but its eye had shut.

"That thing looked at me, I swear!"

Tapping echoed out in the hall, then faded. I ducked behind the toppled mounds of papyrus. No one entered.

"I'm going to see if that's the son of Hapu," Mutnedjmet said. "Stay here. I'll let him know I invited you so you don't get in trouble."

Watching the creature in the jar out of the corner of my eye, I nodded. After she stepped out, I picked my way along, searching the jumbled mess for Nefertiti's gift. Sunlight faded from the windows, leaving only the deep green glow. Akhenaten would be waiting for me. Mutnedjmet had better hurry! The temperature climbed several degrees, and a rotting stench filled the room. Heaving breaths sounded at the doorway, thickening my blood.

Ducking behind a chest, I peeked through a gap between the object and the wall. A figure in a black cloak appeared under green light, leaned over a small object, and whispered. Picking something up, the veiled man placed it deep inside a bag. He buried the sack inside his cloak, his long, shadowed hood—so long that I wondered how he saw out from under it—scanning the room. Stiffening as if he'd detected something, he shuffled closer.

Cold sweat condensed on my forehead, summoning a chilling fear. I shouldn't let this man see me. But who was he and what was he searching for? Could it be the magician? This figure wasn't dressed like the son of Hapu, the man I'd seen in the streets of Memphis before I'd set sail with Akhenaten. And this figure was hunched and wide … And where was Mutnedjmet? Holding my crouched stance burned my muscles, and they screamed for me to move. But the thought of the noise I'd make held me still.

Sniffing sounds snuck out from beneath the man's draping hood. My hand shook upon my broken amulet, my muscles feeling as if they were being stabbed with hundreds of needles. The cloaked man lumbered toward me with conviction. Something scampered past the doorway and hissed. He paused. Sniffing again, he paced back to the exit, peered outside, and slipped into the shadows.

After a minute, I stood to relieve my burning muscles and crept to the doorway. I listened before glancing out. Nothing. A white cat darted past me, its fat rolls swinging back and forth as it fled. I nearly shrieked in shock but covered my mouth. Where had it come from?

Slinking outside, I cast a glance back into the glowing room. Faint movement stirred against a corner, appearing transparent like mist or fog. I needed to get out of here.

Sneaking down the hallway, I passed oil lamps and many rooms. No sign of Mutnedjmet. Residents stirred and grumbled from their beds when my feet scuffed the tiled floors.

Light filtered through a cracked doorway ahead. Akhenaten's room. I stopped in my tracks, not wanting to ponder my punishment the next time he saw me. Inching my head around the door, I strained to see as a streak of light fell upon my peeking eye.

My master sat on the floor with his back to me, pale yellow light flickering on his far side. Contorting shadows danced across the floor as he muttered to someone or something. Was there someone small sitting on the floor across from him?

I leaned in to pick up the conversation, and the smell of something rotten scathed my nostrils. Shuddering, I curled my lip in disgust.

At first, Akhenaten's rambling sounded like gibberish, but then I caught a word here and there. He told a tale of his own, the same one that I'd begun my story with.

"I was dead," he whispered, his voice airy and secretive as he used a knife to cut into his thumbnail. Trickling blood splattered amongst the contorting shadows as he grunted and groaned. "I saw the underworld. I had drowned. By the grace of the Aten, Mahu was granted the power to bring me back to spread truth into our world. I saw exactly what it looked like, and, as I believed, we were very wrong. All of my ancestors were so very wrong."

I waited, mystified by the unveiled glimpse into the crevices of Akhenaten's mind.

"Floating among the clouds," he whispered as his hands fluttered in the air, dripping blood. "But these clouds were enormous and full. Their pink contrasted against the dark blue sky, and I was not alone. A woman adorned in a simple white dress rode with me, a beautiful woman with pale hair and skin. I felt her love. I felt complete. Not desire, but something deeper. The clouds became an array of blues, purples, and oranges, transforming into the wings of a great bird, the phoenix itself. The *ba* of the Aten!

"Then I saw the others." The character of his voice changed as if a different person spoke. "So many of them arced across the dark sky in wisps of gold and silvery light, leaving shimmering trails like shooting stars. A million voices chanted in unison and rained down to break upon me.

"I was one of them. One with all the universe. A minute part of everything linked together, like some intricate spider's web ensnaring all existence. They told me I was one of them and had nothing to worry about. They would take care of me.

"We rode the phoenix over the river, the seas, and even soared through woods I had never seen. Then we entered it, the utter blackness. But the shadow only lasted a moment before light engulfed me. We veered for the brightest point, a brilliant shining sphere. The Aten itself. It must have been! Could it have been anything else?" He threw his hands into the air and laughed. "I had arrived. Any question in my mind was answered by the sphere of light with clarity unbeknownst to this world. I learned and saw more than I had in all my years in Egypt. I beheld great power, and I understood. I saw the past, the present, and I remembered the future! It may have been a short time as determined by this world, but to my mind it was decades. The sphere was the connection to this world and the next. I wanted to know—"

My ankle popped underneath me as I subconsciously shifted my weight off of my bad leg. Terror stopped my breathing, my body going rigid. His head perked up and turned. The fire cast the side of his face into darkness. Huddling behind the doorway, I squeezed my eyes shut and waited. Nothing. Goose bumps arose on my forearms, spreading across my body. Should I wait until he dismissed the noise and started talking again, then run? Or should I run now? If he caught me spying …

Creeping backward, I kept my eye on the cracked doorway. A footfall scuffed the floor within his room. I swallowed.

Chapter 28

Journal Translation

THE FAINT BRUSHING OF A sandal settling on tile whispered through Akhenaten's doorway. But Akhenaten didn't appear. Another footfall. My nerves shattered, my body shaking. He must be creeping toward the opening to see who spied on him.

Wheeling around, I broke into a full sprint down the palace's corridor but glanced over my shoulder before turning a corner. The gangly outline of Akhenaten emerged. Racing on, I dove into my room and slid onto my bed. Croc leapt three feet into the air and hissed, his tail puffing up thicker than my arm. Yanking the blanket over my head, I rolled to face the wall and clamped my eyes shut. I felt like a child, when pulling reeds over me acted as impenetrable armor against the dread of wandering spirits. Waiting, I attempted to slow my breathing.

Several minutes passed in gut-wrenching silence. I lay paralyzed, as if the unknown couldn't hurt me if I couldn't see it. Then, as if with a sixth sense, I felt it.

A looming presence floated into my room, although no footfalls scuffed the floor. Croc hissed and scrambled out the window. The permeation inched closer and closer, a chill sneaking in. Crushing pressure constricted my chest, and all the moisture drained from my mouth. The soft rustle of fabric came from behind. Squeezing my eyes closed, I attempted to create a light snoring sound.

The presence hovered over me. A cold sweat trickled down my back, and my heart raced so fast and loud that whoever this was must've been able to hear it. Light pressure settled upon my shoulder, and my body wanted to leap to the ceiling. But I held fast with a control I didn't know I commanded.

The touch grew heavier, and I grumbled as if waking from a deep sleep. Rolling over, I pulled the covers from my head and groaned as my heart beat so fast I thought it might take flight.

Narrowed eyes glistened in the pale light six inches from my face. Jerking and shoving backwards, I hit my head against the wall. I swallowed and cleared my throat, "D-did I oversleep? Do you need something? Bread, beer?"

Akhenaten glared, his dark eyes unmoving.

I rubbed my head, "Master?"

"I wanted to make sure you were sleeping soundly, after witnessing those terrors on our trip," he whispered. "You didn't go see your father again, did you?"

"No, but another servant offered to serve you dinner tonight," I lied, trusting that one of his others would've fulfilled my duties in my absence. "That's why you didn't see me before bed. It's taken me a while to calm down from the excitement of our adventure, but now I'm exhausted."

He didn't move.

I swallowed, my skin crawling like bugs on my back.

"What did you hear?" he asked, stooping so his face met mine. His eyebrows narrowed to form an upside-down peak at the bridge of his nose.

"What?"

After straightening, he spun around and disappeared into the black. Releasing a long, slow breath of relief, I watched the doorway. I couldn't do that again; the terror was more than I could handle. But who had Akhenaten been talking to? And who was that cloaked figure, if not the magician? And why had Mutnedjmet led me to some magician's lab only to leave? I didn't have any answers, and I had failed to help Nefertiti. Lying back down in frustration, I pulled the blanket over my head and waited long hours before sleep finally took me.

I awoke to a commotion. The early colored rays of the Aten already filtered through the reed curtain. Servants and guards ran up and down the corridors in droves, their footfalls echoing over their yelling.

Stepping into the hall, I witnessed a group of servant men whispering amongst themselves. That was weird; people didn't usually congregate near my room. I inched closer, and one said, "They say he was stricken with plague. But he's been healthy and was fine just yesterday."

A gaunt servant whispered, licking and moistening his thick lips, "How could he have brought the plague?"

"Who brought the plague?" I asked.

The servants spun, their eyes wide. One covered his wetted mouth, accentuating his red eye shadow.

"Who?" I demanded, my mind whisking through possibilities. Akhenaten? Mahu or Suty? "Who brought the plague?" I asked louder this time. "Akhenaten?"

"Please, boy," said a tall man whose eyes filled with pity. He held out a hand to keep me away. "We're not blaming you."

My lower lip trembled. Fearing the answer, I ran as fast as I could to Pharaoh's wing. I shoved past servants and guards and stopped outside an entrance where two soldiers stood watch with brandished swords.

"No!" I cried.

"You can't enter," one said, halting me with an open palm. "The doctor, priest, and magician need to decontaminate and bless the area to wipe away the disease."

I stepped back. What possibly could have happened? Father and I had spent the late hours together just a few nights ago. He hadn't acted as if he'd fallen ill.

After a brief pause to put the guards at ease, I darted between them. They yelled but wouldn't enter the room. A body lay under a brown blanket. Several men performed some sort of ritual, appearing oddly familiar. A heavyset man jotted on a writing palette. Sweat beads dribbled down his face, which resembled a watermelon with no distinguishable chin or cheeks. An elderly bald man adorned in a sash shook a bronze wand, bouncing the fat rolls of the cat perched on his shoulder. His face was covered beneath deep, black lines, running like a tangled spider's web. I'd seen this magician before, somewhere … although not in Thebes. And no priest stood with them.

Angling between the men, I lunged at Father's bed. Shaking the body, I tore away the blanket. The inner strength I'd found on the Nile fled my body as I gazed into lifeless eyes buried beneath a blue fog. My knees trembled, and I slumped onto the ground beside his bed, tears streaming down my cheeks.

The fat doctor said, "Get away, boy! He carries death itself." He grabbed my shoulder, but I shrugged him off.

"Father!" I wailed, tears spraying. Father's skin was the color of ash. When I touched him, the rigidity and cold of his flesh made me jerk away. I shook him again, and a stream of red fluid dribbled from the corner of his lips. Making a fist, I struck him on the chest just as Mahu had done to revive Akhenaten. But his clammy tissue swallowed my blow. A guard wrapped me in a bear hug from behind, squeezed, and hoisted me out. Throwing me to the ground, he blocked the entryway. I sobbed on the cold floor like a baby …

Something nudged me. The plump doctor had stepped out and lowered his writing palette. He said, "I regret to inform you your father has fled to the underworld. But you're not only putting yourself at risk, you're putting all of us in danger by being exposed. We do not fully understand the cause of his death. I fear it's the black plague, although there're no others with signs or symptoms. His eyes bulge, and black circles and yellow spots cover his body. The Aten may be angry."

The Aten? Guilt pummeled my insides. Was this *all* my fault? Memories of the desert night when curses spewed from my mouth came flooding back. God had heard me after all and took Father for it! I was the worst son the world had ever known. Why hadn't he taken me?

The doctor ruffled through sheets of papyrus, his fat face wrinkling with annoyance. His eyes moved back and forth, reading. "Mudads, send the boy directly to his room. There's no woman listed. If he doesn't have a mother, make sure to inform whatever family he still has. Find Akhenaten two servants to replace him. The boy needs a week off duty. He could be a carrier, and until we know more, he must be isolated."

Mudads, a guard with a potbelly and spindly limbs, grabbed my sidelock. Using my hair to stand me up sent stinging pain across my scalp, and I winced. He escorted me back to my room, where no one waited. "You're to stay in here for the remainder of the week," Mudads said in a slow drawl as I fell onto my bed, hid my head, and wept with grief.

Croc landed beside me, although he rarely appeared during the day. Strutting over, he rubbed back and forth against my leg before lying down. It barely lifted my spirits. I sobbed for hours, mulling over recent events as I pet my cat. I needed to see Father, to tell him goodbye. Even if my punishment would be death, I didn't care; I had essentially killed him. I deserved to die. I'd bring the broken amulet to him. Perhaps it would help save his soul.

Standing, I swept Croc up in one arm and peeked under the reed curtain covering the window. The height of the window only allowed me to see the dark sky and pale moonlight. Creeping to the doorway, I glanced into the hall. A single oil lamp flickered against the walls of the empty corridor.

Mudads hadn't stayed on watch, and only a handful of guards would be awake and at their posts. But would Akhenaten be sleeping, or would he be wandering the palace?

With Croc in my arms, I slunk into the shadows, my bad ankle clicking every few steps. Images of punishment filled my mind, and I had to push back my fear, reminding myself Father was dead.

As I approached Akhenaten's room, my hands and knees shook with trepidation. A glimmer of light reflected around the next corner, along with the echo of footsteps.

Chapter 29

Journal Translation

COVERING CROC'S MOUTH AND EYES with my free hand, I froze in the palace hallway. If Croc hissed or if his eyes reflected the light, he'd give me away. I ducked into the closest doorway, one down from Akhenaten's. Inside the chamber, it was too dark to see.

The footsteps paused.

My breathing stopped as I waited, my teeth chattering with dread. After a minute, I scouted out the door. Three figures stood in the corridor, one holding a torch. I recognized the ugly beast of a man with a pig's ear. Suty. I was hiding inside this ogre's doorway, hoping he was headed somewhere else.

Beside Suty slinked two slender women. One wore her white dress tight around her chest, her hair brushed and her makeup done. The other wore no top, adorned only in a white kilt. Their heavy floral perfume wafted down the hall.

The ogre motioned for the dressed woman to enter my master's bedroom. Then he and the other woman turned toward me. As they stepped closer and closer, I was forced to duck back inside.

Their footsteps grew louder. My heart sank with realization. I couldn't be suspected of spying again or I'd be whipped. Dropping Croc onto the floor, I pushed him out with my foot. He hissed and darted off.

"Damn cats," Suty said, his voice higher-pitched, as if surprised. The woman giggled. "Shut your mouth, whore." The sharp slap of skin on skin sounded as they entered. Suty held the torch aloft, inspecting his abode.

Terror had driven me to jump, scramble, and wedge my small frame into the high window. The awkward maneuver was difficult, especially with my ankle. But not many could accomplish such a feat—one advantage of my size. I had inched my frame through the thickness of the sill, and I tumbled out, crashing into the sand with a thud. Pain shot through my shoulder, but I scampered to my knees.

"Thank you for the distraction, Croc!" I whispered. He'd probably want to bite me the next time I saw him.

Heavy footfalls and muttering carried out the window into the pale moonlit night. Then silence. Streaks of light appeared inside. In the guarded palace, no one concerned themselves with our ventilation system, the high windows. Very few men who could jump to reach the window would be small enough to squeeze through.

Running and jumping again, I grabbed the outer windowsill of Suty's room. I scrambled and pulled myself up, peeking through a slit in the reed curtain. Kissing the woman, Suty groped her naked body. She opened an eye, attempting to look at me, but the guard's lips remained locked on hers. She must've heard me. My muscles tensed with fear. Letting go, I fell.

I'd circle around. More guards would be stationed outside than in, but I couldn't risk trying to climb in through someone's window—the person inside would hear my crashing entrance.

Picking my way along the wall of the palace, I avoided the intermittent crackling torches. The window to Father's room loomed ahead, but a guard stood under a lamp ten rooms down. Thank the Aten, no torches sat mounted between the guard and me. Pressing against the white walls to use my kilt as camouflage, I inched on to my objective. The guard didn't budge, his gaze fixed straight ahead. After taking a deep breath, I launched myself at the sill, my bad ankle popping and releasing a stabbing pain. Gritting my teeth with determination, I kicked myself up. Twisting my narrow shoulders, I wedged them through the opening. The remainder of my body slid through.

I fell into the dark, landing upon cold tile with a smack. What if someone had heard me? I listened. Nothing. Faint firelight flickered red down the hallway but didn't advance. Just a lamp.

Over the doorway hung a sheet of red cloth. Easing it aside, I peered into the corridor. Empty. I crept to the light, yanked it from its mount, and returned to scrutinize the room.

Lamplight danced around the interior, above my shaking hands. Father's body was gone, his bed and other belongings also missing. Only strange symbols remained scribbled on the floor, and eerie hieroglyphs danced upon the walls. Images of men, frightening creatures, water, and fire loomed around me.

My breathing hastened as a feeling of being watched crept over me. Where would they have taken him?

After exiting through the window, I froze until I was convinced the closest guard hadn't noticed. I slinked back along the palace walls, the weight of depression settling over me like a heavy load and dragging my shoulders down.

Would I ever be able to apologize to him, to say goodbye?

A glimmer of light grabbed my attention. In the distance, the white walls of the palace perimeter reflected moonlight, but there was another luminescence. Flickering arced from behind one of the pillars of a temple, beckoning me as if I were a curious cat. The Temple of the Aten, with its massive columns and open roof, loomed over everything.

Holding my breath, I scanned around to make sure no one would see me before darting off. The scent of sweet incense wafted into the air as I navigated through a grove of trees, then crunched across a garden. Ponds large and small reflected moonlight in the midst of flowering plants, shrubs, and shade trees. Plastering my body against the closest pillar of the temple, I paused and surveyed the area. Equally spaced torches glowed along the palace's exterior, while moonlight glinted off the perimeter wall and court-yard. No soldiers on patrol.

I peeked into the inner temple, where a single torch crackled. A stone slab and shield of blankets rested beneath a writhing flame. Hieroglyphs similar to those in Father's room crawled across the ground.

Inching closer, I stepped over the writing, taking care not to disrupt anything. My hand froze and shook as I reached for the blankets. Dragging back the covers revealed the bloated body of my dead father. Stinging tears brimmed in my eyes, and my stomach churned with nausea. Fighting off both emotion and reflex, I wanted to scream into the night, to curse the Aten and myself for this life. This time, I held back.

Removing the fragments of Bes from my kilt, I gently laid them on his chest and fit the pieces together to create the complete pendant. Two fragments slid off his clammy skin and clattered to the stone slab. I groaned with irritation. This wasn't going to work; Mutnedjmet was right. Was there anything I could do?

A memory of blood dribbling out of his lips the other morning returned. Perhaps I could stuff the pendant inside his mouth, to hold it together. The idea seemed morbid, but Bes could be there to protect his body forever.

I opened his jaw, fighting against rigor mortis. No more blood dripped out, but something appeared odd with his tongue. Grimacing, I reached in and extracted the tip. The tissue felt dry and hard, like a raw tuber. I forced myself to examine the organ, although my stomach heaved in protest. Gaping wounds had punctured the flesh in short curvilinear fashion. Similar gouges ran across the underside.

These wounds couldn't have led to his death. Slipping out of my shaking grip with a sickening sucking sound, the tongue only partially returned into his mouth. The tip poked out, lining the cuts up with his upper and lower teeth. I bit into the webbing of my own hand, between my thumb and index finger. The marks were identical.

Realization parted the fog in my mind. Placing the amulet fragments in proper arrangement inside his mouth, I forced his jaw closed. His teeth fit into the lacerations. But why would he have bitten his tongue to the point of nearly severing it?

I scrutinized his ears, lips, nose, and cheeks. His eyelids were swollen and red, but nothing else. Opening his eyes revealed a cloudy fluid, and the whites were more bloodshot than any drunkard's. Tortuous vessels protruded around his irises and had bled onto and below the surface. My God, what a horrendous curse!

Throwing the blankets to the ground, I forced my mind elsewhere. The cold glint of metal flickered in the light—his bracelet! Twisting and tugging, I slid the bronze off his arm. I wrapped my hands around the metal, seeing the object with my fingers; it was simple in style with symmetric facets and rounded ends. He had never removed it, and I cherished the object because it reminded me of family, security, and home. Narrowing my hand, I guided the bracelet onto my forearm. The object would be that last thing I'd receive from father.

I inspected his body, sobbing in sorrow again. Black and yellow spots dotted his torso and legs near regions of peeling skin. Lifting his left ankle, I spotted black tissue flowing across a swollen calf. Then I saw the marks.

Faint streaks ran up toward his torso. The lines appeared faded, barely discernable, but I recognized them immediately. "The marks of death," as Mahu had referred to them when on my body. The doctor must've noticed these.

But what could've spread an infection so fast? Father hadn't even acted ill the other night. And my wound from the hippo had festered for a week before reaching that phase. The plague? But what could've planted the disease?

Footsteps slapped onto the mud brick behind me.

Chapter 30

Journal Translation

"WHAT'RE YOU DOING out here, boy?" Suty barked, torchlight on the wall of the Aten temple outlining his monstrous body. My body tensed. Then my heart squeezed in terror as Akhenaten stepped from behind the giant. Eyeing me suspiciously, Akhenaten shook his head and crossed his arms.

"I had to say goodbye to—"

"Get away from the body." Akhenaten's deep voice echoed through the empty temple. "The doctor believes he contracted plague. And you can still catch it from a corpse. The disease festers in his humors and feeds on his blood. He will either have to be buried … or burned."

"No!" I yelled, my knuckles blanching as I clutched my new bracelet. "Don't burn him! His *ba* will have no place to return! His soul may be lost forever. Please!"

"I cannot have a corpse spreading disease around the palace," Akhenaten said. "You have exposed yourself again, this time without the protection of the magician or doctor." He motioned, and Suty stepped toward me.

I spun and ran. But the soldier's legs covered the ten feet between us before I crossed five. A powerful hand slapped down on my shoulder, holding my body fast although my legs continued to move.

Suty picked me up with one hand, as if I were a cat, then shoved me out of the temple. I stumbled and fell into the sand, the grit abrading my skin.

"Whore was right," Suty said, hoisting me by my sidelock. My scalp felt as if it would tear off. I screamed in pain as we marched away. "She heard someone sneaking."

Two guards had been stooping against the rear entrance of the palace but shot to attention.

"The servant snuck out and is a risk for having contracted the plague," Akhenaten said. "Station a guard outside his room at all times. The doctor ordered him to be quarantined. Do you understand the importance?"

"Yes, son of Pharaoh," Mudads said, his thin limbs whirling around a protruding belly before he marched through the entryway.

Leading us down long corridors, the guard glanced back and kept more than a few steps ahead of me. His upper body leaned away, as if it would help him avoid catching the disease. We arrived at my room, and Suty kicked me inside. I crashed onto the floor.

"Stay in there!" Akhenaten said, pointing at me. The notch he'd cut into his thumbnail was crusted in dried blood. "You have been wandering the palace at night, snooping around and making people anxious. Servants who become burdens are relocated, discarded, or put to death."

"I needed to see Father!" I said. "He's all I have … had."

"If this happens again, you will be cast out of the palace," Akhenaten said, covering his disfigured thumb with his other hand. "Then you can attempt to make your way amongst the commoners or live in the slums. It is not as easy as you may think, not as easy as this life."

Akhenaten and Suty left, but Mudads remained outside my doorway. Lounging on my blanket, Croc wore his displeased look of flattened ears and swishing tail. I lay next to him, welcoming sleep, but my mind raced with questions. How could I find out what'd happened to Father?

I peered up at the window. Or should I stay in isolation?

After I tossed and turned for hours, my mind finally drifted into sleep.

Hideous creatures and disease ran rampant throughout Egypt—in my dream world. I alone carried a torch and searched for other survivors, crawling over piles of bodies and through cities of the dead. I found no one. Something rose up before me: a black creature shrouded in fog. Green eyes glowed behind a veil of mist. My heart raced in fear. The creature leapt at me from the shadows. Its linen-bound face appeared in a white flash—

My eyes shot open and I awakened. Just another nightmare of the Dark Ones ... But excited voices carried in from the hall as I rubbed my face and crawled to the doorway. The scent of deep rose mingled with light citrus. My heart fluttered ... Nefertiti! Mudads rubbed his potbelly as he debated with Nefertiti, Mutnedjmet, and Beketaten, their words rattling over each other.

"We'll keep our distance," Mutnedjmet said, her big eyes focused. "But we must speak with Heb; he—"

"Stand on the far side of the hall," Mudads said, his eyelids drooping as he pointed with a spindly limb. "If the royal family falls ill during my watch, I'll be executed."

"We understand," Nefertiti said, her head hanging low.

"Heb!" Mutnedjmet said, spotting me as I stood up.

What'd happened to her the other night after she'd left me in the magician's lab? I couldn't ask in front of the others, since I shouldn't have been in there.

"I'm so sorry about your father!" Mutnedjmet said. "I tried to reason with mine, but the doctor ordered you to be confined. What will Akhenaten do without his most faithful servant?" She winked. "He says you're disposable, but you know his wants and needs better than anyone. He needs you."

Realization dawned on me, making my head feel light. I'd served Akhenaten's bizarre needs most of his life and had a knack for preparing things before he even knew he wanted them. Indeed, no one could care for Akhenaten like me.

Nefertiti's eyes remained dim, the green paint around them absent.

"Nefertiti, how're you faring?" I asked. Beketaten rolled her eyes.

"I'm glad we're under the palace's roof," Nefertiti said, "but we're worried."

"They may burn my father," I said.

"They wouldn't do that," Mutnedjmet said, brushing dark hair from her face. "Your father was one of Pharaoh's favorite servants. Amenhotep would want him preserved so that he can serve in the next life. The doctor and magician are attending to his cleansing, and even the high priest of Memphis has offered aid."

Releasing a long sigh of relief, I asked, "The high priest?" I pictured the man in Thebes in the jaguar cloak. No one in Father's room had been dressed like that.

"The mighty Thutmose, Amenhotep's crown prince, my own brother," Beketaten said, tilting the twitching end of her long nose up.

Thutmose was the high priest? That must be recent, or Akhenaten, in his desire of turning me into a mindless servant, kept me sheltered from many happenings. And other servants hadn't talked much to me, the outcast who'd stood up for Nefertiti against the son of God, in years. "Why are you so sure about my and my father's safety, Mutnedjmet?" I asked.

Mutnedjmet's pink lips moved rapidly. "I'm a little girl, and men often don't notice me. I overhear a lot of things in Father's chambers, or in the throne room, or in the audience hall. I ask Mother and my Aunt Tiye—"

"One thing I overheard," Beketaten said, folding her arms, "is if the disease spreads, they will have to resort to burning. A warning's been issued throughout the palace. All those your father came into contact with have been ordered to look themselves over for lesions, and to report anything suspicious at once."

My anxiety rose as I gave myself a quick inspection. No marks.

Croc stretched and yawned, then sharpened his claws by tearing the reed mattress.

"I love your cat," Mutnedjmet said, kneeling while reaching out an open palm. "Here, Croc."

Croc eyed her as if considering his options but strutted over with his tail sticking straight up. Mutnedjmet scratched under his chin and patted his arched rump. Purring, he lifted his head to give her better access.

Beketaten pursed her lips, as if blowing me a kiss.

I stepped back in shock. Was it my imagination? I needed to figure some things out, and being trapped in this room left me few options. Kneeling as close to Mutnedjmet as I could, I whispered, "What happened the other night?"

"You mean when you were trying to get an amulet for Nefertiti?" she asked at full volume.

Embarrassment burned my cheeks as Nefertiti blushed and diverted her gaze.

"Ay wandered by," Mutnedjmet said. "I've never seen my father near the lab, and he looked surprised, but he dragged me back to my room demanding answers as to what I was doing there so late."

A man stepped into view in the hallway, his muscular body diminishing the size of the women while commanding authority. Thutmose! He slammed the butt of his spear onto the ground, and the gold-embroidered necklace on his chest jiggled.

Chapter 31

Journal Translation

"COUSINS, SISTER, DO NOT touch the cat," Thutmose said as he approached my doorway. His deep voice must've carried into the next wing. "The animal could transmit the disease."

"We were comforting our friend," Mutnedjmet said, jumping back. "He's Akhenaten's servant, the one who lost his father."

Glaring down at me, the god-king-to-be released a long breath and ran a hand over his shaven abdominal muscles. His anointed skin glistened, power and strength exuding from him like scented oils. A sense of insignificance showered me.

"I am truly sorry," Thutmose said, "but we need to remain vigilant until we solve the mysterious death. I have sworn oaths to protect all the men and women of Egypt from enemies, creatures, beasts, and disease of any sort." Studying the magical wards surrounding my doorway, he traced something in the air and placed a firm hand upon my head. "It's my duty," I couldn't hold his gaze, "to keep the kingdom safe and healthy. My cousins and sister are especially important to me. I do not hold you accountable, but I am leery. The magician and doctor are not sure of what claimed your father. They've never seen anything like it."

"I-I understand, my prince," I stuttered, kicking myself for my nervousness. My composure couldn't be flattering in Nefertiti's eyes, and I'd never be comparable to this man.

"I will have Pentju, the doctor, see you," Thutmose said, "and I am sorry for your loss."

"Thank you," I said.

Thutmose strode down the hall, his steps echoing as his cousins and sister jogged at his heels. The difference between him and Akhenaten displayed itself like a lion beside a cat. I suddenly gained a deeper understanding of my master. To be second in line to the throne must invite never-ending, what-if questions, but to also be repulsive compared to a brother so regal … it might feel like a curse. Pessimism and dejection often filled my soul when waiting on Akhenaten, leaving me to imagine how it would be if our roles were reversed. Pity slipped into my heart, but only for a fleeting moment. No, I could never be so vile.

Kicking the floor in frustration, I lay down beside Croc, exhausted. Sleep took me.

"Hello," a voice said, waking me some time later.

The light of the Aten shone bright, its heat stifling. An overweight bald man entered, slinging a writing palette over his shoulder. The pungent aroma of rank sweat followed, along with his watermelon head. "Thutmose insisted I visit."

"Thank you," I said, jolting upright. "Please, tell me what happened to my father."

"I believe he contracted the black plague," Pentju said, tugging at the rolls under his chin, "although we've not seen it in ages. I don't know how or why, but I pray we've not lost favor in the eyes of God."

A great pain grew inside, my stomach aching as guilt twisted upon it like gnarled fingers. God had rained punishment down on Father to make me suffer. "Does the plague cause black and yellow spotting of the skin, and then sloughing?"

"Yes, I believe so." The doctor sniffed, his eyes wandering. "I heard you snuck out and saw the body. The plague is contagious."

"You examined him."

"Boy, you are ignorant in the ways of the world," he snapped, his face trying to wrinkle through the fat of his cheeks. "I wore protective amulets and charms, and the magician shielded himself with his most powerful spells. You were not so fortunate."

"Oh," I said, realizing my mistake. My stomach cramped again. What had I done?

"Now we have to see if you develop symptoms. Do you have marks, pain, fatigue, fever, anything out of the ordinary?"

"No, I feel fine," I lied through the pain in my gut.

"Drop your kilt and turn around."

I did as I was ordered, having to keep my backside exposed for an uncomfortable minute as the doctor examined and prodded every inch of me.

"The bruise on your left shoulder. What's that from?"

"I've suffered restless sleep and haunting nightmares," I lied, knowing the mark was from falling out of the window. But I didn't want to let him know my secret escape route.

"Hmm," the doctor said, his eyebrows narrowing over the bridge of his nose. "Without significant trauma, I'd be more suspicious of—"

"Or from falling!" I said. "Suty has pushed me down a lot."

The doctor nodded, his neck wobbling. "Where'd you get that?" He pointed at my wrist.

"I—" I looked down at Father's bronze bracelet. "Father gave it to me."

"Remove it! If you took it from his body, I'll have it melted down."

I took a deep breath. Images of a black bruise crawling under the skin formed in my mind. Sliding off the bronze armband, I was too afraid to look. I clamped my eyes shut and rolled my arm around for the doctor.

Silence.

I had to see. Opening my eyes … no marks covered the area. Sighing in relief, I pulled up my kilt and asked, "What about my father's bloodshot eyes?"

Pentju remained silent for a moment. "I am not sure about the redness. Struck blind for a sin? I can't find mention of red eyes in any of the old writings from the times of the plague."

"And his tongue?" I asked.

"Bite marks. He … must've been in a great deal of pain."

I shivered in horror with the thought. "Could someone have killed him?"

"There're no fatal wounds from a physical attack," the doctor said. "If there was a struggle, someone would've heard something. He lived in Pharaoh's own wing where guards patrol day and night."

Would someone murder Father? He didn't have enemies, but I hadn't been around much in recent weeks. Memories of the last encounter with

Akhenaten and Father sent chills down my spine. Father had really wanted to tell me something, but my master had interrupted our conversation. Akhenaten could be cruel enough to kill, but why would he care about a lowly servant? If someone with so much power wanted to get rid of Father, there would be easier ways, like public exile or execution. Hatred for Akhenaten must be clouding my judgment. But I needed Father's death not to be my fault; I needed to know I hadn't killed him.

My stomach cramped again, and I doubled over to ease the tension. "Is there anything else, anything in the world that could make those wounds? Animal bites, perhaps?"

He tapped his hidden chin, and ripples ran under his skin. "I've been pondering this from the moment I uncovered the evidence. There's nothing else to link all the lesions together. An infection would have taken days to set in. Just because you were bitten and survived doesn't mean you understand disease or medicine."

"And the plague can kill that fast?"

"Depends on how fast you think it was." He folded his sagging arms. "Remember, you've been gone a long time, and your father could've been hiding an illness, not wanting to worry you so soon upon your return. Was he acting out of sorts?"

"We talked about my trip, and then he wanted to tell me something, but Akhenaten interrupted us and made me go to bed."

Pentju's sunken eyes clouded over. "He didn't mention anything about what he wanted to tell you?"

Should I tell him Father had scouted for unseen ears and claimed it concerned something bigger than this life? "No, but can I please pray to the Aten? I need to ask for guidance."

The doctor turned and whispered to the guard outside, "It may only be the request of a servant, but we may all need prayer now."

A gaunt servant with red eye shadow appeared. He licked his lips, set a meager tray of bread and beer down, and dashed off.

Scooting the contents inside with his foot, the doctor backed out.

"Please don't burn my father!" I lunged at the doctor in desperation, kneeling and reaching for his kilt with open palms. "Only being eaten by the Devouring Monster would be worse punishment. Please bury him!"

"Gracious Pharaoh doesn't want that, either," Pentju said, placing a sandaled foot on my forehead to keep me at bay. "Not until the infection spreads through the palace will I order the burning of bodies. I'm on your side, boy."

"Thank you," I whispered and collapsed over the delivered meal, emotionally spent.

The guard reappeared and tossed a hardened mud object. The idol hit me on the back and clattered to the floor. Scooping it up, I placed the object on my windowsill. The immortal sun-disc being lifted by the scarab now basked in the light of the Aten.

"What if a Dark One attacked my father?" I asked.

The doctor scoffed. "Those are children's tales. They don't exist, at least not anymore."

"I saw one south of Elephantine," I said. "A group of them."

"You saw a Dark One and lived to tell the tale?" Pentju's eyes narrowed.

"They were miles away in the plains, attacking a herd of animals."

"A band of Nubian barbarians," he said, dismissing me with a wave. "If a Dark One attacked your father, he'd have been decapitated and ripped limb from limb."

I nodded, trying not to imagine the horror.

"One last thing," he said, leaning forward and falling to a whisper. "The magician is a very wise man and has faithfully served Pharaoh for years, but if he approaches, be wary! There's something about him, something I've never seen before. Do not share secrets with him, if you harbor any."

My insides turned icy as the doctor left, leaving a trail of suspicion. Even if a magician had helped save my life at Thebes, their occult powers frightened me.

Praying to the Aten, I asked for forgiveness and promised all the devotion and offerings I could gather for the rest of my life—if the plague didn't spread. If it did, the only memory of Father would be of a man who brought a grave disease down upon Egypt.

Night fell. The guard stationed at my room switched with another. I wanted to talk to Nefertiti, to ease her inner turmoil and help her regain happiness. But that wouldn't save Father's soul. I glanced up at the reed curtain over the window. No, I'd better not climb out. Father and I would be burned. I should accept my fate and the orders of my superiors.

A knock echoed outside my open doorway.

Gray eyes glared above a wide, flat face with high cheekbones and tangled veins of black. A white cat perched upon the sash on his shoulder. The magician from Father's room! The same one I'd seen in the streets of Memphis before sailing on our adventure ... The son of Hapu whispered to the guard, and the watchman left without argument. I waited, steadying my trembling hands by squeezing Father's bracelet.

"Come here, boy," the son of Hapu whispered and motioned.

My heart accelerated as I inched over, still gripping the bronze for courage.

Deep wrinkles sank into the man's shaven head, emphasizing his concerns. "There are things you must hear. The doctor's not looking at the entire picture, and I believe he may be misplacing the evidence on purpose ..."

Chapter 32

Journal Translation

S TEADYING MY SHAKING HAND on my bracelet drew the magician's
scrutiny. He stared with haunted, pale eyes as he stepped inside my
room.

"I don't believe the plague struck one man in one room without warning,"
the son of Hapu said. His eyes darkened. "There's something else at work,
something draped in shadows. Magic!" He leaned into my personal space.
"I didn't see any spells, potions, or statuettes, but I felt it when I entered your
father's room. Something was not right, the feeling profound and obscure …
ancient. Did you notice any idols or drawings when you talked to your father
that night? Or did you bring anything back with you? From Thebes, perhaps?"

This man made my skin crawl under the layer of rising gooseflesh.
Could the Bes amulet have had something to do with all this? No, it'd saved
me. And Akhenaten had broken it before I'd ever seen Father. "I didn't see
any hieroglyphs until after you two were in my father's room."

The light in the magician's eyes faded, his pupils scrawling over blank
space.

"What can I do to help him?" I asked.

"There may not be anything you can do," the magician said. "Pray the
disease doesn't spread. And be careful of what you share with the doctor and
any of the royal family; they may not be what they seem. If someone cast
magic that night, it's stronger than my own … powerful enough to conceal
all remnants. I may be limited in terms of what I can accomplish …" He
looked down the hall.

"I've seen the Dark Ones!" I said. He spun back around, his eyes and
hairless brows pulling back. "And I've seen Akhenaten use magic!"

The son of Hapu's forehead tugged and wrinkled. "I must leave!" He disappeared into the hall. The guard returned without a word, but other footsteps thundered down the corridor.

Suty's jutting ear appeared beside his scarred face, reflecting the light of the torch in his hand. "There you are, boy. Making sure you're where you're supposed to be. Not spreading your cursed family's disease."

The monster intimidated me with his stare. But in spite of the terror engulfing me, I didn't tremble. I wished he'd drop over dead, but I'd never be able to physically harm that ogre. Finally, he left.

Laying my head back, images of all I'd witnessed played out in my mind. Exhaustion overcame me, but distressing thoughts and emotions tore at the center my soul. All the drama and threats of the impending burning kept sleep at bay. Formulating a plan to save Father, I hoped I'd uncover the truth …

A scream pierced the silent halls. My eyes shot open. The Aten's early rays streaked through my window, forming haunting shapes against the cracks in the ceiling.

People raced around the palace, this time in larger swarms than in the morning Father had died. Frantic yelling followed. I crawled on all fours and peeked outside. Displaying overwhelming animation, a royal servant with red eye paint licked his lips and spoke to a contingent of soldiers. Shaking, his finger pointed at me. He wailed, throwing his hands into the air. "Another death!"

My throat constricted so tightly I choked, and my mouth went dry. No! Did this mean the end for Father? Who was it?

The guards came with swords drawn and surrounded my doorway. A familiar monster stepped forward. Suty.

"Stand up, boy," Suty said, his pig's ear twitching. "Need to look you over."

I moved slowly, as if awaiting execution.

"Lift your kilt and turn around," he said, and I obeyed. Cold bronze slapped against my bare buttocks, a stinging pain shooting across my skin. "Don't see any black marks. Fetch the doctor!"

Several of the guards dispersed. Suty watched my door as throngs of people sprinted by, screaming in anguish. This couldn't be good.

"I'll be right here when the doctor comes," he said. "If he recommends burning, I'll be happy to light that flame."

I swallowed, and my insides turned cold. "What happened?"

"You're spreading disease," he said, gnashing his teeth.

"Who died?" I asked, clenching my fists with anxiety.

"You don't need to know; you're just a servant." Sneering, the ogre kicked out in a threat to silence me.

The rank smell of sweat preceded the watermelon-headed doctor. "Our worst fears have come true," Pentju said, the writing palette shaking in his hand.

Standing, I bit my lip to hold back a cry of fear. I didn't like the doctor, but the magician seemed … creepy. But who had died to warrant this kind of reaction?

Turning me around, Pentju slapped my dangling sidelock away from my shoulders. "No lesions. You must be a carrier."

My toes curled with dread. Was that why my stomach ached? "What happened?"

His voice shook. "Th-the prince is dead."

"Akhenaten?" The blood drained from my face, and my chest constricted, making it hard to breathe. Exhilaration arose and spread through my limbs.

"No, Thutmose, the crown prince," he said, his fat cheeks wobbling.

Thutmose! My knees buckled in shock, almost sending me crashing to the floor. The man had looked impervious to mortal afflictions. How? He had just visited me. Perhaps I should keep that to myself. "Did he have marks like my father?"

"Yes, a contagious disease is spreading. We must move swiftly in order to prevent more victims. Pray the Aten is not punishing us." The doctor waddled to the door. "Your father will be burned, and if you show signs, you'll be seared alive for bringing this filth."

I collapsed, begging. "No! Please don't take revenge on my father!"

Pentju departed.

Shrieking and weeping carried throughout the palace all day. I couldn't linger in my room another night. This curse was *my* fault! My life hung in jeopardy, but I didn't have much left to live for. The way things were now, I'd never have a future with Nefertiti or an afterlife with Father. Was his soul already lost for eternity, or did they fear going near his body? I prayed Pharaoh still wanted him in the next life and his *ba* flew free. Perhaps I could steal his body and bury it somewhere in the desert.

I peeked out the doorway. A man in a padded cap stood with his back to me. The spear and hide shield in his hands drooped. My forearms tensed in preparation. He was dozing off, and this was my chance. Grabbing the idol of the sun-disc and scarab, I whispered, "Give me strength, grace, and invisibility, and I'll ever be your faithful servant."

Wadding up the reeds of my bed, I shaped them into a pile and covered it with the blanket. I placed a sand-filled excrement pot next to the window and stood on it. I'd have to accomplish this feat without a commotion. Closing my eyes, I sucked in a deep breath.

When I repeated my window technique, the maneuver came easier and my leg didn't hurt as much. I rolled on the descent, softening the dirt landing. Lying still, I listened. Silence. No guards stood in the immediate area. Thankfully, with Amenhotep's peaceful and prosperous reign, other than the recent plague scare, no one was ever on edge.

Jumping back up, I peered through my window. No commotion arose from within, and no torchlight moved into my room. This time, I wouldn't be caught out in the open.

I scouted everywhere, as if I were prey on the vast desert and the sphinx itself tracked me. My heart pounded. Approaching the edge of torchlight, I stepped away from the white walls and inched around the side of a wing. A guard stood staring vacantly into the distance. This was unfortunate. My white kilt, camouflage against the palace's façade, stood out against the night like an albino crocodile. Scraping up handfuls of dirt, I rubbed the grit into my clothing to stain the fabric brown.

After venturing out to the perimeter wall, I crept back on the soldier's far side. Another watchman patrolled between the palace and the Aten temple. His route paced in and out of the rings of light. But I could run through the visible area before he came back around.

Sprinting through the night, I focused my attention on where the watchman should reappear—hopefully not for another minute. I entered the ring of torchlight, still running as fast as I could. After I passed through, the comfort of darkness descended, but I only slowed my pace after arriving at the temple. Anticipatory scenes of Father formed in my head, terrifying me. But the stone slab was bare, his body gone. No sign of being scorched by flame. Empty.

I glanced around, dumbfounded. Where had they taken him? I wanted to scream but was too afraid. *What do I do now?*

I stumbled back through the fragrant gardens, their vibrancy veiled by darkness. Kicking the dirt in frustration, I cursed under my breath.

A black form darted under a rim of light, moving in my direction. Collapsing, I sank my thin frame into the sand. Scooping dirt onto my legs and body, I turned my head sideways so it sat flush with the ground. I held my breath, unable to see. I had no idea if this person was still advancing. My pulse hammered in my ears.

The air turned warm. My muscles contracted, poised to run. What if Akhenaten had gone to my room and found I wasn't there? He wouldn't mind rustling the piled reeds to make sure I actually slept underneath my blanket. Would he burn me alive this time? Perhaps I should run away, flee to another city ... no, I'd be abandoning Father, Croc, and Nefertiti. I could still save her and make her fall in love with me, create the life I always dreamt of.

Footsteps crunched closer. No one could know I was hiding out here, not in this exact spot—not unless God showed them or they wielded magic. My body ached with tension.

The footsteps receded. After waiting a moment, I lifted my head. The whites of my eyes must've stood out in stark contrast to the night and the dirt covering me. The silhouette of a cloaked figure with a draping hood emerged, outlined by distant torchlight. This hunched figure—the same I'd seen inside the magician's lab—lumbered to the perimeter wall of the palace's grounds. Jumping and grabbing the lip of the outer wall, the figure hoisted himself up with ease. Then he climbed down over the other side, disappearing into the surrounding city.

I released a long-overdue breath. Who was this, and why were they going out at night? I'd have to be quick if I wanted to find out. Dashing over, I jumped to catch the edge of the wall.

"Hey! What're you doing?" someone shouted.

Chapter 33

Journal Translation

I DROPPED BACK ONTO THE desert floor and sprinted to my left, running for my life.

"Wait!" a high-pitched voice said.

Stopping, I glanced back. A petite frame with tousled hair stood outlined by torches. The dance of distant flames landed on my face, but shadows concealed hers. She was wearing plain white cloth. Mutnedjmet or possibly Nefertiti disguising as a commoner? No grown soldier stood before me. As I inched closer, fragments of her facial features stood out, gentle and cute. Nefertiti's sister stood in front of me, or some kind of magic betrayed my eyes. I almost smiled despite my suffocating thoughts, but her eyes appeared swollen and red, as if she'd been weeping.

Holding a hand up at me as if to ward off contamination, she said, "What're *you* doing out here?"

"I-I …" Would she blame me and Father for Thutmose's death?

"I won't tell," she said. "But did you see someone run by? Strange things have been happening, starting with your father and then my cousin …" She choked back tears. "I was out in the gardens, where I go when I need to be alone. The place that reminds me of Thutmose. A man draped in black ran by and climbed this wall rather than going through the gates. Then you popped out of the desert like some sort of sand monster. You're not some kind of magician, are you?"

I laughed. "Just a servant. But I was trying to follow the figure you saw."

"Are you infectious?" she asked, stiffening her raised arm.

"I don't think so. I haven't developed any marks."

Her defensive palm relaxed, and she brushed her hair back behind her ears.

"How'd you get out?" I asked.

"I've been doing it for years," she said. "It's not difficult for Ay's daughter to slip or talk her way past a couple of tired guards. My family's so busy trying to comfort Pharaoh and Tiye that no one even notices me. But how did you get out here?"

I remained silent, guarded.

"You'd better hurry, if you want to follow him." White teeth flashed against her shadowed face, forming the inside of a grin. "Because you're going to have to help me over that wall."

Shaking my head in annoyance, I said, "It's not safe for a royal daughter to run around the city at night, especially with me."

"I don't think it's safe for someone exposed to the plague and quarantined to his room to be running anywhere." She folded her arms across her chest.

I sighed with growing frustration, not sure what to do. "Okay, but we move quickly and quietly."

She motioned with an open palm to lead the way.

The palace's perimeter wall was diminutive in comparison to the mighty walls surrounding Memphis itself, but no less white. Slipping on the plaster, I made another attempt to grip the edge. Mutnedjmet giggled but kneeled on one leg, leaving her other thigh for me to stand on. I eased my foot onto her skin, and her eyes became captivated by my hideous scar. Stretching and scrambling with my legs, I pulled, heaving for breath as I finally reached the top.

Torchlight glimmered sporadically within a vast city, but the dark figure had vanished. Disappointment pulled my forehead into my hands.

"Hurry! Pull me up or I'll start screaming."

I leaned back over and shook my head with irritation. "He's gone."

"Goat balls!" she cursed and stomped her foot.

"We can't possibly find him out there."

"Follow me, then!" Mutnedjmet said, spinning around. "I need to tell you something."

After lowering myself down, we crept through the night. Sweet incense from the gardens thickened before the silhouettes of trees and shrubs rose out of the moonlit desert. Grabbing my hand, Mutnedjmet guided me. We skirted around flowers and plants to the edge of a pool, the water like a mirror. Sitting on the bank, she slipped her sandals off and dipped her toes in the water. The crystal reflection of the moon and sky rippled. Fish darted away, their shiny scales gliding beneath the surface like shooting stars.

"The garden's concealed," Mutnedjmet said. "More guards are on night watch, but they're more scared of plague and pestilence than people."

Sitting down beside her, I asked, "Nefertiti or Beketaten didn't come out with you?"

"You'll be disappointed to know," she folded her arms, "your love is sound asleep, as is Beketaten. I'll have to do for now." Tears brimmed in her kind eyes before trickling down her nose. "I miss Thutmose." Sniffing, she wiped the droplets away.

"I miss my father," I said. "He's all I ever had. Did they burn him?" I squeezed my eyes shut, as if the action would shield me from the answer.

"No." She took my hand in hers. "Not yet, but they will tomorrow. The purification ceremony was today."

I almost shouted in relief, but gnawing stress chewed at my stomach. "Where's his body?"

"Heavily guarded, and they won't reveal the location."

We sat in silence, staring into the wavering pool.

"How is Nefertiti?" I asked.

"She walks like she carries the cargo of two donkeys, and her mood is even more sour than the mood of those creatures."

My heart twisted in anguish.

"She was betrothed to Thutmose."

"What?" My mouth gaped open. No, that couldn't have been. I'd have known something so important about her. For royalty, marrying a cousin was not so strange, but it was not allowed among the common people. Had Akhenaten been keeping me in the dark on purpose, and for how long?

"The magician's been acting strange, too," she said, not addressing my surprise. "No wonder we couldn't find him. He's only been seen once in the last week or so, to inspect your father's room. It's like he disappeared."

I'd seen him! He'd visited and warned me about the doctor. Perhaps I shouldn't tell her yet—and I'd better not mention that I'd seen the cloaked figure in the magician's lab, either.

"Akhenaten's distant, even more so than usual. But apart from Pharaoh, no one has more power. He'll become the god-king." Her face paled even under the moonlight.

By the Aten! Motive dawned on my naïve brain. Akhenaten desired nothing more than to become God himself, the immortal. What if the entire plague was a lie? "Do you trust Akhenaten?" I asked, scrutinizing her reaction.

Mutnedjmet grimaced as she kicked the water. "No, he's done terrible things to me, too."

Repulsion churned my guts. I'd have to save Nefertiti from him. "Do you think he could have anything to do with this plague? Or could the deaths have been murders?"

Her eyes grew larger than the fish's in the pond. "I wouldn't doubt he's capable, but through a plague? How?" She took an uncharacteristic deep breath and spoke more slowly. "Akhenaten had the most to gain, but he'd also have to have the Divine's favor in order to ascend as the immortal god-king. He must deserve it, at least in the eyes of God."

"What if he performed dark magic to usurp the throne? But why my father? And how did that relate to Thutmose?"

Her bright eyes wandered in circles, something playing out in her head. Suspicion crept into her tone. "Maybe he needed to test out his plague … or perhaps your father knew something. A disease that only killed his older brother may seem suspiciously coincidental. Maybe your father's death would make you more obedient, as you have no other family."

Her words stung, but the inquisitive girl spoke the truth. Looking away, I fought off tears.

"I'm sorry," she said, cupping my shoulder.

Rage boiled deep inside. If Akhenaten had murdered Father, I'd avenge him. But how could I take vengeance on someone so powerful, someone who arose from death?

"I have to find out if my father was murdered, and if so, who's responsible," I said, punching my knee. Perhaps I hadn't killed Father by cursing the Aten that night. "If Akhenaten's summoning a curse, we have to stop him. Then I have to save my father's soul."

"I'll help," she said, the pitch of her voice rising as the vacant haze in her eyes vanished. "But how?"

"Did you see Thutmose's body?"

"Not up close," she said, squinting. "They wouldn't let me near him after they knew, but his eyes were red like—"

"The same as my father's! We have to see the body!"

Mutnedjmet leaned away. "If you're caught in the vicinity of the body of the son of the Aten, you'll be put to death on the spot."

"They're considering burning me already," I said. "If his wounds are the same as my father's, it'll prove the deaths are related. If not ..."

"Wouldn't the plague kill the same way every time?"

"Probably, but Akhenaten might not," I said. "What else can we do? Wait and try to catch him in the act if he tries to kill again?"

"He might not need to keep killing." She kicked the water again, distorting the moon and rolling its light over the uneven surface. "Today Akhenaten publicly declared himself the co-regent of the kingdom, alongside Pharaoh. Amenhotep seemed numb, like grief had disconnected him. His body is withering, even if his *ka* and *ba* are immortal. It won't be long until an ailment strikes him."

"Perhaps longer than Akhenaten would like?"

"Father says Amenhotep's so broken up by the twist of fate and the death of his favorite son that he's incoherent and has made no attempt to halt Akhenaten's ambitions. Akhenaten already directed palace affairs today."

"Has anyone tried to stop him?" I asked, anxiety escalating within me like the rising sun.

Removing her feet from the water, she clutched her knees to her chest and shivered. "Why would they? The doctor diagnosed Thutmose with plague, silencing any murder suspicions. I can try to convince Father to talk to Pharaoh, but Amenhotep won't take counsel right now. And Aunt Tiye's beside herself ..." Mutnedjmet stood up. "I have a hunch as to where they may've taken Thutmose, but none of the living should ever go there."

My stomach clenched with dread and curiosity, a wave of nausea washing over me.

She led the way through brush, brambles, and darkness as we snuck to the palace's perimeter wall. With her assistance, I scaled the white fortification. After hoisting her up and over, we headed deep into the sleeping city.

"Where're we going?" I whispered.

"I'm not allowed to speak of it." She held a finger to her lips as we crept by the doorway of a modest house. "We went there years ago, after another family member died."

Trailing Mutnedjmet through lamplit streets lined with houses and shops, I became lost. We lowered our heads when passing a strolling man and quickened our pace when nearing a group of adolescent males. They had gathered together in a circle, yelling and cursing. The smell of baked bread intertwined with dust and wafting body odor. Three children ran screaming out of a house. They stopped when they saw us and stared, their faces stained with food.

After what seemed like hours later, the buildings parted and a vast expanse of darkness opened into the west. My eyes adjusted. The massive white walls of Memphis circled beyond the void. Scattered rings of firelight marked the inner side of the barrier.

Mutnedjmet pointed to the silhouette of an enormous temple. A roof lay atop its pillars.

"There's a dark temple in Memphis?" I asked. I'd never seen or heard of this place.

Nodding, she retrieved an oil lamp that was burning outside a house. Then she stepped out into the abyss. "We all have our dark secrets. Stay in the shadows. If someone comes, run or hide. They'll only see me, and I'll tell them I wanted to see my cousin."

Her ring of light stood out like a beacon upon the dark desert. My heart rate quickened and drops of sweat formed on my forehead, but my limbs turned cold. As we walked away from the lights of the city, countless stars emerged upon the encompassing sky. I was only one of millions, a tiny part of an infinite whole. How could I ever hope to accomplish anything?

After we traversed a dirt and rock courtyard, stone steps emerged from the ground. The temple dominated the celestial night, blotting out the heavens. Insignificance came over me like a single worker ant before the hill. I couldn't move.

"Those who defy fate die or lead miserable lives," I said, the code of the kingdom sounding in my mind. Breathing came in shallow gulps as my chest tightened in fear.

"Follow me," Mutnedjmet said. "We won't do anything of the sort. Plus, fate wouldn't even know what to do with warriors as powerful as we are."

Grinning, she ascended the outer steps and tugged me along. We wound between pillars of ancient stone—ten times thicker than me. A shadowing roof extended overhead as we penetrated deeper and deeper into the occult sanctuary. My heart drummed louder and louder.

Mutnedjmet stopped in her tracks. A faint light shifted through an opening ahead.

"They're still here," she whispered. Brushing tangled hair behind small ears, she crept to the edge of a doorway. She peeked into the room, gasped, and stumbled backward.

Chapter 34

Journal Translation

LYING UPON A ROCK SLAB in the center of the inner chamber was Thutmose's body. But beneath twisting shadows, several figures roamed about. No, they weren't in shadow; they were humanoid with the heads of black jackals. My throat constricted and spasmed as I gasped for air, unable to move or look away.

These beings performed rituals of wafting smoke and rubbing cleansing agents on the dead. A sickening smell of caustic liquids and heavy incense floated through the darkness, along with whimpering.

"By the Aten!" I fell to my knees, crushing Father's bracelet in my grip.

"Shhh!" Mutnedjmet put a finger to her lips.

A creature yanked a multi-lobed organ from the abdomen of the corpse, inspected the brown tissue, and dropped it into an animal-headed jar. The tissue slipped inside the vessel with a moist sucking noise. Something heaved inside me, and my stomach fought to let loose. Ducking behind the doorway, I clamped a hand over my mouth.

"It's them!" Mutnedjmet whispered. "Mummy Makers. They prepare bodies for the afterlife. Those who have laid eyes on them do not live to speak of it!"

"Monsters?"

Mutnedjmet giggled. "Just stories. They're priests wearing masks ... I think." She strummed a lock of hair with her fingertip. "When I was a child, I heard stories about jackal-headed monsters looking after the dead. They keep to themselves, never interacting with the living. I don't believe these people want anyone unmasking their true identity."

Fake beasts looking after the dead? I shuddered in horror, the moisture draining from my mouth. This couldn't be true ... but with my experiences recently, I couldn't dismiss the notion.

"If you want to examine Thutmose, you'll have to do it before the Opening of the Mouth ritual. After that, the body will have been treated with so many chemicals and rubs and wraps you won't be able to tell much."

"How long until the Opening of the Mouth?"

She shrugged. "I heard about it years ago: the most important ceremony to allow the deceased to breathe, speak, and eat in the next life. Without it, they'd never pass the trials."

"So these jackal-men actually help people?" I asked.

"But they're supposed to be from the underworld, helping men arrive in the afterlife ... so that more of these creatures can do who-knows-what with men's souls."

My tongue curled at the thought.

Grabbing my shoulder, she whispered, "You have to see Thutmose's body. Tonight!"

"They're in there cutting out his insides!"

"We don't have the luxury of waiting to see if the Mummy Makers leave before daybreak. You have to get back to your room, or you'll be burned."

"But they could be dangerous." I backed away. "If they catch us disturbing their mummy ..." Vivid images of being torn to pieces by a pack of jackals with human bodies sent shivers coursing through my spine.

"A commotion too intriguing to resist?" Mutnedjmet's face turned as white as the walls of the palace. "I hope they don't catch me." Standing, she held her lamp aloft. "You'd better go in." She raced back into the darkness of the temple before I could stop her.

Torchlight sprang to life in a distant hall, followed by another and another. Mutnedjmet screamed, "By the power of the Aten, I will burn this temple! Bathe it in light! Let the sun raze it to the ground!" A sputtering torch clattered to the floor at the far end of a long hallway.

Her yelling would've caught the attention of the dead.

Creatures burst out with a bang as the door slammed against the wall. My eyes squeezed shut with fright. Heat emanated from their sprinting bodies, and their mouths panted like dogs. I didn't dare move from my crouched position in the dark, but I cracked an eye open.

Dark robes billowed around tall, sinewy figures with black jackal heads. The hair on the back of my neck stood up as torchlight flickered in their yellow eyes. Issuing beast-like grunts and barks, the pack sprinted off. I prayed Mutnedjmet had run out into the desert, back to the city. If these creatures could follow scent like a dog, hiding wouldn't be an option.

Within the hazy chamber the body rested, alone. Burning guilt seared the pit of my stomach. I wouldn't be able to live with myself if Mutnedjmet were harmed, especially if I didn't do my part. I crept inside. The combination of sweet incense mixing with medicinal rubs sickened me. An array of bloodied surgical instruments sat upon the slab. Jars lay scattered about, filled with organs or liquids emitting odors so strong they burned the inside of my nose. The body of Thutmose lay still, a gaping hole in his upper abdomen. Two incisions ran on either side of his disfigured nose, penetrating deep into unknown tissues. My pulse thundered in my ears.

Grabbing his rigid jaw, I forced it open. Animal-like barks and screeches echoed. My hands shook as I examined the orifice, identifying punctures in the tongue. But no blood trickled out. Had his blood been drained by the Mummy Makers? Opening the prince's eyelids revealed snaking red vessels upon the whites. I moved down to his legs. No marks stood out. The hole in his belly and those on his face wouldn't have been caused by the plague, but the monsters used incisions to remove organs.

Lifting a stiff leg revealed black and yellow circles across the back of his calf. Hidden in the crook of his knee, dark lines extended upward. The same marks as Father's.

The yipping outside amplified like jackals after a kill, raising goose bumps along my arms. Hopefully Mutnedjmet had escaped.

A vicious snarl erupted behind me. The face of a beast stared, saliva stringing from its curled lips in waist-deep strands. No human hid behind a mask! Sheer terror paralyzed me. But the monster lumbered forward, its fetid breath suffocating. Was it my time to die? The beast's heaving panting warmed the confined space as its flat footfalls slapped stone.

I crouched at the far end of the slab, and something shiny caught my eye. A curved knife sat in a pool of drying blood. Snatching it with trembling fingers, I peeled the handle out of the caking liquid.

The beast stepped closer, peeking around the corner of the slab. My entire body quaked with fear as this thing stared, an inferno burning behind sunken eyes. It snarled, and a string of bubbling spit splattered onto the floor. Death surrounded me.

I sprinted for the exit. But the beast moved faster. As it reached out with a human hand, I drove the knife deep into the webbing between two knuckles. The tip plunged through its palm and the creature yelped, dropping and sprawling across the floor.

I barreled through shadowy passageways, my pounding footfalls echoing. Several monsters wandered distant halls, turning to pursue me. Their yipping intensified again. I'd never make it outside. Statues lined the chamber I raced through. A sputtering torch was on the wall. The eternal stone eyes of men, animals, and animal heads atop human bodies stared. Beside a shadow-laden bird of prey, the stone head of a man relaxed, turned, and glared directly at me. Its eyes twitched. I twisted and jumped away in shock, bounding on. All of the eyes in the room followed me! Was my mind playing tricks? Would I wake up at any moment?

A side passage opened up in the wall to my left. Turning into the passage, I froze. Sniffing filled the stagnant air, followed by heavy breathing. A jackal-beast stood down the hall, its back to me. It dragged long fingernails against the wall, and the grinding created an ear-piercing screech. The roots of my teeth tingled and ached with the sickening noise.

Taking a slow step back toward the hall of statues, I held my breath. Perhaps I'd have a better chance in there. My sandal settled on the ground, and the beast froze, its pointed ears perking up as its head tilted to the side. I stopped. The sniffing returned, and the beast slowly rotated. I bolted as a low growl erupted. Crashing into something, I went tumbling. Another creature that I'd run into smashed into a statue, snarling as he fell. I scrambled up, charging on as barking erupted from the shadows at my heels.

The hall opened up, pillars soaring overhead as the snarls closed in. Leaping from the top of the stairs, I plummeted and collided with the desert floor. Blood-curdling yips carried into the open night.

Sprinting for the city, I glanced back. Three beasts launched themselves from the temple, covering more distance than me. They landed with terrifying thuds, soon to be upon me—a pack of jackals descending upon a single rodent. I'd be torn limb from limb. Hope left me completely as I gasped for air.

I ran across sand and rock, but a strong hand shoved me from behind. Sprawling forward, I managed to spin around to face my adversary. Snapping jaws descended.

Chapter 35

Journal Translation

ACKAL JAWS LUNGED FOR my neck. Grabbing the Mummy Maker's muzzle, I attempted to hold the snapping teeth at bay. But strong hands pinned mine into the sand. A flash arced over us, and the jackal-headed beast sailed into the dirt. Snarling and growling intermingled with hissing and roaring.

I squinted in the moonlight. Scrambling to its feet, the Mummy Maker yelped, and the pack fled back to the temple. I couldn't make anything else out in the darkness as my head spun in confusion, my breaths shallow and rapid. A soft meow called out, and an orange shape pranced up to me. Croc! I jumped in excitement. His hair stood on end, his pupils so dilated they appeared as black holes.

Croc couldn't possibly have knocked one of those beasts off of me. Did they fear cats? What was Croc doing all the way out here, anyway? It couldn't be coincidence. I scooped up my companion, and he glared at the temple and hissed.

Where was Mutnedjmet? I'd be a coward if I left her after she'd risked her life to help. I'd rather die searching for her than live knowing I'd fled for my own safety. But would I be brave enough to return? Perhaps I should carry Croc as a protective amulet. I took an unsteady step toward the stairs.

"Heb!" Mutnedjmet yelled from the darkness to my right. "Don't go back! You already nearly died!"

I jogged toward her voice, and her figure took shape. The whites around her dark eyes stood out, wide and unblinking. She shook violently.

"Let's go," I said, my heart still thundering against my ribs. Had I really just seen monsters and moving statues? What'd happened to the world these last few weeks?

Staring at my chest, she didn't respond. I glanced down to Croc, who kept a wary eye on the pillars.

She pointed. "H-he ..."

"We need to get out of here! It's great they're afraid, but they'll be stronger as a pack."

"N-no, he ... and those things ..."

Grabbing Mutnedjmet above the elbow, I yanked her around. "I applaud your distraction so that I could examine Thutmose's body, but I wouldn't have approved of you risking your life."

She shook out of my grip and stepped back, eyeing Croc.

"I saw something," she said.

"What?"

"I don't know for sure. I couldn't see well, but I saw something ..."

Croc's eyelids closed. I'd been in dire situations before, and he hadn't done anything. But was that why cats were revered as pets? Could they scare away monsters? I shook my head and jogged toward the city.

"I'm terrified," Mutnedjmet said, following, "but I'm glad you're here. I thought you were dead." She attempted to hug me from behind.

"I'm terrified too," I said, trying to divert my thoughts from the snapping jaws of monsters.

"Someone's helping you."

An image of the old magician and overweight doctor popped into my mind, but the jackal heads forced them out. The city wasn't approaching fast enough. Who else was on my side? Mahu? No, he always followed orders. I wished Nefertiti would look out for me but doubted it. "The magician?" I asked, slowing to a brisk walk.

"There's no way an old man knocked that thing over. Magic, maybe. But I've never seen it used and actually work. And the son of Hapu is missing. Do you think he could've been murdered?"

"Why him and not the doctor?" I asked. Did Mutnedjmet know something she wasn't telling me?

"If Akhenaten's trying to become God and is killing those in his way, I don't see how murdering either one would be beneficial. Could the magician be responsible for the plague?"

Howls of anger resounded over the desert.

Moving faster, we reached the city's outskirts. Amulets now hung around the doors. Visages of a stout dwarf with a mane and beard like a lion stared into the streets. Bes.

"Do people know the Mummy Makers are in the temple?" I asked.

"Not sure," Mutnedjmet said, lifting her hands. "They must've heard something and at least thought jackals were about."

The vast city was eerily quiet. "I think we're safe."

Mutnedjmet's soft face and hair glinted in the moonlight. Her eyes, turning to stare into mine, twinkled against pale skin and dark hair. Everything else disappeared.

I yearned to kiss her—the first time I'd had romantic feelings for anyone besides Nefertiti. She smiled. Shaking my head, I buried the thoughts.

Faint light splashed the eastern sky, hiding the stars. My insides cramped with dread, bringing shooting pain. I needed to get back.

Mutnedjmet led the way but glanced about as if beasts would descend from the alleyways.

I'd confirmed similar wounds on the supposed plague victims, but how would this impact Akhenaten and his plans? I couldn't accuse him of traitorous acts; I'd be executed. Could Mutnedjmet? And Father was going to be burned today. "We need something to convince Pharaoh of Akhenaten's depravity," I said. "He'll never believe me. You must try."

"He won't—"

"You're our only hope. Pharaoh has to oust Akhenaten for good. There isn't anyone else with enough power."

Mutnedjmet frowned but nodded. "I'll insist Father and Aunt Tiye talk to Amenhotep. But we don't have any proof, only your and Nefertiti's accounts of his atrocities."

We climbed over the palace's perimeter wall.

I yearned to see Nefertiti alone, missing her beyond words. And I didn't want her to think I'd put Mutnedjmet's life in jeopardy. Fantasizing,

I imagined she'd awaken at my arrival and be elated to see me. She'd invite me into her room, grateful I longed to be her guardian. We'd talk, or perhaps I'd even kiss her red lips …

After clearing my throat, I said, "I should get back."

Mutnedjmet's head hung with obvious disappointment. "Are you going to check on Nefertiti?"

Surprise made me drop Croc. How did she … ? I shouldn't lie to her; I might need her help again. "Maybe."

"I could still go with you," she said, kicking at the sand.

I didn't want to hurt her feelings. "I can't put you in any more danger."

She shuffled off. "I'll look for you tomorrow night in the gardens and let you know how convincing I was with Ay." Croc followed her. Casting him a wary glance, she walked faster. He trotted to keep up.

I smirked, but I felt bad. Not bad enough to ask Mutnedjmet to tag along, though. Sneaking off into the predawn, I maneuvered around the scattered sentries and arrived at Nefertiti's window. No one in sight. I jumped and pulled myself up.

An icy dagger pierced my soul when I laid eyes upon the scene within. My grip faltered.

Chapter 36

Present Day

SLINGING MY MESSENGER BAG over my shoulder, I followed Maddie out into the cramped aisle of the train. We exited with a small number of tourists and emerged from the station into Cairo. Hordes of locals and tourists spilled through the surrounding streets amongst shimmering waves of morning heat that rose like translucent smoke from the metal of nearby vehicles. The stifling temperature and claustrophobia from the crowd nauseated me. I turned around to gather my wits just as two men in *thawbs* exited the station. One wore a beard to his chest; the other's was sparse and patchy—the same men we'd hired, who might've trapped us in the tomb. They pointed at me.

Fear took control of my limbs, and the muscles in my neck contracted in panic. Huddling against Maddie, who probably hadn't seen the men, I kept my head down as I helped shove her through the masses. Fortunately, taxis lined a nearby curb.

Pounding my fist against a taxi window, I cursed and opened the rear door.

Maddie leapt inside, speaking to the driver in broken Arabic. After ducking into the cramped black-and-white car, I slammed the door. Honking, the cabbie waved the locals aside as he tried to maneuver through the pandemonium of travelers.

The driver yelled in Arabic, waving his hands and swirling smoke from his cigarette as I scanned the crowd for the suspicious men.

"Ouch," Maddie said, jerking her hand from mine. I must've been squishing it, unaware I was even holding it.

The cabbie stomped on the gas and the car jolted, scaring people aside. Lurching out into the street, we careened back and forth as the tires squealed a bit. The scene and our two pursuers disappeared as we swerved around a corner. I let out a long sigh, and my body fell limp.

Maddie stared at the passing buildings and congested cars, waving her hand to dispel the cigarette smoke. She coughed.

Should I tell her that I'd seen those same men following us, or would it only scare her more? We'd already been traumatized enough. What were we going to do now? I'd convinced myself that the risk of this adventure would be worth the secrets and treasures we'd bring back into the world, mysteries lost for thousands of years. But we'd failed.

"We'll get Kaylin and the others and fly back to the States," I said, my gaze falling to the dark stains on the car's floor.

The taxi squealed to a stop, flinging us forward in our seats. The Four Seasons on the bank of the Nile towered overhead. I threw money at the driver, and we jogged into the lobby, earning suspicious stares from guests and staff. We climbed into the elevator and rode it to the penthouse suite. I pounded on the entryway.

A moment passed.

The door flew open, revealing a dark-skinned man in a gray suit.

"What happened?" Kaylin's bodyguard asked in his quiet voice, his eyes bulging in shock. His hand ran across his smooth face and then over his bald head.

"Jenkins!" Maddie said, hugging him and shoving past.

I tailed her to the living area. Kaylin lounged on an elegant sofa, the Nile's vast expanse stretching across the window behind her. Sitting curiously close to her was our guide, Mr. Scalone. A twinge of suspicion arose in my stomach.

Kaylin jumped from the cushions, her long legs exposed. Pink lips spread into a radiant smile as she brushed straight blonde hair over her shoulders. Her blue eyes sparkled as they met mine, and she opened her arms for a hug but paused after seeing our grime. "I'm so glad you guys are back! Mr. Scalone shouldn't have left you. Did you have any more trouble?"

Maddie shrugged and shook her head. "Just normal travel exhaustion. After being entombed, I don't think much else is going to seem that big."

"Except the two hired hands from Luxor followed us," I said. "The ones who buried us inside the tomb."

Maddie's head jerked, bouncing her bun as she glared at me. "When were you going to tell me the hired hands tracked us from the train?" she asked, her voice rising a full octave as it echoed off of the walls of the suite.

"I didn't want to scare you," I said, backpedaling, my psychological defenses springing up like shields.

Wheeling on Mr. Scalone, she thrust a finger at him. "Where did you find those two?"

"I didn't know them," Mr. Scalone said, his muscular arms tensing beneath a myriad of tattoos. "A source informed me they had worked with archaeologists and could be trusted. I was trapped too, remember? You didn't see Jenkins running off to help you in Luxor."

Leaning against the wall with interlaced fingers, Jenkins the bodyguard made his presence easy to ignore—despite his size. "My job is to protect Kaylin and her little brother, Aiden," he said. "I'm not here to hunt treasure."

"Who's your source?" Maddie asked, poking Mr. Scalone in the abs.

Folding his colorful arms across his large chest, Mr. Scalone said, "Can't tell," as if he were a respected journalist.

Maddie's cheeks burned, and the heat of my own anger ignited.

"After all we went through?" Maddie yelled, clenching her fists.

Kaylin cast Mr. Scalone a threatening glare with narrowed eyes and a tense jaw.

"All right," Mr. Scalone said. "The Minister of Antiquities. Known him for years … from my line of work. We talked again after our meeting at the restaurant."

"Did he have us followed?" I asked, my mind reeling with scenarios. "To make sure we didn't go digging on our own?"

Maddie spun on Kaylin, her eyes as hard as stone. "I hope your dad wouldn't set up a meeting with someone who'd trap and leave us to die!"

Kaylin gasped, lifting a hand to her gaping lips. "I-I. My dad is very influential, but I doubt he personally knew that man. I feel horrible." She held her hands over her heart. "With a guide and two helpers, we thought you were safe, but I called, like, every day. I even bought tickets to fly down to Luxor … right before Mr. Scalone showed up."

"I don't know much about Egypt," Jenkins said, stepping forward and looking at each of us in turn. The palpable tension ebbed, and my fists relaxed. "But we all need to be more careful and not trust anyone."

A beanpole of a teenager stumbled into the room, his red dreadlocks spilling out from under a straight-billed cap—Aiden. Yanking at the waist of his green basketball shorts, partially hidden beneath an oversized t-shirt, he froze like a deer in the headlights.

"I filled 'em in on what happened to us in the tomb," Mr. Scalone said in his Italian accent, nodding at Kaylin and Jenkins. "But you two haven't told us everything. It's too dangerous to keep secrets, and I've a feelin' that empty tomb wasn't our real objective."

I swallowed in awkward hesitation. There was no way I was going to let this guide know everything about my dad's discovery.

Stepping up beside Mr. Scalone, Kaylin planted her hands on her hips as if she'd wait all night if she had to.

Maddie chewed her lip. "The Hall of Records is still waiting to be discovered …" She recounted our tale, including Dr. Shelsher's letter, and how we had traced clues to the lost tomb in the Valley of the Kings; she only omitted details about the student's journal.

My insides burned with angst as Mr. Scalone had all of our hard-earned information simply drop into his lap. Maddie, Kaylin, and I had made a pact before setting off. We'd be the only ones in the know about the secrets we learned. I didn't even want to inform Kaylin, but Maddie had already divulged a lot in order to receive her help and funding so quickly. But anyone else Kaylin's dad hired would only be given general information. Aiden had been sent along because their dad hated him hanging around the house, not doing anything with his life.

"So, the tomb we found was supposed to be the start of an ancient trail," Mr. Scalone said, running a hand across his dark stubble.

"Cool," Aiden said, his eyes bugging out of his head. He must've thought this was another vacation he'd been forced to go on with his sister. "I'm glad you dudes are still alive. Why do I miss all the cool stuff?"

"Because you're lazy," Mr. Scalone said, his accent thickening. "And the tomb was supposed to lead us to this Hall of Records?"

"But no clues remained?" Kaylin asked, leaning forward. Her thin eyebrows arched in excitement or disbelief.

I shook my head. Maddie nodded.

Kaylin's thin frame slumped. "But, like, there's got to be something. Maybe we should go back."

I dug a stack of folded papers out of my bag, and the dried parchment crinkled. Teasing the pages apart, I said, "I took notes on everything, before the incident. Mr. Scalone photographed it, too." The guide's expression didn't budge, not conveying his intent. "We could go over it, but it doesn't matter now. It's over."

"I unsealed an ancient tomb," Mr. Scalone said, puffing his chest. "We could be heroes, but without real treasure, we should keep going for the final trophy before announcing—"

"Were there mummies?" Aiden asked, his crooked teeth exposed by parted lips.

Why would this boy, born into wealth, have crooked teeth and dreadlocks?

"Only dead and crumbling inside an open sarcophagus," Maddie said.

"Let's contact the media and show them the tomb!" Aiden said.

"Shut up," Mr. Scalone said, shoving an open palm at Aiden's face. "Someone tried to trap us inside, and I had to dig us out. We'll be in even more danger if we advertise our escape and our identities."

Something in my core knotted in irritation. Had he really just said he saved us? That selfish D-bag had almost let us die. "We're lucky the flood broke through, or we'd be dead," I said.

Mr. Scalone laughed. "A miracle! Or magic!" He waved his fingers like casting a spell.

"I don't remember a flood," Maddie said, her eyes moving back and forth as if trying to recall a memory. "Mr. Scalone pulled me out."

What? I searched her face in disbelief. Were my memories of what'd happened only dehydration-fueled hallucinations? "What about the water bottle he told us he didn't have?" I whispered to her.

"Honestly, Gavin," she said, "the entire day before our escape is pretty foggy. I've remembered more from drunken college parties."

No, that couldn't be. My breathing quickened with distress. Mr. Scalone had kept water from us while we'd worked ourselves to death.

✳ ✳ ✳

Hours faded inside the luxurious sitting room amongst a fervent discussion of the ordeal and what we'd do. Aiden disappeared, his curiosity diminishing. Room service delivered plate-covered entrees of blackened seafood, soft rice, and herbed vegetables. I threw back a long swallow of bold red wine, pepper clinging to my palate. Kaylin polished off her third glass.

"Book us a flight back home," Maddie said.

Kaylin's hands trembled, as if she were almost afraid to leave. "Since you guys have been gone, I've run every cipher from a code-cracking textbook on the professor's letter," Kaylin said. "His clues would only lead us to the lost tomb. From there we should find where the Hall is buried."

The young woman was bright, even though she didn't look it.

"Look what I scored while you guys were gone," Aiden said, reappearing and tugging on a leash. A tiny, rodent-like dog appeared on the other end, sniffing. Huge, bat-like ears flicked back and forth above a slender face and a body of tan fur.

My empty glass clinked onto a decorative white plate, shock making me clumsy.

"It's a pet desert fox!" He picked it up in one hand. "Check this out." Pointing to a spiked collar that resembled a fighting dog's, only on a purse-riding Chihuahua, he laughed. "And he's got his own Egyptian souvenir." A prism—no, a glass pyramid—dangled from its tags.

"Poor thing," Maddie said, her eyes fluttering. "Aiden, animals go through hell because stupid tourists want to buy them."

Shrugging, Aiden shoved a jerky treat in front of its nose. The fennec fox, which must've weighed no more than two or three pounds, gobbled it up.

The fox was cute, drawing me in to stroke its wiry fur. I agreed with Maddie, but what could we do now, let it out into the wild? It seemed tame.

Mr. Scalone wrinkled his nose in disgust. "We go exploring and he buys a filthy rat."

"I'm going to bed," Maddie said, standing to leave.

Jenkins and I followed suit. This long bout of social interaction had tired me out almost as much as the recent tomb ordeal.

I shut the door to my bedroom and leaned against it.

"Kaylin," I heard Mr. Scalone say through the partition. "I can locate this Hall faster than a couple kids. Let me help you, instead of being your chauffeur."

"I've told you everything," she replied.

"Let me see the letter. The one from the 1920s."

A few muffled words followed, and then Kaylin said, "We need to talk it over. I don't want us to get ourselves killed, but I'm not running when we have the opportunity to discover more gold artifacts than what's in the entire Museum of Egyptian Antiquities."

"Deal," Mr. Scalone said. "We'll go over everything *domani.* Want to come to bed?"

I held my breath in suspense. The air conditioning kicked on. I jumped. Did this guide plan on bedding Kaylin, the much younger daughter of the man who'd hired him? What a jackass. Mr. Scalone was handsome in a tough, bad-boy kind of way. My fingers crushed the door handle. Was I jealous? Or disgusted?

"Paul," Kaylin said, "not now."

"You can come in anytime," he replied. "Just don't let Jenkins hear you." The soft clap of shutting doors followed.

Releasing a stale breath, I turned to my bed. I threw the outer crimson, probably unwashed comforter on the floor and flopped down. At least the sheets were clean.

Touching the pages of the journal, I felt a connection to this servant and his problems with women, self-worth, and meaning. Could he really push on through all that suffering? No one had that kind of stamina. Yet, the other characters were real ancient Egyptians, even if those jackal-headed monsters who adorned many tomb walls had been priests in masks. And the other unbelievable events, like living statues? Maybe in a time before science, they had referred to the unknown as magic and embellished it. Heb had been freaking out in the temple, and imagination is more powerful than reality.

My eyes closed, visions from the journal running through my mind like nightmares.

A light burst into my room. Someone had opened the door. Whoever it was shut it quietly and crept toward me. Feeling for the steel flashlight I kept beside my bed, my fingers grasped only carpet. The figure stepped up beside me. My heart raced in fear. Who was it, and what did they want? Cold metal brushed my pinky. Snatching the flashlight, I clicked it on.

Chapter 37

Present Day

SQUINTING UNDER MY flashlight beam, Kaylin held up a hand to block the light. A pink stretch top and blue shorts hugged her curves, leaving most of her skin exposed. My heart fluttered with curiosity. Had she snuck into my hotel room to see me or to search my stuff?

"Turn the light off!" Kaylin said, waving.

Clicking the button off, I set the flashlight down. Artificial light snuck through the slits in the curtains. "What're you doing?" I asked, straining to see.

"I want to know what you guys *really* found," she said. "I'm not waiting 'til morning, or until we ditch Paul and Jenkins."

Paul? Oh, Mr. Scalone. "Maybe we should get Maddie," I said, sitting up.

Kaylin placed a tender hand on my arm, her proximity and flowery perfume teasing my senses. "Maddie was frantic. She needs sleep." She ran her warm fingers up to my shoulder, and my body tingled. "The Hall of Records will be one of the grandest discoveries in history. Its ancient riches could make King Tut's tomb look like a servant's grave. This is our Atlantis!" Eyeing me in the gloom, she ran her tongue across her lips. "Gavin, I never saw what I see in you now. I didn't think you'd become so significant; you were just one of the guys ..."

Suspicion tightened my throat. What was she doing? Kaylin dated star athletes or rich guys with flashy cars, even if they had no other redeeming qualities or hope for a career beyond school. Why—

Her fingers stroked my chest. "I-I," I stuttered, grabbing my bag. I'd have to show her eventually anyway. "We found a body, the lost tomb of Amenhotep the first, and this." I eased the journal from my bag.

"What is it?" she asked, her voice airy as she reached out.

Yanking it back, I said, "The student's journal. No clues, but he may've translated a story from another lost tomb … possibly from the Hall."

"I hope there's more in the Hall than a story," she said. "He didn't have any treasure on him?"

I ran a hand across the journal's rough cover. Life stories were preserved in this treasure. But I shook my head. "Like everything else, the Hall may've been raided in antiquity."

"But legend says it was hidden so well it's been lost since being sealed shut," she said, her lower lip protruding. "Damn it. I wanted a sample of the wonders waiting for us." She gazed off into the shadows. "How'd you get Dr. Shelsher's letter, anyway?"

"I …" Had my dad received it from my great-great-grandpa? It didn't matter now. I'd experienced my alternate path, thanks to him. And it wasn't what I'd hoped for. Now I could finally grow up and put these crazy dreams to rest. I needed to get home, grind through medical school, and put my past behind me. Once I was a doctor, my life would be better. Unfortunately, the hospital environment didn't fill me with drive or satisfaction; it induced stress and anxiety. I worried about the one thing such a career was supposed to guarantee, a *happy* future.

Tender fingers caressed my scalp, tugging my short hair. "How?"

"Someone sent it to me," I said, trying to suppress desire. Would she want me if Maddie didn't? Kaylin was more stereotypically attractive.

"Like, why would someone mail you a letter about one of the best-kept secrets in history?"

"I think it was my dad. But dangerous people are involved, and we don't even know who they are or what they want. Plus, we don't have any other clues. You don't know what Maddie and I went through … and I thought medical school was tough. Maddie and I are going home."

"Gavin," Kaylin said in a sultry tone, lingering over my name as she ran her tongue across her upper teeth. Climbing onto my bed, she leaned her chest closer.

Blood flushed into my face. I wanted to touch her but leaned back.

"Do you know how rich and famous we'd be if we accomplished this?" The glow in her eyes stood out like mirrors against the twinkling darkness.

"It'd take over a week to skim this journal and all the hieroglyphs we found. I have to be back to school before then." I swallowed in apprehension, my gaze drifting over her curves. Did I really want her? Blinking rapidly, I took a couple of breaths. "The professor hid his discovery and didn't want anyone to know he'd found it until he was ready. Maybe someone was trying to kill him. And maybe they succeeded."

Kaylin groaned, and her shoulders slumped, which pulled her chest away. "How about we stay here where it's safe and go over everything?"

"Sorry," I said. "If we eventually discover something, we can petition the government and come back, when I'm done with school."

"If you stay, I'll make it worth it for you," she whispered in my ear, her lips lingering. My insides ached as I turned to her. She slipped away. "Goodnight, Gavin."

"Night," I said, watching the door close. My body, now limp from conflicting hormones and tension, flopped back onto the mattress. What the hell had just happened?

After tossing and turning, I downed two prescription sleeping pills. My gastrointestinal disease could keep me up at night writhing in pain, and immunosuppressive medications turned me into an insomniac. My eyes fluttered. The door opened again, a thin light slanting in. Seriously? *What the hell, Kaylin?* Was I dreaming? No, I was far too exhausted to be asleep.

"Gavin?" A shorter figure tiptoed inside, dressed in only undergarments. "Gavin!"

I bolted upright. "Maddie?"

"I can't sleep. All I see are evil men, and I feel claustrophobic, like I'm trapped in the tomb without a flashlight." Sniffing, she fought back tears.

"I'm sorry," I said, dizzy from the medication.

"Can I lie down with you?" Her apprehensive voice barely cleared a whisper.

My heart raced with excitement. Yes! Oh my god, this had to be a dream. "Y-yes." I cleared my throat after it cracked. "I couldn't sleep, either."

She slid into bed beside me, her warm body rustling the covers. Soft hair nestled against my neck as she curled into me. I couldn't move, my breaths coming in gulps. *What do I do now?* Comfort her? Did she want more? Maddie preferred a different type of guy than Kaylin but only dated the same two or three egotistical muscle men from her hometown. Did their confidence convince her subconscious instincts they'd be successful, even if it wasn't true? Since I wasn't born with boldness or arrogance, could I fake—

Her breathing turned steady and shallow. *You idiot. You missed your chance. She's tired, and she doesn't want you, anyway.*

She stretched, and her toes brushed my leg. My heart jumped. Was that a hint? Or did she still only want to be friends? But if she wanted more and I didn't do anything … that would be terrible, although the former would be pretty horrendous too.

Reaching out, I settled a hand on her silky hair. She scooted closer, her warm breath tickling the sparse hair on my chest. My head swooned. Breathing her in, I ran a hand down her hair and tucked it behind an ear. She didn't move. What now? Sliding my fingers down her cheek and under her chin, I applied gentle pressure to lift her lips to mine. She barely groaned. Was that a yes? Pursing my lips, I kissed hers. Soft and plump.

She pushed away. "What're you doing?"

My heart stopped, my blood turning thick with embarrassment. I couldn't speak. Should I play it off as an accident?

The lamp at the bedside table clicked on, blinding me. "What the hell was that?" Maddie asked. "Were you trying to make out with me? After all our trauma? I just wanted someone to help me sleep."

My heart collapsed like a sinking vessel. I jumped back, my face burning. Maddie sat exposed in a baby blue bra and panties. "I-I was just trying to get comfortable."

"By trying to kiss me?"

My eyes closed. Damn it, epic fail. Standing in my boxer briefs, I covered myself with a pillow and headed for the door.

"Where're you going?" Maddie asked. "You don't have to leave."

"I'm sorry," I said. "I didn't know."

"Didn't know what? That trying to kiss me an hour after I came in and finally fell asleep would be a problem?"

I clutched the pillow tight, a hollow feeling of worthlessness filling my stomach. I darted out of the bedroom and shut the door. Seriously? She of all people comes into my room wearing next to nothing, curls up in bed with me, and gets mad when I try to kiss her? I never knew what to do with her. Never the right time, the right place, or the right guy. Hell with it. Anger rose inside my chest, spreading over my face. But I did get to see her in her underwear.

I swung the door back open. Maddie's head lifted from her hands, her eyes popping wide.

"One last thing," I said, indulging on her curves. "There's nothing else really, I just wanted to see you in your panties again." Slamming the door closed, I wandered, looking for another bed.

Chapter 38

Present Day

I DREAMT OF FRIENDS I'D never met, and of a city whose white walls towered over the countryside.

A scream jolted me into awareness. Maddie burst into my hotel room. Actually it was her room, since we'd traded places last night after our awkward encounter. Springing up in bed, I clutched the covers to me. I'd left my clothes behind. Embarrassment over our most recent interaction ignited my cheeks like red-hot coals.

"Relax, I'm not here to check you out," she said, her high-pitched tone piquing my interest. She was already dressed in black yoga pants and a blue top. "I found something in Dr. Shelsher's letter referencing time." Her eyes wandered behind her sheer glasses, as if in thought.

"Time's important when you're looking so far into the past."

She hushed me with a finger to my lips. "I was holding the professor's timepiece when I read the sentence about tracking modern time."

"You mean the mummified student's timepiece," I corrected her.

She shook her head. "This is Dr. Shelsher's. His initials are engraved in it."

Kaylin appeared in pink sleepwear, followed by her brother.

"Bro, why's Maddie screamin'?" Aiden asked, rubbing his eyes and yawning.

Maddie motioned for them to come in. Great, now they could all see me trying to hide my pale body.

Aiden's little fox leapt onto my bed, and I grunted in surprise. Already spoiled. Good for him. He probably needed to make up for lost—

"Look," Maddie said, holding out a piece of silver and a magnifying glass. "There're inscriptions inside."

I twisted my neck to see the Egyptian hieroglyphs that appeared to be etched into the opened backside of the timepiece. Their minute size forced me to focus. A bird—no, a swallow—referencing stars in the Old Kingdom or the dead in the New Kingdom. A man with a finger to his mouth. To be quiet? No, that was what Egyptologists used to think. This signified a child, and the boy parts were included. A circle within a circle lay nearby, but vertical lines were placed between the images. The biggest obstacle in interpreting hieroglyphs was the style of the writer. The images could be read in accordance with the ancient sounds they evoked or with their symbolic representations, and this could change drastically, depending on what symbols were grouped together.

"What do they say?" Aiden yelled, his eyes bugging out of his head.

Kaylin leaned over to see through the magnifying glass. Mr. Scalone and Jenkins appeared in the doorway.

I stroked the fox's soft head, trying to concentrate. "I discovered the—"

"*I* found the path," Maddie said. "His letter mentioned a map drawn by the ancients who hid the Hall of Records! They left a trail for others who were worthy, or for when the kingdom needed guidance in times of grave crises."

"The path begins with the Son of Sety I," I said, guessing the meaning of the remaining images. A rush of excitement made my head feel light. So a clue wasn't hidden as part of Amenhotep's tomb, but with the student trapped inside.

"The Rameseum!" Kaylin shouted, clapping.

My forehead knotted in confusion. She must've been reading about ancient Egypt over the past week.

"I don't think so," Maddie said, her shiny hair bouncing as she paced the room. "Rameses II was the son of Sety I, but he built and usurped more monuments than any pharaoh of ancient Egypt. Even if he doesn't have an enormous pyramid, there're nearly a hundred shrines and monuments to choose from. The Rameseum seems too obvious for something to have been hidden from archaeologists for centuries."

"The Rameseum's the most famous of all Rameses the Great's monuments," I said.

Wrinkling her nose, Maddie shook her head. "It's not that I just don't want to go back to Luxor …"

I scrutinized the remainder of the tiny hieroglyphs. "You've translated everything?"

"Yes," Maddie said. "The rest says, 'From the boy's discovery … bring the sunlight.' I think it might have to do with Rameses being appointed as the prince regent at fourteen and becoming pharaoh as a teenager. I'll have to perform a search of the temples that were constructed when he was younger. The sun's everywhere in ancient Egypt, so I'm not sure that helps."

"What about Tut?" Aiden asked. "The dude was the boy-king."

Something tucked away in my memory unlocked. Tut, a boy, Rameses, Sety I, Rameses II—the longest line of pharaohs shared the name Rameses.

"You're right, Aiden," Maddie said, "but he came before any Rameses and was disgraced by the early Egyptians."

Utilizing the flat bill of his cap, the manufacturer sticker still in place, Aiden scratched his head in confusion.

"The discovery of his nearly intact tomb made him famous," Maddie said, "but he didn't rule for very long. And the reason his tomb was never discovered or raided earlier was because the Egyptians erased him from their records. So years later, no one knew where to look for his loot. Funny now, because trying to erase him made him the most famous pharaoh of our time."

"Why'd they erase the little dude?" Aiden's lips gaped open, as if he were personally insulted.

"It's a long story filled with mystery, death, and scandal," Maddie said. "And it all started with a pharaoh named Akhenaten …"

I touched the cold metal bracelet on my arm, the servant boy from the journal's story popping into my mind. An outcast of society, like me with the university. He'd had his father's bracelet, too. And the mysterious death of his father had sent him on an adventure, following a trail of evidence. A dark thought settled in, one I'd buried and locked up, one I'd not even told my closest friends. The boy's father could've lost his *ba* with the burning of his body. But what about my dad? I told everyone he'd died of complications from his gastrointestinal disease, which was mostly true, but the final dowsing of his flame had come from his own hand. Current religions said such an act would send someone to hell. If I found the Hall, could I save his soul?

But so many temples were linked to Rameses II. Which one had to do with a boy? And what about the sunlight the clue mentioned … A boy had discovered a temple that displays a light and shadow spectacle twice a year.

"Aswan!" I said. "You can give a history lesson on King Tut later. This has nothing to do with him." Leaping out of bed, I covered myself but stopped before the toned and tattooed tour guide. I didn't like him, but maybe he could get things moving. "Get us to Aswan."

Staring me down, Mr. Scalone folded his thick arms. "We could already be there if you weren't keeping things from me."

Kaylin smacked him on the shoulder and smirked. "Make the arrangements!"

Mr. Scalone walked with a swagger back to his room. Darting into mine, I dressed in khakis and a blue, button-down shirt.

"I know you like to leave people in suspense, but you need to tell me now!" Maddie said from the doorway, daggers not veiled behind those thin lenses. "I told you about the timepiece as soon as … well, as soon as I was certain it was real."

I smiled, unable to control my excitement. "Legend says a local boy discovered one of the most famous temples of Rameses II. He saw it when shifting winds scattered the sand and revealed millennia-old statues. The explorers later credited with the find were led there by the boy, whose name was—"

"Abu Simbel," Maddie said, nodding and brushing her hair back as Kaylin entered. "Now the name of the temple. But it's much farther away than many of Rameses' other monuments."

"I read that Cairo's close to ancient Memphis," Kaylin said. "Maybe we should stop by some of Rameses' ruins there and look for images of a boy in the sun."

"We don't have time," I said.

"Because of the thugs who trapped you?" Aiden asked, picking up his pet.

"No," I said. "We don't have time because of the solar phenomenon inside the temple."

"The light!" Maddie gasped, covering her gaping mouth.

I nodded. "What's the date?"

Jenkins pulled back the sleeve of his suit jacket, revealing a silver watch on his thick, dark wrist. "October twentieth."

"Oh my god!" I said. "I think it's the twenty-first when the temple receives the light."

"And February twenty-first," Maddie said. "The mighty king's birthday and his coronation day. The only two days his statues see the sunlight all year." Pausing, she took a long breath and swallowed. "Maybe we should wait four months and come back, when it's safe."

"How could ancient people without technology make a stone temple work like that?" Aiden asked, his red eyebrows peaking onto his pale forehead. "You know, with the sun going up and down the same everyday?"

Anyone without knowledge of ancient Egyptian culture would have a hard time comprehending the notion, like the building of the pyramids themselves. Current society probably thought we were vastly superior in our understanding of the universe compared to past civilizations. But still, I agreed it must've taken tons of planning to only allow light to enter two specific days a year while shielding it all of the others, when the sun's daily change in position was minimal.

Lifting my hands, I shrugged. "All I can say is that they worshipped the sun as a god and tracked its annual trajectory using scientific methods. Even if they didn't know where the sun went at night, they knew the times of sunrise and sunset and where it would be every day of the year—just like scientists today."

Mr. Scalone emerged from his room, running a hand through his gelled locks. "Booked us a flight to Aswan. We should make Abu Simbel tonight or early *domani*."

"Let's go!" Kaylin said, running out. Mr. Scalone studied her tiny, pink shorts from behind. Aiden caught the man gawking and made a vomit sound while sticking his tongue out.

We'd better not miss tomorrow morning's sunlight.

Maddie's smile disappeared and her hands trembled. "I can't go back there." After standing quietly for a moment, she turned to Mr. Scalone. "Get me a flight home."

Chapter 39

Journal Translation

WHAT WAS GOING ON INSIDE Nefertiti's room? My mind reeled, a bitter twinge arising in my throat. I sat in the sand outside her window, having fallen in shock after peeking inside.

Akhenaten had been sitting with Nefertiti on her bed, both of them naked but in the midst of a heated discussion. Nefertiti's face had darkened in distress, but she hadn't been screaming or fighting—not like the night beside the Nile.

I struggled to catch my breath from the haunting surprise, and the voices inside grew louder.

"I heard something," Akhenaten said.

My pulse quickened. Rays from the Aten streaked across the eastern sky, painting the morning with fire. I ran.

Sunlight cast its magic on the sand. I was about to pull myself into my room, but voices carried out the window. Tensing, I glanced in through a gap in the reed curtain.

Akhenaten stood outside my doorway, conversing with Mudads. Suty stood just behind them. Fear's icy hand ensnared my faltering heart with its stinging cold. My master stepped inside. He had nothing to be afraid of if he knew there wasn't a plague. Pausing, he stared at my crumpled blanket. His sandaled foot extended backwards to kick the pile of reeds!

Croc erupted from beneath the covers and hissed. Launching onto Akhenaten's swinging limb, he clawed and bit flesh before darting out into the hall.

Akhenaten screamed, jumped, and grabbed his toes. "Grab that feral! I am going to skin it!"

Mudads didn't react fast enough to apprehend Croc. Hobbling out into the hall, Akhenaten cursed and flailed his limbs in rage.

Flinging myself in through the window amid the ruckus, I rolled onto my bed. My tumbling flattened the reeds, and I grabbed the edges of the blanket, wrapping it around my shoulders. Standing, I yawned.

Akhenaten returned to the doorway and stared. But someone else was already inside—and had seen my entrance. Mahu's tall figure had been concealed in the far corner. His face appeared orange in the morning light as he glanced to the window and then to me. Leaning over, he inspected my kilt.

"Hopefully you can get a wash soon," the captain said.

I nodded, having forgotten about the stains I'd rubbed into my clothing. My limbs trembled.

"Your vile cat attacked me!" Akhenaten punched his open palm.

"I'm s-so, so sorry, master," I said with a cracking morning voice. "You probably startled him." I held a hand up. "Please, I don't want you to catch the plague."

"I am no longer only your master! I am your majesty, lord, god-king, or Pharaoh, and you will address me as such. I am ruling the country alongside my father, and I am now immortal. A plague cannot rot this flesh!"

My eyes opened wide in feigned shock, the irony not lost on me. If a plague couldn't harm him, how had it killed Thutmose? "My Pharaoh! I am blessed to serve the god-king!"

Akhenaten's twisted visage relaxed. As he rubbed his chin, his nail caught my eye. The notch he'd cut into it had grown out, resembling a sphere between two mountains—the sunrise. "You are *very* lucky. And if the Aten sees you fit to serve, you will be released. The doctor says two more days. These temporary servants are useless. But do not think too highly of yourself. You are nothing other than a glorified slave, and I am training your replacement if need be—the tall, gaunt man who prefers the red eye shadow."

"Thank you! Thank you, my god-king," I said, spilling sincerity.

His thick lips lifted into a smirk as his eyes closed, revealing solid-black lids. "My first order to you as your Pharaoh is to detain the feral when he returns. Then alert the guard to bring Suty. I will give you a better specimen. We cannot have a despicable beast who bites God running about Egypt."

Retaining an emotionless face, I said, "Yes, my Pharaoh. The feral sleeps in my room a couple of nights a week. I will call as soon as I see orange. I'm not too fond of any animal, and I'd prefer a better trained one." Hopefully the lie would buy enough time, and Akhenaten would be removed from his new position.

Mahu's deformed foot shifted as he shook his head at me in warning. My stomach sank.

Winking, Akhenaten whispered, "Someone wanted me to check on you. To make sure you were not sneaking about. I do not think she trusts you."

My jaw dropped. What? She? Nefertiti ... or Mutnedjmet? That little traitor. Because I went to visit her sister without her?

"One other thing," Akhenaten said. "Soon I will take many wives. Most are selected because of their special ... talents. You will not allow these traits to appeal to you. If you are ever caught lusting after one of them, you will be castrated."

Swallowing, I nodded with apprehension.

"Even if one is the most beautiful woman you have ever seen, mysterious or exotic, you will not acknowledge her. They will have their own servants. You will not be punished for ignoring these women, but you will be disobeying me if you do otherwise."

I lowered my gaze in submission. Nefertiti ... no one could be more beautiful than her.

Akhenaten exited, Suty's gigantic form lumbering behind. Mahu's knuckles popped upon his spear shaft, blanching white. Opening his mouth to speak, the captain paused—

My heart fluttered with anxiety. He was going to tell Akhenaten I'd come in through the window!

Pressing his lips together, Mahu departed.

I collapsed onto my bed, the scene of Nefertiti and Akhenaten naked together popping into my head and wrenching my insides. My blood boiled with trapped rage, pity, and burning jealousy. Desiring nothing more in this life than to protect and save her, I yearned to be the man she was intimate with. And I longed to rid everyone of Akhenaten ... forever.

Would Nefertiti visit me? I wished to sit by her side and help her through her pain. But she never showed, grief probably consuming her. I counted down the minutes to sunset. Tonight, I needed to catch Akhenaten in some vicious act. But no one had died last night. Had he finished the slaughter? Or was he not even behind it? Hopefully Mutnedjmet could convince her father and aunt. Pharaoh would listen to Ay and his royal wife, but would he believe something so heinous about his son?

Wailing echoed through the corridor, the uncontrolled moaning of a female. Her shrieks drew near.

I cowered in the corner. Was she coming for me?

The royal guard appeared at my doorway, the crying erupting from behind them.

"Step aside!" a female said, between wails of despair.

The soldiers parted shields and spears. Ay, the handsome father of Nefertiti, stepped forward. Then Beketaten appeared, smirking. A vibrantly redheaded woman in a bejeweled dress followed—the queen of Egypt, Lady Tiye. Tears streamed down her cheeks.

I crawled backward in fear, the blood draining from my face.

"You!" Tiye pointed, her face burning as red as her hair. "Your father spread disease in our palace, and it claimed my son!" Her body broke into throes of sobbing.

I huddled against the wall.

Veins popped out on Tiye's neck, and she clenched her fists as she stood over me. "My beloved Thutmose is gone! The next god-king of Egypt is dead! We're all doomed!" Her hands shot up into the air as she dropped to her knees. "Your father will be burned today, and so will you if you so much as sneeze!"

My chest spasmed. Thrusting my palms outward, I begged. "No! Please don't burn him. It wasn't a disease!" Should I mention her other wicked son? No, she wouldn't take that well, not from me. And if I told her I'd inspected Thutmose's body, my fate would be sealed.

"Listen, servant boy!" Ay said, rising up beside the queen while thrusting a finger at me. "I am Nefertiti and Mutnedjmet's father." His nostrils flared under the black wig and thin orange eye paint. My heart sank. If there ever was a man I'd want to impress, it'd be him. But I didn't have a good feeling about our first official interaction. "Stay away from my daughters! If either of them catch your disease, I'll make sure you suffer much—"

"They visited me!" I blurted under the tension. "But they remained safely outside my door." I pointed to Beketaten, who hid behind the queen. "I had no option but to listen. I couldn't leave! But please, before you make a final decision about my father …" I took a deep breath. "If you could find it in your heart, my beloved queen, have Mutnedjmet, the doctor, and magician all provide counsel to Pharaoh, as some are suspicious the deaths weren't the result of a plague."

Queen Tiye's fists fell open. "You will not advise me!" Grabbing Beketaten's arm, she spun around and marched away.

"Ouch!" Beketaten said, attempting to keep up with her mother. "Come to think of it, Thutmose was here with us the other day."

Tiye froze in her tracks, the royal guard nearly running into her.

My eyes closed, my pulse hammering in my ears.

"No one visits this boy!" the queen screeched, an inferno in her eyes. "Burn him!"

My breath ran thin as panic set in. I wanted to yell my accusations, but she'd never believe me. There was absolutely nothing I could do. I sprawled out onto the cold floor.

"You've been cursed," Mudads said in a slow drawl as he shook his head. Leveling his spear, he motioned with the glistening bronze tip. "I don't want to skewer you, boy, but I'd prefer that to touching you. You'd better come along."

"Where're we going?" My lower lip quivered as my fingers clenched my bracelet.

"I'm taking you to your father."

Chapter 40

Journal Translation

I STOOD BARE-CHESTED UNDER THE blazing light of the Aten. Guards held spears around me, aimed at my torso. Suty doused me in lamp oil. Thick liquid rolled over my hair and skin like marsh water, making me gag. A growling wind blew heat into my ears, deafening my tired, trembling body. Father's corpse lay upon a platform behind me, shrouded in oil-laden blankets. Watching, the royal family and council members gossiped amongst themselves.

"See you in the underworld," Suty said.

Terror, rage, and disbelief burned inside me like the afternoon sun.

"No," he said, "you won't be there if you're burned!" His pig-ear twitched up and down as he laughed. The crackle of an inferno blasted behind me. Father's body shot up like a bonfire. Screaming, I barely noticed the blazing torch in the approaching ogre's hand.

The magician and doctor shouted at each other, then yelled at Akhenaten, Tiye, Ay, and the detached Pharaoh. Heat from the flames soaked through the oil on my cheek. Swooning, I nearly passed out. Mutnedjmet screamed and hurled a rock at Suty.

Mahu realigned his spear and advanced, backing Suty away from me as more people bellowed amidst the rising fury. Guards grabbed me, dragging me away.

Taking me to a dark cave in a nearby hillside, they tossed me inside and slammed an outer door shut with an echoing boom. Darkness. But before the light disappeared, it'd looked as if they'd thrown me into a small room in a cavern, alone. Was this a prison of some sort? I curled up, unable to process the burning and what that meant for Father's soul. Could a burned man's *ba* be saved and be reborn in the underworld, as long as the Devouring Monster hadn't eaten his heart?

Screeches from people being held in the darkness, probably inside different cells or caverns, reverberated around me. But covering my ears didn't blot out the stinging stench of urine and human waste.

Consciousness faded, and my vision went black as I passed out.

I stood silently amidst a group of children, in the company of a recently deceased man. A priest motioned with a sword, and we all watched. Before him, a brown bull chomped absently on its cud, unaware of what fate held in store. Perhaps if I were the unsuspecting beast, I'd be less fearful in life.

With a swift stroke, the priest severed the forelimb from the animal, and it collapsed. Two others grabbed the dismembered limb and shoved it against the dead man's face. Blood spewed. The bull bellowed as the priest ended its suffering with a quick cut across the neck.

I screamed, and my tears fell. Laughing, the other children shoved me out from the group. I knew the power the beast transferred to the dead would assist him in the underworld, but my emotions were so strong I couldn't reason it out. Taunting followed. Then the fists and feet of the other children beat me. I curled into a trembling—

A door slammed shut, waking me from this nightmare I'd had over and over again as a child. Drifting through the darkness, a flame floated along with the echo of stomping feet. Lamplight reflected off of a nightmarish face—a tangle of black lines ensnaring a wrinkled countenance. I'd seen this face when marching through Memphis, before the cursed voyage. Perhaps the very first time after rescuing Croc ... the magician! Blue cat eyes peered from atop his shoulder. Gasping, I scooted away.

"Why did you not help me ... or my father?" I asked, my nerves returning and shaking my body.

"Keep quiet," the son of Hapu said. "I convinced them to keep you alive through fear alone. I asked them, 'If God is angry and punishing the boy for something and he is burned, who will be tormented next?' I also promised to study the plague's effects on you. If one person could be an unaffected carrier, then perhaps those stricken could be cured. I especially want to know the first symptoms of this disease. It seems to spring on its victims and kill within hours. Doesn't really sound like a plague ..."

"What do you think it is?" I asked.

Rolling me over with a bony foot, he wrote feverishly and prodded every inch of my body. The white cat leapt from his shoulder and sniffed my feet, its belly dragging the floor. "I must move quickly. The priests of Memphis have systematically gone missing, as well as any with knowledge of magic. This hasn't only affected your father and Thutmose, as we've been told. I'm afraid for my own soul. As soon as I figure out what madness is at work, I'll attempt to remedy the situation. Do you understand?"

"No! I need your help to save my father's soul!"

"I only speak to you for a reason you may not yet understand. But be cautious with whom you associate and what you say. I am wary of many people. I'll see what I can do without stepping in, but I will not be able to assist at all if I'm permanently removed."

Confusion clouded my thoughts. Could I believe anything this strange man said?

Waving a hand over me, he said, "I will visit the slums of Memphis and a man of magic. Several mysterious deaths have occurred there. Pentju will visit you and may have something else in mind."

What did that mean?

The door creaked inward and daylight burst into the cave. The magician faded into the shadows around me, along with the flame of his lamp.

Almost screaming in surprise, I clamped a hand over my mouth. Where had he gone? Could the son of Hapu turn invisible? No, no one could do that. He must've slipped into the shadows ...

Pentju entered, holding a blue statuette in front of him, his cheeks glistening with sweat. Mudads, Mahu, and a third guard followed, their spears trained on me. I remained paralyzed by fright. What did they want?

Mudads and the third soldier pinned me down. My muscles strained in resistance.

"Be careful with him," Mahu said, lowering his spear and shifting his weight off of his scarred leg. "The boy's been through a lot."

"Hold him tight," Pentju said, his sunken eyes burning. "We're all being protected, but the less time we spend with him the better." He cleared his throat, and his voice softened. "Boy, you're alive because I convinced Pharaoh and Akhenaten that we should study you."

My head throbbed. Hadn't the magician just told me the same thing?

Producing a short-bladed knife, Pentju said, "If you hold still, this will be over quickly."

"What're you going to do?" I asked in a high-pitched tone, trying to scoot away.

The guards held me fast. Leaning over, Pentju sawed off my sidelock and placed the hair inside a sack. The soldiers dragged me into the light streaming through the doorway, and the doctor moved to my toes. Jamming the knife under a toenail, he pried it up. I squealed like a pig in surprise and blinding pain, thrashing wildly.

Mahu jumped on me, aiding with my restraint. My head turned foggy, the ground tilted, and the sun's rays bent. Pentju collected the nail and a blood sample from my hemorrhaging toe before cinching a tourniquet down on the digit and applying a quick bandage. "Mudads, make sure he takes his medicine." He dropped a handful of something into the guard's open palm, and they exited.

The door swung shut, leaving me in utter blackness. Wails of despair and anguish carried through the walls. Shivering in pain and horror, I embraced my own body and wept.

Hours later, the door creaked opened again. Mudads stepped inside, holding a jar. He reached out, and I scuttled against the far wall.

"Just here to give you medicine," he said with a drawl, his gangly limbs shoving a jug of water in front of me. "Open up."

Suspicion clamped my mouth shut. I wasn't sick. Why did I need medicine?

With one hand under my jaw, Mudads squeezed my face so hard my teeth bit into my cheeks. I winced and he dumped a burning drink down my throat and over my face. It tasted of dirt and sour herbs. I swallowed, choked, and coughed.

"My apologies," Mudads said, rubbing his potbelly. "Got to get the job done. Got a wife and six children I need rations for."

Curling up against the wall, I sputtered, and he turned away.

"They say if you don't show signs and no one else in here or in the palace comes down with plague, we can let you out. Things won't be this bad for too long." The door clanged shut.

I caught my breath as rage built inside me, twisting my guts. Hunching over, I spat in defiance. Everything I did was wrong and my world kept falling apart, no matter how hard I tried to hold it together. Something black stirred in my soul, along with the loss of hope.

My vision grew used to the darkness. I imagined myself jumping up, ripping open the door, and grabbing Mudads' spear. Driving him into this cell with his own weapon, I'd smile. Then I'd hunt down the doctor and peel off his toenails. The magician I'd trick with lies and deceit before I took everything from him. For Suty ... I'd have to incapacitate him first by binding his arms and legs while he slept. Then I'd casually walk around his bed, pouring oil as he lay there watching. Lighting a torch in front of him, I'd wave it before his eyes. When he begged for mercy, I'd let the torch fall. Then I'd go straight for my master. For him I'd save the most horrendous punishment—I'd need more time to conceive something fitting.

Darkness and shadows intertwined in my soul. Images of green-eyed beings floating amidst a fog returned. I shook my head.

My stomach wrenched inside itself, and I coughed, spitting a trickle of blood onto the floor. But how could I ever take revenge? I was powerless and a weakling. And my master had arisen from death already, unscathed, immortal. I would have to trick them all ... somehow.

Crumpling onto the floor, I cried with my head in my hands. "Why?" I howled.

"There is no why in this place," a crackly voice echoed out of the black before growling like a beast from Nubia.

Chapter 41

Journal Translation

I RECOILED IN FEAR OF THE VOICE within the darkness of the cave prison.

Another prisoner? But a few minutes of silence followed, and my panic subsided. I beat my fists against the wall. "I didn't do any of it!"

"If he really did it, he wouldn't be *here*," a hollow voice called back, followed by a burst of hysterical giggling from a young girl. "There're many other prisons."

Fright drove me to press my back against a cold rock wall. How many others shared these cells—and my fate? "Who's in here?" I asked.

"To whom does it matter?"

"What? What're you in here for?" I asked.

"Nothing! Just like you," a voice said cheerfully. The giggling of the young girl rose and fell, as if she were running back and forth on the other side of a wall.

Reaching out, I felt along the jagged wall, which ran to the ceiling. How could I hear them? Locating a crevice, I tried to peek through, but the room on the other side remained suffocated in similar darkness. The reek of urine stung my nose like a slap to the face. Grimacing in disgust, I pinched my nostrils. I slid my fingers through the opening. Touching the surface on the other side of the wall, I felt around. Something sharp bit down on the tip of my finger. Stinging pain! Yowling, I yanked my hand back.

"He keeps his hands to himself. He keeps them to himself!" A voice chuckled.

Someone had bitten me! Who were these lunatics? Had I been put next to them to see if they'd contract plague? "Keep the noise down," I said, clutching my finger to my chest.

"He wants it quiet! Oh, but he doesn't know the more you lose, the more that goes. And sight is gone. Yes, already gone. And smell." A man chattered nonsense.

Others chimed in, and they continued for hours. I refused to respond.

✳ ✳ ✳

Days and weeks passed in a blur of darkness and the forced administration of medicines. The crazy people giggled and chided me during my examinations. I grew more ill, and my mind contorted. My eyes darted about as I lunged around my cave stabbing hidden enemies.

"Now he sees. Now he does," the crackly voice said.

I paused, wondering. Could he sense the blackness growing within me? The turbulent thoughts and emotions? "I'll kill *my* enemies, madman," I said.

"He's hateful. Oh, yes. We've been there, haven't we?" the hollow voice said, followed by giggling.

Then the female said, "Yes, I killed them. I killed them all." More giggling.

"Who's his enemies?" the crackly voice shouted into the gap.

I leapt back in alarm. "The evil Suty and Akhenaten."

"Oh! The Aten!"

"No, Akhenaten."

"We were his once. We all were!"

Voices cried in glee as clapping filled the darkness.

"You were Akhenaten's?" I asked.

"Yes, we were! We served him. Until that day."

"You were *all* Akhenaten's servants?" Something buried in the recesses of my mind sprang forth. When I'd entered servitude, Father had told me my predecessor went mad, becoming a liar and a lunatic. People referred to the man's name when someone's mind abandoned their body, or if they ended it all by diving into the Nile. I couldn't recall the name …

"Yes, many years ago. Weren't we?" a voice asked.

"What happened?"

"We heard him say something. Something we never should have! No, no we didn't hear it. Did we? Yes. Yes. No!" Giggling followed. "Couldn't go back after we told Pharaoh."

"What did he say?"

"He spoke to no one about God. He forced something upon us. Something we didn't like. And then we suffered. Suty's a gnat! A gnat!"

The door swung open with a drawn-out creak, sending blinding light in to burn my eyes. Rays of sun flashed through the fissure between the two cells. Overcome by curiosity, I peered through the slit to see the other prisoners. Scraggly tufts of graying hair framed a gaunt face with pale, cloudy eyes. His eyes twitched but didn't focus on me. Jumping back, the old prisoner ran around in a circle while giggling like a girl. He was covered in filth, and his bones protruded under naked skin and absent muscle. No one else was in the cell with him, and there were no other cells connected to his chamber or mine ...

Footsteps settled behind me. Straightening my hunched posture to an upright position, I attempted a semblance of normalcy.

A svelte silhouette limped in. "Heb, I hope you're faring okay, given the circumstances."

Mahu? Sneering like a cornered animal, I held my hands up to block the light.

Mahu, my supposed friend who had abetted my torture, now stood before me.

"I've come of my own volition, to wish you well. You only need another week in here," he said, forcing a smile. "You've almost been cleared and appear healthy in every one of the doctor's tests. No one else in the palace, nor the other man in this prison, has been struck with plague, but in the city ..." His eyes wandered.

Disbelief dropped me to my knees as pity filled my heart. How had this one other prisoner made it seem like he'd been multiple people, and how had he spoken with more than one voice at the same time? Echoes, or magic? Would I become like this prisoner if I stayed in here or let my evil take control?

"But the plague in the city cannot be your fault," Mahu said. "Akhenaten has asked for your return, in stages."

"The Aten! Yes, the Aten!" the madman shrieked next door.

Mahu continued, "He believes you were never the carrier, only your father. And by the grace of God, you escaped its wrath because you are *his* servant."

My thoughts floated through a fog of incomprehension. But the sunlight entranced me, reminding me of life and the others still out there. Croc. Nefertiti!

I lunged at Mahu.

Jumping back, he held up a hand and shook his head. "You can't touch anyone until you're cleared." But he grinned and pointed at my ankle. "The hippo left a big scar, but it healed. And you're agile enough for a servant."

The old wound was rarely on my mind, as it no longer ached. But memories of the trip and of Mahu came flooding back in pictures.

"Do you know how I got mine?" he asked.

I shrugged.

"I mean how I lost half of my foot," he said, pointing to two twisted toes filling only half of his sandal. His horrid scar ran up to his knee. "My father had just left my mother and all my brothers and sisters for another woman. He left us poor and shunned. To spite him, I played down by the shore every day, because he told me never to do so. Running along the bank under the bright sun, I laughed and loathed my father. I started to believe everything he told me was a lie. Cursing him, I ran back and forth through the water. Then something snatched me," he clapped his hands, making me jump, "and sucked me into the depths before I even knew what'd happened. They say crocodiles drag you to the bottom of the river, twisting and rolling to break your bones. Then they hold you down there until you stop kicking."

Shuddering in terror, I settled back to a sitting position.

"The next thing I knew, my brothers carried me back to the house, my foot burning like fire. Blood spewed from my leg, and I passed out. Later they told me a wandering beggar used a magical gesture to ward off the crocodile. The hand signal I showed you. The man then dove in and wrenched my small body from the jaws of the beast. My brothers said after he helped place me on their shoulders, he was gone." He lowered his head, but when he looked up, a full smile covered his face. "We are given our positions in life for a reason. Even those you'd never expect to be able to can perform miracles. You saved Pharaoh himself, after all."

A catharsis unleashed within me, almost sneaking tears past my debilitated mental state, a defense against my intolerable situation. But my bitterness resisted. Pharaoh? Did he mean Akhenaten? Was Mahu supposed to be my friend again? The look on my face must've betrayed my emotions.

"Heb," Mahu said, sighing, "I labor for the good of the crown. I don't want you to suffer." He held out an open palm, and something orange fluttered into the radiant sunlight. "Have you seen the monarch butterfly? They float over the shimmering waters of the river, bringing vibrant colors, beauty, and elegance to our world. But even these creatures begin life as a dark worm. They must transform within a suffocating cocoon before revealing their true magnificence."

Intricately patterned orange, white, and black wings drifted out upon the wind.

"You may arise and become the greatest personal servant of the god-king himself … but only if you choose to. What did your father and mother instill in you?"

"My father is dead," I said. Perhaps my resistance was my mother's fault.

"The dead can still be some of the most important people, and they live on inside us. That is why the underworld and death are so important for life and rebirth."

Picturing Father dead made me suddenly realize that turning back for Akhenaten's body was the mistake the mysterious *ba* had warned me about that desert night.

I would become something, all right. I grinned.

Chapter 42

Journal Translation

THE DOOR TO MY CELL of the cave prison swung open with a loud squeal of metal on metal, and blinding light again washed in. Grimacing, I held an arm over my face.

Mudads, the palace soldier, entered this time. "Here to escort you back to your room. The palace is safe." I no longer had a sidelock of hair for Mudads to pull on, so he grabbed my pale arm and helped me stand.

Shuffling out into daylight, I squeezed my eyes shut. Red rays seeped through my closed eyelids, bringing a blinding sensation.

Giggling from the other cell turned into a pleading wail, echoes thundering inside the cave. "No! Don't leave us with—" The man's voices faded with the slamming of the door. Sympathy tugged at my heart. What would become of him? I could've become him. Was this a warning?

A monarch butterfly thrashed around, ensnared within a web outside the corner of the doorway. Reaching up, I plucked the insect from the sticky strands. Mudads shoved me onward, but I peeled away the webbing. The butterfly flapped its mighty wings upon my open palm. Blowing, I sent the creature flying with the wind and into the blinding light.

"You have to stay confined for a few more days, per Pentju's orders," Mudads drawled, guiding me into my old room. Drawings and wards were partially scrubbed from the walls. "Rest and prepare to serve your master. He's been complaining about the quality of his servants. If I didn't know better, I'd think he might even miss you." Smirking, he stepped out.

I shook my head in disbelief. No wonder I wasn't burned. I understood Akhenaten's needs better than anyone. Perhaps that should be enough for this life. Being good at something, even if I loathed it, would be much easier than my other options.

Over the course of the day, I grew agitated. Memories and emotions returned like fire on the empty desert, and questions piled up. I couldn't lie here waiting, or I'd go mad again. No, I should heed Mahu's advice and become the butterfly.

Sunlight made my head ache but cleared the fog from my mind. Something within me desired the comfort of darkness. As I removed the curtain from my window, a mountainous, dark cloud wavered across the sun. My eyes blurred and my mind drifted ...

> *Father's face appeared in the cloudbank but was veiled in shade. I touched his bracelet, my heart twinging with longing. Rebirth in the underworld would be his only salvation. Light streaked through the circular opening of his eye, sparkling in the wind as it landed upon a bare tree. The tamarisk's bark absorbed the glimmer like shadow.*

The daydream, or whatever it was, faded ...

Rare rain washed over Memphis, clattering on the roofs and bringing a dank chill. The moisture released a pungent tang from dry dirt, adding to the feeling of suffocation.

Croc didn't visit, but he typically only showed up at night. And with the rain he wouldn't want to travel. I couldn't consider the other option. No, he wouldn't have let Akhenaten catch him. Anguish and loneliness crept in as I fought off images of the horrendous possibilities.

Darkness finally fell, but the inconceivable rain in the north this time of year continued. A pebble clattered onto my floor. I glanced about in surprise. Where had that come from? Another landed on my stomach with a faint sting. My eyes were drawn to the open window. Jumping up and catching the sill, I hung for a moment. Silence. I scampered up and peeked out.

The silhouette of a young woman cowered in the rain. "Get out here," she whispered.

Wiggling through the opening, I held on to the window's edge with my feet and walked my hands down the wall. I released my toes, attempting to catch myself as the ground approached. Tumbling, I landed on my back with a splat.

Someone grabbed my shoulder. I nearly screamed, my body trembling after the initial spasm.

"It's me." Torchlight reflected off of Mutnedjmet's drawn face and sopping hair.

"Stop scaring me," I whispered.

"Sorry, did you want me to call out to you? By name, perhaps?" Her quiet voice barely carried through the pattering rain. Something orange and white ... Croc rested in the crook of her arm! "Follow me! I've seen Akhenaten and the cloaked man. They're not the same person. The cloak's headed into the city."

She grabbed me by my arm, and we ran into the night. My sandals and feet grew heavy with caking mud as anxiety set in. What was I doing? Mutnedjmet might have told Akhenaten to come check on me before my confinement. Could she be working with him in his dark plot? Perhaps she desired power, too. If Akhenaten didn't have much to gain by killing Nefertiti, Mutnedjmet sure did. Nefertiti was her older sister, like Thutmose to my master. But what other option did I have to help Father and Nefertiti?

"He carried a jar with some sort of creature inside," she said, "and he held a knife made of gold and bone—unlike anything I've ever seen."

Like the weapon Akhenaten had carried at Thebes ...

Climbing the perimeter wall proved more treacherous in the rain. I slipped twice before ascending and struggled to haul Croc and then Mutnedjmet up.

Pointing to the south, she said, "He was headed that way a few minutes ago."

A hush hovered over the city tonight. As we snuck into the maze, a couple of curious faces peeked through open doorways, but no one stood outside. Had something happened, or was it the weather? And how could the cloaked man not be Akhenaten? Was I so blind in my hatred of my master that I only considered one suspect for this plague?

"Strange things have happened these past weeks," Mutnedjmet said as we hugged the shadows of a street. "I've been watching Akhenaten, but he's always busy and is surrounded by people." Extending her arms, she handed over my cat. "And Croc's been following me everywhere. I've had to hide him."

Burying my face in my best friend's warm fur, I squeezed. He meowed and leapt away. "Did you convince Pharaoh of Akhenaten's treachery?" I asked.

"Every day I tried to persuade Father and Aunt Tiye to talk to Pharaoh about it," Mutnedjmet said, hanging her head. "The queen said she couldn't deal with my antics, not after the death of Thutmose. Pharaoh is no longer lucid and won't get out of bed, but the doctor says he has no signs of plague. I don't know if he's overcome with pain from the loss of his son, or if Akhenaten did something to him. But if so, why would Akhenaten keep him around at all?"

I'd already pondered this during confinement. "Perhaps there're too many guards around Pharaoh, or Akhenaten wants a time of co-regency. He probably needs to learn a few things and be accepted by the people. If there isn't a smooth transition, his power may be questioned. It should've been Thutmose, and everyone knows it. Akhenaten pales in comparison."

"Sounds reasonable," she said, dodging a street-swallowing puddle.

"I can't go back to serving the murderer of my father and abuser of Nefertiti …" My fists tremored with anger. "We need to help her." Unable to hold back emotion any longer, tears brimmed in my eyes. But I masked my weakness by looking up into the rain.

Mutnedjmet placed her hand on mine, and lines dug into her soft forehead. "I'll help any way I can."

I wanted to believe her. Her touch comforted me, but there were so many unknowns …

A cloaked form faded from the lamplight directly ahead, his back to us. After pausing with uncertainty, we maneuvered around the flame's conspicuity and trailed the dark figure at a distance. We ventured deep into the bowels of the city, water pelting our backs. Collapsing mud-brick houses lined the streets ahead. Two men wobbled along in opposing directions, apparently unaware of us. One of these drunken men muttered slurred words to an unseen comrade while the other yelled into the night. The crying of babies carried out one window and mingled with the bellowing laughter of people across the street. A couple huddled together against a dilapidated house, trying to find shelter. The woman fell into a fit of coughing.

Apprehension quickened my pulse. I'd never seen this district but knew we walked through the slums of Memphis.

The cloaked figure stopped suddenly and staggered beneath a crumbling doorway—to enter a small house.

Skirting around two drunken men, we raced to the entrance. Mutnedjmet leaned around the corner, peeking inside.

"Be careful," I whispered and jumped for the window of the structure, peering over the sill.

Inside, our suspect crouched, and an eerie green light glowed from within his robes. An elderly man and woman lay together on a bed of reeds, both asleep. The cloak opened like wings of a great bird. I froze in awestruck terror.

Chapter 43

Journal Translation

FROM OUR HIDING SPOTS, Mutnedjmet and I watched the scene within the dilapidated house.

The suspect wearing the black cloak—with a hood so long it carried outward from his face—remained concealed, but a diminutive form danced its way out from beneath the folds of his disguise, into the inner chamber.

Was this thing a summoned demon or the carrier of the plague? It was too big to be a … wait, it was a very large scorpion! The biggest scorpion I'd ever seen, stretching the length of a man's foot. Its tail extended and retracted in a devilish dance. Whirling about in a frenzy, it lowered its head and elevated its rear end while its legs spiked into the air in alternating form.

The hooded man chanted and shook something around the room—and over the sleeping couple. Pulling out a sack, he dumped out the contents. Tangled serpents slithered, a mass of black and red scales. They hissed, their lengths separating into five distinct snakes. The resting occupants still didn't stir. My terror amplified. Flashes of white darted up the jerking scorpion's back. It was giving birth to live babies! The young arachnids twisted and squirmed beneath the mother's protective tail, like eight-legged maggots. Prickling arose on the back of my neck as if bugs crawled on me. I shuddered in disgust. Mutnedjmet clasped a hand over her mouth to stifle a scream as she fell to her rear.

The sleeping woman rolled over in bed, and the cloaked man recited arcane language while drawing symbols in the air with hands hidden by his cloak. Incomprehensible words and intonations rose and fell. Fifteen or twenty scorpion offspring writhed on top of their mother and started to transform. Growing, they altered color from white to desert sand before developing a soft red hue, like the fading light of the Aten. They crowded each other out and spilled onto the floor as they aged weeks in a matter of seconds.

Scurrying about with a strange crackling sound, the scorpions faced the sleeping pair. The cloaked figure's hissing voice rose to a crescendo.

Either the inhabitants couldn't hear, or they lay paralyzed. The serpents advanced.

The sleeping man and woman's eyes shot open, horror sinking into their expressions. The woman's lips parted but only muffled groans escaped, like someone trying to yell under water. Blood flowed from the man's mouth, his jaw clenched. My face turned numb with disbelief, and my stomach boiled with rage as I imagined my own father. I wouldn't be able to stop this attack and survive, but I needed to see the conjurer's face.

Descending upon the prone couple with lashing tails and piercing fangs, scorpions and serpents covered them like hornets. The room fell silent. Uttering a short phrase, the cloaked figure commanded the swarm to scuttle to the doorway. With the mother leading the way, the arachnids scaled the wall.

The moisture drained from my mouth as my fingers trembled with fright. Was this the son of Hapu? The clicking of insect legs inched closer. I wanted to see the magician's face but couldn't. "Hide!" I said, dropping from the windowsill to the ground outside the house.

Already running into the shadows of an adjacent house, Mutnedjmet flattened her body against a wall. I followed.

Watching the residence of the murdered, Croc sat and licked his paws in the middle of the street.

Why would the cloaked man want to kill this couple in the slums?

Scorpions clattered out into the night, followed by serpents. Then a dark figure emerged, holding a walking stick. Something bulged beneath his cloak. After scouting up the street, his attention shifted toward us.

We swung around to the backside of the house and hunched down. The wind died, and the stubble on my arms stood straight up like a defeathered bird. I held my breath. But curiosity burned in my mind. I should take a peek and—

The cloak rustled past, not ten feet away. The air grew hot, and the reek of death floated by. Crunching from his nearby footsteps caused my throat to squeeze shut with panic.

He paused. My eyes locked on him. His head turned …

Then, sniffing, he paced off and disappeared into the falling rain. The insects scattered, but an eerie chanting arose from the shadows. Re-forming into a pack, the scorpions crackled through a doorway to another house across the street. Silence.

My heart raced as I turned to Mutnedjmet. "What should we do?"

"I-I don't know," she stuttered. "But we need to see who he is …"

I stepped from the shadows, in pursuit.

"What're you doing out here?" someone asked.

Mutnedjmet gasped as I spun around, crouching. Elegant features stood out from the slum's shadows like the glistening Nile on the desert. A rain-soaked dress clung to a shapely body. Nefertiti!

"I knew you were up to something, Sister," Nefertiti said as she planted her hands on her hips. "I had to spy on you to see what kind of trouble you were getting into. And I find you with Heb, in the slums!" Green eye paint ran down her cheeks in streams.

"Did you see the cloaked man?" Mutnedjmet asked. "The scorpions and—"

"Heb, Mutnedjmet's been completely out of sorts," Nefertiti said, glaring. "She sleeps during the day and has been spinning all sorts of crazy stories. She has a long history of starting drama with fiction."

"This is real!" Mutnedjmet said, stomping her foot.

"Like when you saw crocodiles walk upright out of the Nile and attack people?" Nefertiti asked.

"I told that story when I was a child." Mutnedjmet grabbed a lock of her hair and started strumming it.

"That was about a year ago," Nefertiti said. "And Heb, what are *you* doing out here with my sister? Shouldn't you be in isolation?"

My face flushed as guilt rose inside me. I wanted to tell my love everything, but what if she didn't believe me? "My father was murdered. And a hooded man is coming and going from the palace at night. We tracked him here and saw him use snakes and scorpions to kill people. We suspect he is the cause of the so-called plague."

Nefertiti's arms fell slack at her side. "Who is it?"

"Akhenaten," Mutnedjmet said. "Or at least he's behind it."

"The hooded man wielded magic!" I said. "We were following him."

Wheels spun behind Nefertiti's eyes. "If all three of us unmask this hooded man, then people will believe it when we tell them who he is and what he's done."

I nodded and waved them on.

"But," Nefertiti said, holding up a hand, "we need to get you back to your room before dawn. I don't know if you're contagious, and I hope you're telling the truth, but you're just a servant and can be executed before we know the facts."

I swallowed in fear. "The scorpion pack went into that house." I pointed down the street. "The cloaked man disappeared in the same direction, but I didn't see him go inside."

"I don't think we can overpower such a man," Nefertiti said. "Let's just try to prove this is not a plague."

Edging around lamplight and through falling water, we approached the entrance. Nefertiti's presence made my steps lighter. But I needed to act the part of a brave hero. If she could help me uncover Akhenaten's treachery and have him exiled, it would be a crowning moment. She'd witness a power within me as I overthrew the traitorous king. Then she'd love me, and her father would accept me with open arms. I would be Egypt's savior.

I waved the group on and peeked into the house.

Chapter 44

Journal Translation

IN THE PALE LIGHT SLINKING through the window, the hovel appeared abandoned—no snakes, scorpions, or cloaked figures. Only pieces of a table lay scattered about the tight confines, covered with dust. Cool air brushed against my wide eyes. "No one's here," I said.

"We saw them go in!" Mutnedjmet said. "Maybe they went out the back. Let's see what they were doing." She tugged at my kilt, and we inched our way inside.

The air turned cold and humid, sending shivers through my body.

Something lay on the floor at the far end, covered by a blanket.

"Be careful!" Nefertiti said in a hoarse whisper, tugging at my shoulder. "There's something underneath."

I reached for a corner of the blanket. Markings were scrawled across the dirt floor.

"Can you read this?" I asked.

Nefertiti shook her head. "They say young women don't need to waste time learning when all we're meant to do is bear children."

"I'm sometimes able to sneak in and listen to my cousin's classes," Mutnedjmet whispered. "But I only know bits and pieces." She examined the images. "I'm not sure, but it doesn't look like typical writing. Maybe a symbol for 'beware.'"

Foreboding caused me to pause, but the girls waited for me to make a move. I eased the corner of the blanket aside with my toes, a cold bead of sweat trickling down my back.

A pile of bug carcasses lay underneath. Curiosity pushed me to inspect them. "What would he be doing with locusts?" I asked, wrinkling my face in disgust.

Mutnedjmet leaned down to grab one. Something rustled within the blanket. A black and red creature slithered out. Screaming, Mutnedjmet fell.

The serpent rose up to look Mutnedjmet directly in her terror-stricken eyes. Trying to scoot away, she smacked her head against the wall. Wing-like structures emerged from the snake's head. Croc hissed, his hackles rising. I flung a broken table leg at the reptile, but a stream of spit already flew from its mouth and hit Mutnedjmet's face.

Mutnedjmet wailed, collapsing against the toppled furniture as her hands covered her eyes. The serpent slithered off into a corner, and Croc stalked it. His hisses echoed off the walls. Spittle frothed around the bridge of Mutnedjmet's nose, already in her left eye, and now running toward her right. She screamed in agony.

My heart pounded with angst. What could I do? Utilizing the edge of my kilt, I wiped the foam from her face before it could slide into her other eye.

She shoved me away and howled, "I can't see!"

Struggling, we lifted Mutnedjmet and hauled her outside.

"We need to get her to a magician or doctor," I said. "I'll take her."

"No!" Nefertiti said, pulling my kilt. "If you're caught, some will suspect you were murdering people. The river's near. Go wash her eye out. I'll be at the palace waiting with help."

I nodded in agreement.

Nefertiti kissed her sister's cheek, staining it green with dripping makeup. "The Nile's that way." She pointed and darted off through the driving rain. It might've been my imagination, but a darkness hovered out from an alleyway and trailed her.

Voices of alarm sounded. Frightened residents appeared under wavering lamplight, staring at the hovel and Croc, who licked his belly at the doorway. Assisting Mutnedjmet, I ran with her into the night. Her breathing came rapidly.

"How is it?" I asked, guiding us through the darkness.

"It burns," she said, a hand clamped over her left eye. "Cobra poison can cause blindness. But at least you stopped it from going into both of my eyes."

I pulled her to the edge of the placid Nile, where the repetitive patter of ripples washed over the dock. Moonlight glinted on the glass-like surface as stars twinkled in the surrounding depths.

After forcing her hands away from her eye, I scooped up cool liquid and splashed the water onto her face. She shrieked and cringed.

"Try to open it," I said.

She forced her eye open with her fingers but winced and cried out. Her eyelid had grown swollen, the white horridly bloodshot. Like Father's!

Cupping my hands, I splashed more water over the area. "It'd probably work better if you dunked your head under and blinked," I said.

"You'll protect me from crocodiles?" she asked.

I nodded, trusting there wouldn't be any inside the city. But I formed the magical ward with my hand, as Mahu had taught me. Bubbles erupted before she plunged her face into the river. My eyes narrowed with skepticism. Magic? Yanking her head out, she sucked in a deep breath and repeated.

"Any better?" I asked.

"It doesn't hurt quite as bad," she said.

"I'll find someone to help you," I said. Memories of the doctor and magician, and how they each said not to trust the other, filled my mind.

"You'll go to your room," Mutnedjmet said, folding her arms across her chest. She bent over in pain. "Nefertiti and I will find the magician … if he's still alive. He's the gifted one. The wisest man to ever live. Imhotep reincarnated—the genius architect of the pyramids. He always knows what to do."

"But we may not be able to trust him," I said, attempting to get her to move.

She shook my hands off. "I need a minute."

Mutnedjmet's soaked hair glinted in the moonlight. Droplets of crystal liquid released their hold on her locks, lips, and nose, falling in slow motion.

Feelings of love and desire stirred, ignited by her gentle beauty. Why did I feel this way for Nefertiti's little sister?

Her gaze fell to the ground.

My eyes must've revealed my attraction.

"Sorry about your father," she said, taking my hand and letting me assist her to her feet. "It all makes sense now. His wounds, I mean."

Scenarios returned of what Father must've gone through before his death. The spitting cobra, the magical silence from biting his own tongue, the scorpions … I clenched my fists to ease my fury as we paced back through the slums. Would Nefertiti believe us now? She hated Akhenaten more than anyone but didn't trust Mutnedjmet.

A man in tattered clothing emerged from the dark street, staggering in our direction. His blurry gray eyes focused beyond cascading rain. I clutched my bracelet.

"You!" the drunkard said through a toothless mouth.

My heart raced as we sprinted away.

"You're the one who's not supposed to be here! But he said you would come!" Long, dirty fingernails scratched at the air.

Bolting down the next side street, I glanced back. The man hadn't followed us.

"Who was that?" Mutnedjmet asked, her left eye clamped shut and swollen like a blistering tomato.

I shrugged as we exchanged worried expressions. We ran on.

As we reached the palace walls, I was overcome by my insignificance and failure at unmasking the cloaked man. Hope crumbled like the houses in the slums. "I'm too weak to stop him!" I said, punching my thighs in absolute frustration. "I'm just a servant, a nobody!"

Mutnedjmet looked at me as if I were the madman running in circles giggling like a little girl. "You've done more than anyone."

My forehead tensed with confusion. What did she want from me, excitement? Bitterness boiled inside me, heating my neck and face. Or did she want me to give up now, to fail? I wanted to yell at her, to yell at everyone for all the horrid events of my life.

Her good eye darted back and forth over my face. Something glistened behind it, something I hadn't noticed before. I marveled at the fiery emotions raging within her own soul and forced a couple of deep breaths. "What can we do?" I asked.

"I'm not sure, Heb," she said. "So far you've led us well. Think on it."

A sense of accomplishment and pride filled my chest. My anger abated like hunger at a feast. My animosity had rendered me unable to think, to speak, and unable to control my thoughts and emotions. I prayed they would not get the better of me before I rescued Father's soul.

Assisting Mutnedjmet over the wall, I felt horrible for her suffering. But Nefertiti awaited us and took her sister's hand.

"I have help waiting inside," Nefertiti whispered before heading to the main entrance.

I sprinted to my room, leapt up, and peeked through the window.

Something within reeked with suspicion. Something was out of place.

Chapter 45

Journal Translation

SOMETHING FELT ODD. Peering through the dripping windowsill into my room, I couldn't locate what created the feeling. It was deathly still.

Would I be thrown back into the cave and end up a madman? My mind darkened, memories choking in a fog of desperation and rage. Fear chilled my bones. I could never go back to that place.

After climbing inside, I smoothed out the reeds of my bed. Something struck me hard from behind. Flying into the wall, I smacked my head and slumped to the ground.

Akhenaten's dark eyes glowed in the pink morning light. My chest constricted so hard I feared my heart would stop beating. "Where were you?" he demanded, towering over me. Gold jewelry and armor encrusted his skin, like a god's.

"I …" I swallowed.

"Do not lie!" His face contorted like a beast's. "Someone suggested I check your room. All I found was piled bedding!"

"I went outside," I said, struggling for breath. "I've been trapped for too long."

"You have placed the palace, Memphis, and all of Egypt at risk."

"I can't spread what I don't have," I said.

"The doctor will confirm or deny that. But someone else wishes to speak to you first. And he may not be as kind as I am."

My stomach knotted with anxiety.

His head whipped up to inspect the window, suspicion dripping from grimacing lips. "You would need dexterity to go out that way, which is not a skill of the servant. Did you have assistance?"

"Only desire," I said. "I was suffocating with thoughts of my father. Please tell me his *ba* can be saved."

"Where did you go?"

"Not far; it was raining," I said. "Only for a walk, to get fresh air."

His eyes narrowed as if he detected the lie, his dark lids growing like hoods of a cloak.

My hands perspired with worry. Had he seen me following the robed figure last night? Or had the figure been him? I attempted to stand.

Kicking out with a clubby foot, my master stomped me to the ground. A crushing force drained the air from my lungs. I coughed and wheezed.

"If the doctor does not order your immediate execution, you will be put back into service. But this time, someone will always be watching. You will be more prepared and efficient in your chores. And if the gaunt servant with the red eye shadow outperforms you, or if you cause the slightest annoyance, you will be dealt with permanently." After lifting his foot from my chest, he exited.

I gasped as air reentered my hypoxic body, burning my lungs. Was Akhenaten keeping me alive to torture me, or so I could serve him in the next life?

※ ※ ※

Soldiers were now stationed at the door and outside the window of my room. If only I could bury myself under the floor and hide. Or perhaps I should kill myself and get it over with.

Croc landed beside me with a quiet thud. Sauntering over, he rubbed against my leg, and I stroked his cheeks. His soft fur calmed my shaking hands. Sniffing the air, he paused as if he knew something was coming.

Footsteps clapped outside. Scooping up Croc, I braced my back against the far wall.

The plump doctor appeared, followed by a familiar man in a pristine wig. Ay. His jaw muscles protruded as his lips grew taut.

I shoved myself farther into the corner, my nerves screaming for me to run.

"So you've wandered outside," Pentju said, tapping his chin, which sent ripples down his neck.

Nefertiti's father squeezed Pentju's shoulder and pulled past. "You are disrespectful scum!" He pointed a long finger at me. "Mutnedjmet said you persuaded her into sneaking around with you."

Disbelief weighed my head down, and my chin hit my chest. *She did?*

"You exposed my daughter to the plague!" His face flared red. "If she dies, you'll be burned alive by my hand!"

Conceding, I closed my eyes. My second conversation with my potential father-in-law was also less than ideal. But what could I do? I knelt before him, my gaze remaining on the floor. "I only have respect for your daughters, Master Ay. If I wronged them, you may smite me as you see fit. But I do not carry the plague. I'd never have risked their lives."

Nothing happened.

When I glanced up, the red hue in Ay's cheeks deepened to purple and his fists balled up. I flinched with anticipation, but I'd take a hundred blows if it meant Nefertiti's father would approve of me. His knuckles landed between my eyes. A flash of white preceded the crack of pain, and I crashed to the floor. Ringing sounded in my ears, and blinking lights floated across the room. I tasted metal. Croc hissed. Rising to shaky feet, I tilted violently. I wouldn't be able to take even another of those punches.

"Let me examine you before you conclude you don't harbor any disease," Pentju said, kicking Croc aside with a meaty leg.

Bracing against the wall, I lifted my kilt.

After a moment, Pentju said, "You still don't have any lesions."

Ay's handsome features relaxed.

"Another day," Pentju said, "and you won't be any more of a threat for disease transmission than Ay or myself."

Ay's orange-lined eyes narrowed. "But if I ever catch you with one of my daughters, or if Mutnedjmet says you cast another lusting stare at her ..." He shook his head.

I inhaled in surprise. Had my brief feelings for Mutnedjmet been that obvious, or was he really referring to Nefertiti? But either way, Mutnedjmet had told him? Anger grew inside. "I never—"

"I don't care for anything you have to say!" Spittle flew from Ay's lips, showering my face. He stomped out.

Slumping down in defeat, I studied Pentju. "What about a swarm of insects?" I asked.

"What did you say?" His eyebrows crawled toward the bridge of his nose.

Did he know the truth? "Could the marks on my father and Thutmose be from venomous creatures?"

"We've already discussed possibilities other than plague," he said, his cheeks jiggling and flashing red. "Hornets and wasps don't fly at night. And no other insects carry that much poison or anger to strike thirty times."

"What if the swarm were scorpions, or snakes that spit poison?"

Recoiling in surprise, he tugged at the fat under his chin. He laughed. "Cobras enter houses in search of small prey, scorpions for warmth, but they don't hunt in packs like wild dogs. You can't arrive at the correct conclusion through ignorance. Why are you so intent on finding an alternate cause?"

"I'm trying to figure out why my father died from this plague no one else has." Desperation took hold of my tongue and lips. "What if I told you I saw such creatures?"

Waving me off, he said, "I'd say you were dreaming, or a liar. And tell me, why wouldn't the victims cry for help? If they had shouted, people inside the palace would've heard something."

"Magic! Do I have to figure everything out for you?"

He slapped me across the face, causing my head to whip to the side. My cheek burned like a bee sting.

Mudads peeked in. "Everything all right?"

"Fine," Pentju said, shoving his bulk out into the hall.

"I irritated him," I mumbled, holding my cheek.

"Doctors …" Mudads said and shrugged before stepping back out.

Recent events played over and over again in my head. Was the son of Hapu under the cloak? The green light was suspicious, and the figure probably couldn't have been the overweight doctor.

Cursing in frustration, I pounded on my bed. A longing for vengeance consumed my frail body, an inferno that could only be quenched with the fall of Akhenaten. Even the love of Nefertiti might not be able to overcome such emotion. And Mutnedjmet, my one supposed ally, had betrayed me. No one could be trusted.

My stomach clenched, burned, and twisted into a knot of tension. Yellow liquid heavy with acid spewed from my lips onto the tile. Grimacing, I wiped my mouth. Was I coming down with plague after all?

Croc climbed into my lap and purred. Petting his back, I traced his deep stripes. My pain subsided. I needed sleep, preferably with Croc so that he could fend off any snakes or scorpions the cloaked man sent after me. Perhaps I'd asked too many questions …

After nightfall, Croc perked up, staring at the doorway as if he saw something. Standing, he stretched and sauntered over.

A voice whispered inside my head.

Chapter 46

A SNAP BROKE THE SILENCE within my room. Faint green light illuminated the magician's deeply lined face, the remainder of his body appearing before my eyes.

Springing out of bed, I stumbled away and clung to the wall in fear.

"Listen carefully," the son of Hapu whispered, his hands shaking. The white cat jumped down from his shoulder, waddled over, and sniffed Croc.

"They'll see your light."

"Be silent!" he said, waving his arms wildly. "People can't see what is covered in darkness. I know what you've gone through, and I've seen your life if you stay. Leave this place … forever."

"What?" I asked, stunned.

"I just spoke with the doctor," he whispered. "He may not remember our conversation … but he mentioned something strange." Leaning closer, the magician stared through my eyes, looking directly into my soul. "I want to know about this spitting serpent."

"I …" Apprehension made me hesitate. I did not want to admit that I might've seen the magician, as the cloaked man, commit murder. What would he do to silence me?

"Even if you saw it in a dream or possess the gift of magic." His pale eyes scanned my face. "Tales from across the sea and from the vastness of Nubia mention serpents spitting venom—a breed of cobra we do not have in Egypt. Their accuracy is superior to that of the skilled archer, and their saliva can render a man blind. Where did you see this?"

"Y-you should talk to Mutnedjmet."

"People are dying!" Rubbing his shaven head, he spoke in a strained whisper as he glanced out the doorway. "Bodies pile up in the slums. This is not concerning for the palace, but people are so terrified, they whisper about the end of time for man. Egypt quakes in utter fear—fear this is the will of God."

"I saw a snake spit poison!" I said. "At Mutnedjmet!"

"A cobra slithered inside the palace walls last night?" he asked, lifting a shaven eyebrow.

"And scorpions! A pack of dark-reddish ones with huge tails and stingers."

"The Fattail? They have been driven to near extinction in the area, but their sting can be deadly." The crevasses on his forehead deepened. "You know more than you're telling me."

Dropping to my knees, I begged, "I'd be put to death for blasphemy. The loss of my soul would be more certain than being burned for a plague I do not carry!"

"They're hunting me as well!" His gray eyes twitched, perhaps with fear.

"Who?" I asked.

"There's no time for questions, boy, only answers. I cannot stay or I'll be caught. Something's amiss in the kingdom of the living and the dead. A plague *is* descending out of the west, a plague of shadows. Shapes roll in on the winds. I was unaware. A great power is boiling over and has masked its coming."

My lips parted in confusion, but no words came out.

"If beasts wander the streets of Memphis under the cover of night, they'd still be incapable of pure evil. Wicked deeds originate in the minds of man. Whispers of a ravaging black death and a deluge of the Nile drift across the land. Those stricken with the plague are those who possess rare abilities. If we lose those who command powers of the unseen, the art of magic will be forever lost. I've tried to contact the others, but I am hearing and seeing only muttering and fog. Some have spoken of atrocities and were sent to warn the people. I cannot locate their *ka*s or *ba*s. They've vanished. The royal family has spread word throughout Egypt that the Aten is dis-pleased. Our civilization will be erased if we do not accept the teachings and communion with Akhenaten's one god. The time of Akhen-Aten," he uttered the name slowly, "is emerging. I fear it's not in the people's interest. And ..." He wrung his withered hands.

"What?" I cried in anticipation, nearly squishing Croc, who released a pitiful squeak.

Mudads peeked inside. After a brief inspection, he turned back to the hallway as if he hadn't seen the magician.

"Quiet!" The son of Hapu held a gnarled finger to his lips. "There're those hidden in this palace who can sense my presence. The soldiers cannot see, but if they grow suspicious and a conjurer arrives, I'll be doomed." He shook his head. "Pharaoh is going to die."

"Akhenaten?" I asked, my face popping with excitement.

"Amenhotep will soon pass beyond the realm of the living. His *ba* will be forbidden to visit this world. It is already cloaked in twilight."

My thoughts swirled in confusion.

"I've risked much for a lonely, poor sap of a child. Your hopes of Mutnedjmet convincing her family of Akhenaten's treachery will not succeed. She is either on his side, or they cannot hear her. Do you understand?"

"I want to save Nefer—"

Throwing his hands into the air, he spun around. "Akhenaten will be pharaoh! Alone! There'll be no one to tell of his murders or conspiracies." His voice fell to a whisper again. "Leave with me this night. You must run as far away as you can. I cannot foresee what such a path will hold, but it doesn't include serving your father's murderer—the road your current life travels down. Such a fate is the most miserable existence any man could be dealt. I won't stand for it. And if my peers believe otherwise, may they halt your journey before your feet leave Egyptian soil."

Croc brushed around his bony ankles. He glanced down and grinned. "You must bring your companion with you! He is something I've only read about. You'll need him no matter what journey you take."

"Why are you helping me?" I asked, folding my arms in suspicion as I studied Croc. But I'd had Croc as a pet since he was a kitten, and besides the weird encounter with the Mummy Makers, I'd never seen him act strangely ... for a cat. "Do I carry the powers you speak of? Am I destined to do something?"

"Destinies turn to dust," he said, shaking his head. "If anyone were destined, it was Thutmose. Now he's dead. You are special because you know Akhenaten better than anyone. There is only one of a certain type of my kind still in existence. Either way, he'll find you and ask you to reveal what you know." The magician stepped back, closed his eyes, and faded into green mist and a flurry of brown moths.

Leaping back, I hit the wall again. This couldn't be!

The faint light and winged insects wisped through the open window. Following, the magician's fat cat struggled to claw its way up to the exit. I shoved its butt up and out the opening. The son of Hapu's voice rang inside my head, "You harbor feelings for Nefertiti, but do not let emotions ensnare you, boy! Now, get out! They're coming …"

After scooping up Croc, I paused, conflicted. I didn't want to serve Akhenaten, but I couldn't allow Father's murderer to thrive and Nefertiti, the love of my life, to be tormented forever. But I also couldn't drive a knife into Akhenaten's back and hope he'd die. He'd already arisen from death. I should run.

No. Even if my weak body and fate wouldn't grant me the life I desired, I *needed* to be part of Nefertiti's. Was that what all naïve boys believed when love struck them with its sharpest arrow?

The magician manipulated the night beyond my window to the deepest shade of black, so the guards stationed outside couldn't witness my escape. Footsteps echoed outside my room.

Chapter 47

Journal Translation

MY HEAD NEVER EMERGED from the window of my room. I would not escape and run. Collapsing onto the tiled floor, I closed my eyes. I couldn't leave Nefertiti to Akhenaten, even if it meant serving the demon Pharaoh. Lying twisted upon the floor for the duration of the night, I contemplated running away, suicide, and worst of all, facing my horrors. Croc's presence saved me from madness.

The morning came too early, and my head throbbed.

"We sail this day," Mahu said as he peeked into my room, his tone apprehensive. "Pharaoh has fulfilled his governing duties in Memphis for now. He and Akhenaten issued orders for the royal family and its subjects to finally return to Thebes—our home and the capital of Upper Egypt. And you're no longer to be isolated!" He held his hands up as if I should be elated. "But you look like you've been crawling through the dirt. Go and bathe, pack, and be ready to disembark by midday."

I nodded, drained and emotionless.

Mahu left. After glancing into the hall, I inched along toward the baths. Flat footfalls followed. I looked over my shoulder. Mudads nodded his capped head as if to let me know he'd always be watching.

Servants eyed me with suspicion, keeping their distance. None spoke to me. I washed my stubbly hair—now without a sidelock—shaved my body, and anointed myself with refreshing oil. After I dressed in a clean kilt, my exterior appeared reinvigorated, but my soul remained drawn.

I found Croc, wrapped him in my blanket, took the amulet of the scarab from my windowsill, and followed the mass exodus and cloud of choking dust toward the Nile. I'd have to keep Croc hidden so that Suty wouldn't kill him. But with all the recent events, it seemed likely that my master might've forgotten about Croc's savage attack. And I couldn't leave him in Memphis.

We arrived at the banks of the river. Amenhotep and Akhenaten—sitting upon thrones borne by servants—were carried aboard the royal yacht. The outer hull of the vessel gleamed gold, its immensity making the men on board appear small, like stones on a mountain. Oars broke water and the jeweled helm led the voyage, a fleet of barges trailing behind.

Time seemed imperceptible as I suffocated in a fog of hate and despair. Life was fantastically unfair. Only the strong could succeed—the meek would always be enslaved and serve them.

As I served Akhenaten—without Nefertiti or Mutnedjmet visiting—many days, or even weeks burned themselves out before a straight artery stood out against the beautiful curves of the Nile. We diverted into the west bank, where a rectangular lake rested before the Gleaming Palace of the Aten.

A passing cloud shadowed the burning walls of light, revealing their metallic surface. My lips parted with awe. Celebrating God's rays in such fashion was ingenious. Perhaps if I helped create a comparable spectacle or monument, I could be forgiven.

"We're home," a servant said to another, rubbing his red eye shadow as we disembarked and marched to the palace.

Twin sphinxes glared at me from beside the gates, and terror pounded in my chest, suffocating me. Three times the size of a man, the stone lions reared into the sky, their manes permanently billowing in the wind. Who could ever control such beasts, as I'd once heard? I scampered beyond the guardians, and an enormous palace crawled across the desert as its multiple stories reached for the Aten. Tattered flags waved in the wind, scattering light with their emblazoned metals.

We marched through a columned hall and under an open roof, where pools of water sparkled and cast reflections upon the walls. Brilliant images of great deeds, nature, and beasts loomed between and beneath the reflections. The throne of Egypt sat at the far end, its golden presence towering over us. Twin sphinx armrests trampled enemies. I paused in wonder.

Someone yelled. I spun as a ceramic ankh fell from a servant's load, as if in slow motion. The most ancient of symbols smashed into the bright blue tile, releasing a wave of energy. A thousand pieces skittered across the floor as the air shook. Holding my breath, I glanced about. To break the symbol of life and dominion was a bad omen.

Akhenaten strode into the room from a back chamber and nodded. Suty towered over the cowering servant as he apologized and scooped up fragments. With one swing of his sword, the ogre lopped the servant's arm clean off at the shoulder. The ping of metal on bone rang in my ears, followed by a hollow thud. Screaming, the servant collapsed as bright blood pulsated from his gaping wound.

"Clean up and get him out," Suty said, wiping his red blade on the victim's white kilt. "Hang him on the walls and let the Aten scorch him for his crime."

Shoving a bucket of water into my chest, the servant with the red eye paint smirked. I sopped the splatter of red from the blue tiles, but the more water I used, the more the blood diluted and spread into larger and larger circles. My stomach rolled with nausea.

✳ ✳ ✳

Visions of the emotionless act performed by Suty haunted my dreams that night.

Waking me early with a prodding foot, my new roommate said, "We have to serve breakfast in the throne room." He applied red eye shadow, studying his gaunt features in a bronze mirror.

My body tensed with nervousness—the competition was sleeping in the same room. I didn't care if he surpassed my abilities at serving Akhenaten, but if I fell behind, I might never see Nefertiti again.

"Did they tell us any more about Pharaoh's upcoming celebration?" I asked, looking down in shame. "I wasn't attentive during the voyage … not feeling well."

"We'll be working non-stop. His sed-festival will be enormous and needs to happen quickly." Licking thin lips, he placed his hands on his hips. "It will rejuvenate Pharaoh."

"Didn't Amenhotep mention visiting Thebes first?" I wished they'd visit Thebes—the actual city on the eastern bank and not just the small western community around us—so someone with authority and power could tell Amenhotep and convince him of the truth of Akhenaten's vicious deeds when we'd last visited—when my master had consumed the high priest's beating heart, devouring his soul. Thus far, I'd not heard that Pharaoh had justly punished his wicked son. But Akhenaten would've kept messengers from his father and probably wouldn't allow Amenhotep to visit Thebes while Pharaoh still lived inside his mortal body.

Shrugging, my new roommate turned his head side to side for the mirror and walked out into the hall. "Akhenaten is hesitant to do so."

I followed. And why was this celebration being rushed? Did Pharaoh or the people wish to delay Akhenaten's rule? But if Akhenaten was running the kingdom because of Amenhotep's debilitated mental state, the event must benefit my master as well.

Endless chores blurred the following days.

I stumbled off to bed early one morning to catch a couple of hours sleep before making the final preparations for guests from all over Egypt and the surrounding world.

"Heb."

Jumping, I spun around as memories of the wrinkled magician made my skin crawl.

A face popped out of the shadows and into torchlight, smiling.

Mutnedjmet. I scowled with disgust. What a charlatan, selling me out to her father while pretending to help oust Akhenaten.

"Why won't you talk to me anymore?" she asked.

I glanced around for the ever-watching soldier with the spindly limbs and potbelly. Nowhere in sight. "You betrayed me!" I said, pointing at her. "And your father threatened me with what he'd do if I ever looked at you again. I'm trying to find a way to Nefertiti. She's all I care about."

Her eyes welled with tears. "I never betrayed you."

I stalked off. Liar.

A group of young female servants spun around a corner in front of me, before I had even made it down the hall, and blocked my escape.

"The wedding was so beautiful," one adolescent girl said, striding along with three others. "I hope mine is half that amazing."

A wedding? Whose wedding had I missed preparing for this exorbitant sed-festival? The couple must not care for attention, given everything else going on at the moment.

"I wonder what it would be like," another girl, this one shorter than the first, said, cupping her breast, "to be with a man like that."

"He's repulsive," the first said. The others laughed.

"Maybe, but he's the crown prince of Egypt," the short one replied, her fingers digging into her dress at her thigh. "That kind of power is intoxicating. He'd make my knees weak ..."

My feet stopped moving in my surprise. Akhenaten had just married? Who would marry him? Poor girl. I'd imagined he'd only ever have his unwilling concubines.

"But the bride was *so* beautiful," the first girl said, placing her palms against her cheeks. "I wish I could be half that pretty. Maybe I'd have men fawning over me."

The new bride's life would soon become a living nightmare. I groaned with sympathy. Hopefully this woman knew what she was getting into.

"Her delicate features with plump lips and high cheekbones aren't fair to the rest of us," a third girl said.

My stomach churned. Strange that—

"I don't think she's that pretty," the short girl replied, shaking her head.

"That's not what all the men were whispering," the first said.

"The princess is the most beautiful woman they'd ever seen ..."

My mind shut down, in shock. Wait ... who were they talking about? My heart fluttered and raced. This couldn't be ... it had to be somebody else. But who else would men think was so beautiful?

"Nefertiti is Akhenaten's," Mutnedjmet said, from behind me.

I couldn't breathe as I slowly pivoted around. "*What?*"

Tears trickled down Nefertiti's sister's cheeks, as if she were overcome by guilt or loss. "Nefertiti is Akhenaten's royal wife. You've been wandering around in a daze."

"She wouldn't do that!" I said, a sharp pain stabbing my chest. "They're cousins, and she despises him!"

"I know," Mutnedjmet said, lifting her small hands in defense. "But she didn't have a choice … and she doesn't despise him like she used to."

My cheeks burned with rage and jealousy, my stomach clenched, and the hall spun. I braced myself against the mud-brick wall.

Heaving for breath, I raced back down the hall toward the throne room. My mind spun with images of my love and my vile master, and the world crumbled in upon itself. This couldn't be …

Scampering feet followed me.

Could I do anything to save Nefertiti now? Tripping, I fell and sprawled out across the hall with a grunt and a crash. I'd tell her everything: how I felt, how I loved her, and how I would finally rescue her. Jumping back up, I sprinted on.

Rounding the corner into the throne room, I stopped in astonishment. Plates and food were strewn across the tables, and chairs were spread everywhere. Grain littered the room as if a celebration had already happened, but only a few bodies lay passed out in the hall. How was I not a part of this?

A woman in a sheer white dress sashayed beside the golden throne, her back to me as her hand brushed the throne's twin sphinxes. No! It looked like her, but it couldn't be Nefertiti …

My master sat upon the chair, as if it were already his. His head was leaned back, his eyes closed. Perhaps he was asleep.

My teeth clenched, along with my stomach, as the room spun. I teetered, knocking into a chair that grated and smacked into a table with a thud.

The woman turned … Green eye-paint and the most beautiful features I'd ever seen! My heart twisted and withered in pain.

Nefertiti shook her head and averted her gaze.

"Nefertiti!" I whispered.

She froze, but her eyes moved, locking on me. Releasing a long sigh, she stepped down the stairs toward me. "Heb, I know this must be hard, but I didn't want you here for your own good. I knew it would cause you too much pain. And Akhenaten let me get my way, this one time."

My knees wobbled.

Akhenaten's head perked up, his black eyelids sliding open as he smirked. "Come, my royal princess and queen-to-be," he said, standing and stepping down beside her. "Join me in my chambers. But don't plan on sleeping much tonight."

My stomach knotted with pain and jealousy, as if he'd struck me in the groin.

Taking her by the arm, he pulled her away to his chambers.

I collapsed to my knees, my soul wanting to flee my body with each breath and never return.

A gentle hand settled onto my back. Mutnedjmet's eyes were misty, sadness embedded in her down-turned lips.

"Please don't hate *me*, Heb," Mutnedjmet said. "Ay was upset with you because he thought you put us in danger. I've told him a hundred times what we saw."

I punched a table, my knuckles popping with pain rather than releasing tension. I winced.

"My eye healed fine, thanks to you. And you're not favoring your leg anymore." She pointed at my ankle. "I saw the doctor. No one's seen the magician."

My forehead tightened in anger. Mutnedjmet was trying to distract me, perhaps to make me feel better. But nothing mattered anymore. "I saw him! And I told him to ask you about spitting serpents. I couldn't accuse Akhenaten of murdering the crown prince! They'd have burned me."

"Oh my god!" Her eyes widened. "He never came. If I see him, I'll tell him everything. I told the doctor, but like the others, he scolded me and told me to stop telling lies."

"Perhaps you'll finally convince someone in the next life," I said, retreating.

"Heb!" She reached out. "Seeking revenge won't help. But we're no longer children who must blindly do what we're told. Now is the time to trust your friends, work together, and fight … before it's too late."

"The people I trust are dead."

Voices echoed down the hall as the outline of a soldier appeared, rubbing his belly—Mudads, still following me.

Dashing off to my room, I lay down but couldn't sleep.

I got up and peeked out into the hall. Mudads stood watch in the corridor and another guard was stationed under my window. Throwing my head back in frustration, I growled. I lived in a cage, a pet slave for the master.

✳ ✳ ✳

The sound of banging pots carried down the corridor, making me jump up in bed. My roommate's gray cat dashed outside, his tail puffed like a bird trying to keep out the cold. Dawn already? I rubbed my tired eyes and headed to the audience room.

Amenhotep slouched upon his throne, facing the long hall. Rubbing at his mouth, he scowled and wiggled a row of teeth with his finger. Not even the royal dentist had been able to ease his suffering.

Entering in file, royalty and councilmen took their seats as I set out spotless dining plates and utensils. A regal man glistening with gold jewelry sat at Pharaoh's right. He looked familiar, but I couldn't place him. A substantial wig hugged his face and neck. Ay? No, Ay sat to Amenhotep's left, beside lady Tiye and his daughters—including Nefertiti. Royal advisors, the vizier, the doctor, royal soldiers, and the extended family all attended. Everyone but Akhenaten.

Rattles, trumpets, and drums rang throughout the palace as guests arrived by the boatload. Handing out wax cones at the entrance, I placed the objects on top of attendees' heads or wigs. These would melt throughout the day and release pleasant aromas of honey, floral, or citrus.

Guests laden with offerings placed their palms out in adoration of Pharaoh. Servants wheeled in rumbling carts overflowing with gold rings, caged animals, and other items I didn't recognize. Lions and tigers roared from behind bars, and monkeys howled as they leapt about their enclosures, eyeing the masses of surrounding people.

A man with a thin moustache and beard held a dagger in his open palms, its sharpened edges glistening gray. "My Aten, we are beyond grateful for the prosperity you have spread across the lands. This weapon was forged of a metal much stronger than bronze and will soon replace the weaker copper alloy. We call it steel." He presented the blade like a proud father, speaking with a thick accent. "A gift from Tushratta of Mitanni. Mighty King sends his regards." He then produced a lock of hair as shiny as silk and as dark as night; the strands fluttered in the wind. "A gift from Princess Kiya. For your mighty son, Thutmose."

The god-king's face reddened and veins bulged from his temples. A short servant seized the items and waved the man off.

The attendees from Egypt and the surrounding world celebrated with overflowing food and drink, the feast dragging on. Topless women danced to the rhythm of deafening drums, weighted discs hypnotically swinging from their hair. Drunken men roared.

Perhaps Mudads would become intoxicated, and I could escape with Nefertiti. I searched for him ... Mudads threw back a cup of dark wine, keeping an eye on me. Damn—

"Did you see who's now sitting in the position of co-regent Pharaoh?" Mahu whispered, nudging me with an elbow as he watched two dark boys backflip across the hall. "Look to his right. It's not Akhenaten! Pharaoh's lucid, and he may yet save Egypt."

Surprise made me gawk. The wigged man beside Pharaoh applauded the act. Who could he be? Had Amenhotep really replaced Akhenaten? My body tingled.

As if he sensed me watching, the man's gray eyes moved beneath his overhanging wig and focused on me. I'd seen that face before ...

Chapter 48

Present Day

MARCHING AWAY FROM OUR rental car with Mr. Scalone, Kaylin, Aiden, his fox—Aiden had paid extra just to bring the animal on the flight—and their bodyguard, I feared the light already shone inside the ancient temple of Abu Simbel. A delayed flight hadn't allowed us to arrive before sunrise.

The sun crested the eastern horizon as the choppy waters of the dammed Nile, Lake Nasser, crashed upon the rocky shore. Crocodiles lurked in the lake's depths, yearning for me to take a cool, inviting dip. Dismissing the sensation, I hiked upward.

Blue water snaked north as a bright ribbon through an unchanging brown landscape. The exception was the mysterious island of Elephantine, the isle Heb had visited. He might've trodden this same ground. Touching the warm dirt at my feet, my spirits lifted in wonder. Should I continue to be driven by the curiosity burning within me? But modern society and its expectations were much different from ancient Egypt's. I'd have to grow up soon.

Stone jutted forebodingly from a cliff face overhead, shadow and light contrasting upon the monument as if signifying the struggle of fear and hope. Howling wind whistled around hordes of tourists, a mob of locals, and a couple of armed soldiers who'd gathered beside the colossal rock guardians. These sentinels protected the southern reaches of the kingdom from Africa, what the ancients referred to as Nubia. Across the top of the cliff, a row of sculpted baboons already danced in the light. So did the central sun god. My pulse quickened and my hands shook in anticipation. I'd better be correct in interpreting the secret message. Too bad Mr. Scalone walked beside me and not Maddie. She'd waited in Cairo for a flight home because she was afraid someone might try to hurt or kill us again.

I shrank as I confronted the massive keepers of the temple, four seated statues of Rameses the Great. If animate, they'd squish me like a roach. A sign at their feet read, "No pictures inside."

Brushing past me, Kaylin pointed to the dark entrance just as the sun's rays arced through the opening and landed upon the inner floor. She slipped through the whispering throngs and stepped between the sentinels. Shoving people out of his way, Mr. Scalone broke into a run. I followed in his wake as the spectators cursed or yelled at us. The wind died, creating an eerie quiet as we entered the stone temple.

Rising sunlight raced across the inclined floor of the pillared hall, guiding a path between eight additional statues of Rameses II. Standing with folded arms, the massive sculptures focused on the ground between them. The hairs on the back of my neck stood up.

"Follow it!" I yelled, pointing to the light already spreading beyond the hall. Visitors cursed as we darted between or pushed around them.

"What're we looking for?" Kaylin asked, her heels echoing off of the wooden walkway.

"I'm not sure," I said, trailing.

"I've never seen anything like this!" Aiden said, running with his fox in his arms.

The light flowed into a narrower corridor. We passed under an archway where passages split off in either direction. But the light swung ahead and settled inside a chamber at the far end. Three pairs of statues' eyes stared back, reflecting the rays of the sun for the first time in eight months.

My skin crawled with fear. Tripping, I crashed to the ground. Kaylin ducked under a rope partition, Mr. Scalone and Aiden following. Harsh words flew from the assortment of tourists and locals, echoing throughout the halls. Jenkins stopped to pacify the masses and obstruct their view of us. I crawled into the sanctuary.

Snapping pictures under the rare setting of sunlight, Mr. Scalone scrutinized the four total ancient statues and the hieroglyphs adorning the walls. Only the statue on the far left with a crumbling head remained in shadow, as intended. Either that statue or the sunbathing Rameses himself would hold the answer.

Kaylin's lips moved, but her voice drowned under the cacophony of the mob. Shouting, three local men marched up to Jenkins. The bodyguard placed a hand inside his suit jacket, probably on a gun. My chest constricted with panic.

Scanning the room, I searched for anything out of the ordinary. Under the moving rays, darkness and light twisted in warfare upon the statues' noses, chins, and chests. Cartouche-encircled names above the statues lit up while images on the adjacent walls remained sheathed in darkness. Nothing leapt out. The shadows the deities cast on the back wall differed primarily because of their headdresses. Sitting in the dark, the one clutched an object to his chest. The others had all lost their limbs below the elbows. Sunken impressions of their forearms stretched along their thighs, casting contorted shadows upon their abdomens. Was it my imagination, or did these shadows resemble hieroglyphs? Either way, they weren't distinct enough to read. Perhaps if all the statues had still been encased in gold, as they were in ancient times, a clue would be more obvious.

Turning off the sound on my phone, I captured a video. The three local Egyptians entered the sanctuary and glared. Thankfully, none of them were the hired hands from the Valley of the Kings.

"No interrupt display," one said, his red face twisted with anger.

"Get out of here," Mr. Scalone said, sticking his chest out.

The locals sneered. Two machine-gun-toting guards with berets pushed through the mob.

"We're sorry," I said as Jenkins's grip tightened inside his jacket. "We wanted to see the light phenomenon. Let's go!" I ducked out with the others, but Kaylin remained inside. "Now!"

I covered my face in shame, and we wound around the mass of screaming spectators and kept as far away from the armed guards as we could. After pushing through the horde near the entrance, we took pictures outside like typical tourists. Maybe we should just say we're Americans. That would explain our behavior.

Following us, the three locals who'd confronted us exited and waited until the sunlight passed over the entrance, returning the temple to darkness.

The temperature climbed. Finding shade under a giant Rameses, we lingered until the gathering dispersed. The armed soldiers took their posts at the entrance, glaring at us beneath dark berets.

Sitting down, I examined the video on my phone.

"What'd you find?" Kaylin asked, grabbing my arm.

"The shadows on the statue's abdomens looked purposeful, but their hands had been removed. If they formed a message, we'll never know." My head sank into my palm as a sense of failure overcame me.

"So that's it?" Mr. Scalone said, throwing his arms up. "I got us all flights out here on a whim, fought off locals, and gave you my time. You let us down."

"The path to the Hall had to be here at one time," I said. The hope of bringing a relic home for Maddie started to fade. But I imagined unlocking the mystery of the shadows, which would turn out to be a mere trick of visual distortion. Letting my eyes blur, I'd read ancient writing from men wiser than anyone in millennia. Their message would guide me to the Hall. I'd bring home the journal and a gold funerary mask. Stepping out of my new car in a sharp gray suit, I'd don aviator sunglasses and march up to the small white house with the blue door. I'd knock and Maddie's roommate would answer. "Oh, she moved out," the redhead with the bouncy curls would say. "She's been depressed since she got back." But Maddie would pull up, returning for something she'd forgotten. She'd stop in her tracks and stare, her expression blank, the sun shining at her back. "Took you long enough," she'd say with a straight face, but then she'd crack a smile. I'd hold out the journal and she'd come running, pushing the book aside and jumping into my—

"Back to Cairo then," Mr. Scalone said, bringing me back to the present as he shook his head in disgust. The sun crested its zenith. Kaylin stomped her feet as she walked off, Jenkins, Aiden, and his fox following.

"Where're you guys going?" a familiar voice asked from the hillside below. *Maddie!* "I couldn't leave all this just because someone intimidated me." She spread her arms open to emphasize the temple and smiled.

"He couldn't figure it out," Mr. Scalone said, strutting past her.

"Maybe if you didn't chicken out," Kaylin said, glaring at Maddie, "and were here when the sunlight came, we'd be off to the Hall of Records. It's too late." She trailed Mr. Scalone.

Grimacing, Maddie asked, "What happened?"

I couldn't meet her gaze, ashamed I'd brought us all here. Staring blankly at the video on my phone, I said, "We didn't find anything. The statues' arms are missing, and some locals pushed us out."

Snatching the phone from my hands, she studied the video for several minutes. "I've got something!" She yanked her laptop out of her messenger bag and clicked violently on the keyboard and trackpad. A sepia-style photograph of the sanctuary inside Abu Simbel appeared, looking a hundred years old. "I ran across this during my thesis research." The hands of the three dismembered statues were intact, their fingers arching from their thighs in atypical fashion.

My heart jumped in surprise. But the shadows cast upon the statues from the camera flash were blurred. Damn it!

Maddie's hands blurred as she typed and clicked on her laptop, her eyes jumping around as she studied the screen. "I have a simulator program on my desktop, and a smaller version here ... to study shadow and light on monuments." Attaching my phone, she imported the video and drew in the arms, hands, and fingers from the old photo. "No one's placed much emphasis on the mobile elements of light and shade in ancient Egyptian art even though they worshiped the sun's life-giving rays above everything." She took a deep breath and whispered, "Gavin, never stare directly into the light, or you won't see its shadows."

What?

Images morphed as she redirected the origin of the light.

"Let's bounce," Aiden yelled. His fox's pink tongue lolled out in a pant, as wide as a soupspoon.

"Give us another minute," I said.

Groaning, Aiden trudged back up the path. "Kaylin's in a mood. She wants to go right—" He stared at the screen. "That's freakin' awesome!" Whirling around, he ran after Kaylin, his green shorts flapping above untied shoes and long black socks.

Maddie completed the reconstruction. The spinning pinwheel of death popped onto her screen. I held my breath in suspense. A minute passed and the pinwheel disappeared. Pixels clarified and shapes appeared. The shadows almost created images.

"And Abu Simbel was moved in the sixties," she said, her glasses reflecting the colors of the screen, her brow wrinkling in thought. "This changed the day that the temple received light from the twenty-second to the twenty-first. The date and change in location would've altered the angles." She played with the light, shifting shadows across the statues. Distorted hieroglyphs emerged on the abdomens of the three bathed in sunlight, like an ancient finger-puppet show.

"My god!" I said. "Were the arms intentionally removed?"

She shook her head. "Transporting the temple was a huge undertaking. Maybe they were damaged in the move."

My forehead tightened with skepticism.

The others wandered back just after the second daily caravan of tourists arrived from Aswan. Aside from these two guarded tours, visitors could only arrive via the nearby airstrip.

"What is it?" Kaylin asked, her eyes burning with either interest or anger.

Maddie squinted and read, "Rameses II, he ..." The image of a standing man holding a walking stick and a scepter followed the part she'd translated aloud. "I may have to check this, but I think his statue obstructs or blocks a secret path or tunnel."

"Or stands on it," I said.

"The Hall is here?" Kaylin squealed, jumping up and down.

We waited for the longest hour or two of my life. Anticipation made my palms sweat. Tourists wandered in, gawked, and listened to their obnoxious guide, who hid behind sunglasses and a wide-brimmed hat. As soon as the first old woman in a purple dress and red hat shuffled out the entrance, we wandered in, attempting to sneak past the guards. But the two men in uniform carrying machine guns followed us. Fear created a hollow feeling in my stomach and a tingling in my neck and face.

Jenkins positioned himself to obstruct the soldier's view, so that we could duck under the ropes and enter the sanctuary. I prodded around the feet of Rameses the Great. The stone was solid.

"We need more time," Mr. Scalone said, glaring at me.

"What do you want me to do?" I asked. "Maybe you should distract them."

"And leave you here to not find the answers again?" His Italian accent hung thick as he shook his head, tossing his lustrous hair.

Aiden pushed by Jenkins, running back down the hallway screaming, "Let's carve our names into those statues outside!"

My eyes closed with regret and irritation. "Most of us will have to leave, or only one guard will go after Aiden," I said. "The other will come in here." I chased after the teen.

Pausing before the guards, Aiden held up his hands. One lunged, snatched his collar, and shook him like a doll before shoving him back toward the entrance.

"Hey, bro, get off me," Aiden said, stumbling away while straightening his shirt.

The guards' suspicious eyes and sneers focused on me. I froze. Jenkins and Kaylin approached, Jenkins holding his hands up while hovering over Kaylin. Strutting by in her tiny shorts, Kaylin winked and rubbed her buttocks.

"It's really hot," she said. "Let's go skinny dipping in the lake." Inching her tank top from her body, she exposed a white lace bra.

Gawking, the guards whispered to each other and followed.

We paraded down to the water. A few lingering locals shouted.

"We can't go in," I whispered. "There're crocodiles."

Bending over, Kaylin slowly pulled her shorts down and exposed her lower cheeks beneath skimpy panties. "Many Middle Eastern men believe Western women are whores and might naturally do this kind of thing. Come on, Gavin, show some skin."

What? Oh. I unbuttoned my shirt with shaky fingers and let it fall. Clutching my pale chest, I reached for my belt and released it. Kaylin sashayed to the lake like a runway model, her glutes jiggling. Locals shouted in Arabic and waved wildly. Aiden gagged. Jenkins turned his back, facing the onlookers.

Slipping off my pants, I shuffled after Kaylin, wearing only boxer briefs and a fedora. The guards still pursued us. What now?

Kaylin dipped a toe in the water, reaching back to unclasp her bra.

Chapter 49

Present Day

"L ET'S GO!" An Italian accent carried over the crowd of onlookers outside the temple of Abu Simbel.

Leaping away from the edge of Lake Nasser, Kaylin clutched her clothes to her chest and hid behind Jenkins. Heat rose in my face as I jumped into my pants. Mr. Scalone approached and stared at Kaylin's exposed body.

"What're you two doing?" Maddie asked, her jaw falling to her chest as she followed behind Mr. Scalone.

After slipping my shirt and hiking boots on, I marched back to our vehicle. "Did you find anything?" I asked, my body tense with anticipation.

"Yes, Paul did," Maddie said, patting the guide's back and squeezing his bulging arm.

A sting struck my chest. Jealousy. Now Maddie was calling him Paul and touching him?

"Found a hollow stone about the size of a floor tile behind Rameses," Mr. Scalone said. "Pried it out with my knife."

"I don't think any of the rest of us could've dislodged it," Maddie said, smiling.

Mr. Scalone put his arm around her shoulders, giving a hug. My insides wrenched, like someone had kicked me in the groin. Now he was going after Maddie? He'd probably take any girl he could get his hands on.

"But get this," Maddie said, blushing and playing with her hair, "some type of epoxy held the tile in place! To hide—"

"A mummy?" Aiden's eyes expanded.

Maddie shook her head. "No, an opening about a foot across. I shone my light inside but couldn't see anything. Paul said he'd take the risk and shoved his hand—"

"There wasn't anything in there," Mr. Scalone said, opening the door of the silver SUV for Maddie. "The rock at the back was solid. I even used my knife, but I didn't get far."

Jumping onto the leather seat, Mr. Scalone started the engine and blasted the AC.

"Nothing?" Kaylin asked. "No Hall of Records?"

So he hadn't found *anything* but was still a hero? I clenched my fists.

"That's when I thought of it," Maddie said, her sparkling eyes running over something in her head. "This temple was moved higher up because of the dam and formation of Lake Nasser. Whatever was buried behind Rameses may've been left at the original site."

Kaylin tugged her shirt down. "They moved a rock temple?"

"With modern machinery and thousands of people," Maddie said.

"Someone may've taken whatever was back there," I said. "Like the arms of the statues."

Maddie adjusted her glasses. "We should find out for sure."

"So now you're the brave one, huh." Mr. Scalone chuckled, flexing his arms as he grasped the steering wheel and tossed his hair back with a snap of his neck.

"Where was the temple?" Aiden asked.

Maddie swallowed. "Under Lake Nasser."

"What?" Kaylin said.

"And that would've been the temple's location when the professor followed the path to the Hall a century ago," I said. "The dam wasn't built yet."

Mr. Scalone gunned it, throwing us back in our seats as we sped off.

Over the next couple of days, we visited the local museum to scrutinize the original position of the temple compared to its present location. Kaylin's dad's secretary overnighted diving equipment. We attempted to hire local guards, but none would venture into the water, not unless aboard a decent boat. They feared the lake. Within its depths lived the last remaining crocodiles of the Nile, perfect predators dating back to prehistoric times.

"I-I can't," Jenkins said at the remote locale, shaking in his shoes and rubbing his bald head. "I'd face any man to protect you guys, but wild animals … I'd die of a heart attack in there."

"I'm up for anything." Mr. Scalone studied his flexed bicep beneath a layer of tattoos. Winking at Maddie, he then did the same for Kaylin. "The more dangerous, the more exciting."

"I can't believe we're really doing this," Maddie said. "The crash course Kaylin gave in the pool at the hotel wouldn't have certified us."

"I've been diving since I was a little girl," Kaylin said. "Aiden's even gone a few times."

Aiden's face was more pale than typical. "I don't know if I can do it either, even with this." He held up a spear gun.

"Just keep a lookout while we dig," I said, trying to be brave in spite of my trembling limbs. "Crocodile attacks are rare, like shark attacks. You're fifteen times more likely to die from a falling coconut …" Recalling Heb's tale, I added, "Don't thrash around like wounded prey, and don't stay near the surface. That's their attack zone. Stay in a group and dive deep."

"The coconut thing is ludicrous," Aiden said. "But if I see a croc, I'll brown my britches."

"Anyone who doesn't want to go, don't," I said. I didn't want to go either, but curiosity plus the need to impress Maddie grew more powerful than fear, at least at the moment.

Gazing into my eyes, Maddie mouthed the words, "Thank you."

I imagined diving through murky water, leading the group. A roar would vibrate the liquid world, and the others would scramble for shore. Fleeing first, Mr. Scalone would climb over the rest. A massive form would emerge from the depths. I'd fire my spear gun. The harpoon would lodge into scaly hide as gargantuan jaws would snap around Mr. Scalone, swallowing him whole. Releasing a growl, the eternally hungry predator would descend upon Maddie. But I'd grab the crocodile's tail, ascending its scales to the spear I'd buried into its chest. As I'd yank the weapon out, a rush of black blood would follow, and the beast's jaws would unhinge for its next victim. Leaping, I'd drive the tip of my spear into the base of its skull and—

"Reminds me of the time I searched a sunken galleon in Shark Alley off South Africa," Mr. Scalone said, tossing his spear gun back and forth between his hands.

"Whoa," Aiden said. "When did you do that?"

"I wasn't much older than you are now," he said.

"Did you see any sharks?" Aiden asked.

"Of course. I even had to shoot one. It was the size of our SUV, and it came right at me. And I had to punch another in the nose, to disrupt its equilibrium."

Aiden's mouth gaped.

Clutching my bronze bracelet with quivering fingers, I stepped one finned foot into the water. I had to be brave. My heart rattled my ribs. Images of my leg being ripped out from under me by a beast with the strength of ten men popped into my mind. Nothing happened. Smiling, I gave a thumbs up and donned my mask and regulator. As I waded farther in, my fear rose higher than the water. Breaths came in rapid gulps. Kaylin and Aiden entered, followed by Maddie and Mr. Scalone. The fox at Jenkins' feet yipped over the sloshing of waves.

Murky water washed in cool against my wetsuit, which I wore more for protection than for warmth, even though it probably wouldn't offer any real defense against a crocodile. My head sank under, and the world fell silent. Debris stirred, swirling amongst the brown liquid and allowing for only a few feet of visualization. Fear escalated to terror, my pulse thundering in my ears. Clutching my flashlight and spear gun, I dove toward the temple's previous location. The others followed, our shaking lights penetrating like candles in a jungle.

Something grabbed my ankle! Whipping around, I whirled my gun in that direction. Kaylin's hands released me, waving in fear. Bubbles erupted from her regulator and muffled shouts drowned in the gloom of the water. I shot her a vile look for nearly giving me a heart attack. But she pointed below. An enormous tunnel ran into the underwater cliff face, darkness spewing out from inside.

Clinging to the stone walls, I led us into the blackness the sentinels would've guarded. A silver flash darted by. Yelling, I flung myself aside. Mr. Scalone's spear shot through the water as if he believed a crocodile were attacking. A two-foot-long fish darted around the sailing bolt, a school following close behind.

Breathing slowly into the regulator, I attempted to calm myself. We swam through shifting plant material into the unknown. Although the statues were absent from this original location, the scrutinizing stares of Rameses still maintained a presence of fear. I felt them like a hot breath on the back of my neck, similar to when inside the lost tomb. The feeling grew until I couldn't dismiss it. I shined my light around, the narrow beam wavering over the dirt floor. White objects lay piled below. I swam closer. Bones! Screaming, I thrashed backward, but Mr. Scalone caught me and held me fast.

I pointed at the human skulls, femurs, and rib cages as my throat squeezed shut. Bubbles erupted from the others' mouths. Aiden spun wildly. Snagging his shoulder, Kaylin held on until he settled and started breathing again.

We needed to do this now, as I wouldn't ever be able to make it down here again. I swam for the inner sanctuary, and the others followed.

Walls pressed in around us. Something inside the dead-end reflected my light. Pausing, I kicked my fins to right myself. A form as long as a boat burst out of the sanctuary. Bubbles and dirt spewed forth like an erupting volcano, disrupting visibility. As fast and as sleek as a shark, a scaled creature whipped its tail through the water. The appendage struck me, sending me careening into a rock wall. The beast disappeared into the swirling gloom. Cold like the darkest winter night gripped my muscles. I couldn't move or even breathe.

Plastered against the wall, I had let my light sink to the floor. Mr. Scalone repeatedly clicked his gun, but it was empty, and the beast had already shot around the others. Aiden, Maddie, and Kaylin had formed themselves into a trembling ball.

The crocodile had fled its lair, but this didn't settle our nerves. Aiden fired a spear into the sanctuary, the bolt sailing over my head as I retrieved my flashlight. Nothing else swam out. We approached, Maddie gripping my arm. Packed dirt the size of a large vehicle lay upon the floor. The bed of the beast. Nothing moved. Pointing to where Rameses II's statue would've sat in this original dead-end chamber, I checked with Maddie. She nodded.

Pulling a shovel from my back, I dug through wet dirt. The sandstone of ancient cliffs lay beneath.

Holding reloaded spear guns, Aiden and Mr. Scalone stood on guard. Maddie, Kaylin, and I used a pick and shovels to discover an irregularity in the cliff face. A rock lay wedged into an opening. We heaved, tugged, and dug for what felt like an hour before a stone the size of my head broke free. The remaining rubble proved much easier to dislodge. Kaylin flashed her light inside the tunnel. Only stone and dirt. Damn it! Not after all this! I swung my shovel at the wall in frustration, but the water slowed the object before it collided at an unrewarding speed.

Kaylin swam into a crevasse barely large enough for her. Fishing around, she paused. I held my breath, expecting her to scream and be dismembered or to be sucked in. Yanking an empty hand out, she shook her head.

My disappointment seemed to add twenty pounds of weight to my body. Maddie pointed, bubbles blowing out of her nose. She tore into her pack and pulled out an underwater camera as she wiped a hand over the inside wall. Peeking over her shoulder, I saw something glisten through the murk.

Chapter 50

Journal Translation

THE MAN BESIDE PHARAOH hiding under his new wig was the magician, the son of Hapu, the old wise man of Egypt! Only now the black lines upon his face had faded to wrinkles, and spider veins engulfed his exposed cheeks. The magician now stood to become Pharaoh after Amenhotep passed—seated at Pharaoh's right at what would probably be Amenhotep's last sed-festival. How could I have been so stupid?

Tripping in bewilderment, I caught myself before falling and spilling mugs everywhere. It must be the magician I couldn't trust, not the doctor. The son of Hapu had told me to run far away, but why? I couldn't stop his ascension and preferred him over Akhenaten.

Perhaps Mutnedjmet wasn't lying … She sat near Ay, and giggled at my recent stumble, her eyes lingering. Shaking my head, I walked on. I'd trust only Nefertiti and Croc.

Music echoed to the far reaches of Egypt. Squat, dark-skinned boys with black, curly hair climbed onto each other's shoulders—five high. The entertainers wore short beards—so, no, they weren't children—and their heads appeared large compared to their body, their limbs short.

"Nubian dancing dwarves," the servant beside me muttered as he moistened his cracked lips with his tongue.

Dancing to choreographed routines, these dwarves performed flips, lifts, leaping, and catching, displaying more strength and agility than I'd witnessed in any man. Smiling as wide as a delighted child, Mutnedjmet clapped, whistled, and hollered. Nefertiti barely opened her green-painted eyes. My heart melted in sorrow. What was going on inside my love's head?

A tall man with feminine attributes appeared, adorned in gold armlets, a chest-encompassing necklace, and a stylized black wig. Akhenaten! The throne room fell silent. Parading past the attendees, my master scooted a chair beside Pharaoh. The wood of the chair rattled as it slid across the tile, as if protesting its movement.

"Hello, Father," Akhenaten said for all to hear. His eyelids closed to reveal black paint that made his eyes appear as empty sockets.

Moist meat fell from the god-king's yellowed teeth, betraying his shock. Akhenaten dangled a lock of black hair shining like silk, the gift intended for Thutmose from the foreigner! Running the strands over his pursed lips, his eyes popped open. "Pharaoh does not need offerings, only fear and respect."

"Much of our wealth comes from friends beyond our lands," Amenhotep said. "The King of Babylon, and of Mitanni, and Hatti bring—"

Cheering erupted as the crowd parted. A black bull the size of ten men stomped forward. A white diamond marking upon its head matched the wings stretching across its shoulders. The beast snorted, its eyes twitching wildly.

"Apis Bull!" Pharaoh cried, his withered lips lifting as he staggered from his seat. "My friend and intermediary to the beyond. They brought you from Memphis for this?" He reached out to the animal. "This is the last time we celebrate on this side."

The bull's hot breath roared from flaring nostrils before the beast barreled away from Pharaoh, parting the spectators. Attempting to give chase, Pharaoh took two wobbly steps and fell to his hands and knees. Akhenaten vaulted over the table and sprinted after the beast, gangly like a newborn giraffe. The people erupted with applause.

I gnashed my teeth in resentment as my stomach burned. Pharaoh was supposed to run with the Apis Bull. Did this foretell of Akhenaten's rise?

✳ ✳ ✳

Morning light, appearing sickly pale, flooded through my open window. Remorse pulled my heavy head into my palms as I sat upon my reed bed. After days of celebration, the visitors had finally departed, leaving only the stench of rotting food. And I hadn't even had the chance to speak to Nefertiti, much less save her. Would my life vanish before my eyes as I performed menial chores? Soon I'd be a grown man still serving a wicked—

"Pharaoh has died!" a soldier yelled to Mudads, who again stood watch outside my room.

Croc sprang from my bed and leapt out the window, his orange fading into the dawn.

My heart froze with apprehension. What did that mean for Akhenaten, for Egypt? And who would now rise as Pharaoh? I shuffled to my master's room. Rattling furniture and voices already sounded within. Emerging, Akhenaten strode straight for the royal baths, where I scrubbed and anointed him in viscous oil. After I assisted him into golden regalia, we marched into the throne room. All of the royal family, guards, and council were already here, standing in silent attention—their gazes fixated on the raised platform housing the throne.

A figure stood beside the raised throne, the morning sunlight reflecting off of his gold-encrusted body and the royal seat beside him, so I could not see his face. With such a display of power, he must have the Aten's blessing.

Akhenaten halted beside me, his knuckles blanching white upon his walking stick as he straightened. Did rage consume him? What would he do?

Ten priests marched a golden sarcophagus into the hall, setting it before the throne with a hollow clunk. Waving gilded wands over the bright red and blue jewels near the head, the hairless men spoke an ancient tongue and blessed the deceased with white smoke and sweet incense.

Stepping forward, the figure beside the throne opened his arms. The blinding rays redirected away from my eyes … The son of Hapu! The next Pharaoh of Egypt … My teeth clenched in anger. That trickster, lying to me the entire time while attempting to gain power for himself.

"My fellow Egyptians," the son of Hapu said, his voice booming, "it is with great remorse that we gather here today. The mightiest of Pharaohs, Amenhotep, has passed into the next world. But Egypt has found its new Pharaoh."

An orchestra of rattles, drums, and stringed instruments hummed. An eerily deep voice carrying a dark timbre rose over the music, its haunting beauty sending chills up my spine and creating goose bumps on my arms. Akhenaten's mouth stretched wide, his tongue flat as he sang! Echoing off the walls of stone, his lyrics and bass vibrato composed a hymn to the Aten. Everyone stood in stunned silence, entranced by dark beauty.

The music faded. "God has ascended to the horizon!" Akhenaten yelled with raised arms, making me jump. His voice boomed and carried to the far reaches of the palace as he strode up to the magician and the throne. Sliding aside, the magician made way for my master. "The king of Upper and Lower Egypt has flown to heaven. The Aten and Amenhotep have merged as one!"

People wailed for the greatest of kings.

My eyes gaped in suspense, and fear. Was the son of Hapu no longer next in line to be Pharaoh? Had he and my master had a confrontation from which Akhenaten emerged as the victor? Please, God, no …

"I am the son of God!" Akhenaten continued, reaching the raised platform and spinning to face the packed hall. "The living manifestation of the Aten. Only I am privy to Father's bidding and desires! If you please God by worshipping my ascension and obeying my laws, Egypt will be supreme again. But if you displease Him, you will all suffer. I will lead the faithful to the greatest glory attainable by man!"

Silence. Then a roaring applause. My body slumped in utter defeat.

An enormous procession led out of the palace, transferring Amenhotep to his final resting place inside the pyramid mountain.

✳ ✳ ✳

Long months followed. I transformed into a wandering mummy cut off from the afterlife—released from one quarantine and placed into another. Days of service blended together in miserable boredom and suppressed rage. Mudads scrutinized me whenever I trailed Akhenaten, serving all of his needs.

Perhaps my best course of action would be to portray the most loyal servant in the entire kingdom. Then, after time, maybe Mudads wouldn't watch me so closely.

But submission poisoned my soul so deeply I never discovered the antidote. The details of life faded. My dead father must've cursed his own living son. Perhaps my only purpose in life was to serve Akhenaten, my miserable fate. I was good at it, better than the others. My stomach heaved and I vomited, streaks of blood appearing in the bile. I lay down and never wanted to get up, but others kicked me and yelled, "Prepare for Akhenaten!"

The magician was right, I should've run. Or I never should've cursed the Aten that desert night, or turned the boat around to pick up Akhenaten's body. The mysterious *ba* had risked its existence to try to save Egypt when it visited me at night and spoke the warning about not turning around. I had failed.

During these endless days, I stood beside the golden throne in the company of the royal council and family. I caught Nefertiti's green-painted eyes watching me. She smiled. Her beauty had only increased after she'd matured into a woman, making my heart beat faster with excitement. What did she think of me now? I served the most powerful man in the world, but my master was her affliction, as well.

"A plague still ravages the land," a withered man at the council table said, his tone pessimistic. The air hung rank with the heat of evening as I fanned the god-king with ostrich feathers bundled into the appearance of a blue lotus leaf.

"Yes, but we do not need to worry," Akhenaten replied, waving the golden crook and flail. "The contagion only strikes blasphemers. The deaths are executions by God himself. If they embrace and worship only the Aten, they will not die. But the defiant ... well, Egypt will only grow stronger."

My head cocked in surprise. But no one else at the table seemed shocked. What barbarians were unfaithful to the Aten? And what did they worship instead?

Honking trumpets broke the tension. Akhenaten stood, wearing the united red and white crowns of Upper and Lower Egypt—the cobra and vulture watching from atop his clean-shaven head.

Mahu entered and knelt in the sand before Pharaoh, kissing the dirt. Akhenaten examined his incised thumbnail, which resembled an image of the sun rising between two peaks. He'd either continued to cut it, or it'd been permanently deformed into that shape ...

"You have returned with her?" Akhenaten asked as he stroked a lock of black hair—the same hair offered to Thutmose and Pharaoh by the foreigner at Amenhotep's last sed-festival.

"We've traveled across sand and mountain to the Valley of the Pine Tree," Mahu said. "The daughter of the king of Mitanni, the Lady Kiya, awaited us. She desires nothing more than to be the wife of Pharaoh."

"Bring her in," Akhenaten said.

Shaking rattles preceded a woman hooded in white. Her skin held a yellowish hue, her eyes were elongated, and her black hair fell only to her upper neck. She was beautiful in an exotic sense, but her allure diminished when she was inside the same room as Nefertiti.

Akhenaten, now always shielded in gold, studied his prize with a hunter's eyes. "I am Akhenaten, Pharaoh, God."

"I am Kiya," the young woman said, not lifting her gaze.

"You will join me in my chambers." Akhenaten strode away as if walking on air. "Nefertiti will join us later."

Kiya hesitantly trailed behind.

Several days or weeks later—I wasn't sure in my numb haze—before the midday heat of the Aten crashed upon western Thebes, I followed the royal family out of the palace. Akhenaten's mother, still sporting lustrous red hair with thick curls, sauntered beside Nefertiti's father and a handful of servants. Nefertiti, Beketaten, and Kiya whispered to each other as they walked. Mutnedjmet was not present. And Mudads didn't follow me. He was nowhere to be seen ... for the first time.

Columns of sandstone appeared, reaching for the heavens. The Aten temple, and as was customary, no roof blocked out the glorious light. Early rays of the sun cast themselves upon the altars. Positioning myself beside Nefertiti, I closed my eyes in silent worship. The warmth of the life-giving beams pierced the ceiling and flowed around the pillars, soaking into my soul. I grew hot but forced out criticism. Requiring the favor of the Aten and Amenhotep, I only allowed gratitude and prayers of forgiveness. Falling to my knees, I opened my palms in divine adoration. My mind fell quiet.

Shouting erupted, tearing me from my prayer for salvation. Two royal guards brandished swords and stepped between us and a man cloaked in black. Tensing with fear, I recalled the nights in Memphis. But embroidered stars dotted this man's robe, as if I gazed upon the heavens in the absence of the Aten.

Limping across the sand with arms hidden beneath his cloak, the man uttered incomprehensible words.

"Stay back!" Mahu said, crouching.

"He wears the black panther's skin!" Akhenaten yelled, pointing with his scepter. "One of the great blasphemers! Kill him!" Squeezing a crocodile-shaped hilt of gold at his belt, he shoved me aside.

The hooded man stumbled closer. I watched, paralyzed. Nefertiti, Kiya, and Beketaten clung to each other and shrieked.

"Your black magic's not welcome in Egypt any more!" Suty said.

The man threw back the hood of night, and shaggy gray hair and a beard tumbled from the dark folds. Ancient wisdom lay buried behind cloudy cataracts. "You!" the man said, looking past Akhenaten. Our eyes locked, and my chin jerked back in confusion. My fingers clamped onto Father's bracelet.

His voice cracked like dry twigs. "Do not fall prey to the lies concealed as teachings! Those about the divine. The answers are right here, but you must see, hear, and feel them!"

Dashing forward, Suty cut the man down with a single slash across the abdomen. The cloak collapsed in a heap and the air shook as if thunder boomed.

Akhenaten raised his crocodile-bone blade with serrated edge of teeth, the golden hilt glistening in the sun. "This magician will trouble us no more." Closing his eyes, he chanted.

Kiya approached the pelt, as if confused.

"His magic will be released!" Ay shouted, shielding himself behind Nefertiti.

Lunging over, Beketaten grabbed Kiya's wrist as she reached for the cloak. A gnarled hand lashed out at Beketaten from under the night sky pelt.

Chapter 51

Journal Translation

SNATCHING BEKETATEN'S ANKLE, the gnarled hand beneath the fallen cloak yanked her leg out from under her. She shrieked as she flopped onto her back. This magician's other liver-spotted appendage shot out, his fingers squeezing Beketaten's belly. Chanting emerged from Beketaten's lips, but the deep, incomprehensible words couldn't have been her own—it was like this magician spoke through her. The aged hands fell limp and retracted, the pelt sinking as if the body beneath melted.

My eyes gaped with wonder. Suty lifted Beketaten's gangly frame, shoved her away, and stabbed the cloak with his sword. Flinging the garment aside with his blade revealed only a black stain.

"He laid his filth in the Grand Temple of the Aten!" Akhenaten said, his face redder than sunset. "And he interrupted our worship uttering those names. This was no random act! I will return to the court and retaliate!" Striding over to the black stain, he rammed his mandible-bone blade deep. The air sucked out of my lungs as if someone had struck me. Beketaten screamed and grabbed her belly, her face pale. Akhenaten marched away.

Curiosity welled up within me. The old man had appeared to be addressing me before Suty had cut him down. Buried emotions swirled. If I searched for answers as this magician had suggested, I'd betray Akhenaten, the Aten, and the life I'd been dealt. This seemed evil. But I felt more alive than I had in months, or perhaps fog-shrouded years.

After Akhenaten called for priests to remove the stain, the group followed him out of the temple. Only Nefertiti and Kiya remained, enthralled with the missing body. I couldn't continue hoping for a perfect moment with my love. Life didn't work in such ways. I needed to make the moment happen, or I'd soon die in this place. Fear and doubt clouded my mind and agitated my hands, but as Nefertiti walked away, I caught her arm.

"Nefertiti," I said, "it's been too long since I've been able to speak with you."

The corners of her red lips turned up into a smirk, her dark eyes sparkling. "I miss our days together." She sighed. "Things were so much simpler only a short time ago, but this seems like another life."

"I miss you. And I'm going to find out what just happened. I-I love you …"

She blushed, and her grin broadened to reveal perfect teeth. "I've loved you too, Heb, but life is complicated …"

Her words rang like the most beautiful music I'd ever heard, and I nearly collapsed in shock. She said she'd loved me! I had worried I'd been living a fantasy. Warmth spread from my heart throughout my body. "I'll find the answers this madman spoke of," I said, beaming. "It must have to do with my father and the son of Hapu. But I will come for you soon and save you. We will create our own lives if we cannot rid the world of Akhenaten."

"I don't see how—"

"Akhenaten, Mahu, and my father have told me what I'm supposed to do with my life, but I'm not settling. You rescued this poor servant the first day I laid eyes on you."

She laughed. Her wide smile was more captivating than anything I'd ever seen.

Kiya yanked Nefertiti away, shouting in a heavy accent.

"Heb …" Nefertiti glanced back, her eyes pleading for me to save her.

"I tried to find Bes," I said, pulling forth my amulet, "but thus far I've failed. I pray the scarab will ease the darkness within you."

Jerking from Kiya's grip, she reached out. But she paused. "Heb," she said, "I have a dozen of these, and mine are made of gold and precious jewels. I don't need one of mud brick."

My heart sank in defeat, a chill replacing its new warmth. Why had I believed a worthless trinket would help her?

Priests escorted the women away. But on the ground lay the black panther skin.

As I snatched the cloak, the coarse fur poked my palm, but its silver stars glistened. Wadding up the garment, I held it behind my back and marched directly to my room. Thankfully, my roommate was gone. Lifting my blanket, I laid the pelt out on the reed mattress and covered it. I strode out to find Akhenaten and report for duty one last time.

The royal court had gathered before their god-king in the audience hall. A feverish discussion raged, so I grabbed a serving pitcher and carried it to my post beside the recessed throne of gold.

"He spoke to Akhenaten's servant," Ay said, his orange eye shadow blurring as he swung his head around to gaze at the members.

Pressing my back against the wall, I attempted to remain inconspicuous.

"He pointed at me!" Akhenaten boomed, his knuckles blanching as he squeezed the heads of his sphinx. "That servant has been mine since he was a child and has nothing to offer anyone. They fear *my* power. We will ensure that all the dark priests and cults are accounted for, those the plague did not wipe out." He closed his eyes, his black lids stretching across his face.

"Dark priests?" Ay gasped, leaning back. "What do they want?"

"To challenge my authority, to challenge God!"

"No one would challenge you, my Pharaoh," Ay said.

Most nodded in swift agreement, but a couple of men gave delayed acknowledgements. Intriguing. Did some in the court not approve of the new god-king? But how could they question the will of the Aten?

"The military will scour Thebes," Akhenaten said. "Every alley and rat hole. Cults cannot hide. They will be tracked," he snarled the rest, "especially those of Amun."

Akhenaten's murder of the high priest at Thebes must've been the first marker of his coming genocide, since disguised as a plague.

"Pardon me, Pharaoh," a withered man said, "but the other cults have been with us since the beginning of civilization, if not longer. We cannot treat them like animals."

Akhenaten glared. "Those priests and their followers skulk around, hiding who they really are amidst the masses. They poison our lands. They and the outside civilizations are the paramount threat to the security of our kingdom!"

"My lord," the man replied in an even tone, spreading arms like twigs, "Amenhotep left Egypt with the greatest wealth and prosperity since Menes received the throne from God hundreds of generations ago. We stand atop the pinnacle of the world."

"What is your point?" Akhenaten asked.

Swallowing, he smacked his purple lips. "Amenhotep formed allegiances outside our borders and within. We didn't live in fear."

Akhenaten's fist crashed onto a sphinx with the sound of a drumbeat. "There are men who could use magic to sear the flesh from your brittle old bones. If Egypt is to continue to achieve greater and greater prosperity, we cannot let others unite and challenge us. I am not ordering punishment. But we need to track the affairs of the cults in our midst, their whereabouts, and their families. Preemptive knowledge is far superior to a post-war history lesson."

The old man's cheeks flushed. "The people thrive. We have all we can eat and drink, a surplus for taxes, trade with the outside world, and more commodities than ever. Perhaps there is a line beyond which wealth becomes detrimental. And the Dark Ones, the Nine Bows, the Sea Peoples," his hands waved wildly overhead, "barbarians, Asiatics, Kush, and the Nubians are scattered. We do not need to account for every Egyptian pagan."

"You may be old," Akhenaten whispered, his thin cheek muscles bulging, "but you still have not learned that you cannot trust those beneath you." Screaming, he pointed over the heads of the council members. "They are always plotting to take power! Whether from the inside or the outside, you must be prepared, or even God may not grant you the favor of victory."

Tense silence reigned.

"Now," Pharaoh said, "we locate every man, woman, and child who puts enough faith in the other gods that they would still utter their names. I have discovered a way to detect them. Find them all!"

The attendees exited, but the withered man remained before the elevated throne and motioned for Akhenaten to come closer. Pharaoh snatched the golden scepter he now used as his walking stick and stepped down.

"Is this why you shipped crates of breeding scorpions to Thebes?" the elderly man asked.

Akhenaten gnashed his teeth.

"A servant opened a box by accident, as he couldn't read the warning." White eyebrows arched onto the councilman's forehead. "Is this plague really what it seems?"

"Listen, my friend," Akhenaten said, his demeanor shifting to one of concern. "The plague is spreading. Soon Egypt will be covered in its darkness, and unless we follow only the Aten and his teachings, we will fall. Come, and I will tell you how I know this." Guiding the man toward the columns, Akhenaten motioned to someone in the shadows. "After the plague comes pestilence, and scorpions are the best defense against the locust …"

A monstrous figure with a scarred pig's ear emerged from the darkness.

Chapter 52

Journal Translation

HOISTING THE OLD COUNCILMAN by his neck, Akhenaten squeezed. The victim's eyes bulged out of their sockets, and a gurgle escaped his lips. Crocodile bone and teeth buried into his stomach. Slumping to the ground, the body writhed and twisted into a mummy in a matter of seconds. Suty scooped up the desiccated corpse as Akhenaten licked his dripping blade.

I recoiled in terror.

"Pentju!" Akhenaten yelled. "Has the plague reached the Palace of the Aten?"

The watermelon-headed doctor waddled back in, sweat glistening upon his brow. Suty placed a large hand over the wound on the dead man's stomach. Councilmen and advisors reappeared with ghastly expressions as they whispered of the plague and pointed at the body.

"Marks of the plague!" the doctor said. "Keep your distance!"

Clenching my jaw, I suppressed outrage at the deceptive doctor. Pentju was Akhenaten's pawn. So perhaps the son of Hapu was not.

Suty set the carcass onto the edge of a dark rug and rolled it up so that the body was hidden inside. Hefting the rolled carpet, he rushed out of the audience hall.

Court members gasped. Perhaps they realized Akhenaten had killed the old man and they couldn't do anything about it. One pointed at a red spot and whispered to another.

"He coughed up blood before collapsing," Pentju said, tugging at the rolls of his neck.

Striding toward an exit, I kept my head down. The Aten faded into twilight.

"Servant!" Akhenaten said. "Stand beside me."

Freezing in terror, I swallowed before shuffling over to my vile master.

As I neared, he whispered, "What did you see?"

"An old man," I said. "He questioned you, but you walked with him as a friend. He choked and collapsed. Suty saved us by whisking the infected corpse away after the doctor's diagnosis." Decay rotted my heart from the inside out like a fruit, and my *ba* shriveled inside my mortal bones.

Akhenaten's dark eyes bored into mine. "What do you believe happened?"

"The plague strikes those who question the Aten and incur his wrath."

Grinning, he patted my shoulder. "You have grown up to become a good servant."

After Pharaoh turned away, I leaned against the wall. Memories of the monarch butterfly filled my mind. I vomited bloody chunks, hiding my face as spittle strung from my lips.

"We've already confirmed another plague death beyond the elderly councilman's, here within the palace!" the doctor said as he lumbered into the audience hall again, heaving for breath.

The room fell silent.

"This one is only a servant," he said. "He'd been complaining of fatigue and retired to his room. Someone just found him dead."

Whispers carried up and out of the open roof of the chamber. Akhenaten bellowed, "We must identify the cults and priests in hiding to win back the favor of the Aten. Now go!"

The councilmen scrambled out. Akhenaten retired to his room, alone.

Exhaling an overdue breath released some of my tension. Was a servant also given the plague to make the old man's death less suspicious? Or perhaps it was the person the old man spoke of, the one who'd seen the evidence in the scorpion crate …

I raced to my room, eager to inspect my new possession. Standing in a corner, Croc glared at my bed with his hackles raised. He stalked around the bedding and sniffed the air as if he detected the dead priest or panther.

Hoping to find answers, I inspected the black pelt and then wrapped it around my body. The panther head slipped over mine, and a chill sank into my bones. Distant screams filled the night sky as my eyes peeked out of the empty eye sockets of the panther's.

Croc reacted in such a slow, drawn-out fashion, it couldn't have been real. His whiskers crawled back over his head, his mouth teased opened, and a hiss rang out. His curse carried on for a minute before he crouched, his muscles tensed, his skin wobbled, and his feet left the floor.

Choking in surprise, I glanced around. What new magic was this? He moved in ultra-slow motion!

Leaping so sluggishly into the air, Croc appeared to float. And his eyes dilated so lethargically, I watched them expand from slits to black circles. Reaching his peak height, he slowly descended. I stroked his orange fur as he glided to the floor, his claws extending as slowly as a snail.

A clatter from the doorway stole my attention, carrying on as slow as Croc's hiss. Pentju stood under lamplight, his eyes moving as if almost frozen. I squeezed Father's bracelet and jumped back.

"I …" The single sound crawled out of the doctor's mouth as moisture from his tongue released its hold. The saliva droplets appeared to hover in the air before tracking toward the earth. "Th …" a new sound began.

Crouching in the shadows, I pushed the hood off so that he wouldn't see my new prize. The distant cries faded.

"Thought he'd have come to bed," Pentju said as Croc landed and darted out the window in a flash.

"Tell him about his roommate tomorrow," a voice outside said. "We can't wait."

I watched the doctor leave, astonished. How had he not seen me? Running a hand across the star-lined cloak, I leapt up. Was it magical? But what about my roommate? Had he been the one who'd discovered the scorpion crate and contracted the plague of—

"Were you hiding?" Mudads asked, peeking inside. "Pentju was just looking for you."

Nodding, I lowered my gaze to veil the lie.

"I understand," he said, stepping away. "I wouldn't want to be blamed and quarantined for the plague again, either."

My skin crawled with eerie delight. I was finally on the right side of magic and could enact my revenge on all those who'd wronged me. Biting my lip, I attempted to control my emotions. Was Mutnedjmet right about friendship and not pursuing vengeance? I was not as ignorant as I had been, but had the wickedness all around me transformed my character?

As I pulled the panther's empty eye sockets down over my own, distant shrieks again carried through the window. I lunged into the hall and waved at the guard. Nothing. I clapped. Mudads' neck turned as fast as the sun moving across the sky, his skin leisurely folding. I didn't possess any more patience. I'd used up all I owned over the last few years.

My pulse quickened as I recalled the nights in Memphis when I'd felt alive, when I'd been able to determine my own fate. I couldn't enact revenge on the immortal Akhenaten, so I'd find answers about these cults and who Amun was, in hopes of saving Father's soul and Nefertiti. Perhaps the city proper of Thebes would hold the answers.

Sprinting out of the palace, I passed multiple watchmen. No one acknowledged me. The cries in the distance grew louder. What made these sounds? Slinking between the sphinxes at the outer gates of the palace, I gazed out into the wild night. My feet were light, my eyes and mind clear.

A black cloud concealed the moon, but pale light reflected off the sky behind. A fierce gale roared, and I tasted the grit of sand. Birds soared across the night sky, like migrating flocks without directional instinct while shrieking like wild animals. Why were so many fowl out? I'd seen nighthawks and owls, but these were different. They arced back and forth with the speed of the wind, in all different shapes and sizes.

Through the wind gusts and screams of the birds, soft whispers rang in my ears, calling out to me. I followed the whispers.

A troop of armed soldiers appeared frozen while climbing aboard a barge on the rectangular palace lake. Sneaking onboard, I hid behind a stack of crates before removing my hood. The screams faded, as well as the swarming birds.

Wind tore at the mast, but the sails didn't open. Picking up oars, the soldiers rowed out of the canal and into the expanse of the river—toward the city of Thebes on the east bank. The quiet breaking of wood on water was masked under the howling gale. We were silent, like a tiger stalking prey. Rain splattered the deck as we docked. Piling out, men armed themselves as if ready for war, broke up into divisions, and followed their leaders into the world's largest city.

I tailed a group into Thebes and watched two soldiers smash down the door of a house. A dazzling bolt of lightning flashed across the sky, and a clap of thunder quickly answered. The soldiers dragged the inhabitants out into the storm, muffling their interrogations, screaming, and shouting.

A glimmer of green flashed to my left, accompanied by whispers like those that had summoned me to the boat. What was making this noise? I turned and followed the sound, and as I approached, the hum grew louder. A green mist cast itself upon a street, which was more than wide enough for pairs of horses and chariots traveling in both directions. But the road sat empty, save for the hundreds of stone sphinxes lining either side. With this many guardians, the path must lead to God himself, but it ran off into darkness to my left and right. Donning my hood, I stepped into the street. Cries filled the night sky, as well as thousands of swirling birds.

Chapter 53

Journal Translation

LIGHTNING FLASHED directly overhead, lighting up the sphinx-lined street. Thunder immediately reverberated in my ears. The clatter of Akhenaten's marauding regiment, barking orders and banging on buildings, carried in slow motion but drew closer. And the voices were not as drawn-out as they'd been when I'd first used the cloak. Could its magic be fading?

"Don't think I cannot see you," a voice said as thunder crackled in the hot wind.

My heart jumped and nearly stuck in my throat in surprise. I glanced left and right.

"I'm right here," the voice boomed. The hawk head of a sphinx turned! Stone groaned but didn't crack, folding like gray skin. As the beast flexed its lion digits back and forth upon its ancient bed, its massive tail flicked with agitation.

I fell backward, unable to comprehend the situation.

"Stand up, you sorry boy," the sphinx ordered.

I scrambled away.

"Run. Now's your chance." Its hooked beak parted, and a gray tongue slipped out.

"W-what do you want?" I asked. Was I hallucinating because of the cloak? But the creature moved at ordinary speed.

"I'm merely the guardian. Isn't it you who wants something?"

"Are you going to tell Akhenaten?" I asked.

"Ha!" the sphinx said. "I haven't served a pharaoh in millennia. I guard the two temples."

"What temples?"

Rearing back as if bewildered, the hawk said, "You're much too ignorant. But do not waste time." Its beak reached toward me. "One man the military is searching for is the one you're trying to save. This victim is either to your left at Karnak or to your right in Luxor Temple. You have the chance to save him."

Rising to my knees in confusion and desperation, I asked, "Who am I supposed to save?"

"You may earn the chance to see, or you may not. But you're wasting precious moments. I own all the time of the ages. You're not so fortunate. The soldiers are coming."

"Stop playing games!" I said, surprising myself as my cheeks grew hot with rage.

"Such anger," a deeper voice boomed. The adjacent sphinx spoke through the head of a ram, its horns tilting forward. "Games are not our forte. A riddle, perhaps? Or you could put up a fight while we tear you limb from limb!"

Battling stone beasts seemed like suicide. "You said I don't have time." I punched the ground in frustration.

"You don't," replied the first.

"Then please tell me which way to go," I begged.

"Let's assume this," the hawk said, the feathers on its neck lifting, "one of the two temples at each end of this road is a temple of darkness. The other is a temple of light. Except these temples are not what they seem. The guardians at the temple of light always lie and those from the temple of darkness always tell the truth in response to your questions. The person you are trying to save is inside the temple of light, and I am the guardian of one of the temples. And you only have time to visit one temple before this person is killed. Decide which temple is which way ... and hurry."

"What do truth and lies have to do with saving someone's life?"

"Everything," replied the hawk.

"And nothing," replied the ram.

Clenching my fists, I stood. The approaching marauders released a drawn-out cry just behind me. The voices were not as slow as they'd been.

To the hawk I yelled, "What way should I go?"

"To your right," he replied.

I sprinted a few feet before stopping in realization. "Which way will help me save someone?" I asked the ram. "Which way is the temple of light?"

"I am merely a guardian of the road and am not part of this riddle."

My eyes closed in frustration. The world always acted against me. "But if he tells me to go right, how do I know if he's telling the truth or not?"

"Because he always lies," the ram said. "Or always tells the truth."

"Which way is the dark temple?" I asked the hawk.

"To your left."

I groaned. If he was responding with the truth I should go right, but if he was lying I should go left. But how would I ever know? "What temple are you the guardian of?" I asked the hawk again.

"The temple of darkness," it replied and then picked at its claws with its beak. "You'd better hurry; this victim doesn't have much time left."

How in the name of the Aten would I know if that answer was the truth or a lie?

Lightning struck the head of another sphinx not twenty feet away. Stone exploded into hundreds of fragments, pelting my skin as I covered my head. The stench of rotten eggs stung my nose. Shouting from the soldiers intensified. Even in this altered state of time, I wouldn't have more than a couple of minutes before warriors swarmed the street.

If I asked the sphinx directly, it didn't make sense. Could I address it indirectly? A moment of clarity came amidst the haunting night. "Which way is your temple?" I asked the hawk.

"To your right."

Doubts filled my mind as I turned to the ram. The ram's stone lips parted as if smiling at me, although it could've been a sneer.

Throwing my hands triumphantly into the air, I ran left. It didn't matter if the hawk lied or told the truth with that question. An honest sphinx from the temple of darkness would answer in the correct direction—the opposite direction that I needed to go. A liar from the temple of light would have to say the opposite of the truth and so would also point to the temple of darkness. Either a liar or an honest sphinx's answer would lead me to the temple of darkness! So I ran in the opposite direction for this temple of light ... The sphinx had originally said that some place called Karnak was to my left.

Passing hundreds of sphinxes upon the road, many different kinds of eyes glared into my soul. I threw off my mask. Lightning arced across the sky, the flash outlining something consuming the landscape before me. The spectacle rendered me immobile, as if I'd turned to stone. More humming whispers beckoned me onward. Taking a few deep breaths, I inched forward.

The gateway to the temple of Karnak, a towering aperture between enormous pylon walls, was fashioned for giants. Images upon the stone showed titans, their radiance muted in shadow, smiting hordes of enemies. Hundreds of unseen flags whipped in the wind overhead.

Cold beads of sweat trickled down my brow and into my eyes, stinging like bees. This complex couldn't have been constructed by mortal men. Bowing my head, I sprinted between the guardians. The wind died and the interior grew darker, the perimeter walls blocking the shrouded moonlight. Creeping around soaring obelisks, I told myself not to look up, just as someone scared of heights would be afraid to look down. But I couldn't help it. I glanced to the sky. Golden capstones shimmered with moonlight against the night and reached for the stars. The crackle of lightning leapt through the darkness, illuminating the engraved faces of the obelisks. These pillars were adorned with images of divine beings, most of them animal-headed men!

I collapsed to my knees, dizzy. What was this place? Faint torchlight wavered in the vast expanse of the open-air temple ahead, in the opposite direction of the approaching soldiers.

Something else was moving too, among the shadows. The air grew warm. Wringing my bracelet, I relived my encounter with the Mummy Makers. I should've brought Croc. Should I run? No, I had to learn whatever it was I'd come here for.

A figure emerged from a crevice and moved as silently as a ghost. Cloaked in black with a very long hood, he carried a sack slung over his shoulder and a walking stick—the same person Mutnedjmet and I had followed in the slums, and whom I'd seen in the magician's lab.

Flattening myself against the wall, I pursued him. He paused, reaching for something around his neck. Sniffing, he held an amulet aloft. Green light burned from within, growing brighter and bringing incomprehensible whispers—like those that'd led me to the boat, to the sphinx-lined street, and now to this temple.

I tensed. Could this medallion detect magic, like Akhenaten had claimed? Would the cloaked figure be drawn to me? Yanking my mask down for protection, I waited. The birds appeared again, screeching and swarming the area as they blotted out moon and starlight. I could only see these beasts and hear their cries when I was wearing the panther's hood … My skin crawled with fear. What were they?

The cloaked figure approached my hiding spot, his movements half the speed as before I'd donned the hood.

I darted across the way.

Crouching low, he sniffed but eventually lumbered away. I lingered to create more distance between us before removing the panther's mask and pursuing him again at normal speed. Passing around a corner, he disappeared. I hugged the edge, my teeth chattering with fear as I gripped the bronze on my wrist. Taking a quick breath, I peeked around. Wind erupted within the confines of the temple and I tasted sand. But the figure stalked away.

The mysterious man exited an even taller gateway on the western front.

My muscles contracted. I needed to unmask him or die trying.

Pacing back toward the river, we arrived at a rectangular harbor. He released a shrill, bird-like call. Hiding behind a crate, I scrutinized the ships and skiffs docked at the port. A figure hooded in white strode down the ramp from a boat. My heart turned icy.

"How many did you find?" asked the one who'd descended from the ship. I recognized his abnormally deep voice. Akhenaten! The cloaked man *was* someone else.

"Something is not right." The other figure's voice was high-pitched with a hissing quality.

"Do not lie to me!" Akhenaten snapped, pointing a long finger.

"I want no part of this, but I cannot be deceitful. The amulet led me to Karnak, where several slept. I assisted their passing." He dropped the sack. It landed with a moist thud. "But the beacon still shines as if there is a magician present, even though there is not enough left in this sack to allow for life. And no others are here. I do not understand." He held the amulet aloft, and it glowed green again.

"You are not here to understand," Akhenaten said, glancing off into the night as if searching for someone. "You are merely a tool. How many did you gather?"

"Four," the enigmatic figure said, pushing the sack over to Akhenaten with a concealed foot.

"There are still more out there." Snatching the bag, Akhenaten ascended the ramp to his boat.

They were both going to leave ... I needed to see what was inside the bag, and who this other man was.

Guards onboard the ship took up oars. Perhaps I gained courage from the powers of the cloak, but before I could think, I pulled the mask back down and ran at Akhenaten. As his foot eased into the boat, I seized the sack and threw it down the ramp. Grunting, Akhenaten turned as several rocks—no, blood-soaked *hearts*—rolled out from inside and bounced down the plank. Convulsing with chills, I stifled a gasp and turned to flee.

"Someone tore the bag from my hand!" Akhenaten screamed in slow motion.

The cloaked figure rose up before me, an inhuman face shadowed beneath. The rank stench of decaying flesh billowed out.

Chapter 54

Journal Translation

MOONLIGHT REFLECTED OFF the lake, shining underneath the draping hood of the cloaked figure. Green scales and a long snout flashed. The face of nightmares, the Devouring Monster itself! Jaws parted to reveal hundreds of yellow teeth, the stink of death wafting out. I couldn't move. Unsheathing a serrated blade of bone, the creature took a battle stance as its reptilian eyes darted about.

It must not have been able to see me. But my blood ran cold in panic. Akhenaten descended the ramp as the Monster blocked my escape route onto shore. I was trapped. Lightning arced overhead.

I kicked one of the hearts from the sack off the ramp and into the water below. A splash erupted. Diving in after it, the Monster swam like a fish. He'd taken the bait. Dashing down the ramp, I leapt onto solid ground and raced into the night. Screams of rage rang behind me, amidst the crying of birds. Emerging from the water, the Monster held a heart into the air. It devoured the organ with moist chomps. Akhenaten chanted.

Three birds swooped down at me, all supporting the heads of men! I ducked just as they grazed my back with sharp talons. More *ba*! And I could only see and hear them while wearing the panther's hood.

"I will find you!" Akhenaten roared. "And the Aten will smite your devils!"

Another winged nightmare dove and knocked me over, releasing an ear-piercing wail. Ripping off the hood to make them disappear, I sprinted into the city.

Those sphinxes had lied, even after I'd solved their riddle! I'd been too late to save anyone. And Akhenaten would discover me missing. He might not believe I could perform such deeds as stalking him and his Devouring Monster while remaining unseen, but he was always suspicious of me. Now, when he sailed back to the palace, checked in on me, and found me gone from my room, he would know or at least highly suspect that I was somehow involved in what'd just happened.

I'd head back for Nefertiti, and we'd never set foot in Thebes or Memphis again.

Waiting for over an hour, I donned my hood and returned to the docks. Cries of the dead, from the *ba*—the birds with human heads—filled my ears. Akhenaten's boat was gone. Jumping onto a reed skiff, I rowed away. No screams of alarm followed, and I didn't want to waste any more magic. I removed my hood and guided the raft through a narrow channel as straight as a city road. The Nile emerged, its dark current grabbing my vessel and almost spilling me over. But I sailed to the western bank and dragged the skiff into thick brush. This would be our escape vehicle, for the three of us—me, Nefertiti, and Croc.

As I hiked toward the palace for the last time, the Aten peaked over the horizon and shot rays of soft light across the ground. Groaning carried across the open desert in sharp crescendos. My eyebrows rose in bewilderment when I spotted two stone giants resting upon thrones in the distance. But they appeared immobile, like enormous statues.

Was this an answer to one of my many questions about the gods and magic, or another trick? As I cut across barren land, the statues rose into the heavens. Basking in the young light of the Aten, their appearance was unmistakable. Both were Amenhotep III, Akhenaten's father. The moaning originated from one of the titans, although neither of their lips parted. Behind them loomed pylon walls and a gateway even more massive than the one outside the temple of Karnak. What waited inside these walls? Another temple?

I paused in the vast shadow of the seated kings, their feet stretching longer than I was tall. What did his grumbling mean? He didn't form distinct words, but his pain was obvious.

The morning sun grew fierce, causing the statue's groan to transition to a roar. Then it ceased.

A troop of singing men approached from the west. Pulling my hood back down, I crouched behind a statue and waited. Great doors of plated gold swung inward at the temple beyond the stone giants. Flags, also of brilliant gold, fluttered from staffs mounted over the gateway. The contingent of singing men bowed their shaven heads and marched inside at more than half-speed. I'd fought my fate with all the strength I'd possessed in attempting to avenge Father and pursue Nefertiti, but now instead of rushing back to the palace to rescue her, I followed the call of something inside this temple.

Stepping between the sentinels, I followed the singing men. A paved trail littered with silver and gold bricks celebrated the rays of the Aten. Overwhelmed with enchantment, I struggled for breath—this was the most magnificent temple the world would ever know.

Priests wandered the sunlit interior. Radiant reliefs adorned pillars and walls, portraying Amenhotep smiting enemies or worshipping animal-headed beings. The representation of a mummy holding a crook and flail was carved from a black stone with mirroring depths.

"Interesting, is it not?" a voice spoke at normal speed.

Lurching, I turned to bolt out of the golden gates. But the magician, the son of Hapu, stood beside me, examining the artwork. He'd abandoned his wig and reclaimed the scrawling black wrinkles, contrasting against the white cat on his shoulder and hiding his consuming spider veins.

"Sculpted from volcanic glass. Obsidian."

"Are you talking to me?" I whispered. And how could he speak at normal speed if I was still wearing my hood—

"Well, I am a crazy old man and sometimes mutter to myself." He smiled, not looking at me. "But don't worry, there're no longer any others inside this temple who can sense you. They've been disposed of by the Hunter … and you've finally seen under his hood, haven't you. The face of nightmares."

"I don't trust anyone, including you."

"I granted you the opportunity to leave, remember?" He reached his palms toward the obsidian Pharaoh.

"You tried to usurp the throne, but Akhenaten prevailed! You're no better."

"We had different reasons for our ambition." He bowed toward the statue. "I attempted to save Egypt in return for you aiding me. But it's late and my powers grow feeble with—"

"How did I aid you?" My face wrinkled with skepticism.

"You stayed to fight when you had no chance and could've run. I saw your raw will, the sheer determination of a mere boy, and realized mighty people still dwell beside the river, even if one cannot spot them with the naked eye. For a moment, you gave me hope. But I still foresee the kingdom's demise. And if you had not solved the sphinxes' riddle, you would've led the Hunter straight to me. He tracked the magic you now command. One of the hearts in that bag would've been mine."

My eyebrows arched onto my forehead. The sphinxes might not have deceived me …

"But you've reclaimed the power to save yourself. Forsake this land and never return."

"I will vanish! I've nothing left here." I paused in the midst of heaving breaths. "But before I leave, please tell me why Amenhotep's statue groans."

"He cries for Egypt, suffering even in death." The magician pointed at me. "The stars are fading."

"What?" I looked down at the cloak. The stars that originally shone like beacons now appeared as embers from a dying fire.

"What became of the original owner?" he asked, a muscle in his neck twitching.

"He was murdered by Akhenaten's soldiers, and he melted into the sand."

He ran a hand across his spotted head. "He may not be dead. Was he shaven as a priest?"

"No, he wore his hair and beard long and gray."

"That one hates bathing and shaving. Believes them to be a waste of time." The son of Hapu nodded at a priest in the distance who was looking this way and smiled. "He is quite odiferous. A time bender. Now his grimy cloak drapes your shoulders."

"A time bender?" I asked, ignoring the itching arising on my back.

"He is about twenty years old, in the time of this world."

"We must speak of different men. The one I saw couldn't have been a day less than eighty," I said.

"The man is one of a kind amongst the current threads of the present. He can control time so masterfully, he could crawl away and yet be moving so fast no one would be able to see him. Slowing down time for others or speeding it up for himself, he floats through the webs like a spider.

Unfortunately, he's used his gift far too frequently and now has no time left. His mortal body has aged even when he's slowed down the fabric for others. Living only two decades in our world, he's spent closer to eight in his own."

Thoughts bounced around in my head, confusing me.

"More importantly, have you seen evidence of the other gods? The Aten is the disc, but what of Re? And Osiris, Horus, Amun? Many others."

"I saw the inside of the temple of Karnak." I swallowed. "Are you a blasphemer?"

Chuckling, he held a finger to his lips. "Yes, but do not tell! No one can force beliefs upon you; Akhenaten's already tried. Now go!"

Tiye approached, her gaze on the ground as her red hair drifted in the wind. Staring with vacant eyes, she faced the obsidian statue and took the magician's arm. "My Amenhotep as Osiris himself."

Dashing from Amenhotep's mortuary complex, his final temple, I hiked until the Gleaming Palace of the Aten arose before me. The sun sank toward the horizon. I donned my cloak and snuck between guards who were withering in the heat like plants. But when I passed the rearing sphinxes of the palace, an ear-piercing shriek rang out.

I froze in fear. The soldiers glanced at each other, their eyes growing wide. Those damn sphinxes were a twisting thorn in my heel! Did Akhenaten control them? I ran into the palace and the comfort of shadows.

I didn't have to wait long outside Pharaoh's bedchamber. Akhenaten and Kiya appeared in the corridor under a servant's lamplight. Their footsteps came at a nearly normal pace. Crouching in a dark corner, I attempted to breathe quietly, but tension racked my body. What if *he* could see me? My heart beat so loud, they must've been able to hear it. They stepped closer and closer. I should run. My hands trembled, and sweat rolled down my brow. His golden scepter struck the tile at my feet, issuing a clap. I flinched.

Akhenaten's eyes focused on mine! His expression didn't change, but his dark gaze told me that he knew I was there and had figured out what I'd done. Run! But before I could flee, they passed into the room and shut the door.

Releasing a stifled sigh, I crept to Nefertiti's private doorway. I quietly opened the door and peeked in. Empty. But within minutes, her beauty lit the hall. My heart sang. Her slowed movement appeared like the enchanting spell of a temptress. Two female servants flanked her. I slipped into her room.

A single lamp flickered as sweet rose and citrus permeated the air. She entered. The servants slid her dress off, revealing her naked body. My pulse quickened, and I felt faint. I'd never beheld such beauty. Biting my lip, I attempted to control myself. Salty blood trickled into my mouth. I shouldn't stare, but I couldn't look away.

After being dressed in a white sleeping gown, she lay on her framed bed, her head cradled into the crescent pillow. Her eyes closed. The servants extinguished the lamp and exited.

Faint moonlight shone through the windows, outlining her figure. Her chest rose and fell under the light fabric. My mouth went dry as fear set in. I couldn't move. She would be difficult to hide as the wife of a commoner. Would it be safer outside Egypt's borders? But where would we go? What would we do? Could I make her happy? Would we be able to remain hidden from Akhenaten?

I clenched my jaw. If she loved me, I could make her happy. My fingers wrapped around Father's bracelet in a crushing grip as I pushed off the panther's mask. "Nefertiti," I whispered. "Nefertiti!"

Chapter 55

Journal Translation

NEFERTITI'S EYES POPPED OPEN. Glancing around under the pale moonlight inside her bedchamber, she rose to her elbows. "Who's there?"

"I-it's Heb," I said, completely sliding off my cloak.

She gasped as I emerged from the darkness. "By Amun, what, how did—"

"There's not time; please listen. I've come for you!" I offered a shaky hand. Damn my weakness. "We can leave forever and find happiness."

She slid her silky palm against mine. "Heb, if you weren't nervous, I'd think I may not mean much to you, or you were blind with arrogance. I've always loved that you care for me so deeply and you've protected me ..." She took a deep breath. "But what would become of us?"

"We can move to a small farm, like where I was born. I'll work elsewhere until we can harvest our own plot. The kingdom's large enough to hide in. We'll be happy."

Smiling, she closed her green eyelids. "We might be able to hide. And you'd be a good farmer. If you can serve Akhenaten, you can do anything."

"But what?" I asked, tapping my foot while watching the door with apprehension. She had told me she loved me. We needed to leave, not have a discussion. Women ...

"Things are different now." She blushed. "I am the Queen of Egypt, the Great Royal Wife. Akhenaten and I ... we will have a child, a daughter, I believe."

"What?" I cried, clamping a hand over my mouth.

"She grows inside me." She placed a hand over her stomach, still not protruding much.

How had I not noticed? "We can care for her as our own. Leaving her with the beast who created her would consign her to a life of misery."

Nefertiti stuck out her lower lip. "I didn't want anything to do with Akhenaten. He made me suffer for my defiance. But things are different now. He is Pharaoh, and Thutmose, my once betrothed crown prince, is dead."

I stood in dumb silence, unable to believe my ears. "He's your cousin. I know that's okay for some of the royal family, but I thought you were …"

"Lie with me, Heb," she said, patting the area beside her. I slowly settled down onto the taut, woven rope creating her bed, and my body grew excited. "This isn't something I can run from. I do have feelings for you, and in another life, you could've been the one for me, but you cannot compare to the greatness of Akhenaten."

"Please, Nefertiti," I begged. "I love you more than life itself. I've suffered this affliction only because I didn't want to leave *you*. Someone tried to help me escape back in Memphis, but I endured misery to save you … and myself."

Tears brimmed in Nefertiti's eyes and graced her cheek as a trickle. I caught the droplets with my fingertip, and she burst into tears. "Heb, I love you for everything you've done and who you are, but there're more important things!"

"Than love and happiness?"

"To be taken care of!" She rolled her eyes. "And my status, child, and life here!"

What? "We'll figure it out! Farmers have large families, and everyone's living in plenty."

"Heb," her tone turned sour as she twisted away, her supple skin sliding against the firm bed, "I had loved you, but that isn't the life I want. I desire *so* much more. I yearn for people to look upon the great Nefertiti with envy and jealousy of all her wealth and power and wish to be me. I hunger for a husband who is God, who can adore my beauty for eternity, even if he doesn't tenderly care for me in this life. One who has everything a woman desires."

"Akhenaten?" I asked in disbelief.

Her voice grew distant. "He's the pinnacle of our world. That's what people long for above all, only most women can't obtain the man at the top." She stared into my eyes, her own not those of the same person I'd fallen in love with. Holding my breath, I dared not inhale her deceitful scent. "I'd rather be struck and scolded while living with all the possessions and power I'd ever dreamed of than be a happy farmer's wife. The sooner you understand, the sooner you'll find yourself an equal woman."

My heart cracked, decay breaking through the surface as it stopped beating for eternity. Nefertiti might as well have cut the pumping organ from my chest with Akhenaten's soul-drinking knife and fed it to the Devouring Monster. Pain beyond the hippo attack, the enduring infection, Akhenaten, Father's death, solitary confinement, disgracing Father by serving the murderous god-king, pain beyond any other that came later in life stabbed me directly in the heart. Lying still, I couldn't respond. Nefertiti exited the room on quiet feet, closing the door behind her. I'd be put to death if she came back with a guard or Akhenaten, but I didn't care.

Stupefied, I couldn't go any further. The pit of my stomach burned and scarred my soul, never to heal.

But the door opened and she stepped back inside, locking the latch behind her. Her white nightgown stood out in the darkness, hugging her curves. Stepping closer, she kissed my cheek. My body tensed in surprise. She kissed my lips, hers lingering. I knew she wouldn't turn down my love! Our bodies melted together, all the parts of her sensuous skin rubbing on mine. We experienced a transcendence I had no idea existed. I could alter my fate, and this world could be amazing ...

✳ ✳ ✳

I awoke with a jolt, and the first rays of the Aten ran across the ceiling. We had to get out of here! And I had to get Croc. I sat up on the floor while Nefertiti slept on the bed above. Sliding my kilt on, I reached for the panther skin. Empty space. Where was it? I rummaged under the bed. Nothing. I tore the place apart. The time-bending garment was our only escape!

I shook Nefertiti, but something else was out of place. She rolled over. My jaw dropped as I screamed.

Chapter 56

Present Day

"You believe there was a talking sphinx?" I asked Maddie from the air-conditioned bus seat that was not covered with a towel this time—which I had typically used as a safe guard from germs on communal fabric seats. We'd sorted through the images within the secret chamber under Lake Nasser and headed north.

"The journal couldn't be written into a history text," she said, rolling her straight hair into a bun. "But how do we know the ancients didn't wield a kind of magic, art, or skill lost to the ages?" Hugging me, she kissed my cheek. "I'm so glad you're okay. I thought the crocodile might've killed you."

Warmth rose and spread throughout my body. Squeezing the armrest, I held back a shout of elation and hugged her back. "I was worried none of us would make it out of—"

Smacking my shoulder, Aiden said, "I can't get over how we entered a giant crocodile's lair and found the clue, bro!" Leaning across the aisle, he squeezed both of us.

The vehicle screeched to a stop at a bus station, and we and the other passengers all unloaded. Heat smacked me in the face with a dusty wind as I stepped into Luxor City and adjusted my fedora to block the sun's rays. The calling of goats pinged around the surrounding desert like the cries of lost children.

"Sorry, guys," Jenkins said for the hundredth time, his feet kicking up dust. "I guess I'm not much of a bodyguard when it comes to wild animals. Never had to contend with that before."

"It's okay," Maddie said, placing a hand on his back. "I almost died of fright, but that was all. I'd like to say the crocodile was more afraid of us than we were of it, but that would've been impossible."

"So now we're looking for the original sun worshipper?" Kaylin asked, leading us around throngs of locals and vendor stations as well as clusters of chattering tourists.

"Yes," I said. "Amenhotep III could be credited with worshipping the sun-disc as the supreme god of—"

"Akhenaten was the first to bring monotheism," Maddie said, wrinkling the bridge of her nose. "But you're probably right. Akhenaten's temples used to reside near here, but the professor couldn't have found clues in his courts if they were destroyed millennia ago."

Maddie finally agreed with me and hadn't even used sarcasm.

"What did the last riddle actually say?" Mr. Scalone asked.

Maddie rubbed her forehead and adjusted her glasses. "I wiped algae off of the carvings in the wall of the secret chamber as best I could and took pictures, but someone had tried to scratch the message away. The writing wasn't hieroglyphic, either. It was hieratic script, which scribes used for letters and records."

"They had, like, multiple languages?" Kaylin asked.

"Multiple ways to write," I said. "Originally they didn't use an alphabet, so there were thousands of hieroglyphs, one for every word or sound. This was so slow to read and write, scribes developed another form."

"How do we know how to read it, then?" Kaylin asked.

"The Rosetta Stone," I said. "The same message was engraved in hiero-glyphs, script, and Greek."

"This path is a test of knowledge," Maddie whispered.

"So what did it say?" Mr. Scalone demanded, clapping to grab our attention.

Irritation sank in. Perhaps he feared his ignorance would lead to a challenge of his authority.

"Something like ..." Maddie's eyes rolled back and forth as if reading the ancient scrawl. "'Follow the path downriver,' which is north, 'to the complex of the sun and Pharaoh who speaks to the sun. Where it began'—or this could mean 'where it ended.'"

"Began!" I said. "Amenhotep's birth room and the *benben* stone, the origin of the earth as it arose from the primordial waters of the universe, are both in Luxor City at Luxor Temple."

We turned right onto a crowded, statue-lined road toward Luxor Temple, and Maddie said, "'The guardians will guide you with light and shadow.' Then there was a bizarre reference to the floating eye of Horus and the *benben* stone ..."

"What's with all the headless lions?" Aiden asked, jutting a thumb at the hundreds of stone sphinxes lining the roadway. His little fox trotted beside him.

"The sphinxes guard the avenue," Maddie said. "The intact faces are of a pharaoh from the last dynasty, but in prior ancient times, they supported animal heads."

"What do they do?" he asked, running a pale hand across the scorched stone of a beheaded sphinx.

"They protect the temples and Egypt," I said, walking on. "They're the most fearsome guardians on earth."

A towering obelisk and two statues of Rameses emerged, flanked by soaring pylon walls—pylon walls created a monumental gateway with the space between them and in ancient times would've been adorned with flags coated in shimmering metal.

"You're not going to, like, run away again, are you, Maddie?" Kaylin laughed.

"That's the same pharaoh dude as at the Simbel place," Aiden said, pointing at the seated colossi of Rameses. "What're we lookin' for here?"

The sun was descending into the west as Maddie's chin slumped. "Shadow and light."

Slipping between the statues, we passed the soaring pylon walls into Luxor Temple and Amenhotep's colonnade and sun court. Long shadows and light spiraled around pillars that resembled papyrus stalks. Searching areas still illuminated and others now in darkness, I wove around standing and toppled columns. How many years had passed since the path to the Hall had been laid? And how many people had browsed this temple since archaeologists had uncovered the structure in the eighteenth century—at the time calling this place "Waset," when it was in fact ancient Thebes? How could all the archaeologists have missed a clue to the Hall?

I scanned thousands of engravings adorning the walls and colonnades, only seeing typical god worship with offerings, or displays of Pharaoh's ultimate power and claim to the monuments.

"That looks like porn." Aiden snickered, pointing. "Egyptians drew that in their temples? Maybe I'd go to church if they still did that."

Maddie sighed. "It's the conception of the divine Amenhotep. This is his birth room. There's his birth." She motioned to another image of the diminutive pharaoh.

"Focus, Aiden," Mr. Scalone said, half smacking the teen on the back of the head. After glancing at the images, the guide winked at Maddie. She blushed.

My stomach twisted in the grip of jealousy.

"I was focused," Aiden said, "but you got in my way."

"Grow up," Mr. Scalone said, pushing his dark locks out of his face and knocking the cap off Aiden's head.

"Why you gotta bust my balls all the time?" Aiden snatched his hat and sauntered off.

Kaylin smacked Mr. Scalone's chest. "Leave him alone."

"The boy's completely awkward," Mr. Scalone said. "He needs a strong male to shape him up. How can he be related to you? I swear, if it wasn't for his red hair, I'd think he and Gavin were separated at birth."

I gritted my teeth in annoyance. Concentrate, the light was fading!

Walking into a cloak of shade, I entered the inner Opet temple. Twelve pillars stood in a cramped hall, representing the hours of sunlight. In the center of the temple, a mound rested in eternal silence, the supposed inception of the earth. My mind grew distant as I traced images of the rise and descent of the sun.

Maddie entered and stared but diverted her gaze. "How long until you're supposed to be back for your next rotation? So you don't get kicked out of med school and have to move in with your mom."

Anxiety wrenched on my insides. "If I leave Cairo in four days, I'll be back in time to make morning rounds the first Monday of my internal medicine rotation." But everyone would whisper to each other about what I'd done.

"We'd better get moving, then."

"Honestly," I said, "deep down I thought this whole thing would've been a sham and we'd have left by now. I didn't anticipate traveling to ancient temples on a treasure hunt."

Maddie shook her head. "Did you think that after all the knowledge they amassed over thousands of years, the ancient geniuses would hide the world's greatest secrets with a single clue? We still can't duplicate their architectural feats without modern technology. Would *you* leave a prize so precious for just anyone?"

Desire for their secrets clouded my mind.

"What happened back at school, anyway?" Maddie asked. "What was so bad that you'd suddenly give up trying to become a doctor and come here to chase what your dad probably thought was a hoax? If he'd believed the professor's letter, why didn't he search for the Hall years ago?"

My stomach cramped with a hollow pain, like someone had kicked me. Memories of the gnarled foot flashed through my mind. Varicose veins bulged like roots above crumbling yellow toenails. The dismembered tissue seeped blood across my hands, staining my soul. The lady's face appeared, a woman old enough to be my grandma. Guilt had made me run. That and the chance to explore Egypt with Maddie. And during the incident, I'd been fantasizing of doing exactly what I was doing at this moment! Was I like Heb? Heb had faced harsher trials than me and yet still called up the courage to chase his dream, even if he'd suffer for the remainder of his days. He'd served his most hated enemy so that he could pursue his deepest desires. I hadn't come close. I'd run to school and then from school. Heb's father had wanted the best for his son, to live the grand life of a scribe. But they'd settled for servitude. Should I just follow the fate society chose for me?

My stomach churned. I shouldn't continue to make the same mistakes of the past. Maddie, like Nefertiti, could turn me down for her own ambitions, or worse, pretend to love me like Nefertiti with Akhenaten. Or she might fall for Mr. Scalone. He was more her type.

"I entered the OR running behind as always, trying to keep up. The anesthesiologist already had the woman under, and the nurse didn't want to wait, so she had already draped the leg. But I was supposed to do it!" My dark tale released suppressed fear, shame, and remorse. Anger, however, took control, anger directed at life, at my dad for taking his life, at

Akhenaten, at Nefertiti, and for Heb. "She draped the left foot the woman was complaining about that day. Maybe she'd sprained it from putting all her weight on it, but it was her other foot that had to go! The nurse didn't notice the discrepancy. It was my job to double-check! I was thinking about you in Egypt and wanting to be there with you! Then the surgeon burst in and started barking orders. I didn't want to upset him by asking questions."

Maddie's eyes bulged.

"And my dad would've wanted to pursue the letter, but his health deteriorated over the last ten years of his life. Maybe he couldn't see himself attempting it, in and out of the hospital all the time, not being able to travel. Maybe he didn't want to give away his secret or didn't need the glory. Maybe he wanted me to do it! Yes, he wanted me to find it when I was old enough, but before becoming too crippled by his disease!"

Chapter 57

Present Day

"SORRY!" MADDIE SAID, stepping away from me after I'd yelled and unleashed my anger upon her for my past medical mistake, and for my dad's disease. Surprise or even panic masked the pity on her face. "I didn't mean to imply anything negative about your dad, and I didn't know about the surgery … it wasn't all your fault."

Heat intensified in my cheeks. I turned away, ashamed and regretful, and studied the inner temple and the twelve pillars representing the hours of daylight. The sunlight overhead waned.

"Gavin?" she asked in a peep.

Running footsteps stopped behind me. "What happened?" Jenkins's quiet voice asked.

I exited the small Opet temple and wandered back through the sun court of Luxor Temple, feeling sick for unleashing my frustrations on Maddie.

There were no obvious clues anywhere in this place.

I wandered out of Luxor Temple, and the heat and dust strangled me. Shadows crawled across the heads and chests of the red granite and the black stone Rameses. Their bodies and the diminutive figures of the queen at his feet—one identical queen for each Rameses—rejoiced in the wavering battle of luminescence versus shade. Stone hands rested in their laps with flat fingers, none arching into weird—

"Could they simply guide us by where they're looking?" Maddie asked, stepping out from the temple with the others.

"That would not be a clear answer to the riddle," I said, feeling better that she would still speak to me.

"But it said the guardians will guide you." She tightened the bun atop her head. "We didn't find anything else." Pulling out her phone, she filmed the seated pharaohs from multiple angles. "I'll put this in my computer tonight."

"Is there anything important that way?" Kaylin asked, pointing north.

"The Karnak Temple Complex," I said, having no better ideas than to look elsewhere.

Hiking the road again, with other groups of assorted tourists, we followed a bend and strode between hundreds of ram-headed sphinxes. Rows of towering walls dominated the landscape before us. Intricately carved images of men, gods, and the winged sun-disc protected the gateway of the temple of Khonsu—a small portion of Karnak.

"We're gonna find a clue in there?" Mr. Scalone asked, spreading his arms to emphasize the enormity of Karnak. "We need to clarify the last clue about guardians first. Let me see it."

He had a point. Karnak was the largest temple complex ever built by man—247 acres—and could take years to search. What would the guardians of Karnak be? The obelisks? More statues of Rameses, or Osiris, or the sphinxes holding Amun between their paws? But the sphinxes and statues of Amun only stared at each other and the road between them. We were lost. Of the holy trinity of temples that composed Karnak—Amun, the father; Mut, the mother; and Khonsu, the son, also known as the moon and 'the traveler'—we chose to start with the most obvious, the temple of Amun.

We entered between massive pylon walls. I examined stone art, spotting desecrated images of Amun, the dirty work of Akhenaten. Stunted palm trees grew beside a sacred but now dry lakebed, where long ago holy geese would swim. We investigated a hidden underground temple but discovered nothing. The tallest obelisk in the world, before the Washington Monument was erected to commemorate George Washington's apotheosis, soared into the heavens. This creation had been ordered by Hatshepsut, one of the only female pharaohs. In ancient times, the glorious monument would've housed a twin at its side, the finest gold of their pyramidions shimmering beneath brilliant rays of sun. Now the base of the single piece of rose granite was worn smooth, the peak dull.

My feet dragged the dirt like lead weights under my growing pessimism. This was too difficult at every turn, and I'd been an ass to Maddie.

Wandering off through halls and courtyards, I arrived at Karnak's Great Hypostyle Hall. An entire forest of stone pillars supported a rock beam canopy, casting dense shadows below. The few remaining clerestory windows created slatted, arcing rays of light and dark in the interior. Maybe this was it! But I had to hurry; the sunlight was fading.

I glanced around for Maddie. Two men in *thawbs* leaned against a wall in the distance, eyeing me and whispering. One man wore a beard to his chest; the other's lay patchy upon his cheeks. Our hired hands from that desert night outside Amenhotep's tomb and at the train station? My heart raced in surprise, fear pulling at the root of my tongue like hands on a rope. Tugging the gray brim of my fedora lower, I strode back to the others.

"Are those the men you hired for the Valley of the Kings expedition?" I whispered to Mr. Scalone, subtly nodding toward them.

"I don't know," Mr. Scalone said, wrinkling his forehead as he stared directly at them. "I found those locals that night. I didn't know 'em and didn't memorize their faces in the dark. Most Egyptians look the same to me, anyway."

"They're definitely the two who departed our train in Cairo," I said. "I don't want to get trapped in here." Rushing adrenaline coursed through my limbs and mingled with fear. How had they followed us to Thebes?

"There's only two," Mr. Scalone said, stretching his legs in his tight jeans. "I could handle both, but if they have weapons, Jenkins and I could each take one."

"Come on, Gavin," Maddie said, her face pale. "These men are obviously watching us."

"It's almost sunset," Kaylin said, tugging my sleeve, her head spinning to follow the radiance filtering through the panels overhead. "We don't want to miss the remaining light."

"Let's come back tomorrow, before sunrise," I said.

Mr. Scalone threw his hands into the air. "You two scared little girls! I can protect us."

Jenkins cranked his head in a motion to leave, his hand reaching inside his jacket.

"C'mon, Gavin," Kaylin said, caressing the back of my neck. "Only *you* can solve this!"

Tossing his head back, Mr. Scalone scoffed and slapped his knee.

I touched the bronze bracelet under my sleeve. This was almost my last chance to change my life forever. "Another minute," I said. Maddie's eyes closed. "But if they come for us, we run as a group in the opposite direction." I grabbed Maddie's hand, my tongue fumbling in an attempt to explain and ease her fear. "I wasn't prepared for all this, either. But I have to be back at school soon. We'll be okay. I'm s—"

Kaylin clapped and kissed my cheek. Maddie pulled away and hid behind the nearest stone pillar as Aiden clutched his fox to his chest.

I studied the moving light. Because of broken strips in the overhead windows, radiance and shade didn't fall evenly on the area. Specific hieroglyphs lit up in columns, while others blotted out. There had to be something here!

"You better mind-hump this place quick," Aiden said, placing his hands on his knees and breathing hard. "Those men are coming."

Jenkins cursed under his breath.

"Gavin!" Maddie said, cupping a hand beside her mouth. "Let's go!"

"They can't trap us in here, right?" Kaylin asked, running her hand down my back.

"No, there're too many ways out … unless someone locks all the gates," I said, still searching as a knot of anxiety tightened in my stomach. The alternating images around me didn't make any sense. Stepping back, I soaked in the entire spectacle.

"Why are you letting her manipulate you?" Maddie asked, removing her glasses. "She's seducing you like her other mindless boy toys!"

I tensed. No, I was more entranced with the prospect of discovery.

Spinning on Maddie, Kaylin's voice escalated. "You're just scared. We have Jenkins and Mr. Scalone to protect us! And you never liked Gavin, just his attention after guys dump you." Her arms whirled as if trying to assist in her verbal assault. "Go after one of your exes who might've been something in high school but now's just a loser."

My entire body stiffened with the awkwardness of the situation.

Maddie stumbled, and her lips moved a couple of times as if she were trying to speak. "Sorry!" She thrust a finger back and forth between Kaylin and Mr. Scalone. "If I believed every arrogant tool who thinks they'll be a celebrity, star athlete, or CEO, I'd be a gullible doll like you!"

Kaylin advanced, her fists curling. "You only might like Gavin now, because he's *finally* good at something—Egyptian treasure hunting—and has shown some potential."

Maddie's face deepened to the color of a ripe tomato as she turned to me. But she swallowed, and her face relaxed. "You wanted to be an Egyptologist more than anyone I've ever known. I couldn't love someone who was too afraid to chase his dreams, who settled. I might be afraid for my safety, but at least I'm not afraid of who I am."

My jaw must've hit the ground in utter shock, my heart sinking like the *Titanic*.

"I want someone who'll fight for what they believe in," Maddie said, tears welling in her eyes. "Gavin, you're naïve if you think you'll find the Hall without being completely committed. But this last little while, you were smart as always, but also determined and even courageous, like during our diving expedition. I was … falling for you." She motioned to Kaylin. "Kaylin's just using you the only way she knows how."

Joy and frustration brought cramping pain in my gut. She had been falling for me? But she didn't understand the hardships of my past enough to judge me. "I'm trying like hell right now," I said, "and *you* want me to leave."

"You're missing the point." Maddie shook her head. "If you committed to this life, you wouldn't need to accomplish this right now when it's dangerous. You'd have plenty of time."

Kaylin struggled to speak as her chest rose and fell. "Gavin, you can't achieve all this, but I've been leading you on and trying to tempt you into staying so that Mr. Scalone can."

Puffing up his chest, the guide shouldered past Jenkins.

"Mr. Scalone is a world-renowned treasure hunter, not a stupid tour guide. My dad hired him so we can lay claim to the Hall!"

Aiden's arms turned limp, and he dropped his fox.

Maddie huffed and stomped off.

Distress forced my shoulders down. Staring at the ground, I prayed to every god I didn't believe in to reveal a clue. I needed to show them I could do—

A piercing shriek carried around the columns. *Maddie!* My heart jumped.

I sprinted toward the cry as Jenkins drew his gun and followed. A man in a hooded *thawb* wrapped a black cloak around a struggling figure. Lifting his victim, he raced away. But Maddie's messenger bag slid out and fell into the dirt.

A gunshot rang out. Echoes reverberated violently off ancient stone. Wandering goats scattered. "Stop!" Jenkins's usually quiet voice roared across the acres as he lowered his handgun from having fired into the air.

The abductor kicked through an outer gate and disappeared, fading into the dwindling rays of light. I raced after him, burst through the exit, and glanced around.

Vendors, locals, and tourists crowded the dirty streets of the city outside Karnak. No sign of Maddie or her captor.

"Go that way!" Jenkins pointed, spit flying from his lips. "If you see anything, scream like there's a zombie apocalypse."

We dashed in different directions, my mind a blur of emotion. As I shoved past a thin man with a turban, I nearly tripped over a stray dog.

"Gavin!" A muffled scream carried by.

I spotted something—a cloaked figure and someone struggling. They ran through a horde of people taking pictures of Karnak and bumped into a parked car. "Maddie!" I yelled as loud as I could. Elbowing through the crowd, I knocked over a stand brimming with leafy greens and red vegetables.

At the edge of the street, the abductor with the patchy beard eyed me from beneath his cloak. Wrapping his arms around his bundled victim, he sneered and fought to keep her moving.

I propelled through a family of tourists, nearly upon him. Maddie's hand reached out from under the black cloak. I lunged for her.

Something smacked into the side of my head. I toppled over. Glaring light filled my eyes, and pain radiated through my skull. I couldn't move. Maddie's cries faded along with the dark outlines of two men. The world spun in ripples of aching radiance and darkness. Her sheer glasses lay upon the stone walk, staring as if judging me. Fighting to stand, I attempted to run after her but collapsed. The crumbling walls of the western entrance to Karnak loomed over me, dissolving into blinding white.

Chapter 58

Journal Translation

THE WOMAN LYING IN BED inside Nefertiti's room, the woman I'd spent the night with, was not Nefertiti. It was Beketaten, Akhenaten's vindictive sister! My toes curled in disgust, nausea rising in my belly. I stared, my mouth gaping in shock. "What're you doing here?"

Smirking, Beketaten brushed black hair from her face. "I hope you're screaming for joy. You took me into your bed last night, remember?"

"This is Nefertiti's bed!" I said.

"I heard voices and listened at the door," she said. "She obviously didn't want you."

Had Beketaten cast magic, or had my mind deceived me into believing what I'd wanted? "*We* slept together last night?"

"I thought you'd want a woman's comfort," she said, her long nose twitching as she talked. "And I despise Nefertiti for always wanting to make me jealous. It brings comfort when Akhenaten shares himself with me, but I wanted to take someone who truly loved her."

Crushing pressure squeezed my stomach, too soon after I'd been reignited by the hope of Nefertiti's love. I needed to think, to get out of here. "Where's my cloak?"

Her forehead furrowed. "You wore only a kilt last night, and not for very long …"

I tossed aside tables and chairs as the daylight amplified. Without assistance, it'd be impossible for me to escape the palace unseen.

Like a smack in the face, I realized the pelt lay beside the bed. I just hadn't recognized it. The stars had completely faded, and the black fur had lightened to a typical jaguar yellow. Throwing it on, I pulled down the mask.

Laughing, Beketaten pointed at me. Her giggling wasn't delayed.

Pain twisted my gut. The magic must've been spent, and I looked like a fool.

The door burst open! Akhenaten glared, a thin snarl creeping across his face. "You have returned, my faithful, loyal servant." His words dripped with sarcasm as he studied the jaguar cloak of the magician who'd approached us in the Aten temple. Clearing his throat, his eyes narrowed, making the black above them grow. "Tell me, do you wield magic?"

My face flushed in horror as my heart let loose. I let the cloak fall to the ground. "I'm just a servant! I don't hold any power, my lord."

Stepping forward, he revealed something from behind his back—a deep-blue feather and an empty sack stained with blood. "This is an ostrich feather of Ma'at. The Feather of Truth. For you to keep for the remainder of your days, and to remember what really happened, as well as your shame. The heart sack, you've seen before—just the other night." He paused, and his chest heaved. My master knew everything I'd done; he knew it was me who'd pulled the sack of hearts from his hands the other night! "You may not command magic, but with the help of the blasphemers, you employ its horrid powers in my own palace! The home I allow you to live your miserable life in!"

I almost vomited and passed out with fear but struggled enough to form words. "All I did was try to learn what the old man at the temple wanted me to."

"Did you succeed?" After kicking the pelt across the room, he threw the sack at me. A bloodstain ran down my kilt.

"No, I have more questions now than answers," I said.

"This world is so full of lies," he whispered, circling me like a panther waiting to pounce. "You could have lived a comfortable life, a life anyone would have desired. You had everything … well, almost …" He made a come-hither motion with a slender finger.

Nefertiti stepped into the room, her head hanging.

"My queen informed me of what you offered her." He chuckled. "You cannot take the world's most beautiful woman from God!"

"I-I am in love with her." My words trembled like my hands, and I was unable to meet his shadowed gaze. "I didn't intend to offend you. I acted only on my feelings for her."

"Well, you have insulted me, the queen, Egypt, and the Aten!"

I wouldn't be able to appease the devil inside Akhenaten this time, and fighting would mean death. Suty also stood outside the doorway, barring any escape. The demon possessing that monstrous body winked, wings and horns almost visible beside the pig's ear. Standing beside the ogre and eyeing me as if I were the vilest of creatures was Ay. He'd never accept me now.

Akhenaten lunged, but not at me. Yanking Beketaten by the hair, he hoisted her into the air. She screeched as he threw her against a wall. Her upper lip struck stone, gashed open, and bled profusely. "Your body is mine, you whore!" he screamed, his face a deep purple. "You have defiled yourself. The women of this palace do not serve other men!"

I backed into a corner, my mind racing. If Nefertiti wanted Akhenaten to avenge her, why not do it as soon as she left last night? Perhaps part of her still loved me. Or had Akhenaten forced her to tell, and then to watch?

I leapt for the window and caught the sill.

"Coward!" Akhenaten roared. His fingers wrapped around my scarred ankle, burning like fire. Screaming in pain, I pulled, but he opposed with fiercer strength. I crashed onto the floor.

Suty's dark laughter echoed.

I pressed my back against the far wall, and Akhenaten snatched a spear from his soldier and threw it in my direction—butt first. The shaft caught me in the stomach and knocked the wind from my lungs, but I held on to the weapon.

"Defend yourself!" Akhenaten said, seizing another glistening-edged spear. "Like when we were children with our sticks."

Fumbling with the spear, I pointed it at him. The depths of his dark eyes consumed the light. I was going to die. My life and friends flashed before my eyes. Father, Croc, Mahu, Nefertiti …

His spear knocked mine out wide, slashing me across the chest. Blood gushed down over my belly. Ay applauded.

"He wanted to take me for a farmer's wife!" Nefertiti threw her head back and laughed.

My tormented heart shriveled as if the soul-drinking blade had plunged into it. If Nefertiti had ever loved me, that time had long passed, replaced by her need for wealth and power.

"Please don't kill him!" another female cried. Mutnedjmet! "Nefertiti, don't be so vile. His only crime was loving you!" Tears streamed down her gentle face, for me.

My head grew light and foggy. Had I been so wrong about Mutnedjmet? Perhaps she'd only wanted to help and had never betrayed me. Perhaps it was her sister all along …

What would become of Mutnedjmet? Another one of Akhenaten's girls? Perhaps I could have helped everyone if I hadn't been so blind.

Stiffening my resolve, I squeezed Father's bracelet, then stabbed with my weapon, utilizing all of my might. I struck for Father, for Croc, for Mutnedjmet, and for myself.

Akhenaten deflected the spear and rammed the end of his into my face. A geyser of blood erupted from my nose as I collapsed, the world spinning with blinding lights.

"I will not kill him," he said, twirling his weapon overhead with a whirling hiss. "He has betrayed and defied me more than I could imagine. Me! The son of the Aten! I no longer trust anyone. And I have bigger plans for him than death. But when he passes, I will be there to devour his tortured soul." He leaned closer. "Did you believe she would choose you over God?"

Gathering all of my courage, which I'd suppressed for far too long, I yelled, "I had hoped she would chose love over the wicked god-king, murderer of his own brother!"

Akhenaten's visage dropped in surprise before twisting like a gnarled tree. His magic ensnared my chest and throat, crushing me as if I were inside the jaws of a crocodile. Then he pummeled me like when we were children. Everything faded to black.

Chapter 59

Journal Translation

HOW MANY HOURS OF THIS world had passed before I woke from Akhenaten's crushing magic and beating? Was I dead? Suty and Mahu were there, sitting inside a small chamber of stone, beneath a sputtering torch. Two men of such different character wouldn't both find peace in the underworld. Aches and sharp pains racked my head and body as if hippopotami had chewed on my torso and stomped on my head and limbs.

"Why do you hate him so much?" Mahu asked the ogre. "Even before this treachery?"

Suty's upper lip wrinkled. "I despise the weak, the chink in our armor. The strong should thrive, not waste resources on the feeble. When I went back for a fallen soldier ..." Touching his scarred ear, he winced. "Should of let him die, but I was ordered to carry him back. Picked him up and a Nine Bow foreign soldier almost cut my head off."

Mahu grimaced. "This boy would never make a soldier, but he's mentally resilient and full of spirit." His chin jutted out, his eyes growing distant. "I liked having him around. Yet he may not last as a slave. Where're they sending him? A tomb or pyramid?"

A *slave*? Would that be much different from Akhenaten's servant?

"No, he's going to help build the new capital," Suty replied.

"Akhenaten's vision for the city of light? Starting with Karnak and—"

"Look who's awake," Suty said, spotting my swollen but opened eyes.

He picked me from the ground like a weed, his vile breath warming my face.

Mahu's hand reached between us, twirling a beautiful blue feather. "Your last gift from Akhenaten," Mahu said, tucking it into my kilt.

Suty shoved me out of the chamber and through the hallways of the palace. I wobbled outside into the predawn glow, heading across the short expanse of desert before the rectangular lake.

"Wait!" Racing out of the palace, Mutnedjmet carried a sack and brushed her hair from her tired face. "Let him take this, please!" She held out the bag. It squirmed.

My eyes narrowed in suspicion. A scorpion or serpent? To grant me a quick death?

Suty swatted the sack with the flat of his sword, issuing a thud. The sack fell. An orange and white cat flopped out, lying still. Numbness gave way to a new pain twisting in my heart. My best friend, my brother!

Mutnedjmet wailed.

Suty aimed his sword to skewer Croc. "There's that damned feral."

"Croc!" I screamed, grabbing Suty's ankle and biting into his Achilles tendon. "Run! Release yourself from me!" My index and little fingers extended to form the crocodile ward.

Bellowing, Suty toppled over, slamming into the ground and sliding across it as if someone had thrown him. Utter confusion froze my limbs. What'd just happened? Magic … in me?

Springing up, Croc dashed off on three legs and disappeared into the desert shadows. My heart melted with sympathy. Was his leg broken, and if so, could he survive in the wild like that?

Grabbing the back of my neck, Suty squeezed.

Pain radiated up into my head as Mutnedjmet sobbed and reached for my hand. "I will see you again, Heb!"

Suty guided me to the rectangular lake with his spear, his eyes wide in fear—an emotion I hadn't thought the monster could feel. Weeping, Mutnedjmet trailed us. I stepped into a rickety vessel filled with disheveled men.

"Choose your path, but don't forget your friends," Mutnedjmet shouted. "There may be different roads to follow, but don't settle for any outcome other than obtaining your—"

"In the real world, good doesn't always triumph over evil," I muttered.

"Only when you believe that does it become true …" she said. Revealing an amulet covered by her dress, she slipped it up and over her head. It was Bes, the dwarf protector with the lion hair. "I would've accepted a broken gift, if it was you who'd offered it to me—hoping to heal *my* pain." She smashed her amulet on a rock, sending fragments shooting into the desert. "I will wear this for you, until there is justice in Egypt."

Suty shoved the boat away from the bank, and we glided away into the orange light.

Men took up oars and rowed. I huddled at the bow in fear while the crew of vile men and other onboard prisoners stared. What crimes had these men committed? Had they fallen in love with the wrong woman? Were they still in love with her? Or perhaps they'd been born into a life of servitude to a monster.

We sailed through the straight canal and across the Nile, my body hunched from a profound sense of failure.

"What'd you do?" someone whispered in a Nubian accent. A dwarf—one of the actual dancing stars from Amenhotep's sed-festival—eyed me in curiosity. He had boyish features and an oversized head that rose just over my waist, his skin a deep shade of brown.

"Look at that scrawny rat, and he stares like *we're* the abomination." Another Nubian dancing dwarf stood in chains, a black beard covering his face. His muscles rippled against bound wrists, his burly frame stretching as wide as it was tall. "And someone already gave him a good beating."

Wallowing in fresh misery, I didn't want to live, much less speak to anyone. But Mutnedjmet appeared in my mind, tears streaming down her cheeks. Tears for me.

"Don't mind him," the boyish dwarf said. "He's as grumpy as a daddy lion with nine cubs trying to suckle him."

"I'm done judging by appearances," I whispered. "I've seen the most beautiful thing in the entire world and the most hideous."

The dwarves raised their eyebrows as they exchanged a glance.

"They can both still hide the same insides," I said.

"So that's how you ended up on this boat?" the friendly one asked.

"I loved the wrong woman." Gritting my teeth, I fought back emotion. I couldn't risk breaking down like a child amongst hardened criminals. "What happened to you two?"

The clean-shaven dwarf shrugged and chuckled, and his eyes brightened. "We were born far to the south where plains and hills roam farther than a man can wander—lands covered with lush vegetation blowing softly in the wind like eternal banners. And animals so extraordinary you'd think you'd fallen into a fairy tale. One day, my brother and I will return home to the thunder of drums and trumpeting of elephants, our families will rejoice, and the world will be right again." His beaming smile faded. "But because of our appearance, we were trapped and taken from our families to be made into Egyptian puppets."

Skepticism emerged in my mind, warning me. "How were you puppets?" I asked.

"It's none of your damn business," the bearded dwarf grumbled. His jaw muscles bulged under his beard, and his teeth ground together.

"Sorry," I replied.

The burly one said, "He's too friendly for his own—"

"Egyptians desire dancing dwarf puppets for their amusement and for heckling," the boyish one said. "But I turned on our master like a tiger on its trainer."

My jaw dangled in shock. "Are you a murderer?"

"If you considered our former master a man, then yes," he said.

The gruff one kicked his comrade. "No, I am the murderer! He is innocent, only convicted because he's my brother. And I'd rather be a murderous slave than an abused jester."

"I think I know how you felt," I said.

"How can you possibly relate, Egyptian?" the brawny dwarf said, his nostrils flaring.

"I also served a wicked man, who murdered my f ..." My gut twisted in pain and I fell silent.

"We were once called Shabaka and Taharqa," the polite one said. "Equals and great soldiers amongst our society. But for these past years I've been Seneb, he Harkhuf. Our Egyptian names."

"Stick with the Egyptian names," Harkhuf said. "I don't want to hear one of your people utter my language, much less my real name."

"My father called me Heb when—"

"Shut your eaters!" a toothless sailor yelled from the rear, "or you'll all swim to the east bank in chains!"

Other rough-looking men glared with angry or fearful expressions.

The sailor continued, "You poor slaves will pay your debt by working beneath thousands of freemen and craftsmen to erect temples for the Aten. Pharaoh has decreed that these be built to grant us favor and abolish the plague. You'll be working under the great wise man, the son of Hapu ..."

My stomach twisted and cramped in rage. The magician gobbled up any crumbs of power Akhenaten would toss his way.

On the far bank, rows of black dots marched in unison like ants on a never-ending trail, pushing stones that looked like houses. We drew closer. Hunched bodies toiled in the predawn light, driven by the crack of the flail. The Aten's crest peeked over the horizon, yellow light radiating across my face. I felt the warmth of a new day. But the light showed something else. A new statue dominated the eastern skyline, stone chiseled into the image of Akhenaten.

The cold, biting pain of the Devouring Monster's teeth sank into my soul. I had defied the way the world wanted things and followed my heart. If only I'd known how much more suffering my path would bring compared to the content man's ... I swallowed with regret.

Shade fell across my face. The great wings of a bird floated beside a billowing cloud, shifting the young Aten's yellow to deep orange. Swooping down, the creature appeared distinct for a moment. Upon its long neck sat the head of a man. Father! My heart jolted. Had he been reborn in the underworld? Perhaps his *ba* raced away from its nightly abode! I clutched my bracelet as the Aten rose, its light streaking across the desert to land upon a tamarisk tree. A pink bud rested on otherwise bare limbs. Father's voice echoed in my head, "Hope can still shape radiant dreams out of the nightmares of the present ..."

How beautiful this world could be, and yet how savage have we the people made it.

Chapter 60

Present Day

I WAS DEVASTATED. I had no idea where to look for Maddie, and the guilt of her abduction scorched my soul like the Egyptian sun on my pale skin. I just prayed she was okay.

We'd spent two entire days searching and talking to the authorities about the abduction, and the local detective assigned to the case assured us his team was doing everything they could. Maddie's family and the U.S. Embassy were also doing everything in their power to help. So far, no one had found any trace of her or those two men, nor received a ransom demand.

If I could discover the clue inside Karnak, those evil men might show up again and try to stop us from locating the Hall. Then I'd devise a trap or track them back to Maddie. I didn't care about the Hall anymore, but following the professor's trail would probably give us the best chance of finding her. These men only showed themselves when we were seeking the path. Otherwise, I'd just have to wait on the authorities. And resting wasn't an option, as memories and emotions battered me until I started searching again.

As I strode through the crumbled temple of Pharaoh Akhenaten, the afternoon sun pounded down through the open-air court onto my back. My head still ached from the cheap shot delivered by one of the abductors, and depression dragged my feet through the dirt.

Had they taken Maddie because she was the strongest link in our group? Her knowledge and computer skills were our best chance at unlocking clues. Now hope dwindled. But how could those men have known, and who were they?

I still hadn't discovered anything in an entire day studying Luxor Temple and Karnak from sunrise to sunset. Growing weary, I staggered along.

"The authorities will find Maddie," Kaylin muttered, scuffing along beside me. "There's nothing more we can do, and you have to fly out tomorrow for school."

My eyes closed in remorse. Today was my last day. What else could I do? Keep wandering, vomiting from my flaring Crohn's disease—which had been happening since I'd gotten up this morning—unable to eat or drink? I'd either be forced into a hospital or die. Eventually I'd have to give up and go home. And I should be grateful for a prestigious career, even if I didn't enjoy the work. But Dr. Banks, the surgeon, had covered up the situation, dragging me further down with his scheming. We'd falsified an old lady's medical records.

"What happened to that dude?" Aiden asked, his voice melancholy with loss. He indicated a smashed statue with the grotesque face of Akhenaten.

"No one knows," I said, barely able to lift my head from my penitence. "He built temples here, but then up and moved the entire capital of Egypt."

"I meant, what happened to his face?"

I studied the distorted features: long countenance, thick lips, and sunken eyes. "Many believe he didn't actually look like that; this was just his style of art. Some think he was deformed."

"Was he bad?" The flat bill of Aiden's cap turned up toward me.

"Yes," I said, thinking not only about all my life's reading, but about the journal. "Depending on whose side you would've been on. But he married the famous and beautiful Nefertiti."

"Nefertiti … I've heard that name somewhere," Aiden said, staring at fragments of broken statues. "Those must've been some 'titis' for her to still be so famous. Why aren't we looking at *her* tomb?" He laughed, his volume barely above a whisper, revealing his despair.

Shaking my head, I ran a hand over an image of Nine Bows, representing the enemies of ancient Egypt. Aiden, petting his fox, lingered over a sphinx with the face of King Tut. Kaylin examined images of Rameses' infamous battle of Kadesh, her guilt crushing her energy. She hadn't spoken more than a couple of sentences in the last three days. Jenkins stood guard while Mr. Scalone rubbed his tattooed forearms.

"I already know Karnak inside and out," Mr. Scalone said, "everything but the alignment of the light with the structural features. I need to see all of the clues. Then I can locate the Hall and help Maddie."

Distrust tightened my core, but I ignored all my nagging doubts, though everything inside me screamed not to. My dad wouldn't have wanted this man to claim his prize, but I slowly handed over the professor's letters in hopes of saving Maddie.

A devious grin spread across Mr. Scalone's rugged cheeks as he read through all of them.

The sun sank toward the western pylons, and my heart collapsed in failure. We'd never find this clue, or her. Climbing the stairs to the sun chapel in the precinct of Khonsu, I barely noticed an upside-down engraving of a chariot. My stomach cramped, and I fell to my knees in literal gut-wrenching pain—my Crohn's disease protesting by creating a blockage in my intestine.

I wished for some magic. Could such power really have died out millennia ago, from a mass slaughter of the few who commanded it? I *needed* to believe the story wholeheartedly now. But where was my mentor or magician? My dad had died years ago. All he'd left was the letter. Dr. Banks, the surgeon? No, I hadn't learned anything from him other than humiliation and how to cover your mistakes with lies.

I pulled the black-and-white photograph from my wallet, the surface wrinkled and cracked, damaged from the flood inside the tomb. Wearing a grand smile, my dad had held my small shoulder. The sphinx towered behind us like we'd witnessed it on our greatest adventure. Too bad it was all fake.

Maybe I was only meant to pass on the tales and excitement I felt, to share the magnificence of the world for the betterment of society—some consolation. A meager flame flickered in my heart. Discovering the tale in the journal should've been enough, but I'd flipped to the end days ago. The entire translation was incomplete, and there weren't enough hieroglyphs to finish the story. I'd only found a portion of a grand, ancient tale. Would that be my life, ending half finished like it had for my dad and Heb? Kaylin was probably right; she could see me for what I was, not through the veil of hope I held for myself.

My stomach clenched, as if squeezed inside a vice. I doubled over, gasping for breath. The pain slowly receded. I reached for pills but instead grabbed the peeling leather of the journal.

"Looks lost," Mr. Scalone said into his phone, stepping farther away to hide his conversation. "I'll head to Cairo after they leave. Okay, see you then, Minister."

Was he still talking to the Minister of Antiquities? After the man might've been responsible for trapping us inside the tomb? How had Kaylin's dad found this treasure hunter?

The wind gusted, flipping pages of the journal. The story of suffering, persistence, forbidden knowledge, and power left me with a bitter taste, sending a chaos of emotions coursing through my tired body. Heb appeared before my eyes, his tale, dilemma, and obstacles, ancient but so similar to mine eons later. What would he do? Could I follow his example? Or could I only hope to avoid his mistakes? For all of his trying and confrontations, he'd only fallen further behind. Should I too allow myself to clash with fate and stay in Egypt, or allow my own soul to be poisoned and finish medical school? Keep fighting against all odds, or realize my error and go home?

I staggered to my feet. A panoramic view swept around me—towering Karnak, the sphinx road, Luxor Temple to the south, and the city sprawling outward. I gazed into the west, where the Nile extended into endless desert. Sunrays crashed upon my face. Anxiety made my heart beat faster as the sun sank toward the horizon. This was my last chance before the light faded and I had to return home. My stomach cramped again, causing me to double over. Maddie's sheer glasses spilled from my chest pocket and clattered onto the stone, facing the horizon.

"Maddie, where are you?" I groaned. A thought popped into my head, something Maddie had said: never stare directly into the light, or you won't see its shadows … Maybe they only appeared in my mind, two massive shadows sitting upon thrones west of the Nile, but fragments of thought fell into place like a puzzle. The answers were all right there, for someone who understood. My body felt light, as if I were floating with awareness. I knew where we had to go. To the Colossi of Amenhotep.

"Let's go," Mr. Scalone said. "There's nothing here."

A fog fled from my consciousness in a burst of clarity. Maddie was right: I retreated every time problems arose. No wonder I never accomplished anything. Gritting my teeth, I took a long, deep breath. What would Heb do? For Maddie and myself, I needed to create my own fate, pick a path, and sprint down it like there was no alternative, no plan B.

"C'mon, Gavin," Aiden said. "It'll be dark soon, and you have to catch a flight in the morning."

"I've been wrong this entire time," I said, standing straighter and tilting my fedora back, my eyes squinting into the descending sun.

"What?" Kaylin asked.

"I'm not going home, not back to that life, not now, not ever," I said, sacrificing the security of my future—and resolving to find Maddie, even if it cost me everything. "Follow me!"

Heb hadn't given up, and neither would I.

Chapter 61

Present Day

L EAPING OUT OF THE PADDLE BOAT we'd docked on the western bank of the Nile, I sprinted through the desert for the twin colossi. I imagined Maddie's torment. Her situation was my fault. I needed to find something in order to save her. The latest clue ran through my mind. "'Follow the path downriver to the complex of the sun and Pharaoh who speaks to the sun. Where it began or ended.'" The word "began" had caught my attention, although Maddie had specifically said it could've meant "ended."

"So now you're sure it's here, huh?" Mr. Scalone shouted.

I kept running, unsure about everything. The sun descended lower toward the horizon.

"Gavin," Kaylin said, sprinting behind me. "Does this place fit the passage?"

"Yes," I said, words coming in streams between heaving breaths. "The so-called Colossi of Memnon are actually Amenhotep III. They guarded his mortuary temple before floods washed it away. Unfortunately, not much remains ..."

"Why'd he build his tomb in a flood plane?" Aiden asked, sweat dripping from his brow onto the tiny fox he carried like a football.

"So his soul could forever experience the birth, death, and rebirth of his kingdom signified by the changing river," I said, my pace slowing. Breathing burned my dry throat. "Like the *benben* stone, his temple became the earth arising from water. It was the most glorious structure ever built in ancient Egypt."

"More glorious than the pyramids?" Aiden asked.

The colossi arose from the barren desert before us, their faces and chests cracked—only shadows of their former grandeur. "Even compared to the pyramids of the Old Kingdom." A sinking feeling of insignificance rose in my soul as I stepped up to the behemoths. Hunting for an answer, I said, "In ancient times, the northern statue—an oracle—spoke with a ringing tone, but it ceased when the Romans repaired damage sustained from an earthquake."

"It spoke?" Aiden asked, his eyebrows furrowing. "How?"

I shrugged. "Stones may've ground together when expanding under the sun's heat."

"How did this complex represent shadow and light?" Kaylin asked, wringing her hands as the sun sank over the western desert.

"Like most ancient structures here, it was aligned with the sun's path across the sky," I said. "The pylon walls of the temple represented the horizon." Stepping behind the statues, I examined the absorbing rays at their backs. Nothing.

"Kind of like how old Catholic churches are cross-shaped?" Aiden asked, brushing his dreadlocks away from his flushed face.

Beyond the guardians, remnants of a massive enclosure were overgrown with sparse brush. "Symbols are potent in religion," I said, scrutinizing the area. Anxiety squeezed my stomach. We needed to save Maddie from her predicament. "We're now in the temple beyond the horizon, where the sun rises and falls, between the earth and the underworld."

Aiden's eyes sprang open, as if he were entranced.

"But back then only the elite could access the temples and pray." Wandering deeper into the ancient courtyard, I rambled in hopes of unlocking some memory or piece of knowledge. "The aristocracy maintained power by only allowing for communion with the gods through themselves." I scooped sand from the base of a decimated statue guarding the solar court. "Hopefully whatever sign we're supposed to follow is still here. Not just from ancient times, but from the professor's day. Someone might've tried to destroy it, too."

"Is anything else here associated with light?" Kaylin asked, her voice thin with stress.

"The southern statue was aligned with the star Sirius," I said. "When Sirius, the god Horus himself, appeared in the night sky, the inundation would begin. We're at the end of the inundation—"

"What's that?" Aiden asked, pointing west beyond acres of rubble to another ruin.

I squinted. "The mortuary complex of the wisest man of Egypt. A magician, architect, scholar, philosopher, court official, and teacher. The son of Hapu. Legend said he was the reincarnation of the architect of the Giza pyramids, Imhotep." Shielding my eyes, I surveyed the area. "It's the largest Theban mortuary complex of anyone besides the eminent pharaohs. But it also dwarfs Pharaoh Thutmose II's beside it. Followers of the son of Hapu's teachings visited the wise man's temple for centuries. There was a basin of water ringed by ancient trees of knowledge, which granted wisdom to those who sought it."

"Maybe we should pay a visit," Aiden said, darting off.

"Damn kid," Mr. Scalone said.

I shook my head in disbelief. What would the son of Hapu have thought of Aiden? Of me? Indeed, we needed some lost wisdom … or magic! I ran after Aiden.

Stopping beside Aiden in a depression where water might've resided, I closed my eyes. I held my dad's bracelet, my avenue to the past. Whether it was my imagination or a real connection, it didn't matter. The sensation was real, like the hand of the son of Hapu, or Heb, or another who had wandered this land eons ago. A tingling rose in my heart and spread out across my limbs, filling me with the magic I'd lost. Hope. The prickling on the back of my neck returned, as if someone's hot breath descended around me. My hairs stood on end, and I shivered.

My eyes sprang open. Everyone stared, waiting for guidance. Except for Mr. Scalone. Irritation ran deep in those narrowed eyes.

My hands shook under the expectation. The middle of the sun sank beyond the horizon. Diving into my messenger bag, I popped open Maddie's laptop, which had fallen with her messenger bag during her abduction, and sorted through stacked images. Maddie had managed to capture the last desecrated message just well enough that its blurry underwater script was legible. "The guardians will guide you with light and shadow." Then there was a bizarre reference to the floating eye of Horus and the *benben* stone. The latter part of the clue about the *benben* stone could've referred to its chamber at Luxor Temple, but we'd investigated there. The "floating eye of Horus" could've been translated as a "protector," like the colossi. But with the eye and the *benben* stone next to each other … This might suggest bringing the actual *benben* stone to the guardians. Or what if the eye was not only a guardian protecting the secret's location, but also a reference to actually seeing! Was a stone supposed to have been waiting inside the secret shaft with the riddle at Abu Simbel's original location? Had someone taken it, along with the arms of the statues?

"What do you see?" Kaylin asked, pressing her chin to my shoulder.

My mind whirred with images and memories. "We need a translucent or transparent rock to catch the sunlight," I said. "In the shape of the *benben* stone."

"What the hell does that look like?" Mr. Scalone asked, propping a hand on my other shoulder. He gazed at the screen and then at a large gold ring on his finger.

"A pyramidion," I said.

"Is that like a pyramid?" Aiden asked.

"Yes," I said. "The capstone of a pyramid."

Aiden held his tiny fox out to me in both hands.

"What are you—"

Dangling from its spiked collar like an identification tag was a small glass pyramid—a tourist souvenir. I reached but Mr. Scalone snatched it, ripping the collar off the animal.

The treasure hunter shook his head. "I'm in charge from now on. You've failed us too many times and allowed Maddie to get kidnapped. People like you are too weak to accomplish anything."

Angry tension built inside my jaw until it burned. I lunged at him, but he threw out a stiff arm and knocked me back.

"Give it to him, Paul!" Kaylin shouted. "He knows something, and we're running out of daylight. Maddie could be hurt!"

Jenkins pulled out his handgun, aiming at the ground.

Reaching into the back of his jeans, Mr. Scalone yanked out a handgun of his own. Pointing its black barrel at my chest, the treasure hunter tossed his hair out of his face. "Where do we go?"

Jenkins' barrel lifted, his sight settling on Mr. Scalone. "Give the pyramid to Gavin."

"Or what?" Mr. Scalone asked. "You're going to shoot me?" He laughed. "I could still shoot Gavin before I die. And I can wait all night with our guns aimed at each other ... but I don't know if Maddie will last that long."

Rage tore through my body like lightning. I gritted my teeth and clenched my fists. "Back to the colossi!" I dashed away, and the others chased after me.

Mr. Scalone's breath rasped through the dry air as I stopped before the guardians and motioned to him. With his firearm firmly in one hand, he held the glass pyramid out to the fading rays of sun. Refracted colored light streamed out in multiple directions, kissing the silhouetted features of both the north and south Amenhoteps. No message revealed itself. But this tiny pyramidion and its position influenced where the light fell.

"Now what, genius?" Mr. Scalone asked.

"Align the stone with the cardinal directions," I said. "Like the pyramids." I brought up the compass on my phone, and he rotated the object.

Light danced in the growing dusk. On the thrones, etching, shallow and worn with time, was highlighted under an array of blue, red, green, yellow, and purple light. Kaylin recorded this miniature laser light show with her phone. Nothing made sense.

"Don't align the sides of the pyramid with the cardinal directions," I shouted, realizing his mistake. "In the New Kingdom, they aligned the corners of the pyramids south to north with the flow of the Nile and east to west for the rise and fall of the sun!"

Mr. Scalone pivoted his hand, and light swept across the timeless monuments. Ringing stung my ears, arising from the northern statue. I stumbled back, and the sound ceased. Was that a message from the colossus? A faint image was illuminated high above on the chest of the guardian, but the lines faded quickly.

Snatching the stone from Mr. Scalone's fingers, I bit down on the dog collar and scrambled onto the base of the northern guardian.

"Give that back," Mr. Scalone growled, grabbing my ankle.

My hands slipped into crevices between the worn stones.

"You've been a pain in my ass for too long." Yanking on my leg, he pointed his gun up at my face and cocked the hammer. "Give it to me."

"Let him go!" Jenkins yelled, cocking his own gun.

Swallowing in fear, I hung on to the monument.

Mr. Scalone's trigger finger twitched.

"No!" Kicking out, I smashed the heel of my boot into the treasure hunter's face.

Collapsing, he grabbed his nose and dropped his gun. Blood gushed from between his fingers in dark streams. He groaned.

I scaled the blocks, my arms throbbing with adrenaline.

"Be careful," Jenkins said, confiscating Mr. Scalone's gun and holding him at gunpoint.

I'd rock climbed in a gym but never outside. Thankfully, the crumbling blocks offered plenty of easy holds. Scaling nearly forty feet, I reached the top of a titanic knee. My companions cheered from below … so far down. The ground swirled as the wind whipped at my clothing with a shrill gale. My fedora took flight, and my head wobbled, as if I'd faint. Stumbling, I nearly toppled several stories to the rocks below. But I clung with a death grip to the knee of Amenhotep. Dripping cold sweat, I struggled onto the lap of the colossus and closed my eyes.

The sunlight! Holding the prism pyramid in front of the statue's body to capture the last rays, I aligned the corners. Colors twisted and dazzled, but no hieroglyphs revealed themselves.

Damn it! "Maddie!" I screamed, almost throwing the stone into the desert twilight as I pounded Amenhotep's chest. But light refracted by an Egyptian pyramid, made up of four symmetric triangles and a square base, would be affected by the sun's position. Maybe I could come back tomorrow and sit here all day, watching as the sun climbed and then fell … or maybe the peak of the stone was supposed to face the sun. Like the *benben* stone, the first mound of earth arising from the waters of chaos, and how it'd beckoned the Aten to transform and fly down as the fiery phoenix, land upon the pyramid, and cry out, marking the beginning of time.

Keeping the corners aligned, I tipped the pyramid so its apex faced the sun. The last strands of sunlight landed upon the stone. A color spectrum refracted back onto the body of the colossus. A faint image glistened in dark green upon the center of its chest. An inverted representation of a sphere between two mountains. The primeval cry of the granite—possibly representing the legendary cry of the phoenix—rang again, drowning out my shouts of elation. The crest of the sun sank below the horizon, blanketing the vast desert and river in purple and orange twilight. Ringing vibrated my ears. The statue quaked.

Chapter 62

Present Day

SLAMMING MY LAPTOP CLOSED with a thud left only a dim lamp to illuminate the cramped hotel room. I'd been searching for sounds from ancient Egypt that could correspond to the ringing groan of Amenhotep. No luck. "I still know where we need to go," I said.

The solace of achievement in the face of almost giving up again filled my mind, body, and soul. Squeezing my Egyptian-style bracelet, I celebrated with my dad's memory. But my thoughts returned to Maddie. It was my fault she'd been abducted. Where was she? I'd wanted to leave and start searching for her tonight, but we couldn't get transportation until morning. If she was dead, then I'd already lost everything dear to me. I shuddered, the cold of the Devouring Monster's bite puncturing my own heart.

Kaylin stood beside me with a thin, raised eyebrow. "I believe we'll find Maddie and she'll be just fine."

A knock sounded at the door. Mr. Scalone peeked in. Black circles surrounded both of his eyes, and his nose was bent. Pressing an ice pack to his cheek, he said, "Kaylin, can I get you anything to eat or drink before bed?"

"No, thanks," she replied with a smirk.

He glanced at me with cloudy eyes, his hand trembling before he ducked back out. Did rage or vengeance lurk under his demeanor? Earlier, we'd discussed what to do with Mr. Scalone for threatening me with a gun, but we'd decided for Maddie's sake, it was best to keep him around and utilize his resources.

"Jenkins still has Mr. Scalone's gun, right?" I asked.

Kaylin shrugged. "I don't think he'd give it back."

I smiled, the joy of triumph washing over me. Usurping the arrogant bully's power meant at least something had been made right.

Tender hands felt their way up my shoulders and down inside my shirt. I tensed. Kaylin wouldn't need to manipulate me now. What did she want, then? Me? I loved Maddie, but Maddie had even admitted she hadn't been able to reciprocate the emotion with the real me ... could Maddie turn out like Nefertiti? Should I give Kaylin a chance? No, at least not until Maddie was back safe and sound.

Breathing onto my neck, Kaylin leaned over, her floral scent strong on my heightened senses. "Where is the Hall, Gavin?"

My body tingled with excitement, but I bit my lip. "One of two places," I said, fighting the urge to turn and kiss her. I shrugged away. "We'll continue along the path and find the men who took Maddie ... or they'll find us."

"And what are these places?" she cooed, running her tongue across her upper teeth.

There was a tomb nearby where the images inside had transformed in style virtually overnight—on one side of the inner tomb, the images appeared as typical ancient Egyptian, but on the other, they'd been carved in a bizarre style, depicting men with elongated heads and distorted figures—the beginning of Akhenaten's Amarna period. I'd look there before heading out to the site of his capital, el-Amarna—the forbidden city of the rising Aten.

"You're, like, so hot right now," Kaylin whispered, pressing her lips to my neck and tearing my attention from the upside-down hieroglyph of the sunrise between two mountains. "Let's take a break." Shoving me back onto the mattress, she climbed on top of me ...

About the Author

R.M. SCHULTZ has been enthralled with ancient Egypt and its lost secrets for decades. He lives with his wife and daughter in the Pacific Northwest.

Note from the Author:

Thank you for reading this book.
If you enjoyed the story, please consider
rating and reviewing it on Amazon.

www.ingramcontent.com/pod-product-compliance
Lightning Source LLC
Chambersburg PA
CBHW031017120726
47905CB00007B/1952